RUN FROM EVIL

A British Murder Mystery

THE WILD FENS MYSTERY SERIES
BOOK 15

JACK CARTWRIGHT

CHESTNUT PRESS

ALSO BY JACK CARTWRIGHT

The DCI Cook Murder Mysteries

A Winter of Blood

A Secret to Die For

The Wild Fens Murder Mysteries

Secrets In Blood

One For Sorrow

In Cold Blood

Suffer In Silence

Dying To Tell

Never To Return

Lie Beside Me

Dance With Death

In Dead Water

One Deadly Night

Her Dying Mind

Into Death's Arms

No More Blood

Burden of Truth

Run From Evil

Deadly Little Secret

The Deadly Wolds Murder Mysteries

When The Storm Dies

The Harder They Fall

Until Death Do Us Part

The Devil Inside Her

RUN FROM EVIL

A Wild Fens Murder Mystery

PROLOGUE

The air brakes hissed, the rubber squealed, and regardless of how hard he pulled on the steering wheel, the lorry just seemed to slide forward in slow motion, as if the filthy tarmac was ice.

And then he felt it. The slight knock as the man on the bike collided with the seventeen-ton lorry, then disappeared out of sight of the wing mirrors. Another car swerved in front of him, knocking an oncoming vehicle from the road. Finally, as if on a delay timer, two more sets of car tyres screeched, and he jolted forward as two cars ploughed into the back of the lorry.

A terrible, deafening silence followed, where the only sound he could hear was the thumping of blood in his ears- a stampede.

That was when somebody screamed. It was shrill and alarming and conveyed everything he needed to know in a fraction of a second. Far more effective than words might have been.

There was a protocol for these incidents. He was sure of it. Stay calm. Turn the engine off, remove the keys from the ignition, and then climb from the cab. He did all this and dropped down to the road. The tiny Lincolnshire village had become a scene from a movie. A woman fell from her open car door and crawled to the side of the road. A man, whose face was smattered in dark red, wrenched open the rear door of his car, presumably to check on his child.

The last screech he had heard had come from a silver Skoda, which had buried itself into the rear of his lorry, and subsequently, another car had driven it home.

And then there was the bike. It was lying on its side with the front wheel slowing to a stop. And beside it, a smear of deep crimson had stained the road, disappearing beneath the truck.

His stomach muscles clenched suddenly, and he leaned forward, spewing the bacon rolls he'd had for breakfast onto the road. Again and again, his body rejected the meal, the kebab he'd bought the previous night, and God knows what other meals he had consumed.

He stayed there, bent over with his hands on his knees and a string of bile and saliva hanging from his mouth.

"He's dead," somebody called; a passer-by, or maybe somebody from one of the other cars. "Call an ambulance," she screamed. "Help me."

But Eamon couldn't move. He wanted to. He wanted to do the right thing. But if he moved an inch, he would heave again.

The man he had seen earlier was carrying a child in his arms. He fell to his knees on the side of the road and screamed for somebody to help.

The driver of the red Vauxhall stared through the windscreen. His gaze seemed to cut straight through Eamon. And then he saw the gash on the man's head. The trickle of blood that seeped from his nose.

There were sirens somewhere. Far off, maybe? He couldn't tell. Nothing seemed real. None of it.

"You okay there, mate?" a voice said, and Eamon looked up to find a thickset, middle-aged man approaching. He spat the remains of the bile from his mouth.

In his head, he had responded. He had told the man to help

the others, that he would be okay, and that others needed seeing to- the man in the Skoda, for instance.

But the reality was that he hadn't uttered a word.

The thick-set man placed a hand on his shoulder.

"Let's get you out of the road, eh?" he said. He had a Scottish accent and a way about him that Eamon felt comfortable with. "Ambulances are on their way."

He let himself be guided and sat in the shop doorway. The Scotsman gave him his coat, wrapping it around his shoulders.

"Now listen, fella. Shock will be setting in right about now. So, I need you to keep talking, okay? I'm a police officer. You're alright."

"You're a..." Eamon started. "You're police?"

"Aye, for my sins," the man said as he scanned the scene of devastation.

"Is he...?" Eamon said, nodding at the lump still beneath the lorry.

"Let's not worry about that right now, eh?"

"He's dead, isn't he?" Eamon said. "I know he is."

The officer looked down at him, appraising him.

"Aye. Aye, he's dead. There's nothing we can do for him now."

Eamon's heart stopped. Every muscle in his body seemed to tense, and every ounce of heat dissipated, leaving his skin icy cold.

"It was me," he said, feeling his lower jaw tremble. "It was all my fault."

"I'm sure we'll get the bottom of it, Mister...?"

"Price," Eamon said. "Eamon Price."

"Right, well, Mister Price. Do you want to tell me what happened? Are you up to it?"

"I was in a hurry," Eamon started. "I should have held back, but the man on the bike..." He took a breath. "He was in the way. We're supposed to give them a metre, but there wasn't room."

"You were overtaking him, were you?" the officer said.

"Yeah. I was behind him for a while. He was taking up the

road. You know how it is. It's what they do? They don't seem to care, do they?" The officer said nothing, but he had begun making notes in his little notepad. "Anyway, I was on the wrong side of the road. I was paranoid about hitting him. Probably paying too much attention to the mirror and not enough on the road ahead. That's when he pulled out of that side turning. I didn't stand a chance. I had nowhere to go except..."

"Who?" the officer said. "Which car pulled out?"

"The blue one," Eamon said, and he looked about him, unable to see much from where he was sitting. "I thought he'd wait. I thought it was obvious what I was doing."

"And he still pulled out, did he?"

A glimmer of hope shone briefly, then faded. It might not be his fault. But it *was*. It *had* to be his fault.

"I ran into the back of the car. Just caught the rear left-hand side. I heard the lights break, but..."

"But what, Mister Price?"

"But I suppose I was more worried about the bloke on the bike," he replied. "Lot of good that did, eh?

"You're sure it was a blue car?" the officer said.

"Positive. It was bright blue. Like the sky."

The officer pulled his phone from his pocket and then took a few steps away to make a call.

Eamon stretched his legs out, doing everything he could to avoid looking under his lorry. The child was now awake and limping with the help of her father. Local residents and shop-keepers had emerged from their houses and shops. A few tended the wounded, but mostly they stood, huddled in groups, shaking their heads.

The officer returned, pocketing his phone.

"Can I get my things before you take me away?" Eamon asked.

"Take you away?" he said. "You're not going anywhere until you've been seen by a medic, Mister Price. You just stay there, eh?"

"I thought you'd want to take a formal statement. At the station, you know?"

"Oh aye, I'll be taking a statement in due course. I'm more interested in talking with the driver of this blue car you mentioned."

"Is he okay?" Eamon asked. "Is he hurt?"

"Hurt?" The officer said. "I'll let you know when we find him."

"Sorry?"

"There's no blue car here, Mister Price," he said. "So, either you're...misremembering the events, or he's done a runner."

"But if he's gone, then—"

"Then you might want to call your family," the Scotsman said. "Sorry, pal, but your day just took a very bad turn. A very bad turn, indeed."

CHAPTER ONE

"Oh, for crying out loud," Freya said, and she let her head fall back onto the headrest as the car in front edged forward three feet, then came to another stop. "I thought the whole idea of living out in the sticks was that we wouldn't have to put up with sodding traffic."

"When was the last time we sat in a traffic jam?" Ben asked from the passenger seat. "It's not an everyday occurrence, is it?"

He watched as she studied her reflection in the mirror, adjusting her hair to cover one side of her face and the scars that had very nearly claimed her life.

"I don't know why you try to cover your scars," he said. "They're not nearly as bad as they were. I think you look great."

"It's probably just some farmer in his tractor exercising his frustration at the government," she replied, ignoring his comment and even the compliment.

"Well, if it is, then all credit to him," Ben told her, and he gave her a look to remind her that he was from farming stock and would side with the downtrodden in a heartbeat. "Well, seeing as we're not going anywhere, maybe we can discuss the wedding?"

"What's to discuss," she asked. "We've set the date; the banns have been read. The only thing we have to do is agree on the holiday."

"The honeymoon?"

"Yes, that."

"You *can* call it a honeymoon, Freya."

"You're forgetting; I've already had a honeymoon, and it wasn't the experience I hoped for. So, if it's alright with you, I'd prefer to refer to it as a holiday. You've got your church wedding. I gave in on that. But honeymoon?" She shook her head vehemently. "It's a holiday, and when I say holiday, I mean a holiday - a break from everyday life. I don't want to lift a finger, not even to make a coffee. I want to open my door and look out onto the ocean. I want my dinners brought to me beneath a stainless-steel cloche, my drinks served precisely the way I like them, and I want to close my eyes and feel the sun on my face."

"So, you're going on your own then, are you?" Ben asked.

"No, I expect you to be by my side the entire time."

"Like a faithful Labrador?"

"Like a faithful husband," she told him.

"Right," he said. "This holiday discussion we're supposed to have. Am I allowed any input?"

"Of course," she told him. "You can pay for half of it."

"Oh, I see. Look out," he said, nodding at the traffic as it inched forward another few feet.

"Christ almighty," she groaned. "If this is a bloody farmer protesting, then I think he's made his point, don't you?"

"No," Ben said. "Personally, I think he has every right to hold us all up. Do you realise how hard the government has made life for farmers? It's a joke."

"It's life," Freya said. "Nothing is surer than—"

"Death and taxes, yes, but if too many farms are forced to sell land, where will all the food come from?"

"Oh, that'll never happen. We'll always have food."

"And who do you think will buy up the land?" Ben asked. "The government. And what will they do with the land?"

"Build an amusement park?" Freya remarked, a hint at how tedious she was finding the morning so far. "To cheer us all up?"

"They'll either build on it or farm it themselves. Tenant farmers, that's what we'll be. It's one step closer to communism, I'm telling you."

"Oh, really?"

"Really," he said. "They won't be robbing you or me, but our kids—"

"Whoa, whoa, whoa," she said. "Kids? When did we discuss having children? I can't have children. I'm far too old."

"I thought we'd make some on our holiday while we're waiting for your flunky to bring you coffee and breakfast."

"Not happening," she said.

"What the kids, or the...you know, while we're waiting thing."

She gave him the side eye and smirked.

"You know I hate vulgarity," she said, exercising her politician's response but avoiding the question altogether. "Oh, go and have a look, will you?"

"What?"

"Go and see what the holdup is. We've been here ten minutes." She settled in her seat, making a show of making herself comfortable. "Go and see your farmer friend."

"I'll do that, shall I? But when you get to the front of the queue, don't be surprised to find me holding a placard saying *Save Our Farms*, or *Down with Communism*."

"Oh, I doubt it very much," she replied nonchalantly. "You couldn't spell it."

He climbed from the car and peered along the line of vehicles. They were half a mile from Martin, a small village between Metheringham and Woodhall Spa. The road was well used, but seldom did it come to a standstill as it was now.

He closed the car door, leaving Freya in the warmth, and made his way along the line of cars towards the village. The lack of oncoming traffic was a telling sign that the cause was far more significant than a disgruntled farmer. A few other drivers had climbed from their cars to have a look, but none were venturing out for a closer look. More than a dozen of them had decided to take an alternative route through Coningsby and were battling with a three-point turn within the confines of the narrow lane.

The walk to the village was longer than he'd anticipated. It was one of those roads that took moments to drive, but on foot, it seemed to take an age. He was just entering the village when an ambulance came up behind him on the wrong side of the road. Then, when he had rounded the next corner, the devastation ahead of him came into view.

"Ah, Christ," he said, taking in the scene. A lorry was blocking most of the road, with a police Volvo at either end. The ambulance that had passed him parked beside another that was there, and beyond the carnage, the top of a fire engine could be seen.

He pulled the phone from his pocket and called Freya.

"Don't tell me, you're running away to join Just Stop Oil?"

"Drive up here," he told her before her amusement could gain momentum.

"Sorry?"

"Drive up," he said. "RTA. We've got a lorry, two cars, and... oh, for heaven's sake, there's a bike under the lorry. It's a bad one, Freya."

"On my way," she said, and he ended the call as he approached one of the traffic officers.

'Everything under control?" he called.

"Sorry, sir," the officer replied, and he reached out to deter Ben from coming any closer. "If I could ask you to—"

"DI Savage," Ben said, flashing his warrant card. "DCI Bloom is just making her way past the traffic. Anything we can do?"

"I see. Well, I won't pretend a few extra hands wouldn't be

welcome. It's a bad time of day if I'm honest. We've got half a dozen uniforms taking statements from witnesses and one more plain clothes talking to the lorry driver. I think he's one of your lot."

"The officer?"

"Aye," he replied. "Big fella. Glaswegian."

"Gillespie?"

"Aye, that's him. He's over behind the lorry."

Ben heard, rather than saw, Freya's Range Rover approaching.

"She's with me," he said.

"What do we have?" Freya called out, pulling on her coat as she started towards them, eyeing the scene with an experienced eye.

"We're still taking statements," the officer replied, then held out his hand. "Souness. Sergeant Souness."

"DCI Bloom," she replied, politely shaking his hand.

"Two fatalities, two more with injuries," Souness started before the sound of an angle grinder filled the morning air. Ben took a step back to peer around the lorry. "I wouldn't if I were you." Souness shook his head gravely. "Not a pretty sight. The fire service is cutting the driver out so he can be carted off."

"What a dreadful way to start the week," Freya mused. "Do we know what happened?"

"Lorry driver tried to get past the bike. According to the driver, another vehicle pulled out of that side turning," he said, pointing up the road. "The lorry driver had to make a split-second decision. Hit the car or risk hitting the bike."

"Christ," Freya said, bending slightly to view the bloodstained tarmac beneath the lorry. "And he chose the bike, did he? Well, for once, I'm glad I'm not SIO, being as this is a traffic incident. So, whatever you need us to do, just tell us."

"I've got reinforcements on their way," he said. "A few local officers are taking statements, but I need to get them off that and managing traffic. This lot won't be cleared up for a while, so we're going to have to turn that lot around." He nodded at the queueing traffic.

"We can take over from them, put them on traffic management," Ben said.

"That'd be helpful," Souness replied. "Names and addresses are what we need. Anything else is a bonus. I've got the Forensic Collision Investigator on his way, so nothing can be moved until they've done what they need to do."

Ben peered past Freya at the tarmac.

"Decent tyre marks," he said. "He certainly put the anchors on. How is he?"

"He's pretty shaken up right now," Souness said.

"Gillespie's looking after him behind that lorry," Ben said.

"Gillespie's looking after him? Crikey, no wonder he's shaken up."

"I've breathalysed him" Souness said. "He had a drink last night but came in under the mark. What concerns me, though, is this lorry."

"Overloaded?"

"Not as far as I can tell, and I can't see any obvious signs of mechanical failure."

"Jesus, he's in for a rough spell," Ben said.

"Not as tough as the family of the man on the bike or the man being cut from his car."

"What about the car in the shop front?" Freya asked.

"We think they swerved to avoid the collision and lost control. The second vehicle failed to brake in time, and the third is nowhere to be seen."

"The car that pulled out?" Ben asked, to which Souness nodded. "That makes me bloody sick. Any description?"

"Yes," Souness said. "It's a blue hatchback."

"Blue?"

"That's all we have to work with," Souness replied. "And if you believe that, you'll believe anything."

"You think the driver made it up?"

"Wouldn't be the first time," Souness said. "That lorry driver is facing two counts of manslaughter caused by dangerous driving. Trust me, they'll try anything to get off with it."

"Well, let's get started, shall we?" Freya said. "The sooner our uniformed friends get that traffic turned around and close the road off, the better."

"I'm grateful," Souness said, then nodded and started back towards the rear of the lorry, where the fire service were cutting the victim from the car.

Freya led Ben to the pavement, where they found Gillespie standing over a man who was seated on a shop doorstep.

"You alright, Jim?" Ben called out as they approached.

Gillespie looked up at them both, his expression grave. He made his way towards them, leaving the man to his own devices for a few moments.

"Aye," he said. "I might be late in this morning."

"Traffic?" Ben asked.

"Aye, it's a killer, Ben," he said. "It's a bloody killer."

"How's the driver?" Freya asked.

"He's in a right state," Gillespie said. "Have you met Souness?"

"Yes, we've just spoken to him."

"He's going to throw the bloody book at that poor sod," Gillespie said.

"Yeah, he did mention a fictitious blue car," Ben said. "Glad this isn't one of ours. I wouldn't fancy having the job of finding that. If it ever existed."

"Goes to show, eh?" Gillespie mused aloud. "Your whole life can be turned upside down in a heartbeat."

"You think he's telling the truth about the car?"

"Aye, I do," Gillespie said, turning back to glance at the man, who held his head in his hands. "I really do."

Freya eyed the wretched man who was sitting not twenty feet away, then addressed Gillespie.

"We're going to take some statements until reinforcements arrive. We'll see you back at the station," Freya told him. Then, in a rare display of kindness that she reserved for special occasions, she placed her hand on Gillespie's chest, leaned closer and spoke softly. "Why don't you stay here with the driver? You might be the last friendly face he sees for a while."

CHAPTER TWO

In Gillespie's absence, the incident room was calm. The only voice Freya heard when they pushed through the double doors was Nillson's, who was taking the new team member through a few of the processes relevant only to Major Crimes.

"Good morning," Freya chirped, avoiding all eye contact until she had deposited her bag and coat at her desk. She perched on the edge of her desk and then gazed around the room until all eyes were on her. "Thank you," she said. "Gillespie will be late. There was an RTA in Martin, and he's been waylaid."

"Oh, I heard about that," Gold said, her gentle and faint Edinburgh accent adding more than a hint of empathy to the statement. "There was a fatality, wasn't there?"

"Two," Ben said. "And a few more injured. It wasn't a pretty sight."

"Some poor sod is having a bad day," Gold replied.

"In the meantime," Freya said. "We are, for the first time in months, in a fortunate position and have time on our hands to do some housekeeping. Cruz, you have two reports to type up from the quarry. How are they coming along?"

"I'll be done by lunch break," he replied.

"Good, Gold, what are you up to?"

"I'm just completing an FLO form, guv."

"Chapman?" Freya said, turning to the bespectacled young woman whose desk was closest to her own. Then she eyed the neat stack of files on her desk. "Statements?"

"I'm preparing a few closed investigations for the archives, guv," she replied. "We're running out of room in the cabinets."

"Very proactive. Perhaps Cruz can help when he's finished?"

"Eh?" Cruz said, looking up from his own laptop.

"It's okay," Chapman said. "I've got a system. I'm working through them."

"Very well" Freya said and turned to the last pair. "Nillson?"

"Morning, guv," Nillson replied. If ever the team was ranked in order of masculinity, the second place would be a close call between Nillson and Gillespie. With three older brothers, she had developed a no-nonsense approach to policing and was one of the few who could give the big Scotsman a run for his money. "I'm just taking Jewson through a few old investigations."

The younger officer peered up at Freya, slightly nervous.

"And how are you finding it so far, Jewson?" Freya asked, running a critical eye over the young officer's attire. The girl's figure was what Freya would call hourglass, but there was very little need for so much flesh to be on show.

"As expected, guv," she replied.

"You have some big boots to fill. Anderson was extremely efficient, wasn't she, Anna?"

"She was, guv," Nillson said. "But I think Jewson will be all right, if she's pointed in the right direction, that is."

"Well, maybe we can start with some more suitable clothing," Freya said. "Perhaps a cardigan or something?"

Self-consciously, Jewson peered down at herself, then fastened another button on her blouse.

" Have you heard from Anderson?" Freya asked, to which Nillson nodded.

"I have. She's back in London. I think she's taking some time off before going back to the Met."

"Can I ask?" Jewson said, and Freya watched as her facial scars caught Jewson's attention, and she hesitated.

"What is it, Jewson?"

"Oh, erm..." she began. "I was going to ask why she left, guv."

Nillson looked across at Ben, who in turn stared at Freya but then spoke for her.

"She went as far as she could with us," he said. "More opportunity in London."

"Detective Superintendent Granger tells me you've made some progress with your exams, Jewson," Freya said.

"That's right, guv. I'm just waiting on my NIE results. I was going to move into CID, but helping you lot out with the body in the quarry last month really opened my eyes. I think I can make a difference here."

"Well, that's the kind of positivity we need," Freya said.

"Does this mean I'm no longer chief door knocker?" Cruz asked.

"No, Cruz," Freya said. "But it does mean you have somebody to walk the streets with."

"Eh?"

"You two are partnering up," Freya said. "I'm reliably informed that it was you two who discovered the second body and the footprints."

"Well, yeah, but—"

"So, pair up," Freya said. "Nillson, you'll be with Gillespie, Gold you'll continue as FLO, helping out where needed, and Chapman, I need you here to keep things in order."

"I wouldn't change it for the world, guv," Chapman said, smiling as she answered her phone.

"Hang on?" Nillson said. "I have to work with Gillespie? He's a moron, guv."

"He's a Sergeant, Nillson, the same as you, and the way I see it, the two of you together make a strong team."

"Surely Jewson would be better with Nillson, guv?" Cruz said.

"Oh, so you want to stay with Gillespie, do you?"

"Oh, well. No, not really."

"There you go. A new start for you."

Cruz dropped his face into his hands, and Jewson looked uneasy.

"Is there something I should know?" Freya asked.

"No, guv," Jewson said, forcing a smile. "No, we'll be just fine, thanks."

"Glad to hear it." Freya clapped her hands once. "Right, before I go and brief Detective Superintendent Granger, does anybody have any questions?"

A sea of disappointed faces shook from side to side.

"Erm, guv," Chapman said as she placed her phone back in its cradle. "That was the front desk."

It wasn't the look in her eye that suggested a spanner had been well and truly stuffed into Freya's morning. It was the tone of her voice. "Someone's found a body."

"Oh?" Freya replied, and all hopes of them catching up on the mounting paperwork faded.

"It's an old man found on his living room floor. Signs of an assault, and the constable who found him discovered signs of a break-in," Chapman said, then hesitated. "You'll never guess where it is."

CHAPTER THREE

"The Gods are against us," Ben laughed as they came to the point that their white-hatted traffic colleagues deemed a suitable spot to close the road to Martin. Freya pulled the large Range Rover to the blockade and flashed her warrant card to gain them access. Further along the road, a small team of uniformed officers were aiding stranded drivers to turn around on the narrow road. "It's going to be hours before that lorry is moved, you know that, don't you?"

"It's going to be a slow morning, Ben," she replied. "Sergeant Souness will want every scrap of detail before it's allowed to move. The tyre marks on the road will be measured; the lorry will be weighed, and every statement will need to be double-checked and attested. That's where we have the advantage."

"Oh, we have an advantage, do we?"

"When that accident is cleared up, and the road is reopened, every scrap of evidence from that point on becomes contestable. It's tainted. At least in most instances, our crime scenes can be locked down for as long as we need them to. He doesn't have that luxury."

"True," he said as they neared the scene of the accident. He checked the address Chapman had provided and then pointed to a side turning. "Here we are. Pound Road."

She made the turn and then slowed when they saw the liveried cars parked outside the house in question. The houses were neat, semi-detached, and well-kept; clearly, the residents took pride in their homes. It was one of those reflections that Ben thought odd to have made, but there were so many places he'd seen where residents made no effort at all, even in far more affluent areas. So, to see such a well-kept street made a mark on his mind and spoke volumes for the neighbours.

Freya pulled her sun visor down to use the mirror and then began adjusting her hair to hide her scar, finding the right balance of disguise and ability to see.

"Why *do* you cover it?" Ben asked, and she paused with her hand on the mirror before snapping it closed.

"It's going to take time to get used to it," she replied quietly. "Just let me manage it in my own time, okay?"

"You know I think you're beautiful, right?"

"Ben!"

"I mean it," he said. "I think you draw attention to it by hiding behind your hair, wig, or whatever."

"And I think we should have this conversation when half your face and hair have been burned off," she said, to which he had no direct recourse. She reached for the door handle, and he stopped her.

"For the wedding; I'd like to see *you* at the wedding," he said. "Don't hide. It's tradition for the groom to actually see his wife at the wedding, you know?"

She thought for a moment but gave no reply. Instead, she barged the door open and climbed out, leaving Ben no option but to follow suit.

"Morning, guv," the first uniformed officer called out as Ben and Freya marched towards the house, keeping the officer on her left-hand side, and her hair down.

"Morning," Ben replied. "What do we have?"

He turned at the noise of a car, and Gillespie's old Volvo came trundling around the corner, followed closely by Nillson's hatchback and Cruz with Jewson by his side in his mum's two-door Toyota.

"Albert Reilly, guv," the officer said. "Ninety-three years old. Neighbours gave him a knock as his bin was still out."

"When was it collected?"

"Friday, guv. It's the couple in the house opposite."

"The one with the twitching curtain?" Freya asked, to which the officer nodded.

"Said they saw it there on Saturday and Sunday, and he's normally quite good at getting it in on his own."

"A ninety-three-year-old man?" Freya asked. Where she had positioned herself with her scars facing away from the officer, she now turned to face him. "Where's the bin now?"

The officer glanced at the injured skin on the right side of her face and hesitated, then tore his gaze away and looked her in the eye. It was, Ben was learning, Freya's way of coping with her new injuries, when there was no way of keeping them undercover; to just put them out there as if daring the individual to comment.

However, this particular officer, as Ben has guessed, was far too professional to comment on another officer's appearance, regardless of the severity.

"Well, that's it. They brought it in for him this morning and then gave him a knock, but nobody answered. So, they called it in."

"Has anybody been here since?" Freya asked.

"Not since we've been here, guv," he said. He was a clean-cut young man with bright eyes and white teeth. The type of individual who might go far in the force so long as he kept his nose clean. "I went around the back. All the doors were locked, but I found the broken window, so I forced entry." He paused, and those bright eyes dulled. "He's lying on the living room floor. I checked his pulse, but..."

"It's okay," Ben said. "You did the right thing. Need a break?"

"No, guv," he replied.

"Well, take one anyway. Go for a walk or sit in the car for a bit." He turned around to find the rest of his team standing beside the cars, awaiting instructions. "Jackie?"

At the mention of her name, Jackie Gold stepped forward, a little unsure as to why.

"Everything alright?" she asked.

"What's your name, son?" Ben asked.

"Frobisher, guv."

"Jackie, can you take PC Frobisher somewhere for a sit-down? Get him a coffee or something."

"I'm fine—" Frobisher argued.

"Help him get his notes up to date, will you?" Ben said, ignoring Frobisher's remark. He patted the young man on the shoulder and let Gold lead him away.

"That was nice of you," Freya said under her breath. "Have you taken a course in empathy without me knowing?"

Ben laughed but ignored her and caught the team's attention.

"Gillespie, Nillson. Ninety-three-year-old man. The couple in the house over the road said they brought his bin in this morning and knocked on the door. Go and have a word, will you? The way the curtains are twitching, I'm sure they'll have plenty to say."

"Aye, Ben," Gillespie said and made a show of inviting Nillson to lead the way despite her obvious displeasure. "After you, m'lady." He winked at Ben and did very little to hide his grin.

"Cruz, Jewson," Freya said.

"Don't tell me," Cruz said. "Door knocking?"

"A crucial element in any investigation, yes," she said, and Cruz let his head fall forward in despair. "I want to know if anybody saw anybody, heard anybody, or even felt anybody. I want to know if-"

"There are doorbell cameras, what time they went to work, what their dog's name is. I know, I know," Cruz said, gesturing for Jewson to follow him as he trudged up the road. "Come on, Jewson."

"Thank you, Cruz," Freya called out playfully. "Just think of the steps you'll be getting in."

"I presume you missed the course on diplomacy," Ben said, and she laughed out loud, which was a rarity these days. But the brief moment of positivity lasted mere seconds. They turned to look at the house. "Shall we?"

Unlike Nillson, Freya didn't wait for the flamboyant invitation to walk ahead of Ben. Instead, she marched towards the front door where she stopped to pull a pair of shoe covers from the box that either Frobisher or one of his colleagues had provided. A few moments later, they were inside, and Ben stopped and took a long, deep breath.

Tentatively, they peered into the lounge, where Albert Reilly was lying on his side in front of an old electric heater, which thankfully was off.

"He hasn't been there since Friday," Ben said.

"Agreed," Freya replied, her tone short and sharp. "A matter of hours, if you ask me. He still has some colour."

"My observation was more to do with the smell," Ben said. "Or the lack of one."

"Call the FME, will you?" Freya said. "And we might as well alert the scenes of crime team."

"Already done," Ben said. "I messaged them on the way here. Doctor Saint will be here within the hour, and Katy Southwell's team are just finishing up somewhere in the Wolds. Apparently, they pulled an all-nighter at some wedding venue. Some poor bloke was fished out of a pond while the bride and groom were having their photos taken."

"Crikey, there's a day they won't forget in a hurry," Freya mused as Ben slipped out of the room and wandered through to the kitchen, which was to the rear of the house, where he immediately found the reason for Frobisher forcing entry.

The window to the side of the back door was broken, and a few shards of glass were lying on the linoleum floor. He smelled Freya's perfume before he heard her or felt her presence.

"Broken from the outside," he said, guessing what she would ask. "Which begs the question—"

"Why did Frobisher have to force entry?" Freya finished for him. "Unless whoever killed the old man took a key with them to lock up."

"We don't know he was killed yet."

"The wound on his head suggests he was."

"What wound?" he asked. "Don't tell me you moved him?"

"I just had a quick look," she said, running a gloved finger across the split wooden door. She prodded the lock, but it held fast.

"Freya?"

"I know, I know. He just looked so...normal," she said, then grinned up at him. "Please don't tell on me."

He shook his head in disbelief and stepped outside into the back garden, retracing the steps of whoever had been there before him.

The rear garden was small but manageable, mostly paved with a raised border, presumably so the old man could get out and tend to them without having to get down on his knees. Snails had claimed the better part of two Hostas, the Salvias had gone over, and the Hydrangeas were looking sorry for themselves, but aside from that, the beds were well-kept.

Near the path that led down the side of the house were the wheelie bins, one each of black, brown, green, and purple, for general purpose, garden, recycling, and paper, respectively. He nosed inside each one, noting the black bin was empty while the green bin was partly filled with packaging from various food items - a few single-serving baked bean cans, a small box of chicken breasts, an empty box of luxury biscuits, and a handful of one-pint milk containers.

"He lived alone, alright," Ben said. "Let's get Chapman onto the next of kin."

"Is that an order or a suggestion?" Freya asked, and he turned to her, eyeing the small patch of wax-like skin that ran from her cheek to her jawline. She flicked at her hair, releasing it from where it was tucked behind her ear, and it fell over that side of her face, casting the wound into shadow.

"It was neither. It's how things should be," he said, and he reached up to tuck the hair behind her ear again. "You know how I'm a stickler for doing things properly."

CHAPTER FOUR

Doctor Peter Saint was a figure to behold, not just in his position as the county's leading Forensic Medical Examiner but in stature, too. Ben was six-foot-something tall, yet Saint had to peer down his long nose when addressing him. Coming from generations of farmers, Ben's hands were often remarked upon as being shovel-like in size and grip, yet Saint's hand seemed to swallow his when they greeted. And had he not been so lean and wiry, his coat sleeves might have reached his wrists.

"How are you, Ben?" he asked with a gentle smile, and his eyes flicked up at Freya, who was discussing the scene with Katy Southwell, the lead CSI.

"We're getting there," Ben replied, lowering his voice so that Freya could not overhear. "She's...adjusting."

"And she still won't go ahead with the surgery?" Saint asked. "They can do wonders now. She knows that, right?"

"Oh, she knows," Ben told him. "I don't need to remind you she is as stubborn as an old mule, do I?"

"Being stubborn is one thing, Ben. But denying help when it's offered? That's just ignorance."

"She says it's the new her," Ben said, leading Saint away to the roadside. "She says her scars are a reminder of who she used to be."

"So, she's changed then?"

"No," he grinned. "And I wouldn't want her to."

"But why, if she's wearing her scars with pride, does she let her hair hang over her face like that? It was always so neat before."

"It's all part of her adjusting," Ben told him. "I think she likes the idea of facing up to her injuries, but in practice, it's far harder."

"And how do you feel about it?" Saint asked. "You are engaged, are you not?"

"We are. And if truth be told," Ben said, turning to admire Freya in deep discussion with Southwell. "I think she's more beautiful than she's ever been."

"Is she ready to be back at work, Ben? From what I hear, the injuries were quite severe."

"She's lost part of her ear, her cheekbone looks like candle wax, and if it weren't for the air ambulance, she would have lost her eye," Ben told him. "She inhaled enough smoke to kill her three times over, she hit her head on the ground hard enough to render her unconscious, and the doctors suggest that she suffered a minor heart attack., though they can't prove it."

"Crikey, Ben—"

"Her right arm is badly scarred, and her hand too, and her hair..." Ben turned to face the older man. "Most of that is a wig, believe it or not."

"And she's back at work? I can kind of understand her not wanting surgery, but surely she needs therapy?"

"Things could have been worse, Peter," Ben said. "The doctors have been amazing, and how the nurses kept her in bed for all that time, I do not know. But she's doing what she's good at."

"Gillespie, Nillson. How did it go?" Freya called out as the big Scotsman and Nillson strode across the road from the neighbour's house.

"This is her therapy," Ben told him. "Being out here. Doing this. If they tried to take this away from her, then I think she would spiral."

Saint nodded but clearly disagreed with her decisions.

"What about Detective Superintendent Granger? Can't he have a word with her?"

"And say what? She's been signed off, Peter. She's even sat with a psychiatrist and given all the right answers."

"Oh, come on. We both know a woman with her intelligence can get through a psych examination with her eyes closed."

"And so, what could Granger do? Force her to take leave because of an injury? Because of a scar?" Ben shook his head. "That's discrimination, Peter."

"Ten years ago, it would have been common bloody sense."

Ben laughed.

"Well, thank goodness for the woke generation," he said as the crime scene photographer emerged from the house. "At least I get to keep an eye on her."

He started towards the front door with Peter by his side. Freya watched them, and it was obvious she was bringing her chat with Gillespie and Nillson to a close.

"Do me a favour, will you?" Ben said quietly. "Look her in the eye and not at her scar. Don't mention the accident, alright?"

"I'm a doctor, Ben. My patients might all be dead, but I do still have a code of conduct."

He beamed back at Ben reassuringly.

"Thanks, Peter."

"Doctor Saint, thanks for coming," Freya said as the three of them pulled on fresh shoe covers. She hurried to finish first, led the way into the house and turned into the living room, calling back over her shoulder. "I've been looking forward to getting your opinion."

"See?" Ben said quietly. "It's like nothing ever happened."

Saint nodded, accepting defeat, and then followed him inside.

He knelt beside the body and pulled on his wireframe glasses, peering down his nose and scrunching his face up as he examined Albert Reilly's eyes. It took him a few moments to tug on a pair of latex gloves. During which time, he was studying every inch of the old man's face.

Freya watched intently, biting down on her lower lip.

"The photographer's finished," she said. "We're okay to move him if need be."

"I see," Saint replied, with his fingers against Reilly's neck and his eye on his watch. "Well, death is confirmed at 11:07 am, though he's been this way for a few hours."

"How many is a few in your book?" Freya asked.

"More than two, less than six," he said, raising Reilly's arm and flexing the elbow joint. "Early onset of rigor mortis. Any longer, and he would have been stiff as a board."

Carefully, he manoeuvred Reilly onto his back, giving Ben a clear view of the wound Freya had mentioned. She eyed him, but he refused to meet her gaze. The idea was for Doctor Saint to come up with his own interpretation of the cause of death without either of them drawing attention to any particular part of the body.

"Well, this one's new," Saint said. "Looks like he hit his head as he fell, maybe?"

"On what?" Freya asked, and she presented the room with a sweep of her hand. "The armchairs are soft, there's no hearth, and the carpet is softer than my Range Rover's. The only thing he could have hit his head on is the electric fire, and there's no sign it's even been touched for months."

"Hmm," Saint replied, studying the wound. "I must say Freya, that was a very speedy analysis."

"I was just thinking aloud," she said, to which he nodded knowingly.

"Well, you're right, of course. There's very little he could have hit his head on in here."

"So, he was hit?" Ben asked.

"Oh, I think he's been hit, alright. Something hard and if I'm not mistaken, something with a sharp corner. An ornament or something similar." He drew their attention to the broken skin. "There's an indent here. It would have been heavy enough to break the skin and quite possibly fracture his skull."

"Shouldn't there be more blood?" Ben asked. "I've seen my share of head wounds. They have a tendency to bleed heavily."

"Very good, Ben," Saint said as if he were the ageing master and Ben was the doting prodigy. "Of course, for blood to be pumped out of the body, the heart would need to be pumping."

"Sorry?" Freya said. "What are you saying?"

"I'm saying this man has been dead for somewhere between two to six hours," Saint said. "But that wound happened after death had occurred."

CHAPTER FIVE

As with most crime scenes, the atmosphere soon became stale and poisonous. The fresh air was welcome, but the sight that greeted Freya on Albert Reilly's doorstep was far from the relaxing antidote with which to pair the sensation. She tugged her shoe covers off, dumped them in the makeshift bin, and then tied her hair back, letting that cool breeze lick at her cheek.

Along the road, Cruz walked four or five steps ahead of a sulky Jewson as they emerged from one property and made their way towards the next. Over where the cars were parked, Gillespie leaned against his Volvo with his arms folded, and Nillson was in her driver's seat with the door open and a long, slender leg stretched out across the pavement.

"Still pleased with your team changes?" Ben asked as if he could read her mind, which, of course, he nearly could, and she winced at the idea of being so transparent. He tugged his own shoe covers off and stepped aside for one of Southwell's team to cart one of their many boxes into the house.

"I was reliably informed that Cruz and Jewson worked well together," she said.

"By who?" he asked, and she sighed.

"Does it matter?"

"Not really," Ben said. "But give them time."

"And the other two?" she asked. "Gillespie and Nillson? They're supposed to lead by example. They're bloody sergeants, for God's sake. Look at them. It's like they've had a lover's tiff."

"You know what you've done, don't you?" Ben said. "You've pitted them against each other. They're both brilliant in their own ways, but see each other as competitors. Trust me, the first chance one of them gets to drop the other in it, they'll take it."

"Oh, come on. This isn't a school playground."

"No, but the stakes are high enough."

"Promotion?" she asked, to which he nodded.

"When you made DCI, and I was made DI, the competition narrowed. Two sergeants, both vying to step into my shoes."

"But you're not going anywhere, are you?"

"That depends," he said. "I can't move up until either you move up—"

"Or move on?" she said, and he smiled reassuringly at her.

"You have to understand, Freya. When you had your accident, there was a lot of uncertainty in the team. We didn't know if you'd be coming back—"

"Well, I am back," she told him.

"But we didn't know that, did we? Bloody hell, Freya, I thought you were dead for the first couple of hours. You spent weeks in hospital. Nobody wanted to see you leave, but the longer it went on, the more people began to wonder. Who would replace you? Would Granger bring somebody else in, or would he move me up? Am I even ready for it? And if I did move up, then what happens to the team?"

"Well, I'm sorry to have disappointed you all."

"You haven't disappointed anybody, Freya. Don't be a victim. It doesn't suit you," he said. "And before you ask, no, we did not discuss it."

"You thought it, though."

"Of course we did,' he said. "And believe it or not, there wasn't a single disappointed face when I told them you'd be back."

"Oh really?"

"It's the truth," Ben said. "Cruz actually cried."

"What?"

Ben laughed and nodded at her. "It's true. But to be fair to him, so did Jackie. Even Gillespie welled up."

There were words on the tip of her tongue, though they shied when she tried to voice them. Instead, she swallowed and let her smile disguise her emotions.

"The way I see it, we have two options," Ben said. "Put the team back into its natural state—"

"Gillespie and Cruz working together?" she replied. "I'm not sure if I can bear the bickering between them anymore. I don't have the patience for it."

"But Nillson and Jewson?" Ben said. "They'd make a decent little duo. Besides, Nillson needs a little prodigy now that Anderson has gone."

"Which reminds me," Freya said. "Are you going to tell me what happened there?"

"She's gone back to London—"

"Don't lie to me, Ben. She was doing well. I had the accident, spent some time in hospital, and when I come out, she's gone." Ben took a step into the garden, and over by the cars, Gillespie raised his head until Ben stood him down with a wave of his hand. "Tell me the truth, Ben. Anderson followed me up here from London. What happened while I was in hospital that was so bad that she upped and left without so much as a goodbye?"

"What happened? What happened, Freya? You nearly died; that's what happened. Do you know what you were to her?"

"I was her Chief Inspector."

"You were her bloody idol," he said. "She worshipped the ground you walked on."

"Well, she has a funny way of showing it. Anna said she was trying to get back in the Met."

"And if Anna wants to believe that, then let her," Ben hissed at her to avoid them being overheard. "She's out."

"What?"

"She's out, Freya. The person she admired more than anyone had come this close to death," he said, holding his fingers an inch apart. "And had suffered..." he stared at her face, and with a flick of her head, her hair fell into place. So, he took her by the hand and held it up to the light, "life-changing injuries." He shook his head sadly. "She'll find something, and she'll do well. It won't be police work, but she's smart and young enough to start over."

"Because of what happened to me?"

He squeezed her hand, and she let him push her hair back behind her ear.

"I don't think you realise how well you're regarded," he said. "Not just by me. Everyone."

"Hmm," she replied, so taken aback by the comment that she sought a distraction. "You said there was another option."

"Sorry?"

"You said that I either had to return the team to the original pairings, or..."

"Oh," he said. "Or reassure them."

"Reassure them how?"

"Reassure them that you're not going anywhere."

"I'm here, aren't I? Isn't that enough?"

Ben grimaced, as he often did when deciding how best to deliver difficult statements.

"I thought the same," he began. "Until I spoke to Peter Saint earlier."

"Saint? What did he have to say?"

"He questioned your..."

"Go on, Ben. Say it."

"Your...decision making, Freya."

"What?"

"He didn't mean anything by it. It was an honest conversation."

"He thinks I'm nuts."

"You have severe burns to your face and arm, Freya, yet you elected not to undergo plastic surgery."

"So?"

"Freya, I've known you to spend hundreds of pounds on a haircut, not to mention your nails and the clothes you buy. Your appearance is important to you."

"What business is that of Peter Saint's?"

"It's not, and he was very respectful. But if he's thinking it, then..."

"Then the team must be thinking it as well. They think I've lost my mind. They do know I had to sit with a bloody shrink before I could come back, don't they?"

"Of course they do, but you could have got through that examination in a coma, Freya. Powers of persuasion are, let's be honest, your forte."

"So, they think I'm mad? Is that what you're saying?"

"No, of course not. But they're likely wondering if the decision you made is final, or if you'll...come to your senses?"

She nodded slowly, digesting the information.

Gold had finished with Frobisher and had joined Nillson by her car. Gillespie was texting somebody or scrolling through Facebook, and further up the road, Cruz was still going from door to door with Jewson trailing six paces behind like a Georgian married couple.

"What I'm saying, Freya, is that there is still some uncertainty in the team. Tell them you're staying, and maybe Gillespie and Nillson will get along better. Maybe Cruz will step up. Who knows? Just get the ship steady again, one way or another." He smiled up at her, but that smile faded with doubt. "Unless of course, you haven't decided yet." She eyed him, holding her mind and all signs of it in check. "Freya?"

His curious expression morphed into one of concern. He opened his mouth to speak, but like Athena, that God of feminine strength and wisdom stepping into the light, Katy Southwell emerged from the house clad in her white hooded suit.

"We're ready for you," she said.

"That was quick," Freya said.

"Of course it was," Southwell said. "There's almost nothing to see."

CHAPTER SIX

"We've lifted the prints from the door handles," Katy began, as Ben and Freya pulled yet another pair of shoe covers on. "The carpets have had a good going over along with the surfaces around the house."

"I'm sensing by your tone, Katy, that we shouldn't cling to hope," Freya said, and Ben watched the two women, both of whom were admirable in their own rights yet worlds apart. Freya had been born into wealth, a mere one rung down the ladder from the aristocracy, or so she led him to believe. Either way, she had worked hard to shed the label that came with her heritage and had earned every step of her rank.

Katy Southwell, on the other hand, was from the far end of the spectrum. Gillespie told him when he and Southwell had first become an item that her parents hadn't two pennies to rub together. Yet, through little more than sheer dogged determination, she had worked her way through college and university, funding her path to become not just a fine crime scene investigator but, in Gillespie's words, a real creature of beauty.

It was as if Freya had taken a step down from high society, and Southwell had taken a step up from the doldrums. And somehow, these two magnificent women's paths had intertwined to create a formidable duo.

"If you're hopeful, Freya, then I'm afraid I'm doing a poor job setting the tone," Southwell said. "The place is clean. The tables have been polished and dusted; the carpet has been vacuumed, the kitchen surfaces have been wiped down—"

"I get the picture," Freya told her.

"Whoever broke in potentially used their elbow or foot to break the glass, reached in and unlocked the door."

"But you've dusted the door handle and the lock?"

"They're clean," she replied.

"Hold on," Freya said. "So, somebody broke the glass, reached in to unlock the door, assaulted Albert Reilly, and then left, locking the door behind them, presumably in the same manner?"

"It fits," Southwell said.

"And presumably, they either wiped the door handles down as they left or—"

"They wore gloves," Ben said. "Which suggests—"

"That it was premeditated," Freya said, finishing his thoughts for him. "Which begs the question—"

"Who would want to murder a ninety-three-year-old man?" Ben said. "Or at least, assault him."

"Well, well. You're quite the duo, aren't you?" Southwell said. "Like one mind split across two bodies."

"No," Freya said dismissively. "No, I just taught him well." She winked, and Southwell laughed aloud.

"Alright, you know the drill. We'll finish up here and get the report to you as soon as we can. I'll liaise with pathology, so toxicology and any swabs taken from the body will be a day or so later. But, be warned, we do have a lot on."

"Right, the body at the wedding," Ben said.

"Right," she replied. "I'll leave you with that little conundrum."

"One thing," Freya said, stopping Southwell in her tracks. "If you're so busy, I suppose you'll be working quite late."

Southwell's intelligent eyes lit up, computing the unspoken question in a heartbeat. She glanced along the hallway and out of the front door to where Gillespie was still leaning against his car, amusing himself with social media.

"If you're asking if Jim can stay out to play, Freya, then yes," she replied. "But he has to be home for his tea and a bath." She grinned at the little joke and ventured into the living room to join her colleagues, calling back over her shoulder. "Especially the bath."

There was something quite liberating about getting the all-clear from CSI. Any paranoia about damaging a crime scene was gone, and Ben was free to lean against the kitchen worktops without fear of a reprimand from either of the two powerhouses.

"How do you want to play this one?" he asked. "Can't be too many people wanting to kill an old man."

"Let's pick this up at the station," Freya replied. "Leave Gillespie here to meet the ambulance. Let him oversee the body being removed."

"It doesn't make sense," Ben mused, staring at the door lock. "Why would you lock the door on the way out when you've gone to the effort of smashing the window?"

"I'm more concerned about why somebody went to the trouble of hitting him after he'd already died."

"Ah, I've been thinking about that," Ben said. "It all depends on the pathology report, but if he died from a heart attack or something, then I wonder if it's possible that he saw his killer, had the heart attack and died moments before he was hit."

"Surely there would be more blood?" Freya said, and she stared up at Ben as if he might know the answer.

He shrugged instead.

"I don't know. It was just an idea," he said.

Freya shook her head, clearly not buying into Ben's wild stab in the dark. She came to a stop at the living room door, and Ben joined her.

"Forget something?" Southwell asked, looking up from the body.

"No, we're just hypothesising," Freya told her, and she pointed to the armchair in the middle of the room and spoke quietly to Ben. "If he was sitting there, he wouldn't have seen the intruder come in."

"And the intruder wouldn't have seen his face," Ben said. "They wouldn't have known if he was just sleeping or if he was—"

"Already dead," Freya replied, nodding. "Okay, this makes more sense than your last effort."

"I was just getting going," he said. "Takes a while to get lubed up, you know?"

She eyed him, clearly not amused.

"Bloody coward," she said instead. "If you're right, then they came in here, saw the top of his head above the armchair, and just clubbed him with something."

"The force would have been enough to knock him off the chair," Ben said, and he re-enacted the attack slowly. "The wound on the head is on the right side."

"Meaning our attacker is right-handed," Freya added. "But all this is little more than conjecture without a motive."

"Right," Ben said. "Who would have wanted to kill a ninety-three-year-old man?" She stepped away from the doorway and back into the kitchen, where she paced back and forth a few times, then returned wearing a helpless expression. She lowered her voice, perhaps keeping her vulnerabilities between the two of them.

"Let's inform the next of kin," she began, working the process through her brilliant mind. "Let's see what the neighbours have to say. Have Chapman look at his bank records."

"And his will?" Ben suggested.

"Yes," she said, clicking her fingers at the idea. "Yes, the will. Phone records. Have Chapman see who he spoke to recently."

"And who he spoke to regularly," Ben said. "My dad used to speak to his brother every Sunday night. It was a social thing. If Reilly had a friend or relative he spoke to or confided in, then maybe he mentioned something to them."

"Good," Freya said, then peered up at him, daring to tuck her hair behind her ear. "We're going to have to go back to basics on this one."

"We always go back to basics," he replied with a laugh. "The day the answer is staring us in the face is the day we've outgrown the job."

"Ben?" Southwell said from behind them, and they both turned to find her raising her goggles. "I think you need to see this."

CHAPTER SEVEN

"Albert Reilly," Freya announced as she wrote the name in the centre of the whiteboard. She turned and replaced the lid on the pen. "Ninety-three years old." She waved a hand across the mostly empty board. "We have some gaps to fill." The mood in the room was peaceful, yet uneasy, as it had been for months now. Uncertainty hung in the air like the way the sound of passing trains becomes a part of life to those whose houses back onto the lines. The sensation barely registered anymore, but it lingered. The question was, Freya thought, whether to waft the odour away or inhale it, embrace it, and use it to her advantage. "Gold, how was PC Frobisher in the end?"

"Oh, he was alright. A bit shaken up," Gold replied. "I think he was trying to put a brave face on it, but it all came out in the end. Sometimes the adrenaline just needs somewhere to go."

"Indeed," Freya said, reading between the lines. "Did he have much to say?"

"Not really. He and PC Lovell were flagged down by the couple over the road. He radioed it in, had a quick look around the back, and that's when he found the broken window. The door was locked, and the window was broken, and given what the neighbours had said about them not seeing Reilly for a few days, he put his boot to the wood. I think he was worried about being accused of overreacting, but—"

"I would have done the same," Ben added.

"He's alright, is Frobisher," Jewson said, and all eyes turned on the newest member of the team. "I worked with him," she explained. "Solid bloke. Good copper."

"And he didn't touch anything?" Freya asked Gold.

"No, guv," she replied. "He was certain of it. He checked for a pulse but touched nothing until we came along."

"Okay, Jewson, perhaps you can avail on your acquaintance with him and ask him to submit his fingerprints and DNA to the Custody Sergeant. The last thing I'd want is for Katy Southwell's team to find a rogue set of prints and come up with a false positive."

"Now, guv?"

"You can wait until we're done here," Freya told her, then addressed the room. "Has anyone heard from Gillespie?"

"He's on his way back," Nillson called out.

"Well, I'm glad to see he's keeping his partner informed," Freya replied, much to Nillson's annoyance. "Cruz, what about you and Jewson? How did you get on?"

"Na, we drew a blank, guv," he replied. "Nobody saw or heard a thing."

"Nothing at all? Not even the broken window?"

"Nope," he said, referring to his notes. "There was a fella two doors away. A Mr Yates. Said he was up early like he normally is."

"What's early?" Freya asked.

"Five-ish," Jewson cut in, referring to her own notes. "He said he got up, stuck the radio on for the news and weather, while he made a cup of tea, then filled his bird feeders and sat and watched them for a bit."

"Christ, if I ever get like that, can one of you lot come round and put me out of my misery?" Nillson said, which raised a few smiles.

"Anything else, Cruz?" Freya asked.

"Most of the other houses were too far away," Jewson replied before Cruz could respond. "Three of them didn't answer the door to us, two said they didn't see or hear anything, and one of them said they didn't even look out of their windows until the police car was there."

"Is your name Cruz?" Freya asked.

"Sorry?"

"Is your name Cruz?"

"Erm, no, guv."

"Good, when I want your input, PC Jewson, you'll know because I'll be looking at you."

"I just thought that—"

"You thought you could demonstrate some kind of ability or acumen by answering before Detective Constable Cruz had a chance."

"No, I—"

"Let me tell you something, Jewson. You are welcome on this team, of course, but the road to success lies in listening and paying attention to those with more experience. Cruz has such experience."

"I didn't mean to—"

"When I ask you to accompany a member of my team on a particular task, I expect you to demonstrate far more enthusiasm than I saw earlier this morning. You do not walk six steps behind; you walk side by side. You do not stand idle while Cruz knocks on the doors; you stand ready. We were attending a crime scene. A murder, nonetheless. Who's to say that whoever murdered Albert Reilly wasn't in one of those houses, panicking, desperate, and volatile?"

"Well, I—"

"In future, Jewson, I expect better. I read the reports from the previous investigation, and on paper, I have to say your efforts seem impressive. But what I saw today leads me to believe that the accounts of how you discovered evidence in the field and how you were responsible for finding the second body are somewhat skewed. Do better, Jewson. Do better."

Jewson's face had turned an ugly shade of claret, but she held her own and met Freya eye to eye.

"Cruz?" Freya said, eventually. "I'd like to see your findings presented on a map, please."

"Ah, yeah. I've done it, boss," he said, waving a piece of paper at her. Freya strode over to him, collected the piece of paper, and he stood to explain. "I've printed off an internet map, marked the house numbers, and all that corresponds to this." He handed her a second piece of paper, on which was a table with two columns. The first column denoted the house number, while the second column was used to provide remarks, such as no answer, or in the case of the house two doors from Albert Reilly's, a full account of how the occupant had woken, made tea, and listened to the news while he watched the birds.

"This is very good," Freya said, running her eyes over the map. Pound Road was U-shaped, meeting the main road through Martin at either end. Albert Reilly's house was situated on the section that ran adjacent to the main road, meaning that very few houses would have afforded the occupant a direct line of sight of the crime scene. "Doorbell cameras?"

"I've marked them on there. There were only two. One belonged to this house here," he said, pointing to a house on the bend in the road. "But it isn't working."

"And the other?"

"This house here," he replied, pointing to the house next door to that owned by the couple who had flagged Frobisher down. "No answer. They weren't home."

"And you knocked on every door, did you?"

"Every door on Pound Road, guv," Cruz said. "Didn't see much point in going through the entire village, but if you need us to—"

"No, that's fine," Freya told him nodding, as the doors burst open.

"Fear not," the incomer announced, brazen and bold. Gillespie beamed at the room. "I'm back." He dumped his bag and coat on his desk, dropped into his seat with a loud sigh, and then looked up at Freya. "What did I miss, boss? Anything juicy?"

Every ounce of Freya's desire to develop a fully functional team hissed and spat inside her but abated when she stared at the big Scotsman, and he smiled at her. She couldn't help but grin inwardly.

"You're just in time, Gillespie," she said. "I was just about to ask Sergeant Nillson about your visit to the house across the road to Albert Reilly's. She placed Cruz's map and the corresponding table on her desk and then perched on the desk again. "Perhaps you can give us an account?"

"Aye," he said, glancing at Nillson as if seeking permission. She shrugged at him like an over-looked little sister, and he fished his dog-eared notebook from his pocket, then flicked to the right page. "Mr and Mrs Armitage—"

"Armstead," Nillson corrected him, her tone as bored as her expression.

"Right," Gillespie replied. "What did I say?"

"Armitage."

He studied his notes, then looked across the room at her.

"You sure it wasn't Armitage?"

"Positive," she said, holding her notebook up. "You did the talking. I took notes like a good little girl, remember?"

"Right," he said, starting over. "Mr and Mrs Armstead. Retired teachers. Said they've known Mr Reilly for more than forty years. Said him and his wife used to look out for their kids when they were wee bairns. Now he's on his own and getting on a bit; they tend to keep an eye out for him, you know?"

"As you would hope," Freya said.

"Said they saw the bin there on Thursday evening. His carer takes it out for him, and he brings it back in, normally. But it still hadn't been collected on Sunday, and they were getting a bit worried. So, they went and knocked, but nobody was home."

"On the Sunday?"

"Aye, boss," he said. "They had an idea his son might have come and taken him out."

"He has a son?"

"Ah, yes,' Chapman cut in. "Robert Reilly."

"Next of kin?" Freya asked, to which Chapman nodded. "Get me his details, would you, Chapman?" She turned back to Gillespie. "Sorry, go on."

"They didn't see any lights that night, so they thought the son must have visited."

"Was that a regular occurrence?"

"Not regular," he replied. "But from time to time. Though, they did say Reilly normally lets them know when he's going away."

"But he didn't this time?"

"No, boss," Gillespie said. "But they said he's normally back on Sunday evening, so when they saw the bin there on Monday, they popped back over to have a look. That's when they flagged down..." Gillespie checked his notes again.

"Frobisher," Nillson said before he could find the right page.

"That's it. They flagged him down, said they were worried, and he went to have a look," Gillespie continued. "The officer with him..." Again, he looked at his notes.

"Lovell," Nillson said, and for the sake of consistency and Jewson's learning curve, Freya gave Nillson a polite stare and gestured that she should tone her attitude down.

"That's it. Lovell took them back to their house and asked them to wait inside, and that's where they stayed until we knocked on their door."

"What time was this?" Freya asked, to which Gillespie flicked through his notes, then begrudgingly looked across to Nillson.

"Don't suppose you—"

"Nine-thirty," Nillson said. "That's when they went across the road to his house. They were back inside at nine-forty."

"That's very accurate."

"The morning program was just starting on BBC One, boss," Nillson told her. "Mr Armstead turned the telly off when Lovell ushered them back inside. He said he saw the little clock in the corner of the screen."

"Thank you," Freya said. "Gillespie, can I ask that you write your notes up as soon as you've finished talking to a witness in the future? Writing them in your car in the station yard before you attend a briefing isn't the example we want to set, is it?"

"Eh?"

"Your car has been parked down there for fifteen minutes, Gillespie," Freya said. "Unless, of course, it takes you fifteen minutes to climb a single flight of stairs?"

Like criminals, there were two types of rogue officers in Freya's experience. The first were the Jewson's of the world, who would argue that blue is black until proven otherwise. The second, of which Gillespie was a prime example, had the courage to admit defeat and accept when they had been caught. Although, they didn't always hold their hands up without a fight.

"Aye," he said. "It was the first chance I had, but—"

"Perhaps you could have written them up while you were leaning against your car for an hour," Freya said. "Or was there something on social media that needed your undying attention?"

He opened his mouth to speak but was clearly out of excuses.

"Aye, you got me there, boss," he said. "Point taken."

"Good," Freya said, and she turned to the whiteboard. "And I don't know why you're grinning, Nillson," she said without looking. "There's no room on this team for good little girls to simply take notes." She noted the names that Cruz, Jewson, Gillespie and

Nillson had mentioned on the board then checked her watch. "Before we move forward and make a plan, I suggest you use the washroom if need be." She turned on her heels and eyed Nillson. "Or should I call it the little girl's room?"

"Point taken, boss," Nillson replied, more akin to Gillespie than she would ever admit.

"And we'll need coffee," Freya said, dragging a twenty-pound note from her handbag. She started towards Cruz, who cringed at the sight of it. But then she stopped before Jewson and laid the note flat on her desk. "Do you know the coffee shop up the road?"

"Sorry, guv? You want me to fetch coffee?" Jewson said, a look of repugnance spreading across her face.

"Mines a flat white," Freya told her, then turned to Cruz. "Cruz, you know what everybody has. Do you have a list?"

"Erm, yes, boss," he said, flicking to the very first page of his notebook.

"Well, seeing as you're no longer at the bottom of the ladder," Freya said, eyeing the newcomer carefully. "Perhaps you can hand over this particular task to Jewson?"

Reluctantly, Jewson dragged the twenty towards her.

"Understood, guv,' she said quietly, and Freya leaned forward to speak quietly in her ear.

"This game is about experience and respect," she whispered. "With the former comes the latter." She straightened and started back towards her desk. "But to gain the former, you must demonstrate the latter." She smiled as friendly a smile as she could. "No sugar for me, thanks."

CHAPTER EIGHT

The room cleared, aside from Ben and Freya, and while she stared at the blank whiteboard with her back to him, he hit the RETURN button a few dozen times, which was the standard practice for getting the bloody thing to wake up from its slumber. The IT Team had assured him time and time again that nothing was wrong and that the laptop would enter into sleep mode if it wasn't used for a period of time. Ben had subsequently suggested that the sleep feature be renamed the *coma* feature, as waking it was nigh on impossible. The little jibe had fallen on deaf ears, however, and they had alluded to the problem lying somewhere between the laptop and the chair, which was six-foot-something tall with fingers like little hammers.

"That was a bit harsh," he said to Freya as the little circle icon entered into its perpetual spin, giving the user hope that something was happening. Ben was sure, however, that it was not.

"Was it?" Freya replied casually.

"Why don't we give her a chance before we scare her off?"

She turned to look at him, clearly perplexed.

"Who's scaring her off?"

"Oh, I don't know," he said sarcastically.

"Don't play games, Ben. What makes you think I was scaring her off?"

"Maybe something about the former and the latter, and vice versa."

"Ah," she said indifferently, her mind on other things. "Well, if that scares her off..." she turned to look at him. "Then she's not the girl for us, is she?" She tapped the board with a manicured fingernail, one of the remaining parts of her limb that still resembled the old Freya. "Help me out here, will you?"

He glanced down at his laptop; even the little spinning thing had given up, as if the joy of giving him false hope wasn't even worth the effort. He hit the space bar a few times to see if he could at least start it spinning again, but the screen flickered twice, then went black.

"Go on," he said, joining her at the whiteboard. She had drawn a horizontal line across the bottom of the board. She marked the centre of the line with an X, then denoted it with Mr and Mrs Armitage knocked on Reilly's door. "It's Armstead, Freya."

"Sorry?"

"The neighbours. Mr and Mrs Armstead."

She eyed her mistake, then rubbed it out with the rag and corrected it, nostrils flaring as she did so.

Then she moved to the far left of the line, marked another X, and noted, Thursday PM - Bins taken out by...

"The carer?" Ben suggested.

"One for Chapman to look into," Freya replied, adding in two more Xs to the left of the first X and marking them as *Estimated time of death.*

"Somewhere between five and nine a.m.."

She tapped the board again, in the middle of that window on death.

"Cruz said the neighbour rose at five A.M., and he heard nothing. He even went outside to feed the birds." She turned to look at him quizzically. "Who feeds the birds at that time of the morning?"

"Someone who cares for birds," Ben replied. "And who doesn't like squirrels or pigeons."

"I don't understand."

"That's because you, my dear," he began, "are a city dweller. Fill those bird feeders up during the day, and the pigeons will have emptied the lot by dinner time. The poor little tits and wrens and whatnots won't have any breakfast."

Her raised eyebrows suggested she was mildly impressed, but she would never give such an opinion.

"He's got too much time on his hands," she mused aloud, then took up Cruz's street map and jabbed a fingernail at a few of the houses. "If anybody saw anything, it could only have been from inside these properties." She highlighted one. "This one is a no answer."

"So, we send Cruz and Jewson back?"

She nodded.

"Later. Maybe whoever lives there works nights."

"And none of them had doorbell cameras, except the one where nobody answered?"

"Not one that is working," Freya replied. She took a breath and ran her finger over her scar distractedly. "This one is going to be difficult. But, for a change, we at least have a very small pool of suspects to eliminate. Unlike some of the other investigations we've had to work through. Working through them will be easier. Proving their guilt, however, that will be far more challenging."

"What do you think about putting Jewson with Nillson?"

"You know what I think about that," she replied, turning her back on him.

"Come on. Look, Jewson needs someone to keep her in check."

"And Cruz?" Freya said. "What does he need?"

"A kick up the backside?"

"Cruz has earned his place on this team. More so than most. He's spent the best part of two years with Gillespie. Don't you think we should give him a chance to lead?"

"Freya, he can barely tie his shoelaces without asking for directions."

"He's earned some respect, Ben," she said without turning to face him. "And while I'm still here, I'll see to it he gets it. Let respect and experience be my legacy."

He laughed the comment off, and she finally turned to share in the amusement. But her expression stiffened, and something behind Ben caught her attention.

"Back so soon?"

Nillson closed the door as quietly as she had opened it and made her way to her desk.

"Just keen to get started, boss," she said, and Ben closed his eyes in dismay.

"You're going to have to say something," he said quietly, which she chose to ignore.

"I trust you didn't take my comments to heart, Anna," she said.

"Comments, boss? About your legacy?"

"About the little girl's room."

"Oh. Oh, no. I've got thicker skin than that."

Freya smiled at her as the door opened once more, and the rest of the team, minus Jewson, filed in.

"That's what I thought," she said. "I need you to lead by example."

"Boss," Nillson replied.

"That goes for all of you," Freya said, louder this time. "I don't want Jewson picking up any bad habits. Cruz, I need you to be firm with her. You know the processes. You know what I like and what I do not. It's your job to convey those to her."

"But boss—"

"And if she proves to be difficult, then you have my permission to try an alternative approach."

"An alternative approach, boss?"

"Be firm with her, Cruz. Fair, but firm. She'll respect you for it."

"Gabby, firm?" Gillespie laughed. "The only time he's firm is when—"

"There's no need for smut, Gillespie, thank you," Freya said, cutting him off. She sought Cruz's attention. "Firm but fair. Think about how Gillespie mentored you."

"Jim?" he said. "You want me to do to her what that lunatic did to me?"

"No, Cruz," Ben cut in. "No, we want you to do the exact opposite."

"Eh?" Gillespie said, but the conversation was cut short by Freya clapping her hands three times. "Seats. Let's get to it." She turned to the board, and Ben returned to his seat, with Gillespie still looking somewhat bemused. "What do we have?" Freya began, and in the top right-hand corner of the board, she wrote a small list, narrating as she wrote. "Broken window, locked door, puncture marks." She stopped and faced them all. That's all we have. From the crime scene, we have an early theory. We think that whoever killed Albert Reilly did so with intent. They broke the window. They used gloves to unlock the door, which means they came equipped. They entered the living room and were presented with Reilly sitting in his armchair. They used a weapon with a sharp corner, such as an ornament."

"What about the puncture marks?" Gold asked.

"They then left the house, locking the door the same way they had unlocked it, and made their escape,' Freya continued, acknowledging Gold's question with a nod.

"I thought he was already dead, guv," Nillson said. "Didn't I hear that?"

"There's a chance," Freya said. "We won't know until we talk to pathology. The fact of the matter is that somebody broke into that house and hit him. They intended for him to die. Whether or not a jury finds the individual guilty of murder is not down to us. We need to find this person."

"I've got a bit of background on him," Chapman said. "Might be nothing, but—"

"No, *this* is nothing," Freya said, waving at the board. "Whatever you have is more than we've got."

"Well, Reilly's wife died five years ago, according to the death records. According to Companies' House, he used to own a light haulage firm based out of Woodhall Spa."

"What did he do with it?" Ben asked.

"Passed it on to his son," she explained. "Who still owns it."

"Anything else?" Freya asked.

"I'm still looking," she replied, to which Freya thanked her with a smile.

"Guv?" Gold asked.

"Puncture marks?" Freya asked, and Gold nodded. "It was something Southwell discovered before we left. He has several puncture marks on both arms."

"He was injected with something?" Gillespie said. "Jesus, it's like that Salisbury thing."

"This is nothing like the Salisbury murder, Gillespie."

"Boss?" Cruz said, sticking his hand up like a schoolboy. "That doesn't make sense. If he brought gloves to break in and murder Reilly, then why would he use an ornament? Surely, he would have brought whatever weapon he planned on using?"

It was a valid point, and Freya's brief look at Ben added weight to her earlier remark about Cruz's experience.

"Very good," she said, finally. "Which would explain why none of the ornaments appeared out of place or missing."

"It was just a thought," he said, clearly not enjoying the public praise.

"First things first," she continued. "Chapman, I need you to do a few things to get things moving."

Chapman turned to a clean page of her A4 notebook and waited for the instructions.

"Find me the details for the next of kin."

"Robert Reilly, guv?"

"Yes, Ben and I will go and see him to deliver the news," Freya said. "We'll also go to the autopsy while we wait for the lab results to come back tomorrow. Meanwhile, I want you to give Nillson and Gillespie Reilly's phone, bank, and medical records." She turned to the two sergeants. "Go through them. Who did Reilly speak to? What medication was he on? Did he make any recent withdrawals? Find trends. Did he have somebody he spoke to regularly? If so, did he confide in them about something?"

"Aye, boss," Gillespie said while Nillson simply nodded.

"When you've done that, Chapman, I want details of Reilly's carer. Currently, whoever it is was the last person to see him alive last Thursday. I'm keen to talk to them."

"What about us, boss?" Cruz asked as Jewson backed into the room carrying a cardboard tray of takeaway coffees.

Freya waited for her to set the tray down on her desk, and she looked up as if realising she was the topic of conversation.

"You can go back to Martin," Freya said. "Knock on all those doors that weren't answered." She snatched up the street map and jabbed at the house with the doorbell camera. "Especially this one."

"What if they're not home?" Jewson asked.

"Then we wait," Cruz said, and Freya nodded at him. "We wait until they are."

CHAPTER NINE

The address Chapman had provided led Ben and Freya to a detached house on the outskirts of Woodhall Spa. Nestled among the trees, the building's east side peeked out from behind an enormous bed of established Hydrangeas, and as they drew closer, Freya was struck by the magnificent symmetry.

"Oh yes," she said as her eyes grazed the sight before her. "This is much more like it."

"See yourself in a place like this, do you?" Ben asked from the passenger seat, but he looked far from impressed. "I suppose this is more like the house you grew up in, is it?"

"No," she laughed casually. "No, this is more like the cottages my grandfather provided for the staff."

His head snatched to one side, and he pulled a crazed expression.

"Staff?"

"Back in the day, yes," she told him. "Not many, but enough. I have faint memories of the last of them. Daddy used to tell me stories about how the footman and butler used to add unrivalled finesse to his soirees." She stopped the car beside an elegant Jaguar and hit the button to turn the engine off. "When I was growing up, we had a gardener, and daddy had a man who helped him; kind of a butler-cum-valet. And there was a cook for a while."

"Jesus," Ben said. "We had a dog. I tried to teach him to do the washing up once, but it was a nightmare." He laughed even though Freya failed to be amused. "So you went from a manor house to a two-bedroom cottage. It's a wonder you have space to ring the bell."

"Do I need to remind you that when I first came to Lincolnshire, I lived in a motorhome on Huttoft Beach? And after that, it was a cottage on your father's land that hadn't been cleaned or maintained since Queen Victoria donned her black dress."

"Practising, were you?"

"Finding myself," she said. "I rather like my cottage. It's funny, isn't it? When somebody comes from nothing and makes something of themselves, they're congratulated. They're heralded as a success. But when somebody seeks a simpler life, they're considered mad, or I don't know, trying to be something they're not; trying to be normal."

Ben laughed again as he reached for the door handle.

"No, I'm not sure if I agree with that," he said. "As far as I can recall, nobody has ever accused you of being normal."

He climbed from the car, and Freya took her time to pull on her coat and checked her reflection in the visor mirror.

Gravel crunched underfoot as they made their way towards the front door.

"It's not that big. Six bedrooms at the most," Freya mused. "I doubt the gardens are bigger than an acre."

"An acre? You do realise that a developer would stuff a few dozen houses onto a piece of land this big. Besides, can you imagine having to cut the grass?"

"Coming from a man who grew up on several thousand acres."

"It's a farm," Ben argued.

"And I suppose your dad cuts the grass himself, does he?"

"No, we have a team who manage the crops and sheep for the grazing plots."

"Right, so who cleaned your house when you were growing up?"

"Mum did," Ben said. "Then, when she died, one of the farm hands wives took over."

"And the cooking?"

"She did that as well. Dad was busy in the fields."

"Right," she said, nodding for him to ring the bell. "I can only imagine your hardship."

"My upbringing was very different to yours."

"Oh, I imagine it was," she told him, then left the statement hanging there.

"We're not the same, Freya."

"I agree," she said, smiling at how easy it was to wind him up.

"I am *not* privileged."

"Indeed," she said as footsteps approached the door. They both found their game faces, and Freya smoothed her hair against the right side of her face, ignoring Ben's questioning eyes.

In less affluent areas, where terraced houses sat side by side, and neighbours heard nearly every conversation and saw almost every visitor, doors were opened with some trepidation, and often only as far as the security chain would allow. Yet, owners of houses such as the one Freya and Ben were visiting, where privacy was in abundance, owners seemed entirely ignorant of the dangers.

The door opened fully to reveal a woman in her early thirties. She had short blonde hair in a boyish style, wore tight jeans, a loose t-shirt, and clean white trainers.

"Hello?" she said hesitantly, and Freya was sure there was a hint of Eastern European in the voice.

She held up her warrant card, and Ben followed suit.

"We're looking for Robert Reilly," she said. "Is he home?"

"Ah," she said, unsure of herself. "Mr Robert?"

"That's right. Is he home?"

"He is," she said, nodding. "Wait, please."

She started to close the door, and Freya held up a hand to prevent it from closing fully, meeting some resistance at first, but it faded when the girl realised she wasn't going to be shut out.

"Bit young to be a girlfriend?" Ben said quietly.

"Maid," Freya told him, and he gave her a knowing stare.

"I suppose yours had uniforms, did they?" he said. "Little black and white numbers?"

"And yours?"

He laughed casually. "Well, she didn't look like that, that's for sure."

The door opened again, this time by a man who appeared to be in his late fifties or early sixties. He wore tan corduroys, smart brown shoes, and a V-neck sweater over an Oxford shirt.

"Now then," he grumbled. "What's all this?"

Freya held her warrant card up for him to see, and behind him, from a doorway off the large hall, the young woman peered out inquisitively.

"I'm Detective Chief Inspector Freya Bloom," she started, then presented Ben. "This is Detective Inspector Savage. I wonder if we might come in."

"Now?"

"I'm afraid it's not good news, Mr Reilly."

He looked between them, settling on Freya.

"Dead then, is he?"

She nodded once and shared a bemused look with Ben.

"I'm afraid so," she said.

He stiffened at the news, inhaled, and then stepped out of the way.

"Tea, Nadia, please," he said, and the young woman slipped off into the back of the house. Reilly closed the door behind them and led them into what Freya assumed was the more formal of several reception rooms -a pair of Chesterfield sofas faced each other, adjacent to a large open fireplace. The ceilings were high, the mouldings were timeless, and the furniture was tasteful. With a sweep of his hand, he invited them to sit on one of the sofas while he assumed a position opposite, leaning forward with his elbows on his knees. "Suppose I've been expecting a visit," he said sadly. "Although I must admit, I wasn't expecting the cavalry."

"Matters such as this are best dealt with face to face, Mr Reilly," Freya replied.

"I'll pay for everything, of course."

"Excuse me?" Ben said.

"The funeral costs," Reilly said. "I doubt he had two pennies to rub together."

"Mr Reilly—"

"I'd like to say something, too. Unless, of course, I'm not wanted there."

"I imagine your presence will be very much needed, Mr Reilly," Freya said, to which he nodded.

"I've reached out to my legal team, but I want it to be known that if there's any shred of foul play or negligence, then I'll accept responsibility."

"Mr Reilly, I must say this is all very..." Freya said, searching for the right word. "Formal."

"What do you want me to say?" he said. "I didn't know the bloke, but I'm not a complete bastard. I won't hide behind lawyers. If we're at fault here, then we'll accept it.

"We?" Ben said. "I'm sorry, we seem to be at cross purposes here."

"Look, I've spent the past thirty years making sure that Reilly is a name people can trust. I'm not going to have it dragged through the mud unnecessarily. Is that clear?"

"Crystal clear," Freya said.

"Good. Well, if you need me to come and make a statement, then I'm free this afternoon. I imagine it'll take your forensics teams a week or two to establish whether or not there's grounds for an enquiry."

"Of course," Freya said.

"In the meantime, I'd like to pass on my sincere condolences to his immediate family, but I'm reluctant to place either of us in a difficult position. I imagine they'll need time to grieve, and the last thing they need is to find me on their doorstep."

"How astute you are," Freya said slowly.

"Have you seen this kind of thing before?" he asked. "What do you think is a reasonable time to wait?"

"I'm sorry?" Freya said.

"For the family," he explained. "How long do you think I should wait before I send flowers or something? I don't want them to think me heartless."

"We're yet to establish any other family members," Freya said, then caught his eye. "Aside from yourself, of course."

"Sorry?"

"You are his next of kin," Freya explained. "As far as we know, you're also his only living relative."

"His next of..." He stared at her as if she had spoken another language entirely. "I don't even know the man. All I've been told is that he was riding his bike through Martin and wound up under one of my lorries." The door opened, and the young woman entered carrying a tray with a teapot and three cups. "Not now, Nadia," he yelled at her, and she scuttled away with a rattle of crockery. He turned to face Freya and Ben. "Next of kin? Are you telling me—"

"That your father was found at his house in Martin this morning, Mr Reilly," she said. "However, it seems our timing has been off."

CHAPTER TEN

Robert Reilly stared up at the ceiling, his head resting on the back of the couch, and his mouth hanging open in shock.

"If there was any confusion, Mr Reilly, then I can only apologise," Freya said, nudging Ben's leg and then gestured for him to fetch the tea.

Ben rose from the couch and left the room unhurried, leaving Freya and Reilly in silence. It was typical of Freya's cold approach to such matters to give room for silence to breed. She would wait for Reilly to pose a question, regardless of how awkward that silence may become.

There were four doors off the hallway and a wide staircase to one side. Only two of the doors were open, one of which he had just come through. From the other, he heard the familiar rattle of crockery.

He paced to the front door, found the recently dialled numbers on his phone, and then hit the green button to initiate the call.

"Ben?" the voice said after a few rings. Ben imagined the big Glaswegian sitting back in his chair with his feet up and the coffee Jewson had fetched for him in his hand. "Missing me already, are you?"

"I need you to do something for me," Ben said. "What was the name of the haulage firm the lorry belonged to this morning?"

"This morning? The RTA, you mean?"

"Yes, what was the name of the firm? Can you remember?"

Gillespie sucked air in through gritted teeth, like a mechanic dreaming up a quote.

"It was Irish," he said. "Donnelly's?"

"Donnelly's? You sure?"

"No," he said. "No, the name was on the driver's door, but to be honest, I was more concerned with the driver."

"Get hold of Souness, can you? Find out for me."

"Erm, Ben? Don't you think we're busy enough?" Gillespie replied. "You know? Dead fella in his living room. Broken glass and all that?"

"Yeah, and do you know who that old man was?"

"Albert Reilly, weren't it?"

"Talk to Souness, Jim," Ben said. "If I'm right, then it's his name on the door of that lorry."

He ended the call, turned and caught a glimpse of somebody slipping into the kitchen, so he followed, passing through a short rear hallway, most likely added to prevent the noise of the kitchen from polluting the frivolities of the owners and their guests.

Nadia looked up at him, wide-eyed.

"Shall I take those?" he said with a friendly smile.

"Oh, no. Mr Robert would not like it—"

"That's okay," he replied, stepping over to the central island. He slid the tray towards him. "He can shout at me all he likes." She smiled shyly, then bowed her head. "Is he always like that?"

"Pardon?"

"Mr Reilly," Ben said. "Is he always so short-tempered?"

"Oh no, no, no. Mr Robert is good man,' she said, her hands coming together in prayer. "But this morning. Bad news."

"Have you worked for him long?"

She stared at him again, fearful, as if he'd threatened her.

"One year," she said, and Ben tuned into her accent.

"Polish?" She cocked her head to one side and eyed him cautiously. "I have lots of Polish friends," he explained. "My dad has a farm. If it wasn't for our Polish friends, I doubt we'd even still have it. Hard-working." She nodded, seeming to ease a little. "And proud."

"Of course," she replied.

"Well," Ben said, grabbing hold of the tray. "You seem to have landed on your feet here."

"My feet?"

"You have a nice place to work," Ben explained. "Big house. Warm. Nice."

"Ah, yes. House. Big, yes?"

"Too big for my liking," Ben replied. "Is it just Mr Reilly?"

"I'm sorry. My English is not so good."

"Living here," Ben said. "Is there anybody else?"

"Ah, no. Only Mr Robert. I think sometimes he..." She waved her hand about searching for the right phrase. "Set in ways, no?"

"Ah," Ben said, nodding emphatically.

"It is difficult, no? New people. Friends. They make mess. They move things. Mr Robert not like this and that here and there."

"I see," Ben said, speaking slowly to be understood. "I think sometimes moving this and that here and there is a good thing, no?" He tapped his head with an index finger. "Keeps us awake, no?"

She laughed once, and it was a sight to behold. But it faded fast as if it was too precious to waste.

"You cook and clean?"

"For Mr Robert," she said, nodding.

"And you live in the house?"

"Me? Live here? No. I live outside."

"Outside the house?"

"Outside, outside," she said, gesturing that she meant some distance away. But the topic of her home was clearly too much for her to discuss, and she turned away. "Please. I must go. I have work."

Ben smiled at her.

"I wouldn't want to keep you," he said. "But maybe stay away from Mr Reilly today." He rubbed his eyes. "Very sad day."

"Sad. Yes. Of course."

She started towards the back door, where a large cupboard door was open.

"One more thing," he said. "You work here every day?"

"Me? Here?"

"Every day?"

"Yes. Every day. Monday, Tuesday, Wednesday, Thursday, Friday, Saturday. Every day."

"Not Sunday?"

"No. Sunday my day. My free day."

"At least you get one day to yourself," he mused. "What time? Eight o'clock? Nine o'clock?"

"Working?" She said, her eyes wide. "No. Six clock. Is big house, no? Too much work."

"Thank you," he told her, then carried the tray from the room.

A few moments later, he set it down on the coffee table that stood between the two couches and took his place beside Freya.

"I'm sorry, I don't know what to say," Reilly said. "This is all a bit of a shock. I thought you were talking about—"

"Again, I'm very sorry," Freya said. "We hadn't realised that your firm was involved in the accident—"

"Can I ask something?" Reilly said. "Was it...you know? Quick? His heart, right? It was bound to give in one of these days. I should have had him here, really. But I'm afraid we would have throttled each other to death."

"I'm afraid we won't know the cause of death until the post-mortem, which should be this afternoon."

"Post-mortem?" he said. "Is that necessary? Can't they tell how he died from... I don't know, examining him?"

"Mr Reilly," Freya said, side-eyeing Ben. "Your father was discovered on the floor of his living room."

"Christ," Reilly said, flinging himself back in the chair. "Sod it—"

"He had injuries," Freya said, cutting his emotions short.

He stared up at her.

"Injuries? What do you mean? He had a fall. Or—"

"There was an injury to his head," she replied. "To his temple. We're treating his death as suspicious."

"What?" Reilly said, almost laughing but not quite. "Suspicious? He was ninety-two years old."

"Ninety-three," Ben said.

"Right," Reilly acknowledged. "He was ninety-three. You know what ninety-three-year-old men do, don't you? Fall over is what they do."

"Mr Reilly, we are neither in the habit of creating further upset for you nor making ourselves busier than we need to be. We found evidence of a break-in, and we have reason to believe the injuries your father sustained are from an attack of some kind. We'll know more after the post-mortem, at which time we'll invite you in to see him."

"See him?"

"We will need his body to be formally identified, and of course, you'll need a chance to say goodbye."

"See him? Me? I don't want to see the old—"

"Mr Reilly, might I reiterate that we are treating your father's death as suspicious. We will, in due course, be conducting an investigation, during which we will need to eliminate his close friends and relatives from our enquiries."

"Me?" he said. "You're accusing me? You come round here, tell me my old man's dead, and then in the next breath—"

"Nobody is accusing anybody of anything, Mr Reilly. It's a process we must follow. It allows us to eliminate those closest to the victim before we take the investigation wider."

"Wider?"

"Close friends," she said. "Was he close to anybody?"

"Dad? Close to anybody? He alienated himself from society, lady. He spoke to a handful of people and nobody else."

"And who were they? I presume you were one of them?"

"He spoke to me out of necessity," Reilly said. "If he had his own way, he'd have scrubbed my name from his address book years ago."

"Anybody else?" Freya asked. "The couple opposite seemed to know him quite well."

"The couple opposite? What, Judy and George?"

"The Armsteads," Ben said.

"Yeah, that's them," Reilly confirmed, then shook his head. "And no, they were not one of the few. Liked to think they were. But they weren't. Dad found them irritating. Had no time for people like that."

"Like what?"

"Interfering," he said. "They like to stick their noses into other people's business if you know what I mean."

"That's odd. I was reliably informed that they kept an eye on you while you were a child playing in the streets."

"Oh, they did. Didn't bloody ask them to, did he?" He shook his head again. "I'll get you a list of people Dad used to talk to," he said. "It'll be short."

"And I'm sorry to have to ask this, Mr Reilly, but do you know of any reason whatsoever why somebody would want to hurt your father?"

Again, Reilly laughed, and this time it was genuine.

"Yeah, I'll get you a list of those, too," he said. "It'll be long."

CHAPTER ELEVEN

"Well, that was a turn-up for the books," Ben said as he climbed into the car. Freya slipped out of her coat, laid it across the rear seat, and then took her time to get comfortable in the driver's seat. "For a minute there, I thought we had a confession coming. Would have been the shortest bloody murder enquiry we've had to deal with."

"It certainly is a bad day for him," Freya agreed.

"Though, I'm dubious as to which piece of bad news has hit him the hardest," Ben said. "He seemed more upset about the fella on the bike than he did his dad dying. It's like he's dead inside or something."

"His dad was ninety-three," Freya said. "What did he think was going to happen?"

"Yeah, well. My old man's no spring chicken, but I'd be devastated if he went. Especially like that."

"I think it all depends on circumstances," she replied. "My father was dying for a long time. I would wake up each day wondering if he was still with us." She shrugged a little. "Then, one day, I got the call, and that was that. I think I did my grieving before he'd even died."

"Jesus, Freya. There's being efficient, and there's being efficient."

"It wasn't about efficiency, Ben. It's how I coped with it." She looked across at him. "You don't get to choose how you grieve. You just do."

"So, if he was to have died suddenly, do you think you would have grieved differently?

"Almost certainly," she replied. "But we can't choose, Ben. You can't hope your father gets ill. Daddy suffered a great deal before he—"

"Not *my* dad," Ben said, cutting her off. "Where's that list of people Reilly gave you?"

She followed the direction he was taking the conversation, then withdrew the slip of paper from her bag and handed it to him.

"Terri James," he said. "That's who we need to talk to."

"The carer?"

"Of course, we could always go back inside and ask *Reilly* if his dad was dying—"

"Okay, okay," she said. "I suppose it'll save Chapman from having to go through his medical records."

"Who else is on the list?"

He perused the list of three names briefly.

"Harriet Underwood, sister," he said. "And Roger Havers." He looked across at her. "Friend."

"And only a number for the sister?"

"Well, she *is* his aunt. He wouldn't have a reason to have his dad's mate's phone number, would he?"

"No, but you'd think he would have some means of getting in touch with the carer."

Ben gave it some thought.

"I suppose," he said, folding the paper and handing it back to her. "Where to now?"

"Well, I was hoping to swing by the hospital before going back to the station," she replied, scrolling through her emails on her phone. "But I haven't had confirmation from Pip yet." She dumped her phone into her bag and dropped it into the footwell at Ben's feet. "But the last thing I want to do is turn up at the pathology department uninvited. We need Pip on our side on this one. You know how volatile she can be. I suppose we can do some background work. It might be worth paying the carer a visit."

"We can't launch an investigation, Freya," Ben said. "Not until we've got a positive ID and confirmation from Pip that the head wound was indeed foul play."

"I'm not talking about dragging anybody down to the station, Ben. I just want to do some digging," she said. "The sister. Surely we can talk to her."

"Did Reilly say he would call her?"

"No, but then why would he? The man is dead inside, remember?"

"Okay, okay," Ben said. "So, Robert Reilly is either emotionally dead, or he knew his dad was on his way out."

"Right," Freya said.

"Or, he had something to do with it."

"Oh come on," Freya said. "Two minutes ago, you said we couldn't start investigating until—"

"I'm not investigating," Ben said, holding his hands up in defence. "I'm just throwing it out there. That whole charade about him thinking we were there for the accident could have been an act designed to throw us off the scent."

Freya stared through the windscreen, spying a thoughtful figure standing in the house's west window where, not ten minutes before, they sat with Reilly.

"Souness seemed pretty switched on," she said, to which Ben nodded as his phone vibrated in his pocket.

"He won't sit around waiting, that's for sure," he replied, pulling his phone out.

"He'll be in an interview room with the driver right now," Freya said. "I know I would be."

"And when the driver claims he did all he could or that there was a fault with the lorry, Souness will contemplate a manslaughter charge for the company." He held the phone up to show Freya the message Gillespie had sent. "It's Reilly Haulage. Same firm. Same man."

"So Robert Reilly is in for a rough ride."

"It'll take a day or so for forensics to come back with any data," Ben added. "Even if the lorry was overloaded or poorly maintained, he won't move on Reilly until he has the data to back the charge up."

"Which means we have until Souness receives the data from the accident forensics team to question him," Freya replied. "If Souness brings him in on the manslaughter charge, then it'll only make life difficult for us."

"Not impossible," he said.

"But difficult," she reiterated. "And I suspect this one is going to be difficult enough as it is."

"So, you want to bring him in as soon as we can?"

"I do," she said. "In the meantime, let's go and see the carer and the sister. Let's see what they have to say. You never know, they might give us something to work with." She turned her head away and stared out of her window at the sleek Jaguar parked beside them. "Get Chapman on the phone, will you?"

She heard Ben scrolling through his phone and took a moment to bring the facts together in her mind, but there were so few, and the possible directions of travel were so great in numbers the task was nigh on impossible.

"And if they tell us that Albert Reilly was dying and has been for years?" he asked.

"Then, I shall adjust my opinion of Reilly Junior accordingly," she said, forcing a grin. "And *then* I'll bring him in."

"Ben?" Chapman's voice was tinny through the phone's loud-speaker, but her efficiency was still evident.

"You're on loudspeaker," Freya called out. "We've spoken to Robert Reilly. Apparently, his father has a sister close by. A Harriet Underwood. Can you find me an address, please? I'd like to pay her a visit before we come back."

"Harriet Underwood," Chapman narrated. "Anything else?"

"Yes, get in touch with Pip, will you? We need to move fast on this."

"Pathology," Chapman said, again speaking the words as she wrote. "Hold on a moment."

A scratching sound came over the line, and Freya imagined her placing the handset to her chest while she dealt with an enquiry.

"Sorry about that," Chapman said. "Hold on, I'm putting you on loudspeaker."

Ben gave Freya a knowing look, and the background noise of the call increased.

"Ben, that you, fella?" Gillespie called out.

"Yes, mate."

"Thought I'd give you a wee update."

Freya could picture the scene at Chapman's desk. She would be sitting back, keeping the top of her blouse from Gillespie's roving eye, while he would be sitting on her desk, creating havoc with Chapman's neat arrangement of stationery and notes. It wouldn't even surprise Freya to hear Gillespie break wind and mutter something like, "Better out than in, eh, Chapman?"

"Go on, Jim," Ben said.

"Well, you were right about the name. It's Reilly's alright. Owned by Albert Reilly's son, Robert," Gillespie said. "I tell you what. He's going to be having a bad day."

"Well, for once, I agree with you, Gillespie," Freya said. "And for what it's worth, we're unsure which of the two incidents he's more upset about."

"Ah, Christ, you've been to see him already? Have you put him on suicide watch?"

"He's not in custody, Jim," Ben said. "He didn't actually seem too surprised to hear about his old man."

"Aye, but you never know, eh? A double blow like that. I mean, it's not like he doesn't know what he's in for."

Freya peered quizzically at Ben to see if he understood the comment, but he simply shrugged.

"Sorry, Gillespie?" she said. "What do you mean, he knows what he's in for?"

"Well, he's been through it before," Gillespie replied.

"Been through what? Start talking bloody sense, will you?"

"Manslaughter, boss," he replied. "This isn't the first time it's happened to Reilly's."

"His firm has been involved in a fatal accident before now?"

"Aye," Gillespie said. "And I'll bet he won't get away with this one."

"No," Freya said quietly, meeting Ben's curious stare. They both turned towards that forlorn figure in the west window, who held a glass to his mouth and knocked it back as if to numb his senses. "No, I don't suppose he will."

CHAPTER TWELVE

The bungalow Chapman's research had led them to was a far cry from either Albert Reilly's old council house or his son's lord of the manor-esque country house.

One of the first things that Ben noticed was how neat the borders were and how well established the rows of Salvias were. His eye was drawn to the little path that led from the little open porch in either direction and presumably met up again to the rear somewhere. While the roads and the verges were covered in a thick blanket of leaves and would be until they rotted, the property they parked outside seemed impervious to the seasonal plague that gardeners loathed. The little lawn had been clipped short, and the path had been swept clear.

It was one of those properties that, before he had met Freya, Ben would have enjoyed. The gardens to the rear and the sides were ample, not extravagant, but large enough to make his own. But more importantly, the house was small. Probably only a single bedroom which in his retirement, would have suited him just fine.

The most appealing aspect of such a home, though, he considered, was the privacy. Robert Reilly's house may have been buried behind trees, but there was still no escaping the neighbour's noise, even if they were a hundred yards away.

But this place, Ben thought, this was the dream. There wasn't another house in sight. Woodhall Spa, with all its amenities, was less than a five-minute drive away, and still, Harriett Underwood could have danced naked in her garden if she wished and sung at the top of her voice, and nobody would be the wiser.

"You seem thoughtful," Freya said, dragging him from his thoughts. He said nothing and shoved his door open.

"You ever think about retiring?" he asked as they walked up the neat little path to the front door.

"Oh, for God's sake, Ben. Not this again," she said. "I'm back. Can't we just leave it there?"

"No," he said dismissively. "No, I didn't mean that. I just meant retirement in general. Do you ever think about it?"

"Given that I escaped death and spent weeks in hospital, Ben, I'd say I've given it more thought than most."

He laughed, and reached up to ring the doorbell, which issued a polite yet classically cheerful, ding-dong.

"I want to live somewhere like this," he said. "No fuss. No visions of grandeur. Just a simple house close to the shops but far enough away to be on my own."

"On your own?"

"On our own," he said.

"You realise you have at least another fifteen years to do," she said. "And let's face it, the way this government is going, even then, you'll have to find a little job to keep us going. Your pension won't be worth much. And if you're thinking of the inheritance from your dad's farm, then you need to watch the news—"

"I just..." he began. "I just want to think about it. I want something to look forward to."

She peered at him, trying to read his thoughts, but he kept his expression opaque.

"Be there in a minute," a voice called out, and so characterful was it that Ben imagined somebody inside impersonating an elderly lady.

Eventually, the door opened a crack, as far as the chain would allow, and a wrinkly little face peered out through the crack.

"Now then," she said, and Ben couldn't help but smile. It was a greeting he hoped he would hear until his dying day.

"Good morning, Mrs Underwood," Ben said, and he held up his warrant card. "We wondered if we could get a few minutes of your time."

"My time? What are you? Not those Jehovah's, are you? Only spoke to you last week—"

"We're with the police, Mrs Underwood," Ben told her, and he held his warrant card closer, allowing her a few extra seconds to examine it.

"I see," she said, and her jaw swung from side to side as she tongued her false teeth. "Well, time I can afford." She disengaged the security chain and opened the door fully. "Donations, however..." She shook her head gravely. "Those I struggle with."

"I can assure you all we need is a few minutes," Freya added, beaming at her.

"My word," the old lady said, leaning forward to get a closer look at Freya. "Been in the wars, ain't ya."

Freya hurriedly turned away, dragging her hair over her face, so Ben assumed the lead.

"Would you mind if we came in?"

"Well, I hope so. I'm not letting all my heat out," Underwood replied. "Took me all bleeding morning to get the place warm."

"I'll..." Freya started. "I'll just wait in the car."

"No, Freya."

"What'd she say?" Underwood asked, her nose scrunching with the effort of hearing.

"Nothing," Ben told her, and Freya stared at him. "She was just about to come inside."

"Well, come on, then. Take me all bleeding day to get the place warm again."

The old lady trotted inside and disappeared into the living room.

"I'm not going in there," Freya said.

"Oh, come on. She's harmless. She's like everyone's favourite grandma."

"Not *my* favourite grandma," Freya hissed back. "My grandma had a handbag full of Werthers Originals. She didn't bloody insult me as soon as she saw me."

"She didn't mean anything by it," Ben told her. "Come on."

Freya shook her head. "This was a mistake."

"Look, if you can't put up with a little old lady, how the bloody hell do you think you're going to manage with the rest of the world? There are far worse people out there, as well, you know."

Freya's shoulders rose and fell, and she sighed heavily.

"If she says one more thing—"

"Then you'll politely distract her with your beauty and intellect," Ben said. "Now. In."

He stepped back, inviting her to lead the way, and then followed her inside, where he was hit by a heat he could only describe as akin to the Sahara desert on a hot summer's day.

"You coming in?" Underwood called out. "Don't stand out here all bleeding day. I've got things to do, you know?" Freya gave Ben a hateful look, but he couldn't help but grin. "Got my washing to put on, lunch to make..."

"Tongues to sharpen," Freya whispered to Ben and then let herself be nudged into the living room.

"Ah, there you are. Thought you'd got lost."

"No, we were just..." Freya started, doing her best to unbutton her coat before she passed out.

"Wiping our feet," Ben cut in. "Lovely carpet."

"Oh," Underwood replied, gazing curiously at them as they both sought somewhere suitable to lay their coats.

"Warm in here," Ben said, tugging on his collar.

"Not when you've skin this old," Underwood told him. "Let's the cold in; it does. Bones like bleeding ice cubes, I've got. Course, it runs in the family. We all run cold."

"Do you have a large family?" Freya asked, and the old lady peered at her injured hand unabashed.

"What happened to you then, missy?"

"I'm sorry?"

"Been in the wars, ain't ya? Nasty business by the looks of it."

"Mrs Underwood—" Ben began but was cut short by Freya.

"I'm afraid we have some very bad news for you," she said. "It's concerning your brother, Albert."

"Oh?" the old lady said. She sat forward in her seat, ran her tongue around her teeth once more, and then waited.

"I'm afraid he was found dead in his house this morning," Freya said, to which Underwood nodded once, then turned her head towards the television. She reached for the remote control, hit the button to unmute the TV, and Ben was surprised the damn thing didn't shake itself from the stand the sound was so loud.

"Do you understand what we're telling you, Mrs Underwood?" he said, but she was unmoving. Her eyes were fixed on some daytime TV presenter with a spray tan and Turkey teeth.

"Mrs Underwood," Freya said. She reached for the remote, sliding it from the old lady's hand, and then switched the television off. Slowly, Underwood turned to her, her eyes accusing.

"You said you had bad news," she grumbled. "So where is it, then?"

CHAPTER THIRTEEN

"We've spoken to your nephew, Mrs Underwood," Ben said. "Robert?"

"That right, is it?" The old lady replied. "Alright, is he? How'd he take it?"

"Much like you did," Freya said. "Although, I'll credit him with a little more sentiment and excuse him for certain distractions."

"Only us left then, is there? Should give him a call, really. Make sure he's alright."

"Were they close?" Freya asked, and Ben frowned at her as Mrs Underwood peered through the window.

"My brother weren't close to no-one, missy," she replied, then mumbled to herself. "Not in this world, anyway."

"Oh?" Freya said, regaining her attention.

"His wife," Underwood said. "Mary. She was the only one who could get through to him. The only one he would open up to."

"I see," Freya told her. "Well, Robert seems to think he opened up to you."

"Did he heck," she said almost immediately. "Thought myself lucky if I got a phone call. Christmas, that was when he called.

No doubt lonely and feeling sorry for himself. But that's when he called. That's when we spoke."

"You haven't spoken to him since Christmas?"

"No, tell a lie. I paid him a visit," she said. "Must have been a month ago, now." She leaned forward conspiratorially. "Wouldn't answer the phone, would he?" She shook her head to add weight to her snarl. "I was out that way, and you know what? I thought, sod it, I'm going to knock on his door. Miserable old beggar."

"And he opened it, did he?"

"No. Not him. His girl did."

"His girl?"

"Yeah, the home help girl. She answered."

"And she let you in?"

"Had no choice, did she? Weren't going to let little upstart turn me away, was I? Oh no. The old bastard damn near fell out of his armchair when he saw me."

"I take it he wasn't pleased to see you?" Ben asked.

"He wasn't pleased to see anyone, so I never took it personally," she replied. "He always was a loner. S'why he did what he did. You know? The lorries, and that. Course, nobody thought he'd make anything of it. But he did, and credit where it's due."

"Are you saying he drove lorries to be on his own?"

The old lady nodded at him.

"Course," she said. "Started out with one. Used to run around for one of them antiques places in Horncastle, he did. Drove all over the country. That was good work back then. Honest work. Then I suppose he got busier. Got one of his mates involved to drive a second lorry, which meant he needed a yard, and before we knew it, he had a fleet of lorries and drivers, and all of a sudden, he weren't doing any driving. He was sat behind his desk in his old portacabin counting his money."

"I'm sorry if this sounds rude, Mrs Underwood," Ben said. "But we were at your brother's house. He didn't strike me as a particularly wealthy man."

"Yes, well," she replied. "He wasn't exactly destitute, was he?"

"And did Robert start out as a driver?" Freya asked. "Did he work his way through the ranks?"

"Robert, drive?" she laughed. "That boy hasn't done a day's work in his life. No, he took it all over, didn't he? He worked in the office with his dad, learned the ropes, and that. Then, when the time was right, he took over." She gazed at the fireplace, lost in thought, then tore herself away. "Course, Robert isn't shy of spending a few quid here and there. Seen his house, have you?"

"We have," Freya said.

"That's what you get when you don't work for it. Spoiled, if you ask me. What does he need all that for? S'not like he's got kids or owt, is it? Just him in there, with that little wench."

"Nadia?" Ben asked for clarification.

"That her name, is it? The maid?"

"She seems friendly enough."

"Oh, she would. Rinsing him for what he's worth, she is. Mark my words, she'll be earning more than you, and what does she do for it, eh? Make tea? Clean the house? Cook dinner for one?"

"Has he never married?"

"Married? No. Too much like his dad, he is. Can't abide people. No patience. No empathy."

"And you, Mrs Underwood?" Freya asked. "Did you marry?"

"Course I did," she replied haughtily, and she nodded at a picture frame nestled among some photographs on the sideboard. "See that letter? That's from the Queen; God rest her soul. Sixty years. Diamond wedding anniversary. We were only a few months from our sixty-fifth when he died." She gave a hard stare. "Cancer got him in the end."

"Well, it's nice to see *you* in such good health," Ben said.

"Good health?" she said. "Didn't you hear me rattle when I walked? Pills for this, pills for that, bleeding injections every week, and do you think I can get in and see a doctor?" She shook her head. "I call up like they ask, but it takes all morning. Bloody woman tells me I'm twentieth in the queue. And then, when you do finally get through, the receptionist wants to know the ins and outs of a ducks arse. Who ever heard of that? Bleeding receptionist. I don't want to tell the receptionist about my piles. I want to speak to a doctor."

"You said you have injections," Freya said. "Might I ask what for?"

"Christ, you an' all."

"I'm sorry, but your brother had puncture marks. I was just wondering if there was a link."

"Sounds about right," Underwood said. "Blood thinners. Can't think of the name now. They change it every so often. But it keeps me going. Stops my old heart seizing up like Dad's did and his dad before him."

"Oh, so it's hereditary, is it?"

"S'pose it is," she said. "Get to my age, and you'll take whatever they give you if it means you can walk to the bathroom and back."

"Mrs Underwood, is there anybody else your brother might have been close to? Somebody he might have confided in?"

She shrugged casually.

"S'pose you've spoken to old Roger, have you?"

"Roger?"

"Roger Havers," she said as if they should have known the answer. "Him and Albert have been mates for years. It was him I mentioned earlier. The mate he got driving for him."

Freya fished the little slip of paper Robert Reilly had given them from her handbag and handed it to Ben, who checked it and nodded.

"I don't suppose you know where we could find Roger, do you?"

"You don't have to look far," she said with a laugh. "Lives opposite. Thick as thieves, them two were."

"I thought the Armsteads lived opposite."

"No, the next one along," Underwood said. "If Albert had a secret, he would have told it to him. Mark my words."

"They must have been close," Freya said. "If they lived opposite each other, I mean."

"You make it sound like some kind of plan," Underwood said. "Well, it weren't. Grew up there, didn't we? Pound Road."

"Albert's house is your family home?"

"S'right. Dad bought it when he was alive. Roger used to come and go as he pleased when we were kids. It was safe back then, though. Could leave your door open. Not like now."

"Mrs Underwood, is Roger still alive?"

"Far as I know, he is," she said, then gave it some thought. "Yeah, he must be. Saw him when I paid Albert a visit. He was out in the garden tending his roses. He always had an eye for gardening, did Roger. Good with his hands."

"Well, thank you for your time," Ben said, sliding a contact card onto the coffee table. "I appreciate you haven't really had time to digest the news, but if you would like the chance to say goodbye to your brother, we can make the arrangements."

"Say goodbye? To my brother?" she said, shaking her head. "Thank you." She slid the card back towards Ben, holding his stare with a confidence that age affords. "But I said all I needed to say when I saw him last."

"Mrs Underwood," Freya said. "You haven't asked how your brother died—"

"He's dead, ain't he?" she snapped, then nodded slowly at Freya's sad expression. "Well, then, I don't see I've anything else to say."

"I do have one more question," Freya said. "Do you happen to have contact details for his carer?"

CHAPTER FOURTEEN

"Bloody hell's bells," Ben said as they climbed back into the car. They slammed their doors in unison, and although he hoped he might find Mrs Underwood staring through the living room window after them, perhaps in a show of emotion to restore his faith in humanity, he found the curtains pulled. "When I die, I'd like to think my brothers might be at least a little bit upset."

"Oh, she was upset," Freya said. "Of course, she was."

"She had a funny way of showing it."

"She had a funny way of showing lots of things," she told him. "Is she sorry? No. Is she saddened at the news? I think she is, yes. In her own way, at least. But it does answer our question."

"Oh?"

"Robert Reilly wasn't the only one to dislike his father."

"That doesn't render him innocent."

"No, but it does give us an insight into his behaviour. I don't think Robert Reilly is emotionally dead, as you put it. I just think that his father wasn't a particularly nice man." She stretched forward to hit the button to start the engine, then settled back into her seat as the big engine rumbled into life. "Let's get the team on the phone, shall we?"

It took a few moments for Ben to find Chapman's direct number and route the call through the car's Bluetooth system.

"Ben?" Chapman said. "Everything okay?"

"Yeah, it's fine, Denise," he said. "Baffling, but fine. How's it going there?"

"Oh, we're making progress," she replied. "We'll pull it all together before the briefing."

"We're having a briefing now," Freya called out. "Get me on loudspeaker, will you? And tell the team to huddle round."

Chairs scraped across the incident room floor, and a low murmur of voices, mostly Glaswegian, grumbled at the disruption.

"We're all here," Chapman announced. "Except Cruz and Jewson. I think they've gone door-to-door again."

"Good, right. Listen up, please," Freya began. "Ben and I have been to see Robert Reilly and the victim's sister, Harriet Underwood. The son, Robert, gave us a list of three people whom Albert Reilly spoke to. The first was his sister, yet she had nothing good to say about him and made a point of concealing her grief."

"Why would she do that?" Gold asked, and despite the interruption, her soft voice was always difficult to shut down.

"It's a generation thing," Freya said. "She's a tough old boot. The point is that Albert Reilly was not a likeable man, which won't make our lives easier. Harriet Underwood, the sister, last saw him a month ago. She visited his house, where the home-help let her inside. Chapman, I'm going to need an address for his carer. We did ask the sister, but she didn't feel the need to keep a record of it."

"Already done," she replied. "Gillespie and Nillson have been through Reilly's bank statements. There's a payment every month to a company called Friends for Life. We've contacted the office, and I've got the address for a Terri James. That's Terri with an I. She was last scheduled to see Albert Reilly on Thursday, which coincides with what the Armsteads told Gillespie and Nillson."

"Did she attend?" Ben asked. "Do they have some kind of timesheet to fill in?"

"She attended, yes," Chapman said. "She was there all day."

"And when's her next visit?"

"It was supposed to be this afternoon, guv,' Chapman replied. "But we cancelled it for obvious reasons."

"So, she's not working, then?" Ben asked. "Or has she been given something else to do?"

"No, they tend to keep to their own regulars," Chapman explained. "Besides, the carers are on zero-hour contracts, so if she's no appointments, her time's her own."

"Thank you," Freya said. "I do want to talk to Miss James, however. If she was Reilly's only carer, then she might know something. He could have told her something."

"And even if she doesn't know anything," Ben added, "she'll know what medication he was on. The sister has admitted to being on some kind of blood thinner, and she alluded to the fact that there's some kind of hereditary condition."

"What does that matter?" Gillespie said.

"If it's hereditary, it could explain the puncture marks on Albert Reilly's arm," Freya said. "At least then we can focus on the unexplained head wound. Speaking of which, has Southwell contacted us yet?"

"No, guv," Chapman said. "And neither has Pip."

"Right," Freya said, growing agitated at the slow progress, "we've one more name for you to investigate: a Roger Havers. According to Harriet Underwood, Albert and Roger have been lifelong friends on that same street."

"Hold on," Chapman said. "I've got Cruz's little map here."

"You won't find the name on there," Freya said. "It's the house with the doorbell camera. If he's still not home, no doubt Cruz and Jewson are sitting outside getting to know each other."

"God, I feel sorry for the girl," Gillespie added. "I've spent many an hour sitting in a car with that lunatic. He's probably droning on and on about his collection of Star Wars figures, all of which I'm assured are still in their boxes and worth a small—"

"I need somebody to get word to him," Freya said, cutting Gillespie off before his idle comment ventured into the realms of a rant. "I need Cruz to know the significance of an interview with Roger Havers, and if nobody answers, tell him to pop next door. Mr and Mrs Armstead will no doubt have a lot to say."

"I'll get onto him," Gold said.

"Thank you," Freya said. "Now then, what about you all? What do we have?"

Nobody said a word, and Freya imagined them all daring the others to speak first. "Come on, I haven't got all day."

"Aye, well, it's like Chapman said, boss," Gillespie said, taking the bait exactly as Freya knew he would. "We took a wee look at the victim's bank statement."

"And?"

"Well, there's a few payments, gas, leccy, council tax, and whatnot. Plus, there's the payments to Friends for Life," he said. "Besides that, the man doesn't seem to spend a penny."

"He's a pensioner," Ben said. "What did you expect to find, payments to strip clubs and coke dealers?"

"Aye, he's a pensioner," Gillespie agreed. "But he's not like any pensioner I know of."

"How's that?"

"Well, for a start, he's worth a few quid."

Freya and Ben exchanged glances.

"How much are we talking here?" she asked.

"Seven figures," Gillespie replied. "Eight if you include assets and shares."

"Bloody hell," Ben said aloud.

"That's close to what I said," Gillespie added. "But that's not all. It turns out that our wee victim, the saintly old man in his nice little ex-council house, sitting on a hoard of money with no friends and no family to give two hoots about, was an ex-con."

"He's a what?"

"He's been inside," Gillespie said. "Manslaughter."

"Don't tell me," Freya said. "Negligence?"

"Brakes failed on one of his lorries back in the eighties," Gillespie said. "Killed an entire family outright."

"But he wasn't driving, was he?" Ben asked.

"No, but as the business owner, he took responsibility. I'm looking at the report now, though I can barely make out the handwriting. It looks, to me, as if Reilly's Haulage was skimping the maintenance side of things to keep costs down. A few of the employees testified against him, and he served eight years."

"What about the driver?" Ben asked. "Did he get off?"

"Erm, one sec," Gillespie replied, and they heard the rustling of papers. "Looks like it. There's a statement from him. Says something about him not having brakes. I can't really read it. It's like Dickens bloody wrote it with a feather."

"Who was he?" Freya asked.

"Eh?"

"His name," Ben urged. "What was the driver's name?"

"Oh," Gillespie replied and then hummed a tuneless melody while he searched the document. "Here we are. Richie Mavis?"

"Richie Mavis?" Nillson said, with clear disbelief in her tone. "It might have been the eighties, but they wouldn't use his nickname in a police report. Give it here."

Freya took a deep breath and, closed her eyes, and was thankful Cruz wasn't there to stir things up even more.

"It doesn't say Richie Mavis, you halfwit," Nillson said. "It says Roger Havers. Roger Havers was the driver of the lorry."

CHAPTER FIFTEEN

Police tape flapped in the gentle breeze, marking Albert Reilly's property as out of bounds. A sheet of plywood had been fixed to the front of the house, barring entry through the front door. Presumably, the rear had received the same treatment.

"Sad, isn't it?" Cruz mused aloud as he pulled the little Toyota to a stop outside Roger Havers' home.

"What is?" Jewson replied.

"The house," he said, nodding at Reilly's property. "You know, somebody made a life there. They made memories." He shook his head sadly. "Now look at it. It's little more than a piece of evidence."

"Do you want a tissue?"

"Eh?"

"You sound like you're about to burst into tears."

"Oh, come on. The old man lived there. His family probably had Christmases and birthdays there. Kids probably played in the street and the garden—"

"Jesus, is there much more of this?"

"You really are a cow, you know that?"

"No, I'm not. I just don't like being sucked into sentimental rubbish about a man I never even knew."

"Somebody loved him," Cruz said.

"Not me."

"Maybe not, but everyone is loved by somebody. He had a mother like the rest of us."

"He was ninety-three years old, Cruz."

"So?"

"So, that would make her one-hundred-and-something. A hundred and thirty-odd."

"But she probably loved him when she was alive," he said. "Don't be so bloody heartless."

He shoved the car door open, climbed out, and wrapped his coat around him while she walked to the footpath.

"You know, this job is about more than ticking boxes or processing people. There's more to it than objective fact."

"Is that right?"

"It's about people, Jewson. One man died, but everyone in this street will be affected to some degree, even if they never knew him. They'll have seen the police cars, ambulance, CSI, and the rest of it. They'll probably have heard about the broken window." He leaned in close and lowered his voice. "They might have even heard about the old man being hit over the head," he said. "They'll be locking their doors at night. They'll be worried."

"Right, you mean the bloke in his forties with tattoos on his face, who lives twenty doors away, will be worried about somebody breaking into his house, will he?"

"Well, not necessarily worried, but—"

"The only thing he'll be worried about is the house prices," Jewson said. "Same as everyone else. People don't care about people. Nobody on this street will be shedding a tear for the old man, and I'm sorry if that sounds harsh, but it's the truth. People don't care about other people. They care about themselves."

"That's just your narrow-minded view. You think everyone is as callous as you."

"Well, I hope they are," Jewson told him. "I hope they are callous. The last thing we need is a street filled with people like you. They'd all be blubbering about some bloke they didn't know and how the world is a cruel place, and it would be down to people like me to tell them to man the hell up, stop snivelling, and get on with it. Crying won't bring him back."

"Jesus bloody Christ," Cruz said, shaking his head, peering along the line of roses to the front door. "Just let me do the talking, yeah?"

Jewson shrugged.

"Whatever you say, boss," she said, and Cruz started up the path. "But just so you know, we're not actually allowed to give grieving neighbours hugs. You know that, right?"

"Just watch and learn, Jewson," he called back over his shoulder. He reached up and pressed the doorbell, spying the little blue light that indicated the video was recording. "You never know; you might even find a heart inside that uniform."

She turned away, pulling a bored-looking expression. A minute passed, and he felt her eyes on him again.

"Well?"

"Give him time," Cruz said. "It's all about patience."

"I thought it was all about people."

"Yeah, well. You need to be patient with people, don't you?"

"Or you could just admit he isn't home."

Cruz sighed, stepped back, and peered up at the first-floor windows.

"Do we even know his name?" Jewson asked.

"Not yet, no," Cruz muttered, pulling his phone from his pocket. He found his recently dialled numbers and hit the topmost entry on the list.

"Ah, Gabby, your ears must be burning," Gillespie said.

"Why's that?"

"Oh, no reason," he said. "We just had a wee call with Ben and the boss, and your name came up. Came up quite a few times as it happens."

"I'm not in the mood, Jim."

"Oh dear. Things not working out with your little prodigy then, eh?"

Cruz turned away and started along the footpath, putting some distance between himself and Jewson.

"She's a psycho," he hissed.

"Ah, a psycho? Not had one of those on the team before, have we?"

"Honestly, she's like the bloody Tin Man. She's heartless."

"Ah, sorry Gabby. You can't call her a Tin *Man* anymore," Gillespie said, then called out to the team in the incident room. "Can somebody tell me what the woke version of Tin Man would be? Tin Girl, maybe? Tin Human?"

"Tin Person," Gold called.

"You hear that, Gabby? Tin Person."

"Whatever," Cruz said. "Honestly, she has a lot to learn."

"Well, thank the Lord she has you as a mentor, eh?" Gillespie said. "What do you want anyway? I'm guessing you didn't call to tell me you've found the tin person but can't find the lion or the scarecrow?"

"No, I need a favour," Cruz said. "Are you in the office?"

"Aye," he said. "I'm just doing a wee bit of paperwork. You know, checking through bank statements and phone records. It's quite fun, as it happens. Better than walking the streets anyway."

"I'm at the house with the video doorbell," Cruz started, but Gillespie seemed to be one step ahead of him.

"Oh, aye. Roger Havers' place?"

"How do you know his name?"

"Ah, just intuition."

"Right, well, that's rubbish. I've seen slugs with more intuition than you," Cruz said. "Anyway, there's no answer again. I was wondering if you could look at the DVLA database for me, to see if there's a car registered to this place."

"Me?" Gillespie said. "You want my help? You just compared me to a slug."

"Oh, come on."

"Isn't this a Chapman job?" Gillespie said. "Since when have you called me to look something up on a database?"

"She's always busy," Cruz told him. "And you're...well, you're rarely busy, are you? Let's face it. If any of us ever need a favour but don't want to interrupt actual police work, we call you."

"I am *hurt*, Gabby."

"Can you just...please, look at my map, get the door number, and see if there's a vehicle registered to this place. There's nothing here, but on the street is a black Mercedes, a white Tesla—"

"Ah, Christ, I can't stand them."

"A red Vauxhall," Cruz continued.

"Ah, you're looking for a silver Skoda Fabia. I'll send you the registration plate."

"A Skoda? I don't have a Skoda here."

"What does that tell you?"

"He's out," Cruz said.

"Ah, you know what? It's times like this that you make me proud, Gabby," Gillespie said. "He's out a lot for a man in his nineties, eh?"

"He's in his nineties?"

"Apparently."

"How do you know that?"

"Oh, yeah, sorry, you weren't on the team call, were you?" Gillespie said. "You were busy finding a wee heart for your tin person."

"What the bloody hell is going on?" Cruz said. "Why do I feel like I'm two steps behind."

"Well, if you have to put a number on it, I'd say it was more like three or four steps—"

"Jim?"

"Ben and the boss spoke to the victim's son."

"Right, so?"

"Well, turns out that the old man only spoke to a few people."

"Right?"

"One of them was his sister."

"Great," Cruz said. "So what? Maybe she has the little Silver Skoda?"

"No, they went and spoke to her," Gillespie said, and Cruz imagined the lanky Scotsman with his feet up, savouring the frustration he was causing Cruz. "According to her, Albert Reilly also had a mate."

"Good. I hope I have mates when I'm ninety-odd years old, too."

"Gabby, you don't even have mates now, and you're in your twenties," Gillespie said. "By the time you're in your nineties, you'll have to pay someone to come and listen to all your boring stories about how you were in the police force for forty years yet were never promoted higher than detective constable."

"Jim, come on," Cruz said, as Jewson slowly edged closer. "Tell me what I need to know."

"Alright, alright," Gillespie said, his grin evident in his tone. "Roger Havers was Reilly's BFF."

"BFF?"

"Best friend forever," Gillespie said. "Mates since they were wee nippers, apparently. In those very houses, I might add. That house you're standing outside was where the two lads used to play eighty years ago, with their wee sticks and hoops and marbles or whatever it was they did."

"Well, if my best mate lived opposite—"

"If you even had a mate," Gillespie added.

"I would hope he'd be a bit concerned about the police turning up with ambulances and bloody CSI," Cruz said, ignoring Gillespie's cheap joke.

"Well, if Reilly was anything like you, Havers is probably pleased about it. No more whinging and whining."

"Right, but Roger Havers hasn't been home since Albert Reilly was found dead," Cruz said, and he shoved himself past Jewson and ran to the front window, using his hand to block the sunlight. "What do I do?"

"Eh?"

"What do I do, Jim?" Cruz asked. "If Havers had been home, he would have seen the bloody circus, and even if he missed the action, he'd have seen the bloody sheet of plywood over the front door. Surely, he would have called it in."

"Unless he's done a runner," Gillespie suggested. "Have a wee look around the back, why don't you?"

Cruz clicked his fingers a few times to grab Jewson's attention and then gestured for her to look around by the back door. She did as he requested, with the enthusiasm of a teenage girl being asked to do the washing up.

"You're going to have to kick the door in," Gillespie said.

"What?"

"Kick it in. He could be hiding under the bed or something," Gillespie said. "You might even find the murder weapon."

"I'm not kicking somebody's door in—"

"Aye, well. You asked what I would do."

"I asked what I should do, not what you would do," Cruz said. "There's a difference."

"Hello?" a voice said from behind Cruz, and he turned to find the old couple, who Gillespie had spoken to, peering over the hedge.

"Hello?" Cruz called.

"Who's that?" Gillespie asked.

"It's the couple you spoke to."

"Ah, right. Mr and Mrs Armitage," he replied. "I mean, if you're too scared to kick the door in, then you should probably speak to them—"

Cruz ended the call, cutting Gillespie off, then smiled as pleasantly as he could at the couple who, due to the height of the hedge, looked like two severed head puppets bobbing about. He flashed his warrant card.

"Mr and Mrs Armstead, isn't it?"

"That's right," the man said. "Having trouble, are we?"

"I'm just trying to find Mr Havers," Cruz replied. "I don't suppose you've seen him recently?"

"Who, Roger?" the man said. "No, we haven't seen him for a few days, have we, dear?"

"No, not since Friday."

"Friday?" Cruz said.

"Saw him take his bin in, didn't we, love?"

"We did, aye," the man said.

"And you haven't seen him since?"

"Well, it gets dark ever so early now, doesn't it?"

"And it's gone seven in the morning before it gets light."

"Right," Cruz said. "So, you haven't seen him."

"No," the woman said. "Although, I thought I heard him."

"When was that?"

"When? Oh, it must have been Saturday morning," she said thoughtfully. Then, she thrust an index finger at her husband. "No. No, it was this morning. I heard his back door go. Always slams; it does. I know it was today because that lovely man does the weather. What's his name?"

"Cruz?" A voice called from down the side of the house.

"Excuse me a moment," Cruz said, following the sound of Jewson's voice to the little alleyway, where she appeared in a hurry.

"Come on," she said. "You need to see this."

CHAPTER SIXTEEN

The second address Chapman had provided led Freya and Ben to a new-build estate on the outskirts of nearby Billinghay. The road was neat and tidy, but like many new-build estates, Ben thought, it lacked trees. It was lifeless.

"Here we go," Ben said, pointing to a neat little semi-detached property, and Freya pulled the car onto the kerb. He watched as she pulled the visor down and checked her reflection in the mirror. More than a dozen times per day, Ben stopped himself from assuring her that she looked great and that she should stop worrying, but there were always going to be hang-ups. He waited for her to flip the visor up before reaching for the door handle. "Ready?"

"As I'll ever be," she said, subconsciously tugging her hair over one side of her face.

Every doctor who had spoken to Ben had said the same thing. In the first instance, she should undergo corrective surgery alongside some kind of therapy to help her cope with the changes. In the second instance, she should join some kind of group or even work with a charity so that she may share her experiences with others.

Freya had point-blank refused to enter any kind of therapy, had disregarded plastic surgery with the view that her scars were a reminder of who she used to be, and had baulked at the idea of discussing her injuries with like-minded people.

The theory behind her contrary decisions had been that her scars would remind her of who she used to be and how individuals should be judged on merit and not looks. The idea was that she would be a different person, less materialistic and more personable.

They were changes Ben had yet to witness, and broaching the topic would be like shoving a stick into a wasps nest and wiggling it about.

He rang the doorbell, then stepped back, and Freya checked her watch.

"It's gone lunchtime," she said. "Pip should be ready for us soon."

"Pip won't be ready until tomorrow," Ben said. "You know what she's like. Besides, she's got two bodies from this morning's RTA to deal with, not to mention whatever other work she has on."

"The RTA?" Freya said. "One of them went under a lorry, and the other drove into the back of it. It hardly needs a post-mortem, does it? One of them will have tyre marks across his chest, and the other will have a Ford badge, or whatever it was, imprinted on his forehead from where he head-butted the steering wheel."

"Freya?"

"What?" she said. "I'm only saying what you're thinking."

"I was not thinking that, for God's sake," Ben said. "Besides, you're a fine one to talk."

"What do you mean?"

"Well, you know," he said, wanting to gesture at her face but suddenly finding himself backing into a corner.

"My face?" she said. "What, I'm an advertisement for Guy

Fawkes night, am I? One of those public service announcements you used to see on the BBC. Don't play with fireworks, kids, you could end up looking like her—"

"Don't take it out of context, Freya," he said. "You know perfectly well what I mean. People bloody died. It's not exactly becoming to make light of a tragic accident, is it?"

She reached past him, hit the doorbell harder than necessary, and then puffed her cheeks out.

"There's no car on the drive," she said.

"Maybe she doesn't have one."

"Maybe she takes the bus," a voice said, and they both turned to find a largish black lady with at least two shopping bags in each arm.

"Terri James?" Ben asked.

"S'me," she said, her voice high-pitched and jolly. "Who's asking?"

Ben fished his warrant card from his pocket while Freya did her best to manoeuvre into a position from where James couldn't see her facial scars.

"Detective Inspector Savage," he said. "This is Detective Chief Inspector Bloom. We wondered if we might have a word."

"Oh. Oh dear," the woman replied, and she waddled down the path, struggling with the weight of her shopping. "I would have been here sooner, but the bus was diverted. Went for miles, we did."

"Here, let me," Ben said, relieving her of her shopping so she could find her keys.

"I suppose this must be about poor old Albert, is it?" The lady said as she opened the porch door and wrestled the key into the front door.

"You've heard?"

She shoved the door open and stepped inside, holding the door for them both.

"Debbie called me," she explained. "Said one of your

colleagues had called her. Dreadful shame. He was..." she hesitated. "Such a...a lovely man."

"Perhaps we can sit down and ask you a few questions," Freya asked as Ben brought up the rear, closing both the porch and the front door with his foot while carrying all the bags.

"I'll just drop these in the kitchen, shall I?" he called out to the living room, where, by the sounds of things, Freya and James were making themselves comfortable. "Don't mind me," he muttered to himself as he wandered back to the hallway, then turned into the living room, where, as he had expected, he found Freya and James sitting comfortably but with one other person sitting in an armchair. "Oh," he said, startled. "I didn't realise we were four."

"Oh, yes, sorry," James said. "This is my father. I'm his full-time carer."

"Well, pleased to meet you, Mr James," Ben said, holding his hand out. But the man's gaze was fixed on the far wall, and his head rested to one side.

"He doesn't speak," James said. "Come to think of it, he doesn't do much anymore."

"That's sad," Freya said.

"No, no, really. He's had a good innings. It would have been nice for him to go out with a little more dignity, but we get by. He used to say that God endows us all with one special gift. Well, mine is looking after people. Caring for them. And I'm pleased that if somebody must care for him, then it can be me."

Ben felt Freya's concerned look, and somehow, James must have picked up on it.

"It's okay," she said. "He can hear, so I'm told, but he can't speak. It's as good as being ignorant."

Freya nodded slowly.

"We just have a few questions about Albert Reilly," she said. "Then, we'll get out of your hair."

"How long did you know him, Terri?" Ben asked.

"Albert?" she asked, puffing her cheeks as she thought. "A few years. Four or five."

"And did he confide in you at all?"

"Well, I wouldn't say he confided in anybody," she said with a smile that lit up her face. Her dark skin shone, and her large cheeks gave her the look of somebody whom young children might run to for a hug. "He ranted," she said with a laugh. "Boy, could that man rant. About anything and everything, he could rant. Nothing was good enough. The noisy cars outside, the size of his dinners, the taste of the water. You name it, he could rant about it."

"And did he rant to you about anything in particular? Anything unusual," Ben asked, to which she shook her head.

"Not particularly. His sister. He ranted about her a fair amount. And old Roger across the road. They played bridge, you see. Him and Roger. Albert would always lose and then spend the next few days moaning about how Roger must have cheated." She smiled fondly at the memory. "They always played the week after, though."

"And what day did they play?" Freya asked.

"Oh, Tuesdays. They used to take it in turns to host, but more recently, Roger pops over to his house. Have you told him? I expect he'll be sad."

"Who, Roger?" Ben asked. "We've got a team there right now."

"Oh, he will be upset," James said with a nod.

"Miss James, I'm sorry to have to tell you this, but Albert died under what we believe to be suspicious circumstances," Freya said.

"Sorry? He died under what?"

"Suspicious circumstances," Freya said again, to which James shook her head.

"That can't be. Debbie said it was his heart, she said."

"Well, yes, that is the case. However, he also suffered a blow to his head."

"A what? Why on earth would anybody do that to him? He was a poor old man. He couldn't hurt anybody."

"I'm afraid that's the question we're struggling with," Ben said. "We're in the process of interviewing those closest to him."

"That won't take long," James said.

"Indeed," Freya replied. "Out of interest, when did you see him last?"

"Albert? Thursday, I suppose. He doesn't have weekend visits. Not yet, anyway."

"And what is it you do for him?"

"Everything," James said. "I make him dinner, I clean his house, I clean his clothes, even clean him - but that's just once a week."

"And medication?"

"That too," she said. "I make sure he takes what he has to take when he needs it."

"Injections?" Freya said. "His sister is on some kind of blood thinning medication, which, as I understand it, she injects. She suggested it may be for hereditary illness and that Albert could have been on something similar."

"Yes," James said. "Warfarin, twice a week."

"And what did that do, exactly," Ben asked.

"Warfarin? It does exactly that. Thins the blood."

"And his last dose?"

"Thursday," she said almost immediately. "Sees him through the weekend until I see him again on the Monday."

"Which should have been today?"

James nodded.

"And do you know if somebody would have wanted to hurt Albert?" Freya asked. "Had he upset anybody?"

She smiled back at her sadly.

"I should tell you how wonderful he was," James said, glancing across at her poor old dad. She looked up at Freya and held her gaze.

"Your father?" Ben asked, to which James snorted.

"No, my father was wonderful. You know, when we first came here, we went out to the beach. He used to love the beach back home. So I took him there." Her face lit up as she recalled the experience. "No buildings, no people, fresh air. It was joyous." She closed her eyes and illustrated her words with wild gestures. "The only sign of man on God's beautiful earth were the big windmills out to sea." She smiled, opened her eyes, and looked back at her father. "I'd like to get him out there one last time."

A message came through on Ben's phone, and he held it up for Freya to see.

"I'm sorry to press you, Miss James," Freya said. "But we do have quite a lot to get through. You were talking about Albert?"

"Albert? Well, he could be a cruel man if you crossed him."

"And did you?" Ben asked. "Cross him, I mean."

"Me, no," she said with a hearty laugh. "No, I was always nice to Albert, and so Albert was always nice to me. He would try, of course, to lure me into his rants. But Terri always keeps Terri to herself. There's no place for hatred in my world." She leaned back in the chair and stared thoughtfully at her hands.

"Was he really that bitter?" Ben asked.

"To others," she said, then smiled fondly. "To me, he was always a sweetheart. I remember his sister came not so long ago. Called him a loner like it was a bad thing. Tell me, Inspector, what's bad about that?" She shook her head sadly. "They just didn't understand him like old Terri did."

CHAPTER SEVENTEEN

"This had better be good, Cruz," Freya said when he and Jewson met them at the roadside.

"It's...not what we were expecting, boss," he replied. "In fact, it throws a whole new light on the investigation."

"Where is it?" Ben asked.

"It's this way," Jewson said, keen to lead. She called back over her shoulder as she walked. "It was me who made the discovery—"

"Only because I told you to go around the back," Cruz cut in, his little legs working hard to keep up with Ben's long strides.

"Yeah, because you wanted to get rid of me," she countered.

"Is there something wrong?" a voice called out, and Freya found the Armsteads peering over the hedge.

"There's nothing wrong, Mrs Armstead," Ben said. "If you could go back inside and keep warm, we'll be around in a little while to speak to you; thank you."

"We did see him, you know?" she persisted. "We told him." She pointed at Cruz. "This morning."

"Well, we heard him," her husband corrected her.

Without breaking stride, Ben gave as polite an answer as he could.

"Thank you," he said. "Why not get the kettle on, eh?"

They entered the alleyway down the side of the house, and Cruz felt obliged to fill the silence.

"Sorry about that," he said. "I was just asking after Roger Havers when Jewson found...well, you'll see."

They rounded the corner onto a small patio with a tiny but neatly trimmed lawn, a small bistro set, and a plastic compost bin, presumably filled with leaves as there wasn't a single one on the lawn or the beds. So well maintained was the garden that it could have been a photo from a magazine.

The house, however, was altogether different. The back door was open, and the view of the kitchen could have been straight from a disinfectant TV advert prior to the actor demonstrating the product's potency. A saucepan lay discarded on the linoleum floor, having spewed its porridge up the cupboard doors and even through the threshold into the hallway. The hot tap was running, and the boiler flue that protruded from the exterior wall gave off a constant plume of exhaust fumes.

"Has anybody touched anything?" Freya asked.

"No, boss," Cruz said. "I called out for him, and when I got no response, I had a look around." He shook his head gravely. "Nobody home."

Freya nodded and let her eyes drink in the scene, capturing every detail regardless of significance.

"Turn that tap off," she said and then gestured for Ben to follow her inside. They stepped over the spilt porridge, and Ben handed her a pair of latex gloves from his pocket supply. "Cruz, get onto Chapman. See if we can track down his car. See if he has any family locally. If he does, you and Jewson can drive round there."

"What about the hospital?" he replied.

"Yes, ask Chapman to contact Accident and Emergency, although I very much doubt they'll have much to report."

"What about me?" Jewson asked. "What can I do?"

"You, Jewson," Freya said, pulling on the gloves, "Can follow Cruz. Listen to everything he has to say, how he says it, and what he does with the information when he receives it." She raised her eyebrows at the young PC, daring her to press for something a little more challenging, but Jewson nodded and trailed after Cruz.

"If there's one thing I cannot stand, it's bullies," Freya said, snapping the glove into place. "Now then, what are we looking at here, do you think?"

"Objectively, or am I allowed to let my imagination run wild?" Ben asked.

"Oh, run wild, Ben. Run as wild as you can," she replied. "We're not going to get to the bottom of this one without a little imagination, I can assure you."

"Well, at first glance, I'm looking at a kitchen in a bit of a mess. Somebody had an accident or was startled, and they left in a hurry."

Freya nosed around the kitchen, spying a little key rack beside the back door, adorned with three ceramic tiles depicting a garden scene with little birds and some colourful flowers. One of the four hooks was empty.

"Okay," she said, urging him to continue. "That would seem to be an objective view."

"Then, if I were to look at the individual in question, I would note that he is an elderly man. However he still drives,' Ben said. "And he is a man who, many years ago, was responsible for the death of a family."

"Was he responsible? Reilly was charged, if you remember?"

"He was driving, Freya. Twelve strangers in a box might have deemed him innocent, but his conscience wouldn't have let him forget."

"We're talking forty years ago, Ben."

"We are," Ben said. "Forty years for his deepest thoughts to be swirling in the pit of his stomach. Time can do strange things."

"They were bloody bridge partners," she said. "I'm sure if he had something to say, he would have said it during the four decades that have passed."

"You said I could let my imagination run wild," he said. "So, I did."

"And does this...vivid imagination of yours have anything else to say?"

"No, except that it strikes me as odd that he goes missing shortly after Reilly is hit on the head with, let's face it, an unknown object. And it's worth noting that there doesn't seem to be anything out of place in Reilly's house, which suggests whoever killed him brought the weapon with them, along with gloves, and..." he held an index finger up to accentuate his last point, "whoever killed Reilly had prior knowledge of the house."

"Sorry?" Freya said.

"Just an observation," Ben continued. "Whoever broke that glass knew there was a lock within reach of the window."

"That doesn't mean they had prior knowledge," Freya argued. "Any experienced housebreaker would know to pull on a door to feel where the locks are."

"True," he said. "Unlikely, but true."

"So, why?" Freya said. "Come on. Why would Roger Havers, whom we understand to be Reilly's only real friend, hit him over the head? And before you say it, that twaddle about the conviction in nineteen-eighty-something is not what I would deem to be a suitable motive."

"It could have been anything," Ben said. "You heard what James had to say. The man was a menace."

"Oh, he was not—"

"She was being polite," he told her. "He was a miserable old scrote who accused his best mate of cheating at bridge, moaned about anything and everything, and, if he's anything like my old man, wouldn't be afraid of speaking his mind. Who knows what he said? It could have been personal, something about his wife, maybe? I doubt we'll ever know what was said, but we cannot rule out Havers because of his age."

Freya hated to admit it, but Ben was right. They couldn't rule Havers out. She ambled through to the hallway, tried the front door and, found it to be locked, then stooped to collect the post.

She browsed the letters and rubbish the postman had put through the letterbox, noting the dates printed on each one.

"This is from this morning," she said as she stepped into the living room. She stood before the window, which offered a full view of the street, including Reilly's house.

"Two old men," she muttered to herself. "What were you doing?"

She returned to the kitchen, glanced up at the key rack once more and then reached out for the set on the first hook.

"What's that for?" Ben asked.

Freya held up a large brass key. "Chubb lock," she said, then raised the key beside it, a little silver-coloured Yale key. "Main lock."

"His front door keys?" he said. "Could be a spare set."

She hung the ring from her finger, allowing him to view the little dog tag with Havers' name and blood type stamped on it. "Unlikely."

"Right," Ben said, following along. "So, something happened. Something that required him to leave urgently. He was cooking breakfast, and then..." he looked about the little kitchen. "Maybe Reilly came to his back door. Maybe they struggled."

"Two ninety-year-old men?" Freya said.

"Well, maybe he got a phone call or something."

"Or..." Freya started. "Perhaps his doorbell camera alerted him to something." She marched to the front door, used the keys to unlock the door, and then studied the doorbell camera. "This might have picked up somebody entering Reilly's house."

"Or Reilly himself," Ben suggested.

"Possibly," Freya said, not wanting an argument to cloud the flow of events her mind was putting together.

"There's no mobile phone," Ben said. "He could have had it on the kitchen side while he was cooking breakfast. Then the alert came through, and he dropped his breakfast—"

"There wasn't time to unlock the front door—"

"So, he ran from the back door, which was already open," Freya said.

"Why was it open?"

"I don't know. Maybe he was listening to the birds," Freya said. "I like my back door open while I cook." She glanced up at the ceiling, then moved through to the hallway again. "Smoke alarm. The open back door lets the smoke out."

"So, he ran from the back door and then what?" Ben said. "He ran over to Reilly's house. Maybe they'd argued, and Reilly was ignoring him? Maybe the doorbell camera caught Reilly bringing his bins in or something, and he ran out to grab him."

"We are talking about two ninety-year-old men, Ben," Freya said. "You make them sound like two teenagers with all this running about."

"I'm just picturing the scene," Ben said.

"Right, well, swap the image of two sprightly cheetahs with two old tortoises and see what you come up with. If Havers ran over there to catch Reilly it would have been in slow motion."

"But, whatever happened, it was serious enough for him not to come back," Ben said. "He left the tap running. That hot water has been running since this morning. Imagine how much gas he's used. He's probably used up his winter fuel allowance. That'll annoy him."

"Christ, Ben, you really should make a point of reading the news," she muttered under her breath.

"Sorry?"

"Nothing," she said dismissively. "Listen, let's prioritise that doorbell camera. Have Chapman contact the manufacturer. There must be some way they can get us the footage without being the account owner."

"That'll take a while."

"So do it now," Freya said. "And let's get Southwell's mob in here to give the place a going over."

"Eh?" he said as she stepped out onto the patio. "It's not a crime scene, Freya."

"It is now," she replied. "Whether or not he had anything to do with Reilly's death, as of this moment, Roger Havers is either a person of interest or he's missing." She took a few steps to peer down the length of the alleyway, then turned back to meet his gaze. "Whichever it is, I want him found."

CHAPTER EIGHTEEN

"All taken care of, boss," Cruz said when Freya and Ben emerged onto the footpath. She leaned on her car, eyeing the Reilly house.

"Thank you, Cruz," she replied, then looked about him. "Where's your shadow?"

"Who, Jewson?" he said, looking more than a little sheepish. "I sent her to speak to the Armsteads. Sorry, but she was getting on..." He hesitated and then cleared his throat. "Under my feet. She was getting under my feet."

Freya nodded, and Ben grinned unabashedly.

"Don't you think you ought to be in there?" she asked.

"Not really," Cruz replied. "They told me most of what they had to say before she found the mess."

"And what was that?"

"Only that they saw him last Friday and heard him this morning."

"What did they hear?"

"The back door," he said. "Slams, apparently. And there's the pot, of course."

"It was definitely this morning, was it?"

"Yes,' he replied. "She said something about a TV presenter being on the telly, so she made the connection."

"So, presumably, if they heard his back door slam and the pot, then they were also at the back of the house?"

"S'pose so," Cruz said.

"Which means they wouldn't have seen him run over to Reilly's house."

"Who Roger Havers?" Cruz said. "Run? He was ninety-odd."

"My thoughts exactly, Cruz," Freya said. "Ben seems to think he'll be hopping over fences and sliding across his car bonnet when he's that old."

"I think nothing of the sort," Ben said. "The fact remains that Roger Havers dropped everything, left his house in a hurry, and took off somewhere. What he did in between all that, we cannot know, but we do know something..." He held an index finger up again, clearly under the impression that he had identified something that neither Freya nor Cruz had.

"He took his car keys," Freya said before he had the chance to finish.

"Eh? How did you know I was going to say that?"

"It's not rocket science, Ben," she told him. "The car's gone, and there wasn't a car key on the key rack, which he clearly uses as that's where he keeps his front door keys. It's unlikely he ran back to get his car keys, which means he must have known he would need them. He must have known he was going to be driving somewhere."

"I haven't ruled out that he and Albert Reilly could have argued," Ben said.

"Eh?" Cruz said. "You are kidding me. Two ninety-something-year-old men having a scrap? Can you imagine it?"

"Yes," Ben said. "My old man isn't far behind them; I can assure you he'd put you on your backside in a heartbeat."

"Your father doesn't require a carer five days per week," Freya said.

"I'm not saying they fought, necessarily, but they could have disagreed on something."

"Like, who gets the last Rich Tea biscuit?" Cruz said, and Freya couldn't help but smirk.

"James said that Havers used to go over to Reilly's house because Albert was too frail to go over to his, which means that Havers would know Reilly's house inside out. He would know where the locks on the back door are, where Reilly used to sit, and he would know that the carer wasn't due until the afternoon."

Freya eyed Cruz, who looked utterly lost.

"It would have to be some argument," he said.

"What about if Roger Havers's brakes failed on his lorry, and he killed an entire family?" Ben asked.

"Eh?"

"You weren't on the call," Ben explained. "But that's what happened. Havers was a childhood friend of Reilly's. He ended up driving a lorry for Reilly and ended up killing somebody because of poor maintenance."

"Jesus."

"Reilly served time for manslaughter as a result," Ben continued.

"Bloody hell. When was this?"

"Forty years ago," Freya said. "It's irrelevant."

"It's not irrelevant until we can prove it's irrelevant," Ben corrected her. "And by the way, do you think it's a coincidence that on the same day Albert Reilly is killed, another of his lorries is involved in a fatal accident?"

"I don't believe in coincidences," Freya said. "But on this occasion, I see no plausible way of connecting a tragedy that occurred this morning with one that happened forty years ago, Ben. What's going on? You're normally the voice of reason. It's usually *you* keeping *my* feet on the ground. Who's going to do that if you're running around with your head in the clouds?"

"I wouldn't mind a shot," Cruz said aloud, which earned him a bemused look from both Freya and Ben. "Just an idea," he mumbled.

"Well, you asked me to use my imagination," Ben cut in. "And from where I'm standing, there are too many similarities. More than one person has suggested that Reilly was capable of upsetting people; his own son didn't seem to be bothered about hearing the news—"

"He'd just learned about the accident," Freya argued.

"His own sister," Ben said, "his *sister* clearly disliked him. She didn't have a good word to say about him."

"Maybe the heart condition wasn't the Reilly family's only hereditary trait?"

"The only person who seemed to understand him was the bloody carer," Ben said. "And let's face it, dealing with a grumpy old man is nothing compared to what she has to deal with at home."

"What's that, then?" Cruz asked.

"Her father," Freya said, bringing him up to speed. "He's had a stroke or something. I didn't want to ask."

"He's basically a-" Ben started.

"He is unresponsive," Freya cut in before Ben delved into his bank of outdated and offensive terminology. "She's his full-time carer, presumably caring for patients to fund an existence around the task."

"Christ, that's awful."

"Yes," Freya said. "Yes, it is."

"He was a grumpy old man who made upsetting people a habit," Ben said. "It could have been any one of them; the son, the sister, the carer. Any of them." Ben moved towards the passenger door as Freya opened her side. "But I'll have money on Havers that he had something to do with it. Why else would he throw his breakfast all over the floor and run out of his house, leaving the tap running?"

"He's missing," Freya spat as she unlocked her car. "We find him, and we get access to that bloody doorbell."

"Guv?" somebody called.

"What is it, now?" Freya snapped and turned to find a wide-eyed Jewson stopped in her tracks. "Sorry, you caught me at a bad time. What is it, Jewson?"

The young PC thumbed back to the Armstead house.

"I just spoke to the couple in there," she said.

"Good, well write it up, and I'll read it while I wait for Doctor Pippa bloody Bell to summon me."

"No, guv," Jewson said, and Freya stared at her accusingly. "They said something. I think it's important."

CHAPTER NINETEEN

It was a rarity when returning to the incident room was a blessed relief, but to Ben, it felt like he had been on his feet all day, regardless of spending much of it sitting in Freya's car. He dumped his bag and coat down, then plopped down into his seat with a loud groan.

"Hard day?" Gold asked from her desk a few feet away.

"No," he said, reluctant to give in. "Just long, and..." he considered a word to suit the experience. "Negative."

"Negative?" Gillespie said, using the conversation as an excuse to stop working. "You work in a bloody major crimes team, Ben. We don't go around smelling roses and tickling children, you know?"

"Tickling children?" Nillson cut in. "Tickling bloody children?"

"Aye, tickling children. There's nothing like the sound of a wee bairn's laughter to cheer you up."

Nillson looked to Gold.

"Is he okay to say that?"

"Of course, it's okay to say that," Gillespie argued.

"I think it's okay in here," Gold said. "But I wouldn't say it outside of these four walls."

"Eh? What's wrong with tickling children?" Gillespie's voice rose in pitch, the way it often did when he was defending something he'd said, which, Ben mused to himself, was fairly often.

"Are they *your* children?" Jewson asked.

"Don't you bloody start," he told her. "The last thing I need is a little upstart telling me what I can and cannot say."

Jewson's face reddened, and she turned back to her laptop.

"She's right," Nillson said. "I mean, tickling your own children is one thing, but somebody else's—"

"I haven't actually tickled *any* children—"

"But you alluded to the fact that you'd like to."

"I did not," Gillespie argued, his voice a full octave higher than usual. "I just said that tickling children is...a joyful experience."

"But you don't have children of your own," Jewson said.

"Not that I know about," he argued and followed up with a playful wink.

"You're not helping your cause—"

"Look," Ben said, bringing the charade to a halt. "Like I said, it's been a long day. Jim, try not to talk about touching children in any way, shape or form—"

"I didn't—"

"The rest of you, be mindful of what you accuse people of. You know how these things can get out of hand. All it would take is an off-hand comment from one of you to somebody on the outside, and the next thing Jim would be sitting on the wrong side of an interview table while the tech guys go through his laptop and his phone. Not good for Jim. Not good for us."

"Good for the children, though," Jewson muttered.

"What was that?" Ben asked.

"I said it's good for the children," she said. "We should be held to account."

"What does that mean?"

"It means," Jewson said, turning in her seat to look him in the eye, "that men who make off-hand comments about touching children should be investigated, and that includes police officers. How many celebrities got away with child abuse under our noses? How many of them used to make seemingly innocent comments."

"Sergeant Gillespie is not a celebrity," Ben said.

"Well, I am in certain areas," Gillespie added, to which Ben gave him a warning glare.

"I'm just saying that if society had picked up on the little clues and investigated these men earlier, then maybe some offences wouldn't have taken place. Maybe some lives wouldn't have been ruined."

"Jewson, you are treading on seriously thin ice," Ben warned.

"What? Because I'm stating what we're all thinking?"

"Nobody is actually thinking whatever it is you're saying, Jewson."

"Well, *I* am," she said. "We've got an officer in our team who made off-hand remarks concerning touching children. I'd say that was quite alarming, and if we slash, you and DCI Bloom, choose to ignore it, and one day somebody comes out of the woodwork with allegations against him, how is it going to look when you had the opportunity to have carried out an investigation, but chose to ignore it?"

Ben eyed Gillespie, who, for the first time in his career, was lost for words. He was sitting with his mouth hanging open in shock and horror while Gold, Nillson, and Chapman simply shook their heads in disbelief.

"I think you should take some time out, Jewson," Ben said. "I'd like you to leave and reconsider the implications of what you just said."

"What? Me? It's him you should be telling to leave—"

"Well, I'm asking you," Ben said, his voice rising, not in pitch, but in volume. "In fact, I'm not asking; I'm telling you. Get out."

"Detective Superintendent Granger will hear of this."

"I don't care," Ben said. "I will not have the name of an innocent officer dragged through the mud by you or anybody."

"Oh, so you know he's innocent, do you?"

"I won't ask you again."

"Maybe you're in on it, too?"

A chorus of hissing air ensued as each member of the team sucked in a breath.

"Jewson, I think you've said what you needed to," Nillson said. "I would advise you to go outside and get some air. Come back when you've got a clear head."

"Oh, I've got a clear head," Jewson said. "What's wrong? If he's nothing to hide, then he shouldn't mind having somebody look through his phone and laptop."

"He has nothing to hide," Nillson said. "You've taken this too far. It was banter, that's all. It's what we do. We take the piss out of each other. It helps, you know? Helps us deal with what we have to see on a daily basis. You're new to the team, so you can be excused for not understanding. But I strongly suggest you apologise to Jim and then take some time to get some fresh air." She looked up at Ben. "I'm sure DI Savage will afford you a little leniency, given how new you are to this. Isn't that right, Ben?"

Ben eyed the young PC, who seemed to relish the attention and her stand on right and wrong.

"I don't think that any of us here need to question the morality of any member of this team," Ben said. "I've seen Sergeant Gillespie save lives. I've seen him take a young boy who was so lost in the system that he daren't utter a single word for fear of being beaten and turn him around. Do you know what that young boy wants to be when he's older, Jewson?" Ben asked. "A copper. Sergeant Gillespie made such an impact on the boy that he's now on a path to being one of us. Do you think that would be the case, had Jim acted inappropriately?"

"That's one instance," Jewson said. "Who's to say there aren't more instances when he did act inappropriately? Even Jimmy Saville did some good things."

"I think you should go," Nillson said, standing to demonstrate that she would escort her if need be.

Jewson nodded slowly, digesting Nillson's subtle diplomacy and Ben's candid defence.

She rose, closed her laptop and collected her bag, ready to pack up her belongings.

"That stays here," Ben said, nodding at the laptop. "Anna, escort her out, will you?"

"You can't fire me for identifying a possible offence."

"There's no offence," Ben said. "It was an off-hand comment with no connotations or suggestion that an offence has taken place. I don't want to see you again, not on this team. I'll discuss the incident with DCI Bloom and Detective Superintendent Granger. I'm sure we can move you back to uniformed work, and this entire episode need not go any further."

"Does everyone feel this way?" Jewson asked, looking around the room. "Does everyone believe that if DS Gillespie has nothing to hide, then he shouldn't mind submitting his phone and laptop? Do any of you see how, if the force took more proactive action internally, then the public might actually begin to trust us?"

"We all do," Gold said. "None of us are here to benefit ourselves. None of us treat this as just a job. We do this to make a difference, Jewson. But what we don't do is point fingers at people who deserve better. Jim deserves better. He's one of us. And if we all pointed fingers at each other at the slightest remark, none of us would be here. What I think you're missing is that we're a team. We see dreadful things. We deal with, quite frankly, awful people. And somehow, we have to take that home and lead a normal life. I have to go home to my son and be smiley and happy. I couldn't do that if I didn't trust these people." It wasn't often that Gold was outspoken, but there were times like this when she demonstrated how suited she was to act as a Family Liaison Officer. Her compassion outweighed that of anybody in the room. "If we can't trust you not to point fingers at the slightest little comment, then I'm sorry, but I don't want to work with you."

Jewson absorbed the comment with very little change in her expression.

"And the rest of you?" she said. "Do you share Jackie's opinion?"

"I do," Nillson said, her arms folded and her expression a picture of disgust.

"We can't go around accusing each other of things like that," Chapman said. "It's not on. One comment like that could destroy Jim's career. Then what? Who would be next?"

"What about you?" Jewson said, turning to Ben. "Still want me to go?"

"What I want, Jewson, is irrelevant," he replied. "As the senior officer here, I am obliged to follow procedure, which in this case is to separate the accuser from the accused and seek guidance from a senior officer, who I might add, would also be affected by these claims and accusations."

"Well," Jewson said. "It was nice working with you, however brief it may have been."

She started towards the door, her head held high.

"I don't," a voice called out, and all eyes fell on Cruz, who, until now, had remained silent. "I don't want her to go."

"Cruz?" Gillespie said. "Mate, you heard what she said, right?"

"I heard what she said," he replied. "And I think she made a mistake. We all make mistakes, and I think she should be given a second chance."

"Well, at least one of you has a backbone," Jewson said. "Although, I'm surprised that it's you."

"Don't think this means I like you," Cruz said. "I don't. I think you have a lot to learn." He nodded his head as if convincing himself more than anybody else. "But if you're going to learn how to work as a team, then this is the place to do it."

The incident room doors burst open, and Freya barged in, coming to a stop when the atmosphere hit her. Her head remained still, but her eyes roved across everybody's faces, reading the expressions.

"Ben, what's happening here?" she said.

"Jewson is just leaving," he replied, his eyes not once leaving the young PC's.

Freya looked between them, then nodded.

"Oh good," she said as she started towards her desk. "That saves me the job of finding a way to get rid of her myself." She set her bag down and slid out of her coat, tossing it over the back of the chair.

Then, in that way that only Freya could, she eyed Jewson, eyebrows raised, until the young woman took the hint and left the room of her own accord. Ben gestured for Nillson to accompany her, then took a deep breath and rested his hand on Gillespie's shoulder.

"You okay, fella?" he asked.

Gillespie said nothing. He simply retrieved his phone from his pocket, laid it on top of his laptop, and held them both out for Ben.

"You'll want these."

Freya's head cocked to one side, and Ben guessed even she couldn't have guessed what might have just taken place.

"No, mate," Ben said, nudging Gillespie's hands and the computer away. "No, I won't be needing them."

"Guv, I've got Doctor Bell on the line," Chapman announced. "She said she's ready for you to see Albert Reilly."

The distraction was welcome, and Gillespie nodded his appreciation, though not without a tear or two in his eyes.

"It's half past bloody five," Freya said as if the entire incident hadn't taken place.

"Shall I tell her you'll be there at six?" Chapman asked.

"No," Freya said almost immediately. "I've just spent the day on the road and had a grilling from Detective Superintendent Granger. She'll have to wait until the morning." She flicked her eyes at Ben. "Come on, I need a bloody drink inside me."

CHAPTER TWENTY

Freya's keys slid across the sideboard and came to a stop when they connected with the vase of dried flowers she had bought from the little flea market at the top of Steep Hill. Ben had barely closed the door when she was rummaging through the utensil drawer in search of the bottle opener, which she found beside the sink and immediately set to work on a bottle of Chianti she had been saving.

Ben kicked his shoes off, dumped his bag down, and fell sideways into an armchair, watching with fascination as she wrestled, expertly, with the cork.

She didn't bother fetching Ben a glass. Instead, she poured herself a half measure, downed it, and then leaned back on the counter, not quite satiated but well on her way.

She gave a loud sigh of relief and closed her eyes.

"Jesus, you weren't joking, were you?"

"Come on," she said, topping the glass up. "Let's hear it."

"Hear what?"

"Whatever it was, I walked into," she said. "And don't tell me nothing happened or that you'll manage it."

He used his toes to slip his socks off, then kicked each one to the floor, much to her chagrin.

"Gillespie made a comment," he began, "and Jewson took it out of context."

"Oh, God, no," Freya said. "Don't tell me he made a remark about her boobs. She doesn't do herself any favours, that girl. I mean, you'd think she'd wear a sports bra or something."

"He didn't comment on her..." Ben started. "On her body, at all."

"Oh?"

"I just said it had been a long day, filled with negativity, and he asked if I expected to be smelling roses or tickling children."

"Right?"

"So, that's it," he said.

"What do you mean?"

"That's it. That's all he said."

"I don't understand."

"No, neither do I," he told her. "Jewson just ran away with the idea that because he's a man and he mentioned tickling children, that somehow he could be...you know?"

"No, sorry. Did I just zone out and miss something?"

"No," he said. "No, that's it. It just kind of blew up. One minute, he was making a joke about my expectations of being an officer in a major crime team, and the next minute, she was suggesting he should submit his tech for inspection and saying that if he had nothing to hide, then he has nothing to worry about."

"Gillespie?" she said. "We're talking about Gillespie, here?"

"Yes," he said, almost laughing but too wound up for the humour to break his annoyance.

"I mean, Cruz, maybe."

"What?"

"Ah, well. You know. He's a bit weird, isn't he? But Gillespie."

"Freya?"

"The question is," he started, ignoring her comment about Cruz, "what do we do? If we keep her on, she'll upset the team, and if we push her onto somebody else, who knows what she'll do. She could post on social media, and the whole thing will blow up."

"She can't post on social media," Freya said. "That would be libellous: a defamation of character. It would be most unjust."

"Right, because the world is so just right now, isn't it?"

"We'll keep her," Freya said.

"What?"

"We'll keep her. She stays with Cruz."

"Don't you think that would be awkward?"

"No," Freya said, staring at her glass in deep thought. "No, I want her where I can keep an eye on her. That little minx has an agenda."

"So, get rid of her."

"Oh, no. You know what they say, don't you? Keep your friends close..." she sipped at her wine, grinning to herself, "and give your enemies to somebody like Cruz to look after."

"You are asking for trouble," he said. "Speaking of trouble, I hope you're ready for Pip tomorrow morning. She won't be happy about being pushed back like that. You know how she likes to wield her wand of power."

"Oh, I can't even think about her right now," she said. "My head is swimming with information."

"About Reilly and Havers?"

"And you haven't helped," she said. "I can't seem to shake the image of two tortoises going at it."

"Yeah, but I wasn't wrong, was I?" he said. "You heard what the Armsteads told Jewson. That supports everything I've been saying."

"Oh, that's right. They saw the two men arguing on Reilly's doorstep last Tuesday," she said. "That doesn't mean anything."

"It means they had a falling out," Ben said.

"Probably over bridge," she said. "James said they played on a

Tuesday night. For all we know, Reilly accused Havers of cheating, and Havers took offence. You know, I thought I'd seen every motive under the sun: infidelity, money, jealousy, racism, even sexism. But never, Ben, never have I ever known anybody to have been killed over a game of bloody bridge. And anyway, it's all hypothetical. We cannot investigate anybody until we have confirmation from Pip that Reilly's death was from anything but natural causes, and then... then, Ben, we need to convince somebody to visit the hospital to formally identify the body. Robert Reilly has enough on his plate right now; his sister is unlikely to volunteer for the role given her reaction, and the only person he actually liked—"

"Roger Havers," Ben added.

"Is bloody-well missing."

"Terri James could do it," Ben suggested, and he reached up, took the glass from her hand, and sipped before handing it back, much to her disgust.

"Terri James?"

"It doesn't have to be family," he said. "She's been caring for him for years. She's probably seen bits of him that nobody else has, let's face it."

"Terri James," she said again, thoughtfully. Eventually, she nodded. "You know, every now and then, Ben," she said. "You have a good idea."

"Well, I *am* a detective, you know?" he said, hoping to raise a smile but failing.

"Call her office. They'll have some kind of twenty-four number," she said as she pulled a second glass from the cupboard and began to fill it. "Tell her to meet us there first thing, will you?"

"We'll need to do the post-mortem first," he said.

"Well, after that. Say ten o'clock?" She strolled over and handed him the glass. "And tell her to bring a list of medications he was on."

"Oh, come on. I thought we'd ruled that out."

"For somebody who is about to marry me, Ben, you don't know me very well, do you?" she lowered herself into the other armchair with far more elegance than Ben had. "I'm not ruling *anything* out."

Ben pulled his phone from his pocket and tugged his notebook from his bag.

"Sometimes I feel like a well-paid secretary," he said, but his comments fell on deaf ears. Freya was deep in thought.

"And while you're at it, give Jewson a call, will you?"

"Eh?"

"Have her meet us at the hospital first thing."

"Freya?"

"If the sight of Albert Reilly's body doesn't have her running back to her uniform," she said, then paused for a long swig of her drink, "then Pippa Bell will." She raised her glass in triumph. "Cheers to that."

CHAPTER TWENTY-ONE

Summer was well and truly over, but Winter had not yet arrived. Autumn was apparently undecided on how close it was to either of the seasons surrounding it. The day before had been grey but mild, but by the time Freya and Ben arrived at the hospital on Tuesday morning, a glorious blue sky played host to streaks of cirrus clouds that stretched from the cathedral and beyond to the distant Wolds.

But the wonderful sky belied the frigid air, which bit into Freya's tender flesh the moment she stepped from the car.

"Bloody hell," she said.

"What?" Ben said, rushing from one side of the car to the other. "What is it?" He looked her over to see where the injury was. "Did you bang your face on the door? Or is it your arm?"

"It's all of me," she said, tugging her coat around her. "It's bloody freezing."

He sighed with relief.

"I thought you'd—"

"You thought I'd what? Hurt myself? I'm a grown woman, Ben. I don't need mothering."

"I know, I know," he said, stepping out of her way as she

started across the hospital car park. "But you know it *is* my job to take care of you. If you don't need me to look after you, then why on earth are we getting married?"

Without breaking stride, she called back over her shoulder.

"I don't need you to take care of me, Ben," she said. "I *want* you to take care of me. Well, of my needs, anyway."

"Your needs?"

"Yes, my needs, among other things."

"Such as?" he asked.

"Christ, you're like a smitten teenager," she said.

"I just want to know what my role is," he argued. "That's not hard, is it? If you're expecting something of me, then, I feel it's my right to know what it is."

"Alright," she told him. "I enjoy your company. You make me laugh."

"Make you laugh," he said. "Right, noted. I'll have my clown suit dry-cleaned."

"I like our lazy weekends. You are... very attentive."

"Understood," he said. "Be attentive."

"And I like nothing more than to have you tear my clothes off and ravage me."

She timed the final statement well enough that an elderly couple, walking towards their car, tutted and shook their heads at Ben.

"Tear your clothes off," he said quietly. "Right, got it."

"Got it?" she asked.

"I've made a list," he replied as they neared the main entrance. "I'll pin it to the fridge so I don't forget."

"Why do I think you'll actually do that?" she said, stopping beside the ticket machines. "Just...do what you do, all right? Just love me for who I am."

"Boss?" A voice called, which marked the end of their little chat.

"Good morning, Jewson," Freya said, still staring into Ben's eyes. She turned to face the approaching PC. "I'm glad the early start didn't offend you."

"I'm used to early starts," she replied, then hesitated. "I'm... not entirely sure why I'm here, though."

"You're here because I want you here," Freya told her.

"And because they don't want me back at the station?"

"It matters not what anybody else wants, Jewson. Now, come on. We don't want to keep Pip waiting."

"Pip?" Jewson said as the automatic doors opened like a bowing and scraping footman. "As in Pippa Bell? The pathologist? Why am I going to see her?"

"Because that's where I want you," Freya said. "Where you can't do any harm."

———

"Now then," Pip said when she opened the door to them. It always amused Ben to hear such a local greeting flow from the Welshwoman's lips so fluently. It added a certain rhythm to what was, when his father said it, a tuneless grunt. She glanced between Ben and Freya, then settled on Jewson. "Who have we got here?"

"This is PC Jewson," Ben told her.

"Jewson, eh?" Pip said and glanced down at the young woman's chest. "What are you, undercover?"

"Sorry?" Jewson said.

"You know? On the game? Integrating with the street girls, are you?" Jewson reddened and pulled her coat around her. There was little point in looking to either Ben or Freya for support, as Ben hadn't said a single word to her since meeting her at the hospital entrance, and Freya was doing very little to hide her amusement. "No? Got it wrong, have I?"

"Jewson sees her future with major crimes, Pip," Freya said.

"Right, well, that's one way of getting people to the station.

Show any more of that chest, Jewson, and you'll have every wanted criminal in the county on their knees, ready to confess."

"Shall we?" Freya said. "I'm sure you have lots to do, Pip."

"Always," she said. "As it happens, I'm in the middle of an RTA victim." She stared into Jewson's eyes. "Lorry drove right over his chest, it did," she said. "Shame he didn't have what you've got under that coat. Might have bounced right off him, eh?"

"We're here to see Albert Reilly," Ben said, not enjoying the topic or Pip's tone despite him not being the target for once.

"Oh, I know," Pip replied. "Had him all laid out for you last night, I did. Even phoned my girlfriend to tell her I'd be late. Supposed to see a film, we were."

"Oh, well, that's a shame," Freya replied. "We had a bit of a bonding session last night." She turned to Jewson. "Isn't that right, Jewson?"

Jewson raised her head, jutted her chin forward, and cleared her throat.

"We did, boss, yes," she said. "Team building."

Despite Pip's casual attitude to her profession and her flippant nature, she was no fool, and the look in her eye suggested she knew better than to pry. Instead, she held the door open and stepped aside.

"You know where the PPE is," she said. "I'll get him ready for you." She pushed open the insulated morgue doors and called out as they closed behind her so that her word was carried on a cloud of icy air. "Again."

Ben opened the relevant cupboards and tossed both Freya and Jewson a smock and mask each. They dressed in silence and Ben turned for Freya to tie his strings, a trick he'd never quite gotten the hang of.

"Ready?" Freya asked them once Ben's smock was secure, and Jewson, who remained entirely impassive, pulled her mask down over her face. Perhaps it was to hide the fear in her expression, or perhaps it was little more than cold-blooded indifference; Ben couldn't tell.

It was usual for Pip to have tidied the room, ensuring that any cadavers had been returned to their respective cold drawers, leaving only the one they had come to see. But of the half a dozen or so stainless steel benches in the room, only three were vacant. The other three each had a blue sheet to provide the deceased with the modesty they deserved.

Pip was waiting patiently at the far bench, watching their every move, especially Jewson, who peered inquisitively at the two other mounds as they passed them.

"Right then," Pip said. "I've a lot to do, so if you're ready, I'll begin." Carefully, she raised the blue sheet and lowered it to the old man's waist. She had already made the Y-shaped incision from each ear down to the chest and then down to the navel. It was a grim sight that Ben would never quite feel comfortable with. Freya, who had likely seen as many bodies as Pip, was unfazed and knew better than to interrupt Pip's little show.

Jewson, however, was mesmerised. She leaned forward to peer into the chasm in Reilly's chest as if she were on the edge of the Grand Canyon, staring down in wonder.

"Albert Reilly," Pip said. "Ninety-three years old. Non-smoker, drinker, but nothing heavy, and a fan of dry-roasted peanuts." Jewson's eyes narrowed above her mask. "I found more than a handful in his stomach," Pip explained.

"It wasn't that," Jewson said before Pip could continue. "I was just wondering how you knew they were dry-roasted."

Pip's mask rose with her smile, and she offered Jewson a friendly wink.

"You don't want to know," she said.

"Come on, Pip," Ben said. "You know what we need to know, so shall we press on?"

"Cause of death and time of death?"

"And any other insights you may be able to provide," Freya

said, clearly playing on the pathologist's ego. "You know how we rely on your experience more than anything else."

"Well," Pip replied. "I can give you a time period. Doctor Saint's estimation was fairly accurate. But given the rate of digestion, the body temperature on arrival, the livor mortis process, and, of course, rigor mortis, I would say this man died somewhere between five and seven a.m. yesterday morning."

"Five and seven?" Ben repeated.

"I can't be any more accurate than that without resorting to conjecture," Pip explained.

"What's livor mortis?" Jewson asked, which was interesting to Ben. Most inexperienced officers would have waited until after the examination to ask questions. But Jewson had a way about her, an arrogance.

But Pip was always happy to demonstrate her knowledge, and she was even happier to make an impact on a young and potentially fragile mind. She leaned forward, gripped Reilly's far side, and rolled him back towards her, thus raising him onto his side.

"See that, do you?" she said, supporting him with one hand and gesturing at the bruise-like areas on the man's back and side. "That's livor mortis."

"It's a bruise, isn't it?"

"Gravity is what it is," Pip said. "Gravity." She lowered the old man back into position and repositioned his arms to give him a little more dignity. "The heart stops," Pip continued. "Which means blood stops pumping around the body. Gravity takes hold, and the blood pools."

"When does that start?"

"Inquisitive, aren't you?"

"Perhaps you should wait until we're finished to ask questions, Jewson—"

"No," Pip said. "No, it's fine." She turned her attention to Jewson. "It starts around an hour after death, but the blood is still fluid. It hasn't congealed yet, and it won't do. Not for another few hours."

"So, the bruises can move?" Jewson asked.

"Not move, but if the body is moved at the wrong time, then livor mortis cannot be relied on. After somewhere like nine to twelve hours, the marks become permanent."

"But he was moved, wasn't he? He was taken out of the house."

"He was," Pip agreed. "He was moved at one-twenty p.m., which is within the fluid window."

"So, we can't rely on livor mortis?" Jewson asked.

"Not for an accurate time of death, but we can use it to determine the maximum amount of time that had passed since death."

"Cause?" Freya said, clearly grown tired of the lesson in pathology.

"That's where things get a little messy," Pip said. "He's not exactly helping me out."

"He's not helping you?"

"No. Struggling, I am, if I'm honest. Doesn't happen often, but from time to time, one of them always tries to catch me out."

"I presume you're talking about the head wound," Freya said to which Pip nodded.

"In Doctor Saint's report, he suggests that Mr Reilly died from some other ailment, a heart condition or a failure of some other vital organ."

"But you don't think he did," Freya said. "You think he's wrong."

"Not wrong, entirely. This man experienced a blood clot, which invoked a stroke, which subsequently led to a heart attack," Pip said, demonstrating her respect for Saint. "It would have been quick." She dragged Reilly's arm into view and, with a marker from her breast pocket, she circled the puncture marks Southwell had discovered. "But before I give you my final analysis, I want to see the toxicology results," she said.

"That's Warfarin," Freya said. "The carer administered it last Thursday."

"He was due another dose yesterday," Ben added.

"Like I told you," Pip said. "I'll need to see the toxicology report before I give you a final cause of death." She glanced at Jewson playfully. "You have to be careful with these two," she said. "They'll take anything you say and turn it on its head."

"Oh, you needn't explain that to her," Freya said. "She's already mastered the practice."

CHAPTER TWENTY-TWO

"So, we're no better off than we were an hour ago," Freya said. "You realise we're in a bit of a position here. We can't start interviewing suspects until we have a cause of death. I need to know if Albert Reilly died from the blow to the head or if it was a heart attack."

"I would suggest it was the heart attack," Pip said. "But I won't put my name to that, not until I've seen the—"

"Yeah, yeah, the toxicology report," Ben said. "What about the head wound? Surely that's a factor."

"Not, the wound, per se," she replied. "But, the experience could have been a factor. As I understand it, somebody broke into his house, didn't they?"

"That's right," Jewson said, which earned her a glare from Freya.

"Well, if somebody broke into your house and swung something large and heavy at your head, your pulse would raise, wouldn't it?" she replied, which got the team thinking.

"So, you're saying that his heart attack could have been induced by fear. Therefore, the best we're looking at is a manslaughter charge."

"Yes, kind of," Pip said. "But not quite."

"But would you stand up in court and state that?"

"I would stand up in court and say that whoever hit him over the head, intended to seriously injure him, if not kill him."

"But there's no bleeding. Surely, if he was struck on the head and the wound didn't bleed, then he was already dead, probably from the heart attack."

"Well, yes," Pip said. "But, he does have some underlying health issues that are quite common in elderly people, but which are...pronounced, shall we say, in Mr Reilly."

"Go on," Freya said.

"Well, this is why I need the toxicology report," Pip continued. "You see, there is some scarring on his heart. If I'm not mistaken, he's suffered more than one heart attack. And I think the cause of these attacks, aside from age, is due to ongoing blood clots."

"Pip, you know we're not actually doctors, don't you?" Ben said.

"Okay, okay," she said. "I believe Mr Reilly suffered from blood clots. It's highly likely he did if he was being prescribed Warfarin. It's extremely common in elderly people when blood flow slows, therefore increasing the risk of clots forming, or thrombosis, for that matter. But clots don't form over long periods of time, not like people think. They're sudden." She clicked her fingers to accentuate the point. "Clot. Stroke. Heart attack."

"Would the heart attack have occurred immediately?"

"Ah," she said. "No. Not necessarily. In fact, there's no way of knowing. He could have been suffering for a day or more."

"Jesus," Ben muttered.

Pip pulled the sheet over Reilly, presumably to preserve his modesty.

"I'm sorry to say I cannot give you a definitive answer," she said. "Informally, I believe this man died from a heart attack. But what part that head wound played in his death, I do not know."

"But somebody has hit him?"

"Oh, yes," she replied. "And hard, too."

"So, in summary?" Ben said.

"In summary," Pip started. "And I'll need to investigate further, but I think Mr Reilly had existing clots which caused the previous heart attacks. I think he was on Warfarin to prevent further clots, and either the dose wasn't enough, or he was due his next dose. But when he heard the sound of that breaking glass, or when he saw the intruder, the adrenaline his body released would have been enough to send his pulse soaring." She stared down at the mound between them. "Poor bloke wouldn't have stood a chance."

"Pip," Freya began. "I'm struggling here—"

"You've got a murder on your hands," Pip said, cutting her off. "You asked if I'd stand up in court and testify to the fact."

"Right," Ben said.

"If somebody hadn't broken into his house, Mr Reilly would still be alive today," she said. "The blow to the head came either during or moments after the heart attack. That's all I can give you. But it's enough."

"It's enough for a manslaughter charge," Ben said to Freya, then turned to Pip. "What about the wound? Can you give us an idea of the weapon?"

"Ah," Pip replied. "Now that I *can* help you with." She drew back the sheet again, and Jewson leaned over for a deeper look until she felt Pip's stare boring into her.

"Finished, have we?" Pip said.

"Sorry," Jewson replied. "I was just..."

"Getting in the way is what you were doing?" Pip eyed Freya and Ben as if warning them to keep their young colleague reined in. "Now, the blow is on the upper right temple, which either suggests—"

"That the attacker was left–handed, or Reilly was facing away," Freya said. "Yes, unfortunately, his armchair was positioned with the back to the door, and he was found on the floor, so we can't really establish one way or another."

"And given there was no real volume of blood," Ben added. "We don't even have spatter on the wall or the carpet to indicate one way or another."

"How disappointing," Pip said eventually.

"You call it disappointing," Freya said. "I call it a bloody nuisance. Any idea of what might have caused it?"

To this, Pip sucked in a breath, much as Saint had.

"Well, it's square," she said. "I can tell you that."

"Brilliant," Freya replied.

"And hard."

"Again, not really much to go on, Pip."

"Imagine the base of a trophy. You know, you get a little square block of marble or whatever it is they use? Or maybe an ornament," Pip said, undeterred by Freya's facetious response. "It's a sharp point and a right angle." The area surrounding the wound had been shaved, and Pip waved them in closer. "The skull has been fractured. I can show you the x-rays if you want."

"I'll take your word for it," Freya said. "And the way in which the flesh has been torn differs from, say, a knife wound which would simply split the skin. You can see here how the skin has been forced apart by the shape of the object."

"It couldn't have been a bat or anything like that?"

"No, too round," Pip replied. "That would have damaged the tissues. It would have effectively squashed them. No, this was done by something with a point and with right angles."

"A brick?" Jewson suggested.

"Similar," Pip said. "But a brick would leave residue. They break up quite easily, especially when they come into contact with something hard like bone." She shook her head. "No, this was hard and clean, and if his house is anything like my old Grandad's, I would say it was an ornament."

"You think the killer was acting in the moment?" Ben asked. "Spontaneous."

Pip nodded.

"If he or she is a house breaker, then they won't have been equipped for a murder," Pip said. "They would have grabbed the first thing they saw."

"What about a picture frame?" Freya suggested, and Pip's eyes lit up.

"It would depend on the size, and it would take a fair swing to crack the skull," she said. "But it's possible, yes."

They each took a few moments to process the imagery.

"Thank you, Pip," Freya said. "Please do let us know as soon as you've investigated further. "We're struggling on this one."

"Aren't you always?" she replied. "Now, if you'll excuse me. I have to get him ready for a viewing in…" she checked her watch. "Ten minutes. Who is it, if you don't mind me asking?"

"Sorry?" Freya said.

"The ID. You said his sister and son aren't interested, and his friend is missing."

"Oh, it's his carer," Freya said. "She's the nearest we can get to a friend or family."

"I suppose she'd know him better than most, anyway," Pip said with a wink. "Probably knew him better than his own mother."

"That's what we thought," Freya replied. "And we'll be leaving Jewson with you for the ID. Ben and I have—"

"I wouldn't do that if I were you," Pip called over Freya's shoulder. She turned and found Jewson standing beside one of the other occupied benches.

"I just wanted a look."

"Jewson, do I need to explain that attending a post-mortem is a privilege," Freya said. "Especially for somebody who hasn't formally transferred to the team."

"Yeah, I know. I'm not going to lift the sheet up or anything," Jewson replied.

"Then can you just move away—"

"It's okay," Pip said, holding a hand up to reassure Freya. "She's intrigued, that's all."

"It's just..." Jewson started. "I've never seen a dead body before."

"Well, you've seen Reilly," Ben said. "And if you actually make it through your probation, then I can almost guarantee you'll have another opportunity."

"Want to see him, do you?' Pip said, and Jewson's eyes widened at the prospect.

"Pip, no," Ben started.

"I can show you if you like," Pip said, ignoring Ben and striding towards the young PC. "It's not pretty, though. They aren't all like Mr Reilly here."

"It's a man? How did he die?" Jewson asked while Ben and Freya exchanged nervous glances.

"RTA," Pip said. "He ploughed into the back of a lorry."

"An RTA?" Freya said.

"No seat belt," Pip said. "Just goes to show."

Again, Ben and Freya glanced at each other.

"Forty miles per hour down to a standstill in..." Pip clicked her fingers. "A nanosecond. One minute, he was alive;the next minute, his face was buried in his steering wheel."

"We were there," Ben said. "The Martin crash, right? Sergeant Souness?"

"That's him," Pip said. "You were there, were you?" She looked up at Jewson and held the corners of the sheet. "You sure?"

Jewson glanced back at Freya as if seeking approval, then nodded at Pip.

Slowly, Pip revealed the deceased's face. There were multiple cuts on the man's forehead, and the midsection of his face was beyond repair, even if he had survived. But there was one noticeable feature that Freya picked up on, even from afar. She strode over to stand beside Jewson.

"He's an old man," she said, then looked up at Pip. "What was his name?"

"Havers," Pip said. "His name was Roger Havers."

CHAPTER TWENTY-THREE

"Well, I didn't see that coming," Ben said when he and Freya left via the main entrance and took a breath of fresh air. "No wonder we couldn't find him—"

"Sorry, Ben, can you just..." Freya said, and she pulled that irritated expression Ben knew so well. "I just need to sort all of this. I need to make sense of it."

They walked slowly, with Freya staring into the distance and Ben idling beside her, ready for when she launched questions his way, which she invariably would. However, whether or not she listened to what he had to say was another matter altogether.

"Roger Havers left his house in a hurry," she started.

"He took his keys when he left," Ben said.

"Right, so he knew he would need his car."

"Unless," Ben said, having already processed this particular conundrum.

"Unless what?"

"Unless he had a key to Albert O'Reilly's place," Ben told her.

"And that key was on his car keys?" she replied. "Why would he keep Reilly's key on his car keys, and who keeps their car keys separate from their front door key?"

Ben stopped, and Freya gazed at him questioningly.

"What?"

"We need to go back," he said. "Pip will have Havers' personal effects."

"Oh, for God's sake. I'm not going back there. Not when Terri James is identifying the body."

"We need to see his keys."

"Well...I don't know. Task Jewson with it. See if she can manage that without pissing somebody off."

"So, you'd allow her to accompany a formal ID, but collecting a set of keys...?"

"She's a liability, and had we been lucky enough to have Robert Reilly or his aunt do the ID, then you and I would be in there. I think she can manage the carer and a set of keys. Besides, I got the impression Jewson rather enjoyed this morning."

"Yeah, far more than most," Ben replied. "She's like one of those little boys who dissects road kill to see what's inside and grows up to be a serial killer."

"It takes all types, Ben. We can't all be like you, can we?"

"What's that supposed to mean?"

"It just means that we can't all be normal."

"Boring, you mean?"

"Normal, Ben," she said. "But she was far more interested in Pip's work than I thought she would be."

"Yeah, so much for her quitting," Ben said. "I was expecting to be on the blower with Granger by now, dealing with another transfer."

"Just message her, will you? Tell her to bag the keys up and to bring them to the office," Freya told him. "No. Actually, let's keep her away from the office. If there are any house keys on the rings, then tell her to go to Reilly's house and Havers' house. You never know; the house keys on the hook at his house might be a spare."

"Oh, you mean I might be right?"

"Ben, arrogance is as vulgar as discussing money."

"Arrogance? I was just directing you to the fact that I said—"

"Just message her, will you?" Freya said. "And tell her to call us as soon as she's out. The way things are going, I wouldn't be surprised if we discovered that the man on Pip's gurney is not Albert Reilly after all."

Ben composed the message to Jewson while Freya fumbled with her own phone. They walked in silence while both of them worked, and by the time Ben had sent his message, they were at Freya's car. He climbed in and waited for her to remove her coat, check her reflection, and then for her to voice her opinion about whatever theory her mind was working on.

She removed her coat and laid it across the rear seat. She did climb in and check her reflection, but when she was done, she didn't voice her opinion. Instead, she dialled a number and routed it through the car's Bluetooth system. She started the engine while they waited for the call to connect, and she set the heater to their feet, which, he had to admit, was glorious.

"Morning, guv," Chapman said, and Freya imagined her greeting was a warning, which calmed any ill-behaviour that was taking place in the incident room in her absence.

"Morning, Chapman," Freya said. "Put me on loudspeaker, will you?"

"Erm, yep. Sit tight." A few clicks flooded, and then the ambient noise changed. "You're on loudspeaker."

"Everyone here?" Freya asked.

"Yep," a few people said, followed by a gruff, "Aye."

"Right, first things first," Freya started. "Gillespie, get your feet off the chair."

"Eh?" he said. "How the bloody hell—"

"You'll be pleased to know that Jewson will be out of the office for the rest of the morning."

"Just the morning?" Gillespie asked. "Can't we find her something to do a little further away?"

"Such as?"

"I don't know. The Isle of Skye?"

"She'll be back this afternoon, and I expect you all to be civil to her. I'm not asking anyone to be her new best friend, but just be civil."

"Oh, right. Am I allowed to accuse her of indecent assault or something?" Gillespie asked.

"Not unless she actually indecently assaults you," Freya replied. "But then, I don't suppose that would bother you too much, would it?"

"Ah, come on. I do have standards, you know?"

"Since when?" Nillson asked.

"We've found Havers," Freya announced before the two of them entered into a battle of witty insults.

"Eh? You found him? Where was he? Don't tell me; he had a few too many at Bingo, and when he woke up, the doors were locked, and he was trapped inside."

"No, he managed to bury his car into the back of one of Reilly's lorries," Ben said. "He's lying on one of Pip's benches."

"You're kidding me," Gold said.

"He's dead?"

"Well, if he's not, he's going to have one hell of a headache," Ben replied.

"Bloody Nora," Gillespie called out.

"I don't know why you're so surprised, Gillespie. Seeing as you attended the scene and even spoke to the lorry driver, I would have thought you might have recognised a silver Skoda hanging out of the back of a bloody great lorry."

"Ah, that's not fair, boss," he replied. "I mean, I saw a silver car, aye, but I couldn't tell you what car it was. It had another hatchback buried into the back of it if you remember."

"Hmm, well, I'll give you that one," she said. "Either way, we need to call off the searches. Gillespie, I want you to get hold of Souness. I want to see what's inside that car."

"What are you thinking, boss?" Nillson asked, her voice cool and calm.

"Well, we've told Jewson to get Havers' car keys from Pip and to see if any of the keys fit Reilly's house."

"What's the point in that?"

"Well, if Havers had a key to the front door, he wouldn't need to break into the back door, would he?"

"You think a ninety-year-old man murdered his mate?" Gillespie called out.

"Actually, no. Ben does," Freya said, and she turned to smile at Ben. "I'm just proving him wrong."

"Hold on, hold on," Cruz cut in. "So if Havers has a front door key, then might we assume he was not responsible for Reilly's death? In which case, we might, hypothetically speaking, assume he *heard* something."

"Something?"

"Broken glass?" Cruz said, and Freya smiled with pride. "He could have been protecting his friend."

"Well, well, well," Freya said. "My influence is finally rubbing off on somebody. That's exactly what I'm thinking."

"But if he doesn't have a key to Reilly's house."

"Then we can't rule Ben's theory out," Freya replied. "As much as it pains me to say it."

"We can't just wait," Nillson said. "The clock is ticking. We're already a day behind on whoever did this."

"I know," Freya said. "We have to accept that there is a small chance that our killer is lying beside his victim in the morgue. But you're right; we can't wait to be proved wrong. We need to act."

"So, you want to see inside Havers' car?" Gillespie said. "I can talk to Souness. He wasn't too bad for a traffic officer."

"He mentioned a blue car," Ben said, which caught Freya's attention. "See how far he's got with that."

"Aye, the one Eamon Price saw," Gillespie added.

"Claims to have seen," Freya corrected him, then turned to Ben. "What is this, plan B?"

"If I'm wrong, and Cruz is right," Ben told her. "Then we might just be able to stop an innocent man from going to prison."

"I'm not sure which of those scenarios I prefer," she replied, then addressed the team. "We're on our way back. Let's make some real progress, shall we? Let's show Jewson how it's done when we all pull together."

CHAPTER TWENTY-FOUR

Albert Reilly's name in the centre of the whiteboard seemed as alone as the man himself. A sea of white space surrounded him, interspersed only with a few distantly connected names.

"Listen up," she said, and the room silenced. She didn't bother turning to face them before speaking; she knew exactly what each of them would be doing. Chapman would have stopped typing and drawn a line across her notebook, ready to list the tasks Freya was about to assign her; Cruz would peer up from his laptop, wondering if he was needed in the briefing; Nillson would be slightly annoyed at having to break her train of thought, Gold would make a display of showing how attentive she could be, and Gillespie would have closed his laptop, ready to engage in a chat. Nothing made him happier than the opportunity for what he called a *'wee natter'*. She called the names out, tapping each one with the board marker as she did. "Robert Reilly, Harriet Underwood, Roger Havers."

"At least we don't have a list of suspects as long as my arm like we usually do," Gillespie said.

"Which significantly reduces our chances of success," Freya replied. "Now, Robert Reilly is currently dealing with a potential manslaughter charge with regards to the RTA in Martin yesterday morning. Given that we had to deliver the news of his father, we are yet to question his whereabouts." She held an index finger up to make a point. "However, there was no love lost between him and his father, so we can't rule him out. We need a link; an underlying motive. Without that, then we cannot pursue him as a suspect."

"I can take that on," Nillson said.

"Thank you," Freya said. "I'm sure that if there is a motive somewhere, you and Gillespie will find it."

She smiled at Nillson, who shook her head disappointedly at the underlying message.

"Really?" she said. "I can do that on my own. I don't need that bloody great—"

"Gillespie, have you spoken to Souness?" Freya asked, ignoring Nillson's plight.

"Aye, I managed to get hold of him earlier. He's got his hands full—"

"Has he spoken to Robert Reilly yet?"

"Eh?"

"Robert Reilly," Freya said. "Come on, don't make me repeat everything, or we'll be here all day."

"No, boss," he said. "No, he's still got the driver in custody. He can't really do anything until forensics get back to him with some data to support gross negligence or a death by dangerous driving."

"Good, I want you both to go and see him."

"Souness?"

"No, come on, keep up. Reilly. I want you to see Robert Reilly. He's had a day to grieve, so before Souness gets his teeth into him, let's either strike him off our list or put a circle around him."

"Aye," Gillespie replied. "Aye, we'll see him this afternoon."

"Harriet Underwood," Freya said. "Albert Reilly's sister. Again, no love was lost between her and her brother, and I doubt she has the strength to swing a stick of celery, let alone a heavy ornament or a picture frame. Nevertheless, she's on our list."

"I can take her if you like," Gold said. "I could maybe pay her a visit to see if she's okay. You know? See if I can get her talking."

"That's probably a good idea," Freya replied. "Thank you. Okay, on your own?"

"What are my options?"

"Cruz," Freya said.

"No, he's needed here."

"What's wrong with me?" Cruz said.

"Or Jewson," Freya suggested, to which Gold scrunched up her nose.

"I'll be fine. She's more likely to open up if it's just me," Gold said.

"Very well," Freya said. "That leaves Roger Havers," Freya said.

"I thought he was dead," Cruz said.

"He *is* dead," Freya told him. "But he wasn't dead when Albert Reilly died, was he?"

"I suppose not."

"Go through everything. Your focus is the doorbell camera. Have we made any progress with that?"

"I've sent a support request through the manufacturer's website—"

"Chapman, can you step in, please?" Freya asked.

"Guv?"

"We can't wait for some spotty little helpdesk apprentice to get back to us via email. Call their head office and explain the situation, will you? Find somebody in charge and pass them on to Cruz."

"Will do," Chapman replied.

"I was going to do that," Cruz said. "I was just waiting to see if—"

"There are two more names," Freya said, turning to the board and popping the cap of the marker. "Terri James." She wrote the name at the bottom of the list. "She's the carer. Her last appointment with Reilly was last Thursday, but let's do our due diligence. I want to invite her in for an informal interview."

"Do you want me to call her, guv?" Chapman asked.

"No, not yet. She should be finishing up at the hospital any time now. We'll wait for Jewson to get in touch, and then you can call her."

"That's if Jewson actually calls in," Gillespie said. "Knowing that little minx, she'll take her sweet time getting back here and swan in like she's next in line for your job."

"Oh, she'll call in," Freya said. "You can trust me on that one."

"You don't honestly think the carer would hurt the bloke she was caring for, do you?" Nillson asked.

"No, but when we have a victim in contact with fewer people than I have fingers on one hand, we're obliged to speak to them all," Freya replied. "Anyway, you'd be surprised at how an interview room tends to invoke memories."

"Must be something to do with the decor, boss," Gillespie said.

"Precisely," Freya replied, then turned to the board one last time and added one more line to the list -*Blue car*.

"Blue car?" Gillespie said.

"Blue car," Freya replied. "We don't have the luxury of time on this one, and given Reilly's personal relationships and the RTA, we have to tread carefully. All of these names need to be ticked off the list. However, we can invest some energy into a more likely resolution."

"The blue car that the lorry driver saw?" Gillespie said, and Freya jabbed her pen his way.

"Yes. How does this sound?" she started. "The owner of said blue car breaks into Albert Reilly's house. Albert Reilly hears him or sees him. He's startled, which invokes his demise: blood clot, stroke, then heart attack, possibly due to his medication being due the next day."

"Jesus, should I fetch us all white coats, boss?" Gillespie said.

"Bear with me," she said. "The intruder panics, hits Albert Reilly, and then leaves the way he came, locking the door behind him."

"Why would he lock the door?"

"To buy time," Ben said. "A burglar would leave the door open. But somebody trying to cover their tracks would do their best to throw us off the scent."

"And then what?" Gillespie asked.

"He ran. He probably parked his car up the road, or somebody would have heard or seen him. But he was panicking. He pulled out on the lorry and caused a fatal accident, but he couldn't stop. What would he say when the traffic police asked him what he was doing there?"

"Bloody hell, how are we going to find a blue car?" Gillespie said. "There must be a million of them in Lincolnshire alone."

"Well, we use our resources," Freya began but was cut short by Chapman, who held her phone in the air.

"Guv, Jewson's on the phone."

"Ah," Freya said. "Speaking of our resources. Put her on loud-speaker, will you?"

Chapman did as she was asked, and they were presented with road noise.

"Jewson, are you there?" Freya said.

"Yes, guv," she replied. "I just came out of the hospital."

"And?" Freya said. "Do we have a positive ID?"

"We do, guv," Jewson replied. "It is Albert Reilly."

"Good, and Terri James? Where is she now?"

"I've just left her at the entrance. She said something about going home to her dad."

"Well, run and catch her up, will you?"

"Guv?"

"Invite her in for an interview. Tell her that we're launching the investigation, and we'd appreciate her input."

"Right," Jewson said. "Listen, guv. I got a message from DI Savage."

"Oh, did you?"

"He's asked me to take Havers' keys to see if they open Reilly's front door."

"That's right."

"Well..."

"Is there a problem, Jewson?"

"No, I was just wondering if I should do that alone. You know, being a crime scene and all that. I thought maybe DC Cruz could meet me there. Or I could pick him up on the way through."

"I think you'll be fine. Cruz has enough on his plate. Besides, CSI have done what they needed to do," Freya said. "You have a squad car, do you not?"

"I do, yes. Sergeant Priest said I could use it."

"Good, well, you should find a tool kit in the boot."

"A tool kit?"

"The door is boarded up," Freya said. "You'll need to remove the board to get to the front door."

"Right."

"But make sure it goes back on. We don't want any local yobos breaking in."

"I see."

"And when you're done doing that, I want to expand the door to door," Freya said, thinking aloud. "Go up the main road, will you? Somebody must have a bloody doorbell camera along there."

"What? On my own?" Jewson said. "That'll take all day."

"That should keep you busy then," Freya told her. "Call in to Chapman when you've assessed the key situation. If Havers had a key, we can't strike him off, but we can demote him from the number one spot on our hit list."

"Erm, yeah, sure," Jewson replied, her tone sombre. "But, I have to say, I feel like I'm being targeted for something here."

"Targeted?" Freya replied, and she stepped closer to the

phone. "I hope I heard that wrong, Jewson. It sounded to me like you were accusing me of malpractice or... dare I say it, misconduct."

"I just..." Jewson started. "This is because of what happened yesterday, isn't it?"

"Yesterday? I wasn't here when whatever happened happened, so I'm afraid I can't answer that."

"Right," Jewson mumbled.

"Oh, and one more thing before you go," Freya said.

"Guv?"

"Welcome to major crimes, Jewson."

CHAPTER TWENTY-FIVE

Lincoln City Centre police station was almost otherworldly compared to the dilapidated old building Gillespie had grown used to. Housing the police, ambulance, and fire services, the facility was sprawling, giving Gillespie the feeling he was guilty of something as he entered the reception. Even the security cameras were modern. No doubt some outsourced security guard was watching him, wondering what kind of crime he had done and if he was there to hand himself in. Gillespie imagined the crackle of radios as the guard alerted the actual police inside, something along the lines of, 'there's a big scruffy rough-looking bloke on his way. Standby, standby'.

"Now then," the uniformed officer behind the desk said, his expression blank and unreadable. "Help you?"

"I'm looking for a Sergeant Souness," Gillespie said.

"And you are?" he replied, making a show of looking something up on his computer. Given the huge resources that had been allocated to the facility, they no doubt had some flash software that kept track of visitors and officers going through each door. Back at his own station, Gillespie knew that a manual log was maintained in case of a fire. Officers still had to swipe in and out, but with less than thirty officers, an A4 sheet of paper on an old clipboard was far easier to grab when all thirty of them were running for the fire exit.

"Oh, my name's James Gillespie. I was involved in an accident this morning. I understand he's the CEO."

"The SIO?" The officer said. "Senior Investigating Officer."

"Right, yeah," Gillespie said, clicking his fingers. "That's it. The SIO."

"And can I ask the purpose of your visit?"

"Well, I would imagine he would want to speak to me," Gillespie said. "I mean, he let me go, as I needed to get to work, but he made it clear that I should report to him."

"So, he requested to see you, did he?"

"Well, he just said that I shouldn't leave the country if you know what I mean," Gillespie replied with a wink.

"Right," the officer said slowly, as if unsure of the protocol. He snatched up his desk phone, eyed the computer screen to get Souness's extension, and then held his hand over the mouthpiece as he spoke.

"Ah, yeah, Sergeant Souness?" The officer said. "I've some bloke down here who says he was involved in that RTA. Said you wanted to see him."

"Is that him?" Gillespie asked, leaning forward to hear the conversation better. The officer turned away.

"Big fella. Said his name is James Gillespie?" The officer said. "Scottish, if that means anything."

"Glaswegian," Gillespie corrected him.

"Alright, sarge," the officer said, then replaced the handset and made a show of clicking a few buttons on his computer.

"He coming down then, eh?" Gillespie asked.

"If you could just take a seat," he replied. "Someone will be down shortly."

"Souness? Is it him coming?" Gillespie said, and he tapped on the glass screen between them.

"Sir, if you could just—"

"Is this bulletproof?"

The officer stopped.

"Sorry?"

"Bulletproof, is it?"

"Why would you ask that?" The officer said, but Gillespie was looking around the ceiling.

"Three cameras?"

From the corner of his eye, Gillespie watched with glee as the officer reached to his shoulder radio. He hit the Push-To-Talk button just as the door to the corridor opened. Nearly all the stations Gillespie had been to had a similar layout. The reception was segregated by an electro-magnetically locked door that led to a main corridor, off of which was the custody suite, the cells, and the interview rooms. Offices and incident rooms were often housed on first and second floors, away from the eyes of prying prisoners or suspects.

"That's him," the officer said, abandoning his radio call as Souness stepped into the reception. "Do you know this man, sarge?"

Gillespie toyed with the officer behind the desk for just a few moments longer by pulling the best guilty expression he could muster, which wasn't far off his resting face.

"Gillespie?" Souness said.

"Aye, sarge. How's it going?" Gillespie replied. "I met you at the RTA this morning. Remember?"

"You were the officer dealing with the lorry driver for me."

"Aye, that's it."

"You're a police officer?" The officer behind the desk said.

"Aye," Gillespie replied. "Aye, sorry, didn't I mention that?" He fished his warrant card from his pocket. "Sergeant Gillespie. Nice to meet you, mate."

The uniformed officer's face reddened, and he dropped back into his seat, tossing his pen onto the desk. It was a big station, and if he couldn't deal with a little wind-up like that, the fella had no chance. Gillespie turned to Souness. "Wondered if I could have a wee word with you about the RTA?"

"Well, it's a live investigation," Souness replied. "And we haven't had any reports back from—"

"It's about that car."

"What car?"

"The blue one," Gillespie said.

"Ah, right. Well, if you believe that, you'll believe anything," Souness said. "We've got the driver in custody now, but trust me. There was no blue car."

"What if I told you there was," Gillespie said. "Or at least, there might be."

"Then I would have to ask you to substantiate that claim."

"He's looking at manslaughter, aye?"

"He's heading that way," Souness replied. "He's not giving me much reason to believe otherwise."

Gillespie grinned.

"So what do you reckon?" He said, nodding at the door to the corridor. "Any chance I could have a wee word?"

CHAPTER TWENTY-SIX

Exactly as the guv had said, an eight-by-four sheet of plywood had been installed over Reilly's front door.

Jewson stared at it from inside the car. Part of her wanted to start the engine, turn around and head back to the station.

But there was another part of her that provided a compelling argument; even if she walked directly to Detective Superintendent Granger's office and told him she had changed her mind, she would still have to face the team at some point. She would still have to admit that she couldn't handle being at the bottom of the ladder, and besides, quitting wasn't in her nature. She would have to prove herself, and the best way of achieving that was to disprove somebody else.

She looked across to her left, to the Armstead's house, where the living room curtain twitched. She turned away, pretending not to have noticed, and then climbed from the car to find the tool kit in the boot. She had always found it bizarre that whoever selected the cars the force used selected an already sluggish diesel car and then loaded it up with two adult officers and a boot full of kit. There were provisions for roadside emergencies, such as cones, wet weather gear, cold weather gear, a first aid kit in a huge bag, spare breathalyser tests, drug tests, torches, evidence bags, DNA kits, and even bags she had never bothered looking inside. The tool kit was, of course, beneath the mountain of gear, which meant that Jewson had to unload the car, access the tool kit, and then reload the car. She left the boot open with the tool kit on the roadside and strolled over to Reilly's house, armed with a little electric screwdriver that looked like it had been bought from the centre aisle of the local Aldi store.

It was then that she discovered that whoever had installed the sheet of wood had clearly meant business. It was either that or they were paid by the screw. She counted twenty-something screws before she lost count; one every six -inches.

"Morning," somebody called, and before she had even turned to face the visitor, Jewson knew who it would be.

"Good morning," she replied without turning and making a show of struggling with the first screw.

"Forget something, did you?" the man said as Jewson let the screwdriver whizz around inside the screw head.

She stood and graced them with a polite smile.

"Just following up on some evidence," she explained, to which Mr and Mrs Armstead peered at her quizzically as if she might go into further detail.

"On your own, are you?" the wife asked.

"I am, yes," Jewson said, refraining from waving an arm around to present the otherwise empty street.

"And you've got to get that off, have you?"

"If I want to get inside, then yes," Jewson explained, adding just enough exasperation into her tone to signify that, although capable, it was rather a chore.

"Give her a hand, George, will you?" the older lady said to her husband.

"Oh, that's—" Jewson began.

"Nonsense," Mrs Armstead replied, nudging her husband forward. "George'll do it. He'll have it off in a jiffy."

"Well, I suppose—"

"He's always been good with his hands, has my George."

Jewson made a show of relenting and held the screwdriver out for Mr Armstead.

"Thank you," she said. "I'm very grateful."

"Oh, think nothing of it, lovey," he said, taking the screwdriver off her. "The trick is to start at the bottom and work your way up."

"Oh?"

He dropped to his knees carefully and looked up at her. "Otherwise, it'll fall on your head, won't it?"

"Ah. I hadn't thought of that," she admitted.

"So..." Mrs Armstead said. "What is it you're looking for?"

"Sorry?"

"You said you were following up on something, dear."

"I'm afraid I can't really go into detail."

"Oh, of course. Sorry, I shouldn't have asked," she said. "It's just such a shame, isn't it?"

"About Mr Havers, you mean?"

"No, about Albert. Why? What's happened to Roger? Has something happened to him?"

"No, no. I was just. Sorry, I misunderstood."

"But you have found him, haven't you?"

"Well, actually, we're still trying to locate him."

Mrs Armstead suddenly gasped.

"You don't think..." she said. "No. He couldn't have. He wouldn't have, would he?"

"At the minute, we just want to speak to him, Mrs Armstead, that's all."

"But you can't find him?"

"We're looking for him. For all we know, he could be visiting family."

"But he doesn't have any family," she said. "Only a daughter and she only lives up the road."

"Oh, is that right? I don't suppose you have her address, do you?" Jewson asked, pulling her notepad from her pocket.

"Oh, you don't need that, dear," Mrs Armstead said. "It's the house on the main road. The one with the camper van. It's one of those old ones, you know? The hippy van."

"It's a Volkswagen," Mr Armstead cut in, busy removing the last of the screws. "Can't miss it. Blue and white thing. Looks like it's been around the world twice. Anita, her name is. Not sure of her last name. She's married."

"I'll pop by and have a word with her. Thank you," Jewson said.

"There we go," Mr Armstead said, and he did that thing that Jewson's own father did and made a fuss of heaving the sheet of wood out of the way, grunting and groaning just to let them know it was heavy.

He held the screwdriver out for her.

"Keep hold of it," she said with a smile. "You'll need that to put it back on when I'm done."

"Oh, I see," he replied, and thankfully he saw the funny side.

Jewson pulled Havers' keys from her pocket. There were four keys in total: the car key, a small key that could have been for a padlock, and two keys that could have been for a front door. She tried the first one, twisted it, and met resistance.

"Those Roger's keys, are they?" Mr Armstead asked. Jewson looked up at him.

"Why do you ask?"

"The car key," he replied and nodded at the bunch in her hand. "It's a Skoda key."

"Is it?" she said.

"Albert never drove a Skoda, even when he still had a car."

"Oh," Jewson said. "To be honest, my boss gave me them. I presume they're Mr Reilly's."

"No, they're Rogers," he said.

"Well, if I could just..." she started, trying the second of the front door keys.

It turned, and she pushed the door open, immediately met with the smell of vanilla from a plug-in air freshener.

"I wonder," she said. "Would you mind just waiting here while I pop inside? I'll only be a moment."

"Crime scene, eh?" Mrs Armstead said. "Don't want our grubby fingerprints contaminating the scene. I know. We watch enough of those documentaries to know how it works."

"Thank you," Jewson said, and she stepped inside. The hallway was dim, despite the open door, as if the life of the old house was ebbing away with every moment it was vacant. She stopped at the living room door, spying the spot where Albert Reilly had been found. As the guv had explained, the armchair was facing away from the door, and there was very little in the way of furniture that Reilly could have hit his head on.

She moved through to the kitchen, which, due to the sheet of ply over the door, was ever darker than the hallway. Nothing seemed out of place except the broken window. The shards of glass had no doubt been collected up by CSI for analysis.

She put herself in the intruder's shoes. As far as she could tell from what the team had discussed, there were two schools of thought. The first was that an intruder had broken in to rob the old man of whatever meagre possessions or cash he had. The second was that somebody had meant to harm him. She'd spent enough time in uniform to know that intruders who break into elderly peoples' houses ransacked the kitchen first, knowing that any cash was likely to be stored in a biscuit tin, a teapot or something similar.

Yet, nothing in the cupboard appeared out of place. It was almost impossible to tell if somebody had been rummaging through the cupboards.

If it had been an intruder, Albert Reilly may have heard them.

He might have called out, which would have spooked the intruder.

But somebody who had intended to hurt Reilly would have gone straight to the living room to find him.

"Jesus," she said. "This is impossible."

"What's that, dear?" Mrs Armstead said from the living room doorway.

"Mrs Armstead, I thought I asked you to—"

"I thought I'd have a quick nosey," she replied, then nodded at the living room. "It's bigger than ours, you know."

"I'm afraid I'm going to have to ask you to leave—"

But Mrs Armstead was already inside the living room.

"Oh, yes," she said as Jewson caught up with her. "It's bigger, all right. But ours is nicer."

"You really can't be here—"

"And there's little Robert," she continued, pointing to a framed photo on the sideboard beside the door. She looked around the room quizzically. "That's funny."

"What's that?" Jewson asked.

"Well, I…" Mrs Armstead started, hunting around the room with her eyes narrowed. She stopped and looked up at Jewson. "Well, if I'd have got a framed letter from the Queen, I'd have it up for everyone to see, wouldn't you?"

CHAPTER TWENTY-SEVEN

"Miss James," Freya said as she and Ben entered the interview room. "Thank you so much for coming in."

"That's quite alright," James replied. She was sitting on the far side of the interview room table, her heavy coat wrapped around her and her large tote bag by her feet. "I haven't got long. I should really get back to Dad."

"We won't keep you," Ben assured her. "There are just a few questions that have arisen since we spoke that could really help our investigation."

"Okay," she replied. "I suppose if it helps Albert's family, then I'll do what I can."

"That was one of the things I wanted to begin with, as it happens," Freya said. "You see when we have an incident like this, it's vital that we act fast. The more time that passes, the less chance there is of us getting to the truth. It's a sad fact, but there it is."

"Okay," James said, making a show of following along.

"The vast majority of murders that take place in the UK are carried out by somebody the victim knows. Did you know that?"

"No," James said, a little surprised. "No, I didn't."

"It's the same with sexual assaults, believe it or not," Freya explained. "Now, in the case of Albert Reilly, there are very strong factors that lead us to believe that his death was caused by somebody who did not know him."

"A stranger?"

"There was some broken glass beside the back door," Ben explained.

"We think an intruder gained entry, perhaps startling Albert. The pathology report suggests he experienced a heart attack at around the same time. Now, whether or not he died from that heart attack is to be determined, but the fact remains that he suffered a severe head injury, either shortly before death or shortly afterwards."

"Oh, good Lord," James said, and she took a deep breath to control her nerves.

"You okay?" Ben asked, to which she nodded.

"Our problem is this," Freya continued. "We can't really take the investigation wider until we've eliminated his close friends and family."

"Right, so me then?"

"Yes, you, but also his son, Robert, his sister, Harriet, and then there's Roger Havers."

"Okay?"

"We have officers with Robert Reilly and Harriet Underwood as we speak, working to eliminate them from our investigations, but I wondered if there was something you could tell us that might help us. Anything at all."

"Like what?" James asked.

"Like, when did you last see Robert at Albert's house?"

She sat back, looked up at the ceiling, and then shook her head.

"Months ago. They weren't very close. Albert rarely even mentioned him unless he had to."

"And you have no reason to believe there was any recent communication?"

"None whatsoever," James said. "The same goes for his sister. She's getting on now, but even when she was more mobile, he rarely ever mentioned her. Sad, really."

"It is," Freya agreed. "Which leads me to Roger Havers. When we last spoke, you mentioned they used to play bridge."

"That's right; on Tuesday nights."

"And they regularly fell out. Is that right?"

"Well, I wouldn't call it falling out. Albert would just rant about him. To be honest, I was never there that late."

"And did he rant when you saw him last, which was the Thursday, is that right?"

"That's right," James replied. "And no, not that I recall. He was actually quiet. He was quite a thoughtful man. You know? Conversation wasn't always easy. I had to work at it. Sometimes he would open up, but others..." she shook her head sadly. "Other times, he would snap at me. Tell me to mind my own business or to just get on and do what I'm bloody well paid to do, and bugger off."

"Charming."

"He was okay. It was just his nature. If he snapped, he never held a grudge, and although he never really apologised, he made a show of being sorry. Like I told you yesterday, I seemed to have a way with him. I understood him."

"And Roger?" Freya asked. "Did you understand him?"

"I don't really know him. He seems nice enough. He used to wave if he saw me coming or going. He popped in once or twice while I was there, but there were never any real arguments; not while I was there, anyway. But I think he had a way with Albert, probably just like I did. He has this air of authority about him. He never backed down from Albert and would...not bark orders so much, but he would offer his opinion quite freely. I always got the impression he was somebody who was used to getting his own way."

"That's interesting," Freya said, then eyed Ben to prepare him for what was to come. "Miss James, were you ever aware of Albert's time in prison?"

"Sorry?"

"It was a long time ago now, but Albert Reilly was charged with manslaughter and served nearly a decade in prison."

"No," James said slowly. "No, he never mentioned it."

"Why would he?" Freya asked. "I just wondered if it was something that maybe you had found out. It could be on his record, or—"

"I don't have access to his criminal records or anything like that. I was just given a patient sheet with his or her details on it. I'm told what needs to be done, cleaning, cooking—"

"Medication," Freya added.

"Yes, that's right. I have access to his prescriptions, so that I can collect them on his behalf, and I'm permitted to administer them. But there was never any problems."

"I'm sure," Freya said. "But just going back a little to when you first started caring for Albert, can you remember who set the whole thing up? Who requested Albert to have a carer? Was it Robert or Harriet, maybe?"

"It was Robert," James replied. "He met me there on the first visit. I'm sorry, but I feel like this is going all over the place. You said you needed to, what did you call it, eliminate close friends and family, and I feel like we're jumping from topic to topic. Are you trying to catch me out or something?"

"Why would I catch you out?" Freya asked.

"I don't know. But all of a sudden, I feel like I'm not simply helping you with your investigation, but I'm being interviewed."

"Well," Freya said, offering as pleasant a smile as she could muster. "I apologise if I've made you feel that way. It wasn't my intention. The sad truth is, Miss James, that we really don't have much to go on. I suppose we're clutching at straws in the hope that something you say might point us in the right direction."

James nodded, seeming to understand.

"Well, I really ought to get back to my dad," she said.

"Of course," Freya said, waving her hand at the door. "You're free to go, of course."

James smiled graciously and stood, collecting her bag as she did. She made it to the door before Freya stopped her.

"Oh, one last thing, Miss James," Freya said, and she beamed up at her. "Where were you on Monday morning?"

"Where was I?"

"On Monday morning," Freya asked. "As part of our elimination, you understand."

"I see," she said. "So, it wasn't just a polite chat then?"

"I just want to cross your name off our list," Freya told her.

"I was running errands. I left my house early. I had some clothes to drop off at the charity box behind the Co-op before seeing to my dad. Mornings are quite difficult. There's not many buses, and I've the breakfast to do. Dad always likes a good breakfast. It's one of the things he likes about this country. He doesn't go for English food much, but he has to have his breakfast."

"Hear, hear," Ben said.

"So you didn't visit Albert?" Freya asked. "Just for the record, you didn't swing by?"

"Swing by? Why on earth would I swing by Albert's?" James said, exposing her large teeth as she pulled a face of absolute outrage. "You said somebody broke a window. Is that right?"

"That's how the intruder gained access," Freya said. "Or so we believe."

"Well, why on earth would I need to break a window?" She rummaged in her bag, found her keys, and then held one up for Freya. "When I've got my own key?"

CHAPTER TWENTY-EIGHT

The previous morning, when Gillespie had lent a hand at the scene of the accident, Eamon Price had been pale with shock; he visibly shook, and his eyes had been red raw from the horrors of both what had happened and what was in store for him.

But when Souness led him into the interview room, where Gillespie was waiting, Price was little more than a shell of the already terrified man Gillespie had met.

"Ah, Mr Price," Gillespie said, and he rose from his seat to shake Price's hand despite the handcuffs with which the Traffic Officer was leading him. "How are you coping?"

With a coercive nudge, Souness encouraged Price to take a seat opposite Gillespie. Then, he moved to the seat beside him so the two officers faced the terrified driver.

"How am I coping?" Price said. "I'm being charged with death by dangerous driving."

"Not yet, you're not," Souness said.

"I've been here nearly twenty-four hours," he replied. "This is the fourth interview I've had. I'm not daft. I watch the bloody telly. I've had about two hours sleep and a cup of warm water."

"Well, that's not entirely correct, is it?" Souness said. "You were offered food and drink, but you turned it down."

"Aye, I turned it down. I can't bloody eat a thing. I'm petrified, man. Do you get that? I'm just a bloke. A normal bloke. I've a wife and a kid to support. What are they going to do?"

"Well, perhaps that's where this little chat might be in your favour," Gillespie said. "I'm not actually part of the investigation, but I could help you."

"Right, yeah," Price said, sitting back in his seat. "Help me, eh? You can start by removing these bloody things." He held his cuffed hands up.

"While you're out of your cell, I'm afraid we'll need to keep those on," Souness said.

"Mr Price, I want to cast your mind back to yesterday morning," Gillespie started.

"Cast my mind back? Cast my bloody mind back? What do you think I've been thinking about while I've been here? Christmas? Do you think I've been going over the list of jobs I'm to do around the house? I've got a leaky gutter that'll no doubt cause damp over winter; I need to give the lawn one more cut, and I've a pile of bloody cardboard I need to cut up and somehow fit in the purple bin. Is that what you think I've been thinking about? Not, the poor bloke that I..." He took a breath, and his nostrils flared. "That I crushed to death with my lorry, eh? Which of those do you think has occupied my mind for the past day?"

"You've been given access to a solicitor, aye?" Gillespie asked, to which Price simply scoffed. "And what's he or she going to do for me, eh? They've got no magic wand they can wave."

"Can you just..." Gillespie said, holding his hands out to calm the man down. "Can you just talk me through what happened in your own words?"

Price reached up to scratch his chin with both hands, then settled into his seat.

"There was this fella on a bike. I'm guessing you both know

the rules about leaving a metre and a half when overtaking them, right?"

"Let's go back," Gillespie cut in. "Where were you coming from, and where were you going?"

"I was coming from the yard," Price said. "I'd just picked the load up, and I was on my way out to Grantham. Was only supposed to be out for a few hours."

"And where is the yard?" Gillespie asked.

"What?" Price said. "Just down at Woodhall. Kirkstead Bridge. Why does that matter?"

"And you were heading out to Grantham. What route were you taking?"

"My route? What does that matter?"

"Please, Mr Price," Gillespie said. "Just humour me, will you?"

He nodded slowly, then licked his lips and cleared his throat.

"From Woodhall, I was heading out through Martin, Metheringham, and Navenby, and from there, I'd pick up the 607. It's a clear run down, or at least it was supposed to be."

"But soon after you got going, you encountered the cyclist. Is that right?"

"Yeah. I was coming into Martin when I saw him. Most of them are alright, you know? They keep to the left. But this fella was just in the way." He leaned forward and jabbed an index finger at the interview room table. "If I'd have given him a metre and a bloody half, I'd have been driving through the bloody houses."

"Did you make your presence known to him?"

"It's a lorry, mate. Seventeen tons of metal sitting on a twelve-litre engine. If he didn't know I was there, he must have been deaf and blind."

"But you didn't sound your horn?"

"It was early doors. People were sleeping," Price said. "I'm not a complete moron, you know? Besides, I figured I'd bide my time and get past him in the village when the road widens."

"And that's when you made your move, is it?"

"Sergeant Gillespie," Souness started. "I'm sorry, but you asked for a few minutes with my suspect, but it seems you're going over the same details we've been through time and again. I could have just given you access to the interviews."

"No, I need to talk to him," Gillespie said, turning back to Price. "I need to look in his eye when I ask him the next question."

"Go on, then," Price said. There was a reason that officers had to attend training before interviewing suspects. But even then, there were tiny details that only experience could translate. The way Price stared at him instead of finding a tiny spot on the wall with which to busy his gaze, the way he fiddled with his fingers as if any hope of being released any time soon had been well and truly quashed. And the look in the man's eye. The look of a man who had resigned himself to a fate he didn't deserve. "Ask me."

"When I saw you yesterday, shortly after the incident, you told me there was a blue car—"

"Oh, not this," Souness said.

"Aye, this," Gillespie replied, keen not to let the remark dilute the line of questioning. He spoke to Price with as much sincerity as he could muster. "Is this accurate?"

"I told you I saw it, didn't I?"

"And since you've thought of little else since the incident, have you been able to recollect any more details, Mr Price? Anything at all that could help us track the owner of that car down?"

Price shook his head.

"It was a hatchback," he said. "Japanese or Korean, probably."

"I need facts," Gillespie said, and Price shook his head.

"I don't have them," he said.

"This could be your ticket out of here, Mr Price," Gillespie urged. "Anything at all?"

"I don't know," he said, verging on tears. "I can't remember. I thought they'd stay there, but... they just pulled out. I'd already committed. I had nowhere to go. Don't you see? I had nowhere to go but..."

"I understand," Gillespie said. "It's okay. It was a split-second decision."

"I've replayed it over and over, and I know I should have hit the car. But it was instinct, you know?"

"It's fine, don't get upset."

"I can tell you this much," Price said. "Whoever it was, they were in a bloody hurry."

CHAPTER TWENTY-NINE

However irritating and interfering the Armsteads were, the man's description of the blue and white camper van was spot on. It did indeed look as if it had been around the world twice. The house was modest but well kept, which, for Jewson's purposes, mattered not one iota, but she had come to learn over time that there was a direct correlation between the pride in an owner's house and their receptiveness to a visit from the local police. There were, of course, the outliers. On more than one occasion, she had been barked at by individuals who took the utmost pride in their property, but for the most part, the correlation was accurate. The camper van was the only real stain on the property, but from the stickers on the windows and the soft toys inside, it was clearly a family treasure.

She knocked twice, then stepped back as a voice called out from inside.

"Mum!" a child said, who was young enough that their voice was no gauge of gender. "Door."

"Well, get it then," the mother replied.

"I'm watching telly."

"Can you just get it," the mother called out again.

"I can't. I'm sick, remember?"

"If you're sick, I'm a bloody giraffe," the mother said as her form approached the frosted glass. The door was torn open, and she peered down at Jewson, quite flustered. "Hello?" she said, leaning out of the drive to see if Jewson was alone. She was dressed casually in a pair of jeans and a loose-fitting blouse. Her hair had been pulled up on top of her head as if she had pulled it out of the way to do her makeup. Jewson did something similar. "Can I help you?"

Jewson withdrew her warrant card from her pocket, realising that she was no longer in uniform and the liveried car she had borrowed was still parked outside the old man's house.

"I'm with Lincolnshire Police," she explained. "I wondered if I could have a few words."

"Oh, God. Not you lot again," she said. "Does it have to be now? I'm about to go out."

"It won't take long," Jewson said. "It's just that—"

"Oh, for God's sake. Alright, alright, you'd better come in." She stepped back and held the door open. "Sorry, the place is a mess. We still haven't got it straight."

"Oh, that's okay," Jewson said. "You should see the state of my —" She stopped just inside the door and was immediately confronted with a pile of boxes in the hallway, each one over-flowing with clothes. A rolled-up carpet occupied the other side of the hallway, and the whole house smelled damp. "...of my place," Jewson finished.

"This is for the insurance," she said. "I don't suppose you're any closer to catching the bastard, are you?" she leaned into the lounge as soon as she spoke the words.

"I heard that," the child called out.

"Just watch your TV," the woman replied.

"I'm sorry, I wasn't aware that anybody had spoken to you. It must be a difficult time for you."

"Difficult?" she said. "Difficult? Downright bloody inconvenient, is what it is. We're supposed to be going away in the van."

"Mum!" The child said from the next room in a warning tone, likely pertaining to the woman's language.

"Oh, shut up," she said, pulling the living room door closed. "Come through to the kitchen, will you?" She stepped over the boxes and the carpet and into the kitchen, leaving Jewson to follow with care. "We had someone come round yesterday morning. You know, to give us a crime number."

"A crime number?"

"Then, somebody popped round last night to see how we were getting on."

"Ah, right. A Family Liaison Officer?"

"I don't know," she replied. "It's all hand-holding stuff. My husband dealt with her. We don't need anyone round here while we're dealing with all of this, and especially not when we're away for a few days."

"Everything happens at once, doesn't it?" Jewson said. "Have you been asked to...you know? Visit the hospital?"

"Sorry?"

"Has anybody asked you to view the body?" Jewson asked. "I realise it's difficult, but it is a vital part of what we do."

"View what body?" she said, and Jewson hesitated as the woman peered at her curiously. "View what body? Is somebody dead?"

Jewson stared down at the carpet and the boxes, suddenly feeling quite out of her depth.

"I just thought that you know—"

"Sorry, can I see your identification again, please?"

"Yes, yes, of course," Jewson said, and she opened her warrant card for her to see.

"PC Jewson. You're not in uniform."

"No, no, I'm in the middle of transferring to a new team."

"A new team?"

"Major crimes," Jewson said.

"Major crimes? This isn't a major crime, and if it was, I'd expect more than a bloody crime number to give the insurance firm."

"I'm sorry. May I take your name again, please?"

"My name? You don't even have my name?"

"No, I was sent here by Mr and Mrs Armstead. They said you lived close by."

"Mr and Mrs who?"

"Armstead. They live next door to your dad."

The woman paused, processing the information. Her mouth hung open, and her intelligent eyes suddenly opened wide.

"You're not here about the burglary, are you?"

"And you haven't been made aware of the accident," Jewson replied. "I'm so sorry. I'm so, so sorry."

"My dad?"

Jewson nodded.

"I thought you knew. When you let me in, I thought—"

"Is he...?"

Jewson nodded again.

"Yesterday morning," Jewson said. "There was an RTA—"

"He's dead?"

"I'm afraid so—"

"What's an RTA?"

"A road traffic accident," Jewson explained. "He was..." She stopped herself before the woman interrupted again. "Look, I'm sorry. This has been a mistake. Somebody should have told you. They should be reaching out to you."

"I've been getting calls," she replied quietly. "To be honest, I didn't want to be contacted after yesterday. I just ignored them."

"Why don't we sit down?"

"I don't want to sit down," the woman snapped. "An accident? The one up the road?"

"I'm afraid so."

"But it was a lorry. I walked past it—"

"There were several vehicles," Jewson said. "One of them was your father's."

"And he..." the woman's voice trailed away.

"He died at the scene, Mrs..."

"Stone," she replied, distant and lost in thought. "Mrs Stone."

"Is there somebody we can call? Somebody who might sit with you?"

"I don't need anybody," she replied, and then dropped down onto a breakfast stool and stared at the hallway, perhaps wondering how she would tell her son the bad news. "Bloody hell."

"Can I make you a tea?"

"No," she said. "No, I'm fine. Honestly, it's one of those things. You know it's coming one day. I just didn't expect it to come today. Not after..." she nodded at the mess. "Not after we've had a break-in. I thought this was about the robbery, you know? I thought this was all part of the process that you lot carry out. I didn't even stop to think—"

"It's not your fault," Jewson said. "Somebody should have told you by now. I expect it's taking longer than usual due to the circumstances."

"What circumstances?"

"Well, there was another death."

"Oh God, no."

"A young man on a bike. As far as we can tell, the lorry was passing the bike when somebody pulled out, so the driver had to swerve. He hit the bike and slammed his brakes on. Two cars drove into the back of the lorry at thirty miles an hour."

"And one of them was my dad?"

"I'm afraid so," Jewson said. "Are you sure there's nobody I can call to sit with you?"

She buried her face in her hands, sobbed once, then immediately gained control of her emotions and sniffed loudly.

"No, no, I'm fine. Who else knows?"

"There's nobody to tell," Jewson replied. "Only Mr Reilly over the road, and well..."

"Well, what?"

"Oh, nothing."

"No, go on."

"I can't go into details," Jewson said. "It's a live investigation. We have rules about what we can and can't say."

"Like how you inform somebody their father has just been killed in a crash, you mean?" Jewson took the comment on the chin and offered a sheepish smile in return. "It's probably better you don't tell him, anyway," the woman said. "The way those two used to go at each other, he'd probably jump for joy and die from a heart attack."

"What are you saying?" Jewson asked. "Were they friends or not?"

"Oh, they were friends," she replied. "But it was a love-hate relationship, if you know what I mean. To be honest, my husband and I used to bet on which one of them would kill the other."

CHAPTER THIRTY

There was noise coming from inside the house, of that, Gold was sure. There were no other houses in sight, let alone close enough for the Bargain Hunt theme tune to be heard.

She rang the doorbell again, and the traditional ding-dong reminded her of her childhood when everyone's doorbell seemed to be the same. Modern doorbells just lacked nostalgia.

It wasn't one of her favourite things to do, but she resorted to bending down and calling through the letterbox.

"Mrs Underwood?" she said. "Mrs Underwood, are you there?"

The Bargain Hunt presenter's voice grew quieter and quieter until she couldn't hear it at all.

"Mrs Underwood? My name is Jackie Gold. I'm with Lincolnshire Police. Could I have a word?"

The elderly lady stepped out of her living room, and peered down at Jackie, her face screwed up in absolute revulsion.

"You what, love?"

"My name is Jackie, and I'm with...look, do you think you could open the door, Mrs Underwood? I'm with the police."

She closed the letterbox and straightened as Mrs Underwood approached the door and peered through the frosted glass.

"I'm on my own," Jackie called out, holding up her warrant card ready for when the door opened. To Jackie's surprise, she didn't use the security chain. She opened the door fully, stared down at Jackie, and then studied her identification.

"You lot? Again?"

"I just wondered if I might have a few minutes of your time," Jackie explained. "I'm really sorry to hear about your loss."

"My loss?"

"Your brother, Mrs Underwood," Jackie said. "I'm sorry, I was led to believe my colleagues had told you—"

"Oh, they told me. But it's not much of a loss. One less Christmas card to send. Saved me a bob or two on a stamp."

"Well, I couldn't really comment on that—"

"No. No, you couldn't, could you?" She leaned out of the door. "Didn't know him like I did, did you."

"So, can I come in?"

The old lady seemed reluctant and hardy, but her good nature shone through and she stepped to one side.

"Come on then. I don't know what you want to know, mind. Told them other two everything I know."

"Ah, DCI Bloom and DI Savage, you mean?"

"Oh, I don't remember their names," she replied. "She looked like she'd been in the wars, but he was quite handsome."

"That's them," Gold said, hoping her smile would convince Mrs Underwood to open up. She followed the old lady through to the kitchen and watched as she filled the kettle without even asking if Jackie wanted a tea. "It's not unusual, under these circumstances, for a friend or a relative to remember something. Often, the news can be quite shocking."

"I see," Mrs Underwood said, flicking the kettle on. "But if you think I'm shocked, then I'm afraid you've got me all wrong."

"Well, I—"

"Somebody was going to get him one of these days," she said. "Couldn't go to the bleeding shop without insulting somebody."

She opened the cupboard door and reached up for a biscuit tin, the barrel type Jackie's nan used to have, which was decorated with little flowers and birds . "We always thought he'd amount to nothing," Mrs Underwood said. "I mean, he wasn't so bad when we were growing up, but he was always a bit...I don't know, different, if you know what I mean."

"I think I do."

"Course, when he started the firm, we thought he'd get bored, and it'd fizzle out. But you know what? It didn't. His boy runs it now, but I suppose you know that."

"We do," Jackie said. "Robert."

"Yes. Yes, he's a miserable sod, too," Mrs Underwood said. "Runs in the family, I'm afraid. Like a lot of things."

"You can choose your friends," Jackie said.

"That's right," Mrs Underwood replied as she pulled two cups down and set them out on the kitchen side. "Then, just like we knew it would, it all went wrong."

"How so?" Jackie asked.

"Oh, you know? Prison," she said, as if the word was meant to startle Jackie. "It was bound to happen one day. He was either going to say the wrong thing to somebody, or he was going to cut corners and wind up on the inside. Manslaughter, they called it. It's another name for greedy and lazy if you ask me."

"Yes, we heard," Jackie said, and Mrs Underwood shook her head sadly.

"But you know what," she continued. "He did the right thing. He could have got a better lawyer. He could have argued the case and let old Roger take the rap, but he didn't. Surprised us, he did. He took the whole thing on his chin, served his time and came out."

"And was he different when he came out?"

"Different?" Mrs Underwood said with a laugh. "Worse, more like. It was like he was tired of life. Ended up handing the whole business over to Robert. Imagine that. You spend your life building something up, and then you just walk away."

"You mean he passed the business to Robert?"

"The business, most of the money, the lorries, the yard. All of it. It was like he'd given up. I mean, I dare say he had a few quid tucked away; he wouldn't sell himself short. But it was as if he'd just had enough of it all. You know? He had no real passion for anything. Spent the last God knows how many years sitting in that old house on his own."

"On his own?" Jackie said. "I thought he had a wife."

"Oh, he had a wife, alright. But they weren't really... you know?"

"No. No, I don't."

Mrs Underwood sucked in a breath as the kettle clicked off, and set about pouring the water into the cups.

"They slept in different beds for a start. If my husband and I slept in separate beds, we wouldn't have lasted a week. You're married. You sleep together," she said. "Even had separate rooms, they did. Separate rooms, I ask you." She pressed the tea bags and binned them, and being close to the fridge, Jackie made herself useful. "I don't know what happened when Albert was locked up, but something in him changed."

"How sad," Jackie said.

"When you get to my age, you stop pondering on these things. You can't change people, you know? You take them on face value, or you leave them."

"And that's what you did, is it? You left him to it."

"What did you expect me to do? There was no talking to him. No getting through that thick skull of his. I saw him when I needed to. When I had something to say, but that was it."

"And Robert?" Jackie said. "What was their relationship like?"

"Robert and Albert? Well, put it this way," Mrs Underwood said as she slid the tea towards Jackie. "Robert has put up with more than you or I will ever know. When Albert handed him the keys to the business, he should have handed them right back."

"Meaning?"

"Meaning, my dear," she said. "That firm of his will kill him one of these days." She looked over the rim of her tea and gave it a gentle blow. "You mark my words. It was started with bad blood and it'll end in bad blood."

CHAPTER THIRTY-ONE

"You took your time," Nillson said when Gillespie returned to his car. "You said you'd be ten minutes." She checked her watch. "That was forty minutes ago."

"Aye, well," Gillespie replied as he pulled his seat belt on. "I needed to get the bigger picture, you know? You can't just blurt it out. You have to build up to the point."

"You said you wanted to ask him about the blue car he said he'd seen, not take his inside leg measurement."

"Well, next time, maybe you could come with me instead of sitting here like Lady Muck."

"Lady Muck is pretty apt," Nillson said as she adjusted the seat into an upright position again. "Have you seen the crap in the back of your car? There's a smell coming from somewhere, but I can't find the source."

"Hey, you leave my car alone. You're as bad as Ben. He's always going on about the state of my car."

"Jim, it's a tip. Look," she said, pointing into the rear. "I cannot see one inch of carpet."

"Why do you need to see the carpet?"

"I don't *need* to see the carpet—"

"So, what's the problem?"

A response sat on the tip of Nillson's tongue, ready to launch itself at Gillespie, but it would be futile. If somebody couldn't see how unhygienic it was to have so many takeaway wrappers, chocolate bar wrappers, and drink bottles in their car, then to argue against them would be little more than a waste of breath.

"Does Katy come in here to practise?"

"Practise what?"

"You know? Forensics? Maybe there's some kind of disease or bacteria that's growing in here. She could make a scientific breakthrough."

"Katy doesn't come in here," Gillespie said, scrolling through his phone.

"Out of choice?"

"Aye, my choice," he said. "If we go somewhere, we take her car. It's nicer, and she's got heated seats."

"And it harbours less diseases?"

"Just..." he started. "Just shut it, Anna, eh?" He hit the button on his phone, and the call routed through to the car's loudspeaker.

"Jim?" a familiar voice said. "How did it go with Robert Reilly? He's a character, isn't he?"

"Well, aye. We haven't actually been yet."

"You haven't been? Freya's lining up a debrief this afternoon. You need to get your skates on, mate."

"We swung by Lincoln nick," Gillespie replied. "I wanted to speak to Eamon Price about the blue car."

"Despite Freya's specific instructions?"

"I had nothing to do with it before you ask," Nillson said. "I waited in the car."

"It's a lead," Gillespie argued. "Besides, she didn't specifically tell me not to talk to Price."

"No, she told you to talk to Robert Reilly, which you haven't done," Ben said with a sigh. "What did he say anyway? Anything?"

"Well, Souness is adamant it's a figment of Price's imagination."

"As is everybody else," Nillson said.

"And Price?" Ben asked.

"Firm believer," he said. "I mean, you should see him, Ben. The man's resigned himself to spending the next decade of his life inside. He hasn't run. Every statement he's given has been identical, and by all accounts, Souness has given him a hard time since yesterday. If he's lied, then where's the lie?"

"I don't know," Ben said. "It's not our investigation, so I'm not really up to date on it."

"But that's just it. He saw the bloke on the bike. He tried to go around him. He even said how he faced that split-second decision: crash into the blue car or swerve out of the way."

"And he chose the former."

"I don't think choice is the right way to describe it," Gillespie said. "It was instinct."

"But if there *was* a car, then—"

"He said he was speeding, Ben. He said the car came to the end of the road, and he thought it would stop. But it didn't. It was speeding. The driver just pulled out and buggered off."

"If he's right, then the driver of the blue car could be charged with causing death by dangerous driving. Price would probably walk. Not a bad way of planting some doubt in the jury's lap."

"But if he *is* telling the truth and the driver *was* speeding, then it's more than likely our intruder. Anybody in their right mind would have stopped if they'd caused an accident like that."

"They could have been oblivious to the accident," Nillson said.

"Look, they came out of Pound Road, failed to stop at the end of the road, and caused a seventeen-ton lorry to anchor up. Have you ever heard the sound a lorry makes when it has to make an emergency stop? It's not something you could miss."

"What do you suggest, Gillespie?" Ben asked.

"We need to find them," he replied. "They pulled out of

Pound Road and turned left. At the top of the road, they either turned right towards Dunston and Metheringham or left towards Walcott and Billinghay. There are cameras at the old timber yard that would have got him if he turned right, and there's bound to be a camera at Walcott. There's a kid's nursery there, not to mention a pub and a few dozen houses. Someone must have a security camera." He paused for a moment, and even Nillson had to admit to herself that his argument was compelling. "It's worth a shot, Ben, eh? Even if it's not the intruder, we might just save Price from spending the next part of his sorry life behind bars."

"We're not traffic police, Jim."

"Aye, we're not. But you know what? We deal with enough bloody death and grief to know the difference between right and wrong. Souness is waiting for the forensics report, but you can bet your backside he'll be pushing for a manslaughter charge. Whether that's against Price or Robert Reilly, I don't think he cares."

"I can run it by Freya," Ben said. "She won't like getting involved in a traffic investigation. It muddies the waters, and it's not like we don't have our hands full."

"Yeah, well, I'm not really fussed about a bit of muddy water. We're talking about prison, Ben. He's got a kid, for God's sake."

"Alright, alright," Ben said, and his breath rasped across the phone's speaker. "I'll see who we've got—"

"Jewson," Gillespie said.

"Sorry?"

"Jewson," he said again. "Send her. It'll keep her out of the way for a bit longer."

Ben was silent for a few moments, but his heavy breathing was loud and clear over the line.

"You there, Ben?"

"Yes," he said. "Look, mate, there's something you should know."

"Aye, go on."

"It's Jewson," Ben said. "We think she's arranged a chat with Detective Superintendent Granger."

"What?"

"Freya was in his office earlier and saw an appointment in his calendar for tomorrow. She's arranged a meeting with him."

"So? That could just be one of those, how are you getting on, chats."

"You're right, it could be," Ben said. "Only, I don't know about you, but I've never requested a legal rep to attend a, how are you getting on, chat."

"What? A legal rep?"

"Sorry, mate. We were hoping this would blow over, but it looks like she's hell-bent on causing a scene," Ben said. "We're trying to contain it, but you know how it is. It's like boxing up a litter of kittens. One of them always gets out."

"If I'm honest, mate, I've never boxed up a litter of kittens."

"Jewson's no idiot, Jim. She knows you were keen to progress the blue car theory. If this lead of yours is a dead end, it'll be another arrow in her quiver against you. You know she'll probably spin it into some fabrication of the truth, where you were making a fuss of saving an innocent man from prison in the hope of garnering some positive light."

"Jesus, you think?"

"It's your reputation, mate. If this turns into nothing, she'll use it against you," Ben said. "Think about the conversation with Granger. First of all, you made an off-hand comment about children."

"It was nothing. I just said—"

"I know what you said," Ben told him. "I was there, remember? But look at it from Granger's perspective. You said something that she found inappropriate, and instead of following up on it, Freya and I have done nothing. It'll look like a cover-up."

"Cover what up?" Gillespie said. "There's nothing *to* cover up."

"Granger doesn't know that."

"Oh, come on. He knows me as well as you do."

"The next thing is that Freya sends her out on her own for the day. That'll look like we're bullying her or buying time to clear up the mess."

"There is no mess," Gillespie said. "There's nothing to clear up. I'm not a bloody—"

"She'll develop a smear campaign first," Ben said. "She's probably already started it. Everyone in the station will hear her side of the story."

"Aye, but you heard what I said. I didn't mean anything by it. It was nothing. Just an off-hand comment. You know that, right?"

"Jim, everyone on the team knows that she is merely trying to cause a scene to further her own good," Ben said. "People like her don't care who they tread on to get where they want. The problem is, the rest of the station will hear her side of the story, and she's bound to make a few embellishments. Before you know it, you'll have the IOPC knocking on your door, wanting to examine your computer and phone."

"Well, let them look. I offered you my phone and laptop."

"And then there's social media. All she has to do is make a seemingly innocent comment."

"She can't do that, surely? That's slanderous."

"It's not related to an investigation. There's nothing stopping her from planting a few well-placed lies without mentioning names. You know how it works, mate. She plants the seeds, and social media grows the seed."

"Aye, and then I get whacked by the fully grown plant."

"And then she talks to Detective Superintendent Granger and tells him how you managed to convince Freya and me to keep her out of the office, or how you've got some kind of vendetta against her because she touched a nerve."

"You really think she's that bad?" Gillespie asked.

"*I* do," Nillson said. "She's rotten. I don't want anything to do with her."

"I agree," Ben said. "The trouble is, getting rid of people like that is harder than it looks. They know how to play the game. Freya is aware of it, but with the investigation, she can't really give any time to it."

"What a cow," Gillespie mused. "Not the boss. Jewson, I mean."

"This is your reputation, Jim. Do you still want me to action it?" Ben asked. "I can send Cruz to look into the cameras and find something else for Jewson to do."

Gillespie looked across to Nillson as if seeking some kind of support, and as annoying as the big Scotsman could be, there was a kindness about him that nobody could argue against.

She nodded once, and he smiled his appreciation.

"Aye, Ben. Send her out looking for cameras," he said. "I've done nothing wrong. Just keep her out of my bloody way, or I'll give her something to actually complain about."

"You do realise that Granger will likely be forced to take action," Ben said. "Your phone and laptop will be reclaimed, and you'll be suspended with pay."

"Ah, Christ," Gillespie said, and Nillson felt for the big brute. He didn't deserve it. Nobody deserved their career to be ruined. "You know what, sod her. Let her talk with Granger. Let them take my laptop and my phone. They'll find nothing on them."

"You'll have a mark on your record whatever the outcome," Nillson told him. "You know that, right? Even if they find nothing, there's a chance your days could be numbered. Reputation is everything."

Gillespie let his head fall back onto the seat and closed his eyes.

"She's right, Jim," Ben said. "I mean, Freya and I will back you all the way, but we can't stop the IOPC coming in."

"This is nothing," Gillespie said. "I just made a comment. It was nothing, for God's sake. How can this be happening? How can she destroy my career over a comment?"

"We can't be seen to be doing nothing about it," Ben said. "We don't have to act immediately, but we're obliged to follow up on it as soon as she makes a formal complaint."

"Well, follow it up, then. I have nothing to hide. My laptop is clean. My phone is clean. I'm not a bloody wrongun. They can look as hard as they like. They won't find a bloody thing, and you know what? When this is done, and I'm found to be nothing more than a bloody nice guy, I'll be going after her for damages."

"There is more," Ben said. "And they don't need to look very hard."

"Eh?"

"Remember the witness you...became friends with?"

"Witness?"

"The mother of the boy we were investigating."

"You slept with a witness?" Nillson said, and she stared at him like he was a trash monster emerging from the rubbish on the back of his car.

"Aye, well. I didn't know who she was, did I?"

"And the woman you had an affair with in Haverholme?"

"What?" Nillson said.

"She was an ex," Gillespie explained. "I was going door to door. I didn't know she lived there."

"She chased you down the street in her bra," Ben said, and Nillson shook her head in disgust.

"And then there's the girl in Horncastle. The barmaid," Ben said.

"Jesus, Jim," Nillson said.

"Alright, alright," he said. "But this was all before I met Kate. I'm a red-blooded male. I didn't knowingly break the rules. How did she find all that out anyway? Has she hired a bloody private eye?"

"She's been talking to people," Ben said.

"Cruz," Gillespie said. "Bloody Cruz."

"Cruz wouldn't have said anything to get you into bother."

"He's a gob on him, Ben," Gillespie said. "He might not have meant to, but he did. Stupid bastard." He shook his head and then suddenly lashed out at the steering wheel. "That's why he was the only one who stuck up for her. He knew what he'd told her. He knew he'd given her the ammunition she needed."

"You can see how all this looks, though," Ben said. "We have evidence of an officer with a...large sexual appetite, who broke the rules in order to satiate said sexual appetite and made inappropriate comments regarding small children, who then went to great pains to ensure the offended officer, a.k.a. Jewson, was kept out of the office on minor duties. It looks like you're up to no good, and we're covering for you."

"Aye. Aye, I can see how it looks."

"I could always get her in the office helping Chapman. We can keep an eye on her in here," Ben said.

"No. No, send her out. Keep her away from Cruz before he opens his gob again. I've nothing to hide," Gillespie replied. "If the last thing I do for the force is stop an innocent man from serving time for manslaughter, then so be it, Ben." He started the engine and tugged on his seatbelt. "And God help her if things don't go my way."

CHAPTER THIRTY-TWO

"Here we go," Cruz said excitedly. He turned his laptop around for Freya to see and then slammed the palm of his hand against the desk. "Roger Havers' doorbell. He clearly runs from his house towards Reilly's house at..." he leaned in and scrunched his nose. "Six-twenty-eight on Monday morning."

"That's within the time frame," Chapman said.

"And can we clearly see him walking towards Reilly's house?"

"Yeah," Cruz said. "Clear as anything."

"And does the video show him accessing Albert Reilly's rear garden?"

"Well, no," Cruz said. "Havers' rose hedge is in the way. I can see Reilly's front door. But you can't really see anything past the hedge."

"Okay," Freya said. "And can we see Havers entering Reilly's house through the front door?"

"Yeah," Cruz said. "He goes in and then comes out thirty seconds later. Look." He gestured at the laptop, but Freya was loathe to be sucked into another of Cruz's unsupported fantasies.

"And what does he do when he comes out of Reilly's house?" Freya asked.

"Hold on," Cruz replied, forwarding the video a little more. He slapped his hand on the desk again. "He gets in his car and speeds off down the road."

"To his death," Ben added.

"Right, but he still went in the house."

"So, what you're saying is that the video shows Havers running from his house at around six-thirty. He goes into his friend's house and emerges a few moments later when he climbs into his car and speeds off?"

"Yeah," Cruz said.

"Was he carrying anything?" Freya asked, glad that Ben had at least seen the flaw in Cruz's findings.

"Erm, no. Nothing."

"Right," Freya said. "And you would be happy for me to submit this to the CPS, would you? Perhaps we can play the video at the inquest."

"You don't think it's enough?"

"Tell me," Freya said. "Those doorbell cameras don't usually just record everything non-stop, do they? They're triggered by movement, is that right?"

"Yeah, usually," Cruz replied, and Freya made a point of waiting for him to catch up. "Oh, I see."

"There we go," she muttered while he rewound the video to the trigger point.

"Oh," he said.

"What is it?"

"The video," he said. "It was triggered by him walking past the camera." He waved his hand at the screen.

She looked to Ben, hoping he would add some insights to her questions, but found him gazing into empty space. "Ben? Are you joining us, or..."

"Sorry," he said but looked uncomfortable.

"What is it?"

He winced and took a deep breath.

"If Roger Havers' doorbell camera was triggered by him walking past it, then surely it would have been triggered every time somebody walked past. My mate Snowy has one of those doorbell cameras, and whenever somebody comes to his door, his phone goes off. If that had happened every time somebody passed the house, that would have driven him bananas. His phone would have been going off every five minutes."

Freya cocked her head, aware of the nuances that accompanied doorbell cameras.

"That's very true," she said.

"Seems a bit daft to me," Cruz said. "You know you can adjust the sensor on them, right?"

"Sorry?"

"In the app that comes with the doorbell, you can go into the settings and adjust when something should trigger the alarm. If your neighbour's property was in view, for instance, you could tell the camera to ignore any movement in that area."

"So Havers could have adjusted it so that the alarm went off only when somebody stepped onto his drive?"

"Yeah," he replied. "I had to do it for my mum. Her doorbell went off every time her neighbour cut the lawn or put the bins out. They must have thought she was mad, opening the front door, peering along the street and then going back inside." He laughed to himself, but Freya failed to see the amusement. Her mind was far too busy piecing the facts together.

"So, from where the camera is installed, you can see Reilly's house on the other side of the road?"

"Yeah," he said. "Well, half of it. The roses block the view of the side entrance. But you can see the front door."

"And the footage," she said. "How far back does it go?"

"Oh, I think that all depends on the package you choose," Cruz said. "That's how they get you, see? I think the standard package only keeps a day or two of data. But if you want more, then you pay a monthly subscription."

"And did Havers pay for a subscription?"

Cruz clicked a few buttons, pulled a few strange faces, and then shook his head.

"No. This goes back as far as Friday morning," he said.

"And what was it that triggered the camera on that morning?"

"He was bringing his bin in," Cruz replied.

"Play me the video of when he walks over to Reilly's house," she said.

Cruz navigated to the video, hit play, and then sat back so that Ben could see as well. They watched as Havers came out, walked across the road rather briskly, and entered Reilly's house. He was inside for no more than a few moments and then came out, walked back to his car, started the engine and then sped off in the direction of the main road.

"Go back," Freya said, and so Cruz rewound the video so they could see it again. "There. Look. When he comes out of Reilly's house, he looks up the road. He sees something out of the camera's view." Freya said. "What does he see?"

"The blue car?" Ben suggested, which Freya doubted. "And what made him come out?"

"He could see Albert's house from his front window," Freya said. "The roses block the camera's view, but from the front window, you can see it all."

"Okay, so maybe he saw something."

"He was cooking," she said.

"Alright, maybe he put his porridge onto cook, strolled through to the living room and saw something?"

"The question is," she mused. "What did he see?"

"A blue car?" Ben said again, and again, Freya ignored him.

"So he knew," Freya said. "He must have known. He saw something, was worried about his friend, and went to investigate."

"So he knew whoever it was, and he knew they were up to no good."

"This sounds like fun," a voice said, and Freya looked up to find Jewson in the doorway. "Can anyone join in?"

"If you can explain why you're here and not doing as I asked, Jewson, then yes."

"I have some news," Jewson replied, and she sauntered over to her desk. "I think you'll find it very interesting."

"What I will find interesting is why you haven't called in," Freya said. "You are sailing perilously close to the wind."

"Roger Havers had a front door key for Albert Reilly's house," she said.

"We've established that, thank you," Freya replied. "You're a little late, I'm afraid. Is that it?"

"No. Roger Havers and Albert Reilly spent most of their lives at each other's throats."

"We've also established that," Freya said. "I was hoping for something of substance."

Jewson smiled and rested on the edge of her desk.

"Okay then," she started. "Roger Havers has a daughter who lives around the corner."

Freya looked at Chapman, who held her notepad up.

"I was going to tell you at the briefing," she said. "She was his next of kin."

Freya nodded and smiled at Chapman, then turned back to Jewson.

"Again, nothing of any real substance."

"Well, it is, and it isn't," Jewson said.

"Jewson, if you have something to say, then I wish you would just come out and say it—"

"She was burgled," Jewson said.

"She was what?"

"She was burgled. Monday morning."

At face value, the news seemed irrelevant. But there was something in there, some kind of connection that linked to Reilly's broken window.

"Did she report it?"

"She did," Jewson said. "And guess who attended?"

"I'm not into guessing games, Jewson," Freya said. "This is a murder investigation, not a bloody Christmas get-together."

"I'll give you a clue," Jewson said, staring at Freya. "He was the first one on the scene, and instead of hearing what he had to say, you sent him off to be consoled by Gold." Freya opened her mouth but refrained from speaking the words on the tip of her tongue. "It's a shame we didn't get his statement earlier, really," Jewson continued. "We could have actually made progress by now."

CHAPTER THIRTY-THREE

"PC Frobisher," Ben said, and Freya rolled her eyes at him for falling into Jewson's trap."

"First prize to the tall, dark-haired man in the corner," Jewson said.

"Frobisher?" Ben repeated, then silenced for a minute to interpret the details. "The Armsteads said they flagged the police down."

"Sorry?" Freya said, not following.

"At the crime scene," he said, his voice growing with excitement. "They didn't call the police. They said they flagged them down. I didn't think anything of it. But Frobisher must have been coming from Havers' daughter's house."

"Pound Road is a U-shape. He must have been trying to get around the traffic caused by the accident," Cruz added.

"Right, Ben, get hold of Sergeant Priest. See if we can get Frobisher up here for a chat."

"Is that substance enough for you?" Jewson asked. There was something about the girl that Freya found utterly repugnant, but she couldn't quite put it into words. "Did I do good, boss?"

"I don't know what you did, Jewson," Freya said. "But I can

assure you it is almost certainly not good. I asked you to call when you'd tried Havers' keys, yet you failed to do so. I asked you to knock on the remaining doors, yet I've heard nothing."

"I was going to," Jewson said. "I was just following up on a lead."

"You..." Freya said, jabbing her finger in Jewson's direction, "do not follow up on anything unless I tell you to. You do as instructed and nothing else. Is that understood?"

Jewson shrugged.

"If that's what you want."

"What is it, Jewson?" Freya asked as she perched on her own desk. "What is it that you don't like about this team?"

"Who said I don't like the team?"

"Detective Superintendent Granger," Freya replied. "I know you've scheduled a meeting with him."

"It's just a meeting," she said. "Why, you're not worried about something, are you, boss?"

"Oh, I'm not worried about a thing. It's you who should be worried—"

"Freya—" Ben warned.

"No, sorry, Ben. She needs to hear this. She helped you out while I was in hospital, and by all accounts, she did well enough to be invited to work with us. Yet, after a few short weeks, she's taken an off-hand comment from a respected police officer and blown it out of proportion—"

"That's a matter of opinion," Jewson said.

"And it's my opinion that counts," Freya snapped. "In this team, at least."

"I suspect Detective Superintendent Granger might have something to say about that."

"Do you realise that an inquiry into Sergeant Gillespie could spell the end of his career? Even if the IPOC finds nothing but rumours, he could very well be finished. Do you realise that?"

"I can't be held accountable for what happens in the future, boss," Jewson said innocently. "But he did make a comment about touching children, and, in this day and age, that's hardly appropriate, is it?"

"He said nothing of the sort—" Ben started.

"And then there's *your* behaviour," Jewson continued. "Trying to cover it up to protect your precious team."

"I have done no such thing," Freya said.

"Sergeant Gillespie is still working, isn't he?"

"What are you suggesting? That I suspend him until we've investigated him? He's a good man."

"But still," Jewson said. "Doesn't look good, does it?"

"I'm not obliged to take any action until a formal complaint has been received," Freya said. "Which I assume is the reason for your meeting with Detective Superintendent Granger tomorrow."

"I can see why you're a detective," Jewson said.

Freya slid from her perch, found Jewson's confident stare, and held it as she stepped slowly across the room.

"I want you out of here," she said. "You're not welcome."

"You're kicking me out?" Jewson replied with a laugh. "For what? For flagging a potential predator? Is this nineteen-seventy?"

"Sergeant Gillespie is one of the best officers I have ever known—"

"But you do have doubts, don't you?" Jewson said. "I mean, I am going to meet with Granger tomorrow. I am going to make a formal complaint, and Sergeant Gillespie is going to be investigated. They *have* to follow up on it."

"Then they'll do what they need to do."

"But can you imagine how it would look if you kicked me off the team, and they did find something?"

"I can assure you they won't find a thing—"

"Even if his comment leads to nothing, and I hope it does, but something will. He's a predator. He's too sexual not to be."

"There's something wrong with you, Jewson," Freya said.

"No, there's nothing wrong with me," she replied. "I'm just

doing what women should have been empowered to do decades ago: calling it out when I see it."

"Get out," Freya said.

"Really? If I go and Gillespie is found guilty," Jewson replied. "That's the end of you." She looked around the room at Ben and Chapman. "That's the end of all of you."

"You know, there's a word for people like you," Freya said. "You're toxic. That's what you are."

"Well, perhaps from your perspective, but look at this from the outside. All I'm doing is raising a flag. If nothing comes of it, then great. We can all go back to being best buddies."

"You don't honestly think that you'll be welcomed on this team or even in this station after all of this, do you?"

"I'm leading the way, Inspector Bloom. I'm a young, strong female officer, raising the flag on a potential predator," she said. "I'll be celebrated. There'll be dozens to follow. All it takes is for one to be caught, and officers who, until now, have been too scared to raise their hands, will be calling them out all over Lincolnshire and beyond."

"You know, I find your behaviour quite aggressive, Jewson."

"I can adjust my tone if you prefer," she replied, playing the game as well as she could. "I was led to believe you enjoyed direct communication. Apologies, I'll work on my soft skills in future."

"You come in here, threaten one of my officers and potentially destroy his career, then threaten me?"

"Well, it's not meant as a threat—"

"I am a Detective Chief Inspector. One call from me to the Deputy Chief Constable, and you'll be back walking the streets."

"The day before I make a formal complaint?" Jewson said. "I don't think so. I think you'll find the top brass will be keen to keep this under wraps for the time being. Putting me back out on the streets is a risk. One little social media post, and you'll have the nationals on you. You'll have The Sun and the Mirror on the doorstep, and let's face it, you're hardly difficult to spot."

"What's that supposed to mean?"

"Nothing really," she said, touching the side of her face. "It's just...well, let's face it, your ability to lead a team after your accident is questionable, at best. You were in the tabloids yourself only a few months ago. You've been through a psychiatric program, I assume."

"That's none of your bloody business."

"I'll take that as a no, then."

"Get out," Freya hissed.

"Hold on," Ben said, raising his hand and stepping between them. He coaxed Freya back to her own desk.

"Jewson, you're a trouble maker," he said. "But I get it. You know the rules. You're playing the game. I don't know what you're hoping to achieve, but I get that you're playing the game."

"I'm not playing any game," she replied.

"Well, I am," he told her. "I've got a job for you. I want you to go and look into the cameras on the B1189. We're looking for a little blue hatchback—"

"Ben, she is not a part of this investigation," Freya growled.

"She is, Freya," he said. "Until she's spoken to Granger, she has to be."

"At least somebody in a senior position still has some judgement," Jewson said.

"Jewson, get out. Go now," Ben said. "I want to know if that blue hatchback turned left or right out of Martin. Chapman will send you the details."

Jewson slid her bag from her desk and sauntered over to the door.

"I take it this is another solo task?" she said. "Maybe Cruz could keep me company?"

"I'm playing by your rules, Jewson," Ben said. "The least you can do is toe the line."

"Alright," she said after a few tense seconds of silence. "I'll call in when I've got something."

"Oh, and Jewson," Freya said as she opened the door. "I will be reporting every word of what you just said to the Deputy Chief Constable. Regardless of the outcome with Sergeant Gillespie, you realise that you're finished here, don't you?"

"I agree that one of us is finished, Inspector," Jewson replied. "I'm sure the DCC will judge this for what it really is."

"And what is this?"

"From the top down? Well, the DCI clearly needs psychiatric help and is incapable of running a team; the DI is unable to recognise the difference between right and wrong, mostly because he's infatuated with said DCI. Sergeant Gillespie has a flag against him for being a sexual predator, not to mention the relationships with witnesses and parents of suspects, Sergeant Nillson has a history of police brutality—"

"That's unfounded—" Ben said.

"Yeah, but how hard would it be to contact the suspects she's arrested in the past year or so to ask how she handled them? I heard rugby tackles are her speciality." She grinned at Freya. "Shall I go on? DC Gold is too weak to do anything but act as a Family Liaison Officer, yet she's still studying for her Sergeant's exam; DC Cruz is a feckless waste of skin and bone who lives with his mum and who, twenty years ago, would have been too short to even join up—"

"Oy," Cruz said, clearly hurt at the comment.

"And Chapman," Jewson continued. "As good as you are, Chapman, you seemingly have a phobia of leaving the office. You spend all day on the phone or typing up reports."

"Have you finished?" Freya said. "Perhaps you should turn that mirror on yourself."

"Oh, I do," Jewson said. "And do you know what I see? I see a young female police officer with the potential to be part of a new major crimes team. I see a woman who isn't afraid to call out inefficiencies in public spending and raise the flag against potential predators. I see what the public wants and deserves to see in the force: honesty and trustworthiness." She shook her head at them all. "You? You're all corrupt. You're all so in love with each other that you're covering up crimes just so you can all stay together. It's all the same. It's men abusing women, playing with power, retaining control. I would have thought you'd have seen through it. But you're part of it. You're a part of the reason the force has a bad name. You're the reason people don't trust us anymore. Me? I'm going to change that."

Freya sidestepped Ben, and before he could grab her, she strode over to where Jewson stood, squared up there, and gazed into those smarmy eyes.

"I used to be confident like you," she said.

"It's not confidence," Ben said. "It's arrogance."

"Confidence, arrogance. The lines blur." Jewson smiled at what she perceived to be a compliment. "Sometimes it takes a little heat to recognise your own flaws."

"Heat or flames?" Jewson said with a grin, and she eyed Freya's scar.

"Don't get burned, PC Jewson," Freya told her. "Trust me when I tell you there are some paths to walk that no matter how much you want to, you just cannot return from." She reached out and held the door. "Do what you need to do. But just don't get burned."

Jewson flicked her eyebrows up once, then turned and started down the corridor. Freya let the door swing closed behind her and then turned and faced the room.

"What the bloody hell is she on?" Cruz asked. "Bloody hell, I stuck up for her."

"What are you going to do?" Ben asked, to which Freya gave some thought as she paced back to her desk.

"Burn her," she said, and then looked up at Ben so that he knew she meant business. "I'm not going to play her game. I'm going to burn her."

CHAPTER THIRTY-FOUR

The young woman who opened the door had large eyes, dark hair, and was forlorn. It was as if she had long since forgotten what it was to smile.

"We're looking for Mr Reilly," Nillson explained, holding up her warrant card. "I believe he spoke to our colleagues yesterday."

The girl studied the ID card, looked at Nillson and Gillespie in turn, and then nodded once.

"Wait, please," she said, in what Nillson deemed to be an Eastern European accent. She pushed the door to, then slipped off in search of Reilly.

"What do you reckon?" Gillespie mumbled. "Bit on the side, or just a helping hand?" He nodded at the door in case she hadn't quite followed.

"What do I reckon?" Nillson said. "I reckon that, given your current situation, any reference to bits on the side or anything sexual should stay well and truly inside that thick head of yours."

He opened his mouth to argue, much as he normally would have, but he must have thought better of it.

"Ah, you're right," he said. "Bloody woman."

"She's not a woman, Jim," Nillson replied. "She's a girl. A

spiteful young girl who has been brainwashed by... nonsense. Nothing more than nonsense."

Gillespie laughed it off, which was more an act of bravado than anything else.

"You know what's funny," he said. "I'm normally on the side of the downtrodden. I'm a fan of women's rights. I hate reading those stories from way back when men got away with God knows what." He jabbed a finger at his chest. "I *was* the downtrodden, if you remember? I grew up in a different bloody care home every month. I had to fight for what I've got now, so when I see somebody else trying, I'm right behind them."

"You're preaching to the converted," Nillson said. "But if it means anything, we don't believe her."

"I know that," he said. "It still stings. I mean, one word from her, or anybody for that matter, and that's it. My life is on hold. My past is dragged through the mud, and what about Kate? What if she finds out?"

"Finds out about what?"

"Hello?" Somebody said from the doorway, and they found a man in a v-necked sweater peering down at them.

"Ah, Mr Reilly," Nillson said, flashing her warrant card again. "I'm Detective Sergeant Nillson, and this is Detective Sergeant Gillespie. We wondered if we could have a quick word."

"Come to take me away, have you?" he asked, which came as a surprise.

"Actually, no," she said, then hesitated; doorstep conversations were rarely conducive to results. "Can we come in?"

"I've got to go—"

"We'll be quick," Nillson said. "And, it's important."

"This about my old man, is it?"

"It is," she said.

He looked Gillespie up and down as if he was sizing him up.

"Five minutes," he said, eventually, then stepped out of the way.

The girl waited in the doorway to what looked like a huge kitchen.

"Mr Robert, should I make tea—?"

"No," he snapped. "No, they're not stopping." He stopped in the doorway to a spacious living room with two large sofas and a fireplace to die for, and as Nillson and Gillespie edged past him, he spoke to the girl again. "Nadia?"

"Yes, sir?"

"No interruptions," he said, then closed the door after them and moved towards the far sofa, offering the other with a sweep of his hand. "I told your friends everything I have to say, so I don't really know how else I can help."

"It's more about the procedure than anything," Gillespie said.

"Ah, he speaks, does he?" he replied and crossed one leg over the other.

"Mr Reilly, since you spoke to our colleagues, we have made some progress, which we think you should hear."

"Oh?"

"Well, your father has undergone a post-mortem, the results of which are, as yet, inconclusive."

"What does that mean?"

"It means there's some conflicting evidence regarding the cause of his death."

"I thought it was his heart. I'm sure that's what they said. It was his heart." Nillson did her best to display a neutral expression but was finding the man increasingly irritating. "They said he had a head wound, but it was likely he died of a heart attack."

"It's not as simple as that—"

"Well, how complex can it be?" he said. "And let's face it, if he had a head wound, it matters not one bit what he died from. Some bastard hit him. End of." He stared at them both. "Have you found him?"

"No, we're investigating now—"

"So, why are you here, telling me stuff I already know, for God's sake?"

"Because, believe it or not, Mr Reilly, we know what we're doing," Gillespie said, his tone far harsher than Nillson would have hoped. "I'm sorry for your loss; truly I am, but you have to let us do things our way. We have a procedure to follow—"

"Procedure my backside," Reilly said. "You should be out there talking to people, the neighbours and suspects."

"We are," Gillespie told him.

"No, you're not. You're badgering me. I'm supposed to be at my solicitors. You do know what I'm going through right now, don't you?"

"Oh, we're fully aware," Gillespie said. "In fact, I've just been to see Eamon."

"Eamon?"

"Price. Eamon Price. Your driver?"

"Oh, that Eamon. Right," Reilly said. "How is he?"

"Terrified," Gillespie told him. "He's looking at a death by dangerous driving charge; or manslaughter, if you prefer."

"Jesus," Reilly said, shaking his head. "Is there anything I can do for him?"

"Until we hear back from the forensics team, there's not a lot anybody can do," Nillson said. "But I'm afraid traffic incidents are dealt with by a specialist traffic team. They'll only provide information to the officer leading the investigation."

"And that's not you?"

"No, that is a Sergeant Souness," Nillson told him. "We're with the major crimes team."

"I suppose you realise the possible outcomes," Gillespie said. "I mean, you've been through this before, haven't you?"

Reilly glared at him, but what menace was in his eyes faded with the unavoidable truth.

"You're talking about my old man, aren't you?" he said, to which Gillespie shrugged.

"You have to admit, the similarities are more than evident."

"Similarities?"

"Your father held his hands up to a negligence charge, Mr Reilly," Nillson said. "His actions prevented Roger Havers, an innocent man, from going to prison."

"So?"

"Of course, they didn't have the technology we have now, but if the forensics reports show evidence of negligence, will you follow in your father's footsteps?"

"What? Look, if there's evidence of something being wrong with the vehicle, then I'll make sure the right person is in the firing line."

"The right person?"

"Whoever signed it off," he said. "Which, by the way, was not me."

"But you are accountable, surely? It's your responsibility to ensure procedures are followed—"

"I'm sorry, I thought you were here to discuss my father," he said. "But if you're here on false pretences, then I'm afraid I have nothing to say without my lawyer—"

"We *are* here to discuss your father, Mr Reilly," Gillespie said. "A bit of background never hurt, did it?"

"That depends on whose background it is," he replied.

"Your father's," Nillson said. As much as it pained her to admit it, she was enjoying the informal interview with Reilly. Gillespie was a formidable sparring partner, whereas Anderson had very often remained silent until spoken to.

"But you don't have any suspects," Reilly said. "I mean, your mates said you were treating his death as suspicious. That's copper talk for a murder, right?"

"Potentially," Nillson said. "Suspicious means we are yet to find evidence to support a cause of death."

"Right, so if it was murder, or manslaughter, or whatever, then you must have somebody in mind."

"Oh, we have a few names we'd like to eliminate before we take the investigation wide," Gillespie said.

"And?" Reilly replied. "Who are they?"

"We're talking to one of them right now."

He frowned as if he couldn't quite believe what he was hearing, then laughed once.

"Sorry? Me? I'm a suspect?"

"Everyone your father knew is a suspect until we can eliminate them from our enquiries, Mr Reilly," Nillson said.

"I'm his bloody son."

"So help us," Gillespie said. "I mean, all you have to do is tell us where you were on Monday morning between the hours of five and seven and tell us who can corroborate that, and we'll strike you off. Believe me, Mr Reilly, nothing would make me happier than removing you from our enquiries."

"And why's that? Sick of me, are you?"

"No, it's because I would rather you focused on doing the right thing for Eamon Price and his family, Mr Reilly," Gillespie said. "Like your dear old daddy would have done."

CHAPTER THIRTY-FIVE

The incident room door squeaked open, and for a moment, Ben thought it might be Jewson returning for round two with Freya. But Frobisher stood there, his eyes wide.

"PC Frobisher," Ben said, and Freya turned from where she was wiping the whiteboard clean to start over. "Thanks for coming up. Come in."

"Never been in here," he said. "I've heard the..." he hesitated.

"Rumours?" Freya suggested.

"No. The shouting," he said. "Seems quite calm now, though."

Ben grinned at Freya, who appeared less than impressed.

"Come on, sit down," Ben said. "There won't be any shouting today."

"No, we're all out of shouts," Freya added. "I need to replenish my stock."

Frobisher seemed like a fish out of water and was quite unable to interpret Freya's humour, so Ben pulled a chair out for him.

"We just wanted to go over a few things regarding your discovery yesterday morning," Ben said. "On Pound Road?"

"Right," he said. "Yeah, I figured it was to do with that, but to be honest, there's nothing much I can say. I went around the back, saw the broken window, and kicked my way in. I mean, it wasn't hard."

"May I ask why you didn't reach in and unlock the door?" Freya asked. "Presumably, that's how the intruder gained access."

"I thought of it, guv," he said. "But the couple were worried about the old man. Besides, the door was an old wooden thing. It didn't take much to get it open."

"If only every officer had that foresight," Freya replied.

"To be honest, Frobisher," Ben cut in. "I didn't ask you to come here to tell us about what you saw or how you gained entry."

"So I'm not in any bother then?"

"What? No, of course not," Ben said. "Is that what you thought?"

"Well," he started, then glanced at Freya before looking Ben in the eye. "You hear rumours, don't you?"

"I don't know, do you?" Freya asked, and Ben sought an exit from what could otherwise have been a difficult corner for Frobisher to return from.

"What we really wanted to understand, Frobisher," he said, "is your movements before you arrived at Mr Reilly's house."

"Sorry?"

"You were flagged down. Is that right?"

"That's right. By the couple over the road."

"So you weren't called to the scene?"

"No," he said. "We were called out to look at a break-in round the corner. We were making our way back, but there was that accident—"

"And so you tried to get around the accident by using Pound Road?"

"Well, yeah. We couldn't see how far up the road the accident was, so it was worth a try." He grinned a little. "We did consider switching on the blues and twos, but you know what traffic police can be like."

"No," Freya said. "How can traffic officers be?"

"This break-in," Ben cut in before Frobisher scooped another shovelful of soil from his hole. "Do you happen to have the details on you?"

"Eh?"

"You said you were attending a break-in. Who was the victim?"

"Oh," he said, tapping his pockets for his notepad. He flicked it open to the right page. "Mr and Mrs Stone." He looked up from his pad. "They live around the corner on the high street; why's that?"

"Never mind," Ben said. "We were keen to understand how the intruder broke in."

Frobisher cocked his head. His nerves were settling, and the confident young man Ben had met at the crime scene was beginning to show himself.

"A UPVC window was forced. To be honest, that's how most burglaries are carried out these days."

"And you saw no resemblance to the broken window at Mr Reilly's house?"

"Well, no," Frobisher said. "The window was broken. It was entirely different. Besides, that's not his style. He seems to have a knack for getting in through downstairs windows."

"What do you mean, he has a knack?" Freya asked.

"The suspect," he said. "We've been watching him for a while. He's been operating in the area for about six months now, but we're closer now than we've ever been. He stays low for a few weeks, then pops up in one of the local villages, does a few houses, and then we'll hear nothing from him. He's smart, too. He's quiet, so he never attracts attention, wears gloves and presumably a hat, so he never leaves prints or hair."

"And you know who this man is, do you?"

"Oh, yeah," he said. "We just can't pin anything on him. Do you know how feeble I feel when all I can do is have a look at the damaged window frame, make a list of the missing items, which is usually jewellery or cash, and then leave the victim with nothing more than a crime number? We'll get him, though."

"Surely if you'd just been to a break-in and then discovered a broken window in the next street, you would have put two and two together?" Freya asked.

"Not really, guv," he said. "See, he targets families, and to be honest, usually those with money, nice cars, etc. Pensioners rarely keep cash in the house, and let's face it, the house doesn't scream wealth, does it?"

"Still, if he's an opportunist—"

"And then there's the body," Frobisher said. "Our man has been interrupted on more than one occasion, and never once has he hung about long enough to get into a fight. He's usually straight out the front door and on his toes."

"Out of the front door?"

"He doesn't mess about," Frobisher explained. "We think the first thing he does when he gets inside a house is to unlock the front door. He normally exits the way he came in, but there have been a few victims who have discovered the front door unlocked, which suggests—"

"He was making preparations," Freya said. "Yes, I wasn't born into major crimes. There was a ladder to climb, you know?"

"Right, sorry, guv."

"So, what's his name?" Ben said. "We might need to look into him."

Frobisher seemed uneasy at first. He shuffled in his seat and eyed Ben.

"What?' Ben said. "What is it?"

"We don't want him scared off, guv," Frobisher replied.

"Well, we're investigating a murder, PC Frobisher," Freya said. "And regardless of whether or not you feel the links between Mr Reilly's break-in and the Stone's break-in are weak, *I* see a link. I want him sitting in front of me in an interview room. We don't have to mention the Stone's case, but I want to talk to him, and you're going to help me do that."

Frobisher sighed and looked to Ben, who shrugged.

"Please don't force me to pull rank, Frobisher."

"Samuel Harris," he said. "His name is Samuel Harris. He's got a flat up in Hykeham. Never works his own area. He prefers to hit the little villages."

Ben looked up at Chapman, who took the hint and set to work investigating the name.

"Previous?" Freya asked.

"A list as long as your arm," Frobisher replied. "He was recently released as part of the early release scheme the government brought in to make room for...well, to make room for other prisoners."

"So, he's not thought to be dangerous," Ben asked.

"I don't think volatility was a factor when whoever it was made that decision, Ben," Freya said. "Tell me, Frobisher, how does our man usually get about? Presumably, he doesn't take the bus from Hykeham."

"No, he drives," Frobisher said. "Most of the time, it's a stolen car, something he can chuck away or leave if he has to."

"There's nothing on the DVLA database," Chapman said.

"Like I said, he used stolen motors. We've found a few of them burnt out after his sprees." He eyed Ben knowingly. "That's how we know he's going to ground."

"Where does he steal the cars from?" Ben asked. "Local?"

"As it happens, yes. He's had a few from a little car dealer on Tritton Road, but most of the others have been private."

"And now?" Freya said, coaxing him along. "Presumably, you've been monitoring the stolen vehicle reports to see if you can link him to a car theft?"

"We have," Frobisher said. "We believe he's currently using a Ford Fiesta stolen from the garden centre car park. He doesn't keep it local, though. He'll stash it somewhere down a side street and either walk to it or get a bus or something. I told you, he's smart."

"Colour?"

"The car? Silver," he replied, and Ben felt Freya's stare.

"You're sure it's silver?"

"Well, that's the only unsolved car theft we've had in his area during his last spree. I mean, he could have expanded. He could have gone wider, but we don't have the resources—"

"Yes, I know all about resources; thank you," Freya said, perching on her desk. "Well, thank you, PC Frobisher. You've been a great help."

"Is that it?"

"For the time being," she said. "Of course, if you do come across him, we'd be grateful if we could have a little go with him before he's released on bail or on a suspended sentence."

"Of course," Frobisher said with a laugh. "Although, we reckon if we can get him for one, we'll have enough to put him away this time."

"Oh, do you?" she replied. "Well, not if I get him first."

"What's all this," Gillespie called out as he barged into the incident room and slung his bag onto his chair from a good seven feet away. "Interviewing for Jewson's replacement, already, are we?"

"Actually, Jim—" Ben started, but Gillespie, who was clearly in a good mood, was already sizing Frobisher up. "Well, we'll need to feed him up a little." He reached out, took hold of Frobisher's left cheek, and squeezed it as if he was buying meat for dinner. "And he's a bit wet behind the ears, but I reckon we can knock him into shape, eh, boss?"

"This is PC Frobisher," Ben said. "He's been working on a spate of robberies in the area. We might have our man."

"Oh, are we going wide already?" Gillespie said. "Shame. I was just about to nominate Robert Reilly for the prime suspect spot."

"On what basis?" Freya asked, then nodded at Frobisher, indicating that he was free to leave.

"Oh, only that he told us he was at home on Monday morning," Gillespie replied.

"And can anyone corroborate that story?"

"Yes, but she's a risk," Nillson said as she entered the room, picking up on the conversation immediately.

"She?" Ben asked. "Reilly didn't strike me as somebody who... entertains."

"Unlike you, you mean?" Freya added, reminding him that before he met her, he was also a fully fledged batchelor.

"Did we get a name?" Ben asked, ignoring her. "Have we been to see her?"

"Oh, we didn't have to look far," Gillespie replied. "It's his maid. Nadia Bartosz."

CHAPTER THIRTY-SIX

"Nadia Bartosz," Ben said. "His maid? What a dirty—"

"Okay, okay," Freya cut in before Ben entered into a rant. "We can all connect the dots here. A wealthy white male uses his position to manipulate a female subordinate. Not exactly headline news, is it?"

"I don't think the colour of his skin has much to do with it, Freya," Ben replied. "Or his gender."

"But you have to admit, there does seem to be a theme. Perhaps he could get a job on TV. He'd fit right in."

"Oh, come on. We're not all misogynists."

"No, not all of you," she replied, gazing at Gillespie, who was unusually quiet. "But some of you need to be very careful."

"Speaking of," Gillespie said. "Are we expecting a certain somebody back anytime soon?"

"I sent her out to look for cameras like you asked," Ben told him.

"Aye, thanks," he replied and turned his attention to Freya. "Listen, boss. I don't want to put you in a difficult position. If you want, I can just get my things and bugger off for a bit, eh?"

"And why would you do that?" she asked.

"Well, you know? In case anything comes back to bite us in the backside. You should suspend me by rights—"

"For what?"

"Well, you know. I made an inappropriate comment," he said. "And, well, you know the other stuff."

"You mean, the alleged relationships with witnesses and parents of suspects?"

"Aye," he said. "I'll understand if you ask me to go."

"Gillespie, I hope you don't think I'm too much of a bully," she told him. "I might be harsh under certain conditions, but I am loyal, you know that."

"Aye, I do, but—"

"And when have I ever backed down from a bully?" she asked. "Because that's what she is; a bully. She is one of those individuals who lacks any real substance to get her anywhere in life. Therefore, she intends to tread on the hard work of others, using shame and guilt to climb the ladder. Not your shame or guilt. The shame and guilt of those above us. I'm afraid one word from her will cause a panic in the upper echelons. They will be forced to take action, and no doubt they will request that you be placed on suspension; but until that happens, Gillespie, until I receive a call or I'm asked to take action, I need you beside me. The two things you have in your favour are character and experience." She snatched up her whiteboard marker and removed the lid. "And I'm pleased to say you have oodles of both." She smiled at him affectionately, hoping her words carried through that thick skull of his.

"Aye, thanks, boss," he grumbled.

"So, you will stay in this team and use every available second to prove me right. Am I understood?"

"Aye, boss. Loud and clear," he replied.

"As for the rest of you, PC Jewson is to be treated like

everyone else in this team," Freya said. "At least, until I can figure a way through this. Got that?"

"Yes, boss," Cruz said, and Ben gave a nod. Chapman simply smiled, and Nillson, who ordinarily would have taken the opportunity to twist the knife in Gillespie's side a little, remained silent; that was enough of a sign for Freya to recognise where her loyalties lie.

The last to arrive was Gold, who entered tentatively as if she was disturbing a sermon.

"Sorry," she whispered as she made her way to her seat. "I got stuck talking to Mrs Underwood."

"Not to worry, Gold," Freya said. "We were just about to start, so you haven't missed anything." She turned to the whiteboard, which she had wiped clean save for Albert Reilly's name. "Elimination time," she said as she wrote the name of the first suspect. "Roger Havers. Neighbour. Friend and foe, by all accounts." She turned back to the team. "Unfortunately, Havers is now dead, so we're limited to whatever we can find out about him from others and from his doorbell camera, which I am pleased to say Cruz and Chapman have now managed to access."

"Oh, that's good," Gold said, and she leaned forward to get Cruz's attention. "Must have been hard work."

"It was surprisingly easy," Chapman cut in. "They've had so many requests from various regional police forces, that they now have a department to deal with the warrants and requests. It seems doorbell cameras are proving to be quite an asset."

"Well, I don't want one," Nillson said. "Did you hear about that lady from up North somewhere? Somebody hacked into her doorbell account, waited for her to go out, then popped round and nicked everything."

"How did they know it wasn't just a normal burglary?" Gold asked.

"Because they had the gall to delete the footage showing them breaking in," she said. "I tell you. They are not all they're cracked up to be."

"Nevertheless," Freya said, bringing them back to the briefing. "In this instance Havers' doorbell has proven useful, and I believe we can strike a line through his name."

"On what grounds? Nillson asked.

"On the grounds that he emerged from his house through the back door at six-thirty in the morning, walks briskly over to Reilly's house, then leaves empty-handed less than twenty seconds later. He sees something up the road, jumps in his car and goes after them."

"So he did have a key then?" Nillson asked.

"Looks that way," Freya said.

"So, who or what did he see?"

"We don't know," Cruz said. "His rose hedge is in the way. We can see the left-hand side of Reilly's house and the front door. Everything else is obscured."

"From inside Havers' front room, he had a full view of Reilly's house. We think he saw something and went to investigate."

"Saw what?" Gillespie said, suddenly part of the conversation. "A blue hatchback, maybe?"

Freya beamed at him and held her hand up.

"Let's just say that I'm beginning to come around to the fact that there may have been a blue car," she said. "We also discovered that PC Frobisher, the officer who the Armsteads flagged down, was on his way back from attending a break-in on the high street."

"A break-in?" Gillespie said. "You don't think—"

"He's given us a lead. Chapman is following up on it, and although there are various discrepancies in Reilly's break-in and his usual MO, it's worth looking into."

"Hence why Jewson isn't here," Ben added.

"Aye, that'll please her."

"I'm not concerned with Jewson's happiness, right now," Freya told him. "What's concerning is that the victim of the break-in is Roger Havers' daughter, who lives in the next street."

"What?" Gillespie said, always the first to vocalise his astonishment. "You couldn't make this up."

"So, the daughter reports a break-in," Nillson said, keen to understand the theory. "Frobisher attends, leaves there, gets flagged down by the Armsteads, and then discovers Reilly?"

"That's about the size of it," Freya said. "Meanwhile, Havers sees something, runs out of the house, and goes after someone or something."

"There is one flaw in our theory," Ben said. "The suspect that Frobisher and CID are going after—"

"Samuel Harris," Chapman added. "For the record."

Freya smiled gratefully and added the name to the board.

"Right, Harris," Ben continued, "steals the cars he uses for the burglaries, so we have no real way of pinning him to the scene. According to Frobisher, he's smart. He stashes the car down side streets, never near his house. He picks a village, does a few jobs, and then disappears for a while. Never leaves a fingerprint or hair sample."

"Selfish bastard," Gillespie muttered.

"So, what you're saying is that Havers could have spotted this Harris bloke from across the street," Gillespie said.

"If indeed it was Harris," Freya said.

"And he could have been driving a blue car?"

"Possibly," Freya said.

"Well, there is a God," Gillespie said.

"You really do believe Eamon Price saw a blue car, don't you?" Freya asked.

"With all my heart," he replied. "And if it's the last thing I bloody well do as a copper, I'm going to stop him going inside."

"How very noble," Freya told him, but his face screwed into an expression of discomfort.

"What is it?"

"Just something that's been bothering me, boss," he replied.

"Okay, we're a sharing team, aren't we?"

"Aye, well. You see, Havers had one of those doorbell whatsits, eh?"

"That's right," Freya said.

"Right," Gillespie said. "See, I thought you had to have a phone for them things. Where's his phone?"

CHAPTER THIRTY-SEVEN

"You and your big mouth," Nillson said as they pulled into the car park in front of the secure commercial unit where the traffic-based forensic work was carried out. "You do realise I have a date tonight, don't you? I cannot be late."

"Oh, aye? You kept that quiet."

"What did you expect me to do, share it in a briefing?" she said. "It's my personal life." She cut a vertical line in the air with her hand flat like a blade. "Personal life, professional life."

"And never the twain shall meet, eh?" Gillespie said. "I thought you were seeing that copper, anyway? What happened?"

"Stop fishing, Jim," she sang as if he was a child.

"Ah, come on. Where did you meet? At least tell me that?"

"La la la laaa," she replied, blocking him out.

"Alright, what's his name?" he asked. "Surely you can tell me that."

"Who said it was a *he?*" she replied as he drew the car to a stop.

He stared at her in disbelief, mouth hanging open.

"Eh?"

"That's got your mind going, hasn't it?"

"It's a lass? You mean you're a..." he hesitated, as if unable to say the words, either out of excitement or embarrassment. She hoped it was the latter, but knowing Gillespie it could easily have been the former.

She shoved the car door open before he could dig for more clues and met him at the rear of the car, where the scene before them outweighed their previous conversation. There were several cars parked in a row in various states of mutilation, and to the far end of the line, the lorry had been parked.

"Well, there's the silver Skoda," she said, then checked her watch. "Come on. Let's get this over with."

"A lass," he mumbled to himself as they walked, and he shook his head at the prospect. "Bloody Cruz owes me twenty quid."

"Why's that?" she asked.

"Well, I don't suppose it matters now, does it?" he said as they walked. "About a year ago, I bet him that you were...you know?"

"You did what?"

"Ah, it was only playful. Nothing malicious, like."

"You bet money on my sexuality?"

"Aye, well. I mean, we couldn't be sure. Cruz said you couldn't be because of the way you looked at Ben. But me?" He tapped his temple knowingly. "I knew. I always knew."

"What bloody business is it of yours?"

"Well, none, I suppose. Like I said, it was just a friendly bet. We went for months without knowing, and then you got with that traffic copper, and I had to shell out."

"You..." she stopped herself from entering into a tirade of abuse. "Jim, you're about to be investigated for making inappropriate comments regarding children."

"Aye, don't remind me."

"I bloody stuck up for you. I sat there in the incident room and fought your corner, and now you tell me you made inappropriate bets on my bloody sexuality."

"Not just you," he said defensively. "We tried to guess everyone."

"Oh great, so at least I'm not the sole target of your fascination. That makes me feel a lot better."

"And I was right, I might add. I was right about everyone," he said. "I mean, Cruz had no chance, did he, against a man of experience?"

"Yeah, and that experience is about to land you in a whole lot of bother," Nillson told him. "You slept with the mother of a boy we were questioning for murder, Jim."

"Aye, I mean, when you put it like that, it sounds bad—"

"And you slept with a barmaid who was a witness in another murder investigation."

"Well, I didn't know, did I?"

"Jim, have you ever considered that you might have a problem?"

"A what? A problem?"

"You have sex on the brain. I dread to think what Katy would say to all of this."

"Well, you can ask her if you like," he replied proudly. "She's never complained."

"Jim?" Nillson said. "Too much information. Just... there are topics that you just don't discuss at work, alright? It's not the eighties or the nineties. You have to be careful what you say."

"What, I just meant that our sex life is—"

"Stop it, Jim," she said. "For Christ's sake. I don't want to know. Imagine I'm Jewson, a young twenty-something-year-old. Would you discuss your sex life with her?"

"You're kidding, aren't you? I wouldn't give her the bloody time of day, let alone talk about the outfits I bought—"

"Just..." she began and forced the image from her mind. "Just imagine I'm her, and let's..." she gazed over to the open workshop door, where a man in a white lab coat was waiting for them. "Let's just get this done, eh?"

"So you can meet your lover, you mean?"

Nillson ignored him and strode across the forecourt. The place was like a back street mechanic's or a scrap yard, except there were no car parts strewn about, no old gearboxes resting on pallets, or car doors leaning against the building.

"Mr Glover?" she called out, holding her warrant card up. "I'm Sergeant Nillson; this is my soon-to-be ex-colleague, Sergeant Gillespie. I believe Sergeant Souness has arranged access for us."

"Aye, he has," Glover replied. He was a lean man with short-cropped hair and a breast pocket filled with pens and utensils. "You'll have to be quick, though. We're shutting up soon."

"Music to my ears," she replied.

"It was the Skoda, wasn't it?" he asked. "The car you needed to see."

"Aye," Gillespie said, wandering over to the wreck to their left. "Must have been going some, eh?"

Nillson and Glover followed him, and together they inspected the damage. The bonnet was folded up, the wings were crumpled, the engine was clearly out of place, and the windscreen had shattered.

"Jesus," she muttered.

"Shame, eh?" Glover said. "Safe cars, these are. If he'd have hit a brick wall, he'd have probably walked away." He waved a hand over the fold in the bonnet. "Front end went beneath the lorry as far as this point. Poor bastard never stood a chance."

"You've been through the vehicle, I presume?"

"Not yet," he replied. "Our focus has been on the lorry. Souness calls us every hour on the hour, wanting updates."

"And what can you tell us about it?" Gillespie asked.

He studied Gillespie for a moment, then grinned.

"You don't mince your words, do you?"

"It's my Glaswegian charm," Gillespie replied, to which Glover gave a laugh.

"Well, it's an eighteen-year-old, seventeen and a half-ton curtain sider."

"Great," Gillespie replied dryly. "What was it carrying?"

"Oil tanks," Glover said.

"Oil tanks? Plastic oil tanks?"

"Steel, commercial grade," he said.

Gillespie walked to the side of the truck and pointed to the rear wheels. "Looks like it's carrying the weight of the world."

"That's just how they look," Glover said. "It looks overloaded, but I can assure you it's not."

"What about the tyres?" Gillespie asked. "Or the brakes? All in good nick?"

"The Skoda is open," Glover replied, and he gave Gillespie a look as if to suggest he had divulged all the information on the lorry he was prepared to. "Do you need gloves?"

Nillson tugged a couple of pairs of latex throwaways from her pocket and waved them at him.

"We come prepared," she said.

"Right, well, I'll leave you to it, then," Glover said, "before I say too much and you go running to Souness with half a report. We haven't cleaned the mess yet, so just take care, won't you."

"Come on, Jim," Nillson said, beckoning him away from the lorry so they could focus on the Skoda. She tossed him a pair of gloves. "You take the back; I'll take the front."

"Is that what you say to your date—?"

"Enough," she said, cutting him off before he could make yet another lewd and inappropriate comment.

He opened the boot and appraised the sight before him with a sigh, while Nillson leaned into the open passenger door.

"Clean as a whistle," Gillespie muttered. "Jesus, I can't wait until I'm retired. Everything's always so clean, isn't it? It's like they have nothing better to do but clean stuff."

"Is that a sweeping statement concerning the UK's entire

retired population, Jim, or is it an observation you can substantiate with fact?"

"Eh?"

"Nothing," she said. "Just get your head down; see what you can find so we can go home."

He tugged the parcel shelf out and dropped it to the ground beside him while Nillson put her shoulder to the carpet and rummaged around blindly beneath the passenger seat.

"There's bugger all here," he said. "Look, even the bloody toolkit is still intact. It's still got the little seal on it."

Nillson moved around to the driver's side, checked the door pockets, and then set about performing the same routine she had previously. She found nothing and was carefully retrieving her arm from the space when the entire car suddenly sagged.

"Spacey back here," Gillespie said. "It's decent, this. I'll bet nobody's ever sat back here."

She looked up to find him in the back seat, appraising the space as if he were at a car showroom, envisaging his family on a road trip.

"See that?" she said, pointing to his feet.

"See what?"

"Carpet," she said. "*That* is what a car's carpet looks like. You'll notice there's no drinks can, chocolate wrappers, or underwear."

"Yeah, it does lack the personal touch, doesn't it?" he replied, then leaned down. "What's this?"

"What?"

He straightened again and, wearing an expression that suggested he had just solved the mystery of the universe, waved a mobile phone in the air.

"Havers' mobile," he said. "See, I told you he must have had one, didn't I?"

"Is it on?"

"Aye," he replied, tapping the home button. "Oh, Jesus."

"What?" she said, but he said nothing. "Jim, what is it?"

He turned the phone around for her to see. On the screen, there were two numbers. Nine-nine.

"He was calling the emergency services?" she said. "Bloody hell."

"They say not to use your phone while driving, don't they?" He said. "There's proof if ever I saw it." He tapped a few buttons, and then the humour drained from his face. "Ah, would you look at that?" He turned the screen again so she could see.

"We need to call this in," she said. "Get the boss on the phone."

CHAPTER THIRTY-EIGHT

"I've just locked up," the man said as Jewson strode towards him. The car park was empty, except for one Toyota pickup parked close to the farm shop entrance. "If it's just a few bits you want, then I can squeeze you in. Otherwise, I'm afraid you'll have to come back."

The shop was set back from the road, and the car park was little more than a large patch of weedy gravel. A range of old calor gas bottles were housed in a locked cage, and to the right of that were several pallet loads of firewood in mesh bags.

"I'm not a customer," she replied and discreetly flashed her warrant card. "I'm actually looking for some help."

He eyed her identification and then let his shoulder sag.

"There's nothing to find here," he told her. "There're receipts for all of it."

"I've no doubt there is," she replied. "I'm more interested in that." She pointed to the camera mounted atop a pole at the corner of the building.

"The camera?"

"Does it work?"

He shrugged.

"Course, it bloody works. Got a shop full of stock in there, I have."

"I'm part of the major crimes team dealing with a recent incident," she explained. "We're looking for a particular vehicle that passed by here on Monday morning, sometime between five and seven. A blue hatchback."

"Nobody came in here, love," he said. "Don't open up 'til ten on a Monday." He winked at her. "Need my beauty sleep."

"They wouldn't have come in here, Mr..."

"Rosford," he said.

"Thank you. They came from Martin and would have either turned right towards Metheringham or left, in which case, they would have had to pass your shop."

"You want to see the camera, then?"

"You'd be helping us out tremendously," she told him.

"Right, I know well enough what that's short for," he replied as he unlocked the door. He shoved the door open and started towards the sound of a beeping alarm. By the time she had stepped inside, winced at the stench of the dog chews and animal feeds on sale, he was entering the code into a pad on the wall behind the counter. "Best come this way," he told her. "Though, I don't know that you'll see much. It's not exactly a crisp image. It's more a deterrent."

"Is it colour?" she asked, to which he seemed a little taken back. "The car in question is blue."

"I see," he said, nodding. Aye, it's colour. "He woke a computer up with an impatient shake of the mouse and then tapped on the keyboard far too often for it to be effective. Jewson heard the sound of the discs beginning to spin, and the screen lit up with the familiar sight of the green hills and blue sky. He peered over his shoulder at her to make sure she wasn't watching him enter his password, so she made a visible point of looking the other way.

"Here," he said, eventually, as the CCTV software came onto the screen. "When did you say it was?"

"Monday morning," she said. "Between five and seven."

His tongue was almost cobra-like as Rosford navigated the software, but clearly, he'd had little cause to use it often as he clicked twice and lost the screen he had been on.

"If you go back—" she started, but he waved an irritated hand at her.

"I know, I know," he said. "Had some spotty teenager in here showing me how to do it."

"And when was that?" she asked, to which he glared over his shoulder at her.

"Some time ago," he admitted returning to what he was doing.

"It's the little camera icon," she said, pointing, and he slapped her hand away.

"I know, I know," he said. "I was going to click on it."

"Well, you weren't," she said. "You were hovering around the password settings."

"Look, do you want my help or not?"

She held her hands up in defence, and while he figured it out, she perused the shelves.

"Get busy in here, does it?" she asked, studying one of a few dozen boxes of dog biscuits.

"Busy enough," he said. "Now, can you not touch those..."

She set the box down.

"Candles? Must do a roaring trade in those," she said, not daring to touch one of the boxes on the next shelf.

"You'd be surprised," he told her. "Everyone needs candles, everyone needs a tin opener, and everyone needs thirteen amp fuses."

"Tin opener, yes," she said. "As for candles and fuses, I order them online if I need them."

"Thankfully, there are still plenty who support local businesses," he replied, then jutted his chin at the screen. "Here. This what you're looking for, is it?"

She stepped back to the little cluttered desk and saw that he'd managed to pause the footage to show a little blue Mazda passing the shop coming from the direction of Martin.

"Could be," she said. "Can you zoom in? I can't make out the driver."

"That is zoomed in," he told her. "You can see the number plate. That what you want, is it?"

Using her camera phone, she snapped an image of the screen; it was far easier than making notes.

"Any more?" she asked.

"Plenty of cars. Not many blue hatchbacks," he replied as he zoomed out and scrolled through the timeline so that the passing cars appeared to be travelling at warp speed. "There was a blue van somewhere around here." He wrinkled his nose as he studied the footage."

"No, it was a hatchback. Definitely a hatchback," she said. "Do you mind if..." She pointed to the mouse. "I'm quite familiar with CCTV software."

It was as if she had asked him to pull his pants down to conduct a cavity search, but he relinquished control and stood from the seat.

"What did they do, anyway?" he asked. "The driver, I mean. Rob a bank or something? Not much of a getaway car if he did."

"I hope you can understand that this is a live investigation, Mr Rosford—"

"Ah, right. Important enough to keep me from my tea, but you can't give me a clue? Not even a hint?"

"Not even a hint, Mr Rosford," she said as the same blue hatchback passed by the camera. She checked the timestamp and then snapped another image on her phone.

"That them, is it?"

"I won't know until I've done a little digging," she told him, then followed his eyes to the screen. "They are just a witness," she said. "You understand that, don't you? I'd hate for you to think that the driver of the car had actually done anything."

"Just a witness, yeah?"

"Just a witness, Mr Rosford. Just a witness."

"Why should I believe that? They could be a killer for all I know. I could be in for a reward, couldn't I? For helping you lot."

"Mr Rosford, believe me when I say that if your CCTV camera had picked up a murderer, you would have had a team of officers knocking on your door, and this computer would be in a lab being picked apart by a spotty teenager with a degree in computer science. As it happens, the driver is just somebody we want to speak to, somebody who may or may not have seen something. Therefore it's just me here." She looked around the room, making sure to display her disgust at the eclectic collection of household items and animal feeds. "And believe me, I'm as unhappy about being here as you are of having me."

She moved the mouse to the corner of the screen and clicked the little bin icon.

"No, don't—" he started, but it was too late. The software closed, and they were faced with that family wallpaper image: green hills and blue sky. "You idiot."

"Excuse me?"

"You just deleted the footage."

"No, I—"

"You did. You just deleted it."

"I closed the application, that's all."

"You clicked on the waste paper bin. That's it. It's gone now."

"Oh, really?" she replied with as much sincerity as she could muster. She waited for him to turn back to her. "That's a shame." She waved her phone at him. "Still, I've got what we need." She rose from the seat and made her way to the door. "Thank you for your help, Mr Rosford," she said, casting her eye over the filth and toot. "It's been an experience."

CHAPTER THIRTY-NINE

"Wine?" Ben asked as Freya flopped into her armchair. She flicked her shoes to the floor and flexed her toes.

She didn't reply; there really was no need. She closed her eyes, savouring the darkness, and she heard the drawer open and close, then the satisfying torment of the corkscrew working its way into the cork. A soft *phluck* followed as the cork was removed, and then the best sound of all, the glug of wine being poured into a glass. She felt his presence and raised a hand to take the glass.

"I hope you don't expect me to feed it to you," he said.

"You would if I asked," she told him knowingly. "Or if I couldn't."

"If you couldn't?" he said with a laugh as he dropped into the other armchair and kicked off his own shoes. "The day you can't hold a wine glass to your mouth is the day you ask me to end it all."

"In sickness and health," she said. "If I lose the use of arms, then I would need a flunky to aid me, and who better than my loyal husband?"

"Speaking of," he said. "We really ought to set a date."

"I told you. Three months from now."

"It'll be winter," Ben said. "It's getting cold now. Do you really want to wait?"

"The one thing I would like when I look back at the photographs, Ben, is to see my own hair." She held up a lock of somebody else's hair from her face. "I'd rather not be forced to wear a wig."

"Freya, you know I think you're beautiful, don't you?"

"So you say," she replied, sipping her wine.

"I do. I just want you to feel comfortable. I don't want you to feel that you have to hide your scar."

She said nothing but fingered the smooth skin on her cheek. It had healed far better than she had hoped, but there would always be a reminder of that terrible day."

"You know, Ben, some wounds never heal." She eyed him and smiled weakly. "You have to learn to either learn to live with them..."

"Or?"

She sipped again, savoured the taste, and then swallowed.

"Or give in to them," she replied. "I'm not a quitter."

It was obvious the answer didn't appease him, but he knew better than to press.

"We should think about the invitations," he said. "Maybe we can take a walk over to the church on Sunday? The banns are being read, so they'll know who we are."

"They won't think we've come to join the congregation, you mean?" she said, then relented. "I suppose we *should* show our faces." He peered at her, questioning her comment. "No pun intended," she added. "I've been looking into makeup artists. There's a girl in London I'd like to talk to."

"London? For makeup? Blimey, Freya. I thought it was just going to be a quick ceremony in the church, then a bit of a meal in the Red Lion?"

"She specialises in..." she paused, then waved a hand over her scar. "This type of thing."

"I see," he said, and then he quieted, as he often did when she spoke of her accident.

"She's done a lot with victims of acid burns," Freya continued. "I'd like to see what she can do for me. Let's face it; it's only my cheek now and a little around my eye. Some of those poor girls have had their entire faces destroyed."

"I was under the impression you were going to own your scars," he replied. "You said that you weren't going to hide from them."

"I'm not hiding from them," she said, subconsciously dragging her wig over that side of her face. "But it's my wedding day." He gazed at her in silence and then averted his eyes when she caught him. "What? What is it? You think it's too bad to conceal with makeup?"

He shook his head and laughed nervously.

"We've never really spoken about it, have we?"

"About what? The fire?"

"We've discussed your healing and the hospital and all that. But we've never really discussed what happened."

"It's not a memory I relish," she replied.

"I know," he said. "But you know I saw it all. I saw the blast, and I saw you hit the ground. I saw the flames from the side of the van. You know, if you hadn't been knocked to the ground, you wouldn't be here now. It was only the distance between the mud and the floor of the van that saved you."

"So you say," she said.

"I was laying flat on the ground, Freya. I had to pull you out of the flames."

"For which I am eternally grateful," she said. "There have been times when I wished you had just left me there, but for the most part, I'm grateful."

"Your face was on fire, Freya." He said the words flatly as if he were reprimanding her for some banal wrongdoing. "I'll never forget it. I'll never be able to un-see it. Your skin was charred like... like burnt meat, and your eye was swollen and red and angry and... It was horrific, Freya."

"You paint such a pretty picture—"

"Don't make light of it," he said. "Do you know what it was like to see you like that? I thought I'd bloody lost you."

"It wasn't my favourite day either," she replied. "I told you. I'm not a quitter."

"What I'm trying to say is that everyone knows what you've been through. Everyone knows that you're..." he waved a hand at his own face.

"Disfigured?" She suggested, to which he nodded.

"And I've never loved you more. So don't feel like you have to look how you used to look. Don't do it for me anyway because I don't want the old you. I like the new you."

She smiled and reached a hand out for him to hold.

"You're a silly sod, aren't you?" she said. "But, this is my wedding day. I am going to have my own hair, albeit somewhat shorter than it used to be. I am going to have the best makeup artist I can find to make me feel pretty, and I am going to get as drunk as a skunk, and I am doing all of that..." she paused to ensure she had his full attention, "for me."

He let go of her hand and leaned back in the chair.

"Why did I ever think otherwise?" he muttered as he fished his phone from his pocket. He answered a call and then routed it to loudspeaker. "Gillespie, your timing is impeccable. How's it going?"

"Oh, you know, mate, living the dream. Looking forward to being cast into the same pit as Jimmy bloody Saville."

"It'll work itself out, Jim," Ben said, but as much as Freya wanted to join Ben in his optimism, she couldn't. She gestured for him to move the topic along before Gillespie said something he would regret or, worse, let his nerves get the better of him. "How did it go anyway?" Ben asked. "Did you get to see the car?"

"I did," he replied. "Bloody awful mess, mate. There was no way anyone was walking away from that."

"Well, I'm guessing you didn't find a weapon of any sort?" Freya called out, and Gillespie hesitated as if he hadn't realised she was listening in.

"No, boss," he said. "No weapons. Just an old phone."

"A what?" she said, swinging her legs to the floor and leaning in. "A phone?"

"The forensics team hadn't got to the car yet, so it hadn't been found," Gillespie told them. "It was on the floor in the back. Looks like Havers dropped it on impact."

"What makes you say that? He could have just dropped it when he got in."

"He was halfway through making a call," Gillespie said. "I'll give you a clue; it's a number everyone knows. It starts with nine and ends in nine, and there's one other number in between."

"He was calling the police?"

"Well, we can't be entirely sure, boss," Gillespie said.

"Oh, for heaven's sake, just spit it out, Gillespie, will you? Where's Nillson?"

"I dropped her off in town," he said. "She's had to go and meet somebody. A date with a girl. But I didn't tell you that, alright?"

"About the emergency services call," Freya said. "What are you thinking?"

"Well, I had a wee looky-loo back through his call history. He got a call at six-twenty-nine a.m.."

"So?" Freya said. "Who was it from?"

"A mobile number. I think it's Albert Reilly's."

"He didn't have a mobile phone," Ben said.

"No, we didn't *find* a mobile phone," Gillespie said.

"But if he had a mobile, Chapman would have found it. She contacted all the providers."

"Unless it was a pay-as-you-go," Freya added.

"Exactly," Gillespie said. "I think Albert Reilly heard the

intruder breaking the glass and called Havers. I think he was scared."

"This adds up," Ben agreed. "The doorbell video shows him looking up the street when he comes out of Reilly's house."

"So, he *did* see the killer," Freya said. "He went after them and was calling the police as he drove."

"And then bam!" Gillespie said, and his clap sang out over the phone line.

"So Havers is in the clear," Ben said. "We need that blue car."

"We don't know it was a blue car," Freya said. "Sorry, boys, but we don't know."

"How did Jewson get on?" Gillespie asked. "Did she find it?"

"I don't know. I find that I'm loathe to speak to her," Freya said. "Perhaps you could call her?"

"Not likely," Gillespie said. "It's nothing that can't wait until the morning, that's for sure."

"Speaking of the morning," Freya said. "I have a job for you and Nillson. Ben will send the details through later this evening."

"Oh, aye?" he said. "Anything juicy?"

"Get a good night's rest," she said. "It's going to be an early start."

CHAPTER FORTY

It was the same incident room Ben was familiar with. He'd spent most of his career in the place, and now he thought about it, he'd spent most of his career at the same desk.

The very first day he transferred from uniform under the watchful eye of Sergeant David Foster, he was given the desk, and he had never even considered taking another. Chapman's desk was a home from home, with a photo of her parents, a little pen pot and all the little bits and bobs she surrounded herself with. Even Gold's desk had been personalised with a framed photo of Charlie, her little boy. Gillespie's desk was little more than a footrest when Freya wasn't around, and Ben's was just a space to store the stack of files he'd been meaning to work through. Most of them were completed investigations that would be filed when one or two documents had been returned from CPS or post-trial.

For the most part, he shared that room with the same people. Gold and Chapman had been on his team for the longest time. Gillespie, Cruz, and Nillson had been on an adjacent team under DI Standing, who, for many reasons, was no longer a police officer.

The only two caveats were Freya, who had been drafted in to

replace David Foster when cancer had finally taken him, and Jewson, who had been lined up to replace DC Anderson, who had moved back to London when Freya had her accident.

Despite the familiar place and people, Ben thought there was a difference; something in the air, brooding like a storm cloud.

There was none of the usual banter, no laughing or joking, no anecdotes. Everyone had their head down - except for Jewson, who leaned back in her chair, toying with her pen, watching Freya as she worked the whiteboard prior to the briefing.

He wondered if Jewson recognised the ill-feeling she had created or if she was so hell-bent on destroying the team that her surroundings didn't even register.

"Right, listen up," Freya said, finally taking a step back to appraise the whiteboard. She turned to face them, sliding the pen lid back on and eyeing them all in turn to ensure they were all paying attention. "We've made some significant progress," she began. "But we aren't there yet. Now—"

"Where's Sergeant Gillespie?" Jewson cut in. "And Nillson. Aren't they coming?"

"Excuse me?" Freya said.

"We're not a full team," she said. "Wouldn't it make sense to wait until they're in? Otherwise, we'll have to go through it twice."

Freya glanced to the back of the room to where Ben shook his head discreetly, advising her not to reprimand Jewson but to let it go.

"They're doing something for me," she said. "Or should I have run that past you?"

Jewson shrugged.

"It just makes sense to have the whole team together," Jewson replied. "But what do I know, right?"

"Precisely," Freya said. "What *do* you know?" She left that comment hanging and indicated the top name on the board. "Unless we receive evidence to the contrary, I'm eliminating both

Roger Havers and Terri James from the investigation, which means we can focus on the remaining individuals, namely Robert Reilly and Samuel Harris—"

"We haven't even looked into James, have we?" Jewson asked. "And as for Havers—"

"Terri James doesn't drive, there are no buses she could have possibly taken at that time of the morning, and she has no reason to murder Albert Reilly. In fact, his death has resulted in loss of earnings for her. She also has a front door key and, therefore would have had no need to break in," Freya began. "For the purposes of educating you, PC Jewson, that translates to her having no means, no opportunity, and no motive."

"And Havers?"

"Again, he had a key. He was in the house for a matter of seconds and, as his doorbell footage indicates, he did not emerge from the house carrying any type of weapon. Evidence that came to light last night indicates that he was in the process of calling the emergency services when his car slammed into the back of the lorry, killing him instantly. So, when I say that I am eliminating them from our enquiries, Jewson, I do so with confidence."

Jewson nodded slowly and thoughtfully.

"Fair enough," she said with a wry smile.

"May I continue?"

"Sorry, boss. Didn't mean to hold you up. I just needed to know the details. I was out all day yesterday if you recall." She ran her tongue around her teeth slowly, then smiled innocently. "On my own."

"Why don't you just leave it?" Gold asked. "We just want to get on."

"What's the matter, Jackie? No poor victims to console today? No cups of tea to make? You'll have to do some real police work—"

"That's enough," Ben said from the back row. "Jewson, stop making waves."

Jewson didn't turn to look at him. Instead, she stared dead ahead, grinning to herself.

Freya waited for a moment before continuing until Jewson had composed herself.

"Robert Reilly," she said quietly. "Son of Albert Reilly. Now, we know there was no love lost between the two of them, but as yet, we have not identified a motive. He has suggested that he was with Nadia Bartosz, his housekeeper; Ben and I will be paying them both a visit after this briefing." She circled Reilly's name and added B&F beside it. "The rest of you will be focusing on Samuel Harris. PC Frobisher, who was the first on the scene, has suggested that Harris is a known suspect in an ongoing spate of burglaries. He had been attending a burglary in the next street when he was flagged down by Mr and Mrs Armstead, who, if you remember, live opposite Albert Reilly and next door to Roger Havers." She reached up and indicated the Armstead's house on her rough sketch of the roads around the crime scene.

"Don't you think it's weird that the robbery he was attending was Havers' daughter?" Jewson asked, and with her back to the team, Freya closed her eyes and took a deep breath.

Eventually, she turned and faced the smarmy little madam.

"I don't see the relevance, Jewson," she said. "Perhaps there's something you could share? An insight, maybe?"

Again, Jewson shrugged.

"No, I just think it's a bit odd. A coincidence, if you like."

"I don't like coincidences," Freya replied. "But I fail to see how the victim of the burglary being Roger Havers' daughter is of any significance. True, a potential theory is that when Harris was done with his first house, he then moved onto Albert Reilly's house, but any relationship links have no bearing at all."

"Until we receive further evidence," Jewson added.

"Until we receive further evidence," Freya agreed. "Jewson, is there something you wish to share?"

Jewson shook her head nonchalantly. "No, boss. Not really."

At the back of the room, Ben shook his head, warning Freya to remain calm.

"Points to note," she said, addressing the room. "Roger Havers received a call from an unknown number moments before he ran from his house. Chapman, anything on that?"

"Actually, yes," Chapman replied. "The number was registered to Reilly Haulage, but before we run away with the idea that Robert made that call, there were only half a dozen calls made from that number in the past six months, and most of them were to Roger Havers."

"So, Robert got a SIM card through his business account and gave it to his Dad?" Ben said for clarity.

"Looks that way," Chapman replied.

"What other numbers did he call?" Freya asked, seizing a loose end she saw blowing in the breeze.

Chapman read from her notes.

"He called Terri James a few times and the caring company. Aside from that, nobody."

"Which begs the question, where is his phone?" Freya said. "Can we assume that whoever knocked Albert Reilly down saw the phone and took it?"

"Can we trace it?" Ben asked. "There's a chance it's still switched on."

"Tried that," Chapman said, shaking her head. "Mobile phones issue a hello signal to the nearest mobile mast every few minutes. The last contact was around six-thirty-two on Monday morning."

"So they turned it off?" Freya said. "Whoever it is is smarter than we thought."

"Harris?" Ben suggested. "Frobisher seems to think he's sharp. He's certainly smart enough to evade arrest despite several burglaries."

"Right, so this is where we are," Freya said, nodding at Ben to acknowledge his comment. "Ben and I will go and speak to Reilly and his housekeeper. The rest of you will be working on Harris, who I might add is due any minute now."

"He's coming in?" Jewson said. "What, did you send him an invitation?"

"Yes, it was hand delivered by Sergeant Nillson, Sergeant Gillespie, and half a dozen uniformed officers at seven o'clock this morning." She checked her watch. "Ben, give Gillespie a call, will you? See how they're getting on. In the meantime, let's do some background work on Harris. We know he's been inside. Who does he know? Is he working with anyone? Frobisher said they didn't have the resources to monitor all stolen vehicles from a wider area. Let's take that wider. I really hope, by the time Ben and I return from seeing Reilly and the maid, you'll have a stolen blue hatchback somewhere that we can link to Harris and maybe one of his acquaintances who is corrupt enough to talk to us." Gold, Cruz, and Chapman each looked at Jewson, then at each other, and then finally to Freya.

Nobody needed to say a word. She could read their thoughts to the letter.

"Jewson, perhaps it's best if we find something else for you to do," Freya said. "Why don't you get hold of Katy Southwell for me? We're still waiting for Albert Reilly's toxicology report and the DNA report from his house. I doubt she'll find much, but you never know."

"I'm afraid I can't do that, boss," Jewson said, checking her watch.

"I'm sorry?" Freya replied. "I just gave you an instruction."

"And I apologise, but I'm afraid I can't do that," she said. She rose from her seat, shoving it back so it free-wheeled across the room. "I've got a prior engagement, and I do hate to let people down." She grinned at Freya and let her gaze rove around the room before resettling on Freya. "Especially Detective Superintendent Granger."

"Jewson?" Freya said as the young officer sauntered towards the door.

"Boss?" She replied.

"You made such a fuss of being left alone yesterday afternoon I almost forgot to ask you what you found."

"What I found, boss?"

"Cameras. Blue car?" Freya said. "What do you want me to do, wait for you to write up your report?"

Jewson grinned again, a sight that Ben was beginning to loathe.

"If I had something to report, boss, I would have reported it," she said. "There *was* no blue car. Gillespie is wrong. Eamon Price is a liar." She gazed back as if daring Freya to press for more information, and Ben prayed Freya would see sense. "I'd better run," Jewson said. "Mustn't keep the big man waiting."

CHAPTER FORTY-ONE

The doors swung closed behind Jewson, and a chill ran through the room. Even in the shadow of her wig; Freya's eyes were cold and fixated.

"Leave her," Ben said.

"What a bitch," Gold muttered.

"I said, leave her," he said again. "She's not worth the headache."

"She's going to destroy Jim," Gold said. "We can't just stand by and watch."

"That's exactly what we're going to do," Freya said, which caught Ben off guard. "As much as I hate to admit it, Sergeant Gillespie has not done himself any favours."

"It was just a comment," Chapman argued. "It was nothing."

"Oh, believe me, if Gillespie is suspended for something, the comment he made about tickling children will not be the reason. It'll be his... extra-curricular antics that get him into bother. The comment was little more than something for Jewson to get her teeth into. Something to open the doors."

"It's so spiteful," Chapman said, who was usually very mild-mannered. "I hope she rots in hell."

"Unfortunately, if Jewson gets her own way, we can expect more of the same," Freya said. "If Gillespie is investigated, we'll be under the spotlight. It means that everything we say and do will be analysed. Every decision we make will be scrutinised, and every action we take will be questioned, which means that, while this is going on, we must not speak, think, or do anything that could be deemed unprofessional. We follow protocol. We carry on as if nothing has happened."

"It's so wrong," Gold muttered.

"Strike one," Freya said. "It'll be my decision-making that will be scrutinised more than anything else, which means that I will be forced to take action on any comment you make." Gold nodded and turned away. "Think it. Don't say it," Freya added and winked at her.

"Jim?" Ben said, finally getting through to the man in question. "How's it going?"

He held the phone to his ear, but judging by the look on his face, he was struggling to hear.

"Hold on, mate. I'll put you on loudspeaker," Ben said, and he came to Freya's desk, placing his phone down. "It's Gillespie."

"Oh really?" Freya said. "Not the other Jim, then?" Ben laughed the comment off and let Freya take over. "Gillespie, give me some good news."

"Well, if it's good news you're after, then I'm not your man, boss," he began. "No sign of him."

"What do you mean? There's no sign of him."

"He's not home, boss. Hasn't been for some time by the looks of things. Either that, or he really does have a hygiene issue. I thought my place was bad, but this? Jesus, it's a whole new level of filth."

"You gained entry then?"

"Oh aye, we gained entry, alright. Had the boys, with their wee battering ram, knock the door in. But honestly, boss. I've been over this place, and he's not hiding. Even checked the loft."

"Bugger," Freya said, although Ben thought that wasn't the original B-word she had in mind. "What have you got then?"

"Well, it's early days yet," Gilespie said. "The place is a hole. Every piece of clothing is on the floor, every dish and plate he owns has food in it, along with God knows what, and every surface I can see has something on it."

"What are you saying?"

"I'm saying this isn't going to be a quick in and out," Gillespie replied, and then they heard somebody talking to him.

"Who's that?" Freya asked, never one for patience.

"It's Nillson, boss. One of the uniformed officers has found something in the living room. It's an initial contact letter from his probation officer."

"Date?" Freya said, almost immediately clicking her fingers and gesturing for Chapman to take notes.

"Two months ago," he replied.

"Send a photo of it to Chapman," Freya said. "Chapman, get onto the probation officer and see what they know."

"Will do," she replied.

"What do you want us to do?" Gillespie asked.

"I'm thinking," Freya replied. "Stay there, do as much as you can, then come back here." She looked at Ben, and he instantly knew her reason behind the delay. "We're building a case against Harris. Anything you can find to help us will be appreciated."

"Right, so the theory is that Harris robbed the house round the corner, then did the old man's?"

"That's it," Freya said. "Albert Reilly heard the broken glass and called Havers, who came running over and startled Harris, who must have slipped out of the back door."

"Locking it behind him?" Cruz said. "That's a bit odd, isn't it?"

"If he heard Havers' key in the door, it's not unreasonable to think Harris was trying to throw him off the scent."

"Aye, so Havers finds Reilly, runs out of the house and sees Harris scarpering up the road in his car, then goes after him."

"It adds up," Freya said. "We just need to link Harris to the blue car. There must be something, Jim."

The comment made Ben sit up. It was the first time he had ever heard her address Gillespie by his first name, and the silence that ensued suggested Gillespie had also noted the change.

"Aye, boss. I mean, there's all kinds of junk in here. Beer cans, takeaways, you name it, it's here. There's a bag of weed upstairs."

"Not worth the paperwork," Freya said. "Leave that for the uniformed team to deal with."

"I haven't even found a laptop yet, but I'm guessing his search history will be questionable when we do find it. There's no car keys, nothing."

"What about cash or jewellery?" Gold said. "If he robbed Havers' daughter's house beforehand, then maybe there's something to link him to that."

"I've got an old pair of hair clippers," Gillespie said, and Ben pictured him poking his way through the junk. There was nothing worse than having to rifle through somebody else's belongings, especially when the conditions were far from optimal. "Puncture repair kit, Cruz, I'll nab that for you if you like, for when your mum needs her car back."

"It's *not* my mum's car—"

"A puncture repair kit?" Ben said, cutting him off.

"Aye, you know, one of those things where you stuff the inner tube in a bowl of water, put a wee sticky tab on the hole, put it all back together only to find out you still have a puncture."

"He has a bike then?" Ben continued.

"Aye, he must have had a bike, Ben, unless he nicked a repair kit for the sake of nicking it. You know what these kleptomaniacs are like."

"Gold, call Katy Southwell, will you?" Freya said, picking up on Ben's lead. "Get her on the line and tell her it's urgent."

"What's going on?" Gillespie asked.

"How old is the food in the dishes?" Freya asked.

"Eh? I don't know."

"Is it yesterday's dinner or older?"

"What do you want me to do, boss, bloody taste it? It's old. I don't know; a week or something?"

"I've got her," Gold said.

"Put her on loudspeaker," Freya instructed. Gold did as instructed and then handed the phone to Freya, who placed Gold's phone beside Ben's. "Katy, thanks for taking our call. I have your boyfriend on another line on loudspeaker. He's carrying out a search of a property west of Lincoln as we speak."

"Well, I hope he changes his clothes before dinner," Southwell said. "The last time you sent him to do a search, he came home stinking of cannabis and vomit."

"I heard that," Gillespie said.

"I need a favour," Freya said before the two entered into the realms of domestic conversation. "We encountered an RTA on Monday morning. There was a lorry, a few cars, and—"

"One of my team is working on it," Southwell replied, but there was a hesitation in her tone. "But, I'm not aware that you're the SIO. It's a Sergeant Souness if I recall."

"I know," Freya said. "It's just that something has come up, and well, we wondered if you could share the identity of one of the victims."

"Freya, look. I would, but it's against—"

"Gillespie, talk her into it, will you?" Freya said.

"Eh? She won't listen to me, boss."

"He's right," Southwell said. "I'm afraid it's against procedure. If it got out that I shared sensitive information with an officer outside of the investigation, we'd all be investigated."

"The way things are going, Katy, that might just be the case."

"Sorry?"

"Nothing," Freya said. "Look, I just need one of the names of the victims. I know one of them was Roger Havers. But I need the other one. If I say his name, cough once if I'm right and twice if I'm wrong."

"Freya—"

"I wouldn't ask if it wasn't important, Katy," she said, and a terrible silence followed. "Katy?"

"I could add in that I'd do the washing up," Gillespie chimed in, and Ben smirked at his negotiation skills. "For a week, I might add."

"You don't need to do the washing up," Southwell said. "In fact, I'd rather you didn't. The last thing I want is salmonella, thanks."

"It's Samuel Harris," Freya said before anyone could drag it out any further. "Once, if I'm right, Katy, twice, if I'm wrong. We'll love you forever."

"Is this a secure line?"

"It's Gold's private phone," Freya said, and they heard Southwell flicking through some notes. "Samuel Harris," Freya repeated. "Cough once if I'm right."

"I don't need to cough," Southwell said. "You're right. It's him."

CHAPTER FORTY-TWO

It wasn't often that Ben was beaten by an investigation. He was one of life's curious individuals, and it was one of the reasons Freya admired him. So, to see him flop into his seat and let his head fall back was difficult. He tossed his pen blindly, letting it scatter across his desk, deflect off the files and the drop to the carpeted floor.

"Three down," Freya said, waiting for him to raise his head so she could direct his attention to the whiteboard. "Only Robert Reilly left."

"It doesn't mean Harris didn't do it," he said. "It just means that if he did do it, then it's going to be A, impossible to prove, and B, meaningless. We can't charge a corpse with murder, so what's the bloody point? Not to mention the blue car theory."

"Is that why we do what we do?" Freya asked. "For the gratitude of charging individuals? Or do we do what we do for the benefit of the victims' families? To bring them closure and to let them know that whoever murdered their loved one is paying the price for their crimes."

"Loved ones?" Ben said. "Albert Reilly's son couldn't stand him, his sister couldn't stand him, and even his best mate over the road was always rowing with him. The man was a loner. The only person who had some kind of relationship with him, as far as I can see, was his carer, and let's face it, all she had to do was keep him alive and wipe his backside. She didn't have to smile or enjoy his company. She just had to turn up at his house, do some cleaning, feed him, give him his meds, and then bugger off until next time." He leaned forward on his desk. "It doesn't matter who killed Albert Reilly, Freya. Nobody gives a hoot. All we're doing is ticking a box."

"That's no reason to let somebody get away with murder, Ben," Freya told him. "There's a murderer out there somewhere. They could kill again."

Ben relented, letting his head drop into his hands.

"I know, I know. I was just... venting, that's all." He looked at the concerned faces around the room. "Sorry, guys. A momentary lapse of reason."

"I think we're all feeling the same," Gold said, ever the compassionate one. "Doesn't help that Jewson is in there trying to tear us apart." She looked up at Freya. "I hope Granger stands up for us."

"Oh, I hope he does, too, but I'm afraid his hands are tied. Jewson is playing the game. All she has to do is raise the question of Gillespie's suitability and Granger will be forced to take action. If he doesn't take action, then he'd be opening himself up to a whole world of scrutiny. Don't forget he doesn't simply sit in that office managing us. He has teams of officers across the district. All it would take is for one of them to make a mistake, and his dismissal of an internal complaint would be seen as gross negligence. I doubt he would be fired, but somebody up above him would have a little word in his ear, asking him to take a step down. It's the way things are done when you reach a certain rank."

"Well, I think it's out of order," Gold said. "And I don't mind saying so; jumped up, little cow. I think there needs to be a change in the law."

"Oh, really?" Freya said. "I didn't realise we were branching out into politics."

"I think it should be illegal to falsely accuse somebody of something."

"Christ, if they bring that one in, we'll be busy," Cruz said.

"And the penalty should be whatever the penalty is for the crime they accused somebody of," Gold said. "So if somebody makes up a load of stuff about somebody... I don't know, engaged in domestic violence, for example, then the accuser should stand trial for the same sentence. That would put a stop to things like this."

"Whilst I appreciate your passion for these matters, Gold," Freya said. "We have to remember that Jewson is merely reporting the fact that Gillespie made an ill-timed comment regarding children. She won't be making a complaint, she won't be accusing him of anything, and she certainly won't be demanding action be taken. She will merely be recording the incident. But *we* know, and *she* knows, that Granger will be forced to take action. Jewson's hands will be clean. She will, no doubt, swan in here innocently, safe in the knowledge that I will be powerless to move her on."

"What?" Cruz said. "Can't you just nudge her into another force? I hear there's a spot in the Outer Hebrides."

"I can't nudge her anywhere, Cruz," she replied. "Else, I will be seen to be covering something up. No. No, we've got to play the long game on this one." She grinned at him, then shared the smile with the team. "I need you all to trust me. I'll work something out. I'll get something on her."

"Get something on who?" Gillespie said as the doors banged closed behind him. He peered at them all as he dragged his coat from his broad shoulders and slung it over his chair.

"Oh, the housekeeper," Freya lied. "Nadia Bartosz. I don't trust her."

"Eh?" he said. "When did she come into the equation?"

"When we learned that Harris is dead," Freya told him. "Anyway, what are you doing back so soon?"

"Oh, we were just getting in the way," Gillespie said. "It's not exactly a palace, you know?"

"Where's Nillson?"

"Ah, she's just taking a sl..." he cleared his throat. "She's in the ladies."

"Thank you," Freya replied. "Well, even though Harris is dead, we do need to alibi him."

"Actually, I've got something on that, guv," Chapman said. "His probation officer got back to me. He attended on Friday and Saturday but failed to turn up on Monday."

"Aye, that's because he was squished by a bloody great lorry," Gillespie said.

"Get back in touch with Katy Southwell, will you? Ask her to swab his hands, gloves, or whatever. There weren't any fingerprints in Albert Reilly's house, but perhaps there's some glass dust or saliva. Christ, even a shoe print on the carpet would make me happy right now."

"Will do," Gold replied.

"The thing is," Ben cut in. "If Harris did break into Reilly's house, and Havers chased him off, blahdy blah..." He raised an index finger, as he did when he had a point to make. "Then who was driving the blue car."

"Or was there even a blue car?" Cruz said. "Jewson checked CCTV cameras but couldn't find one."

"Oh, there's a blue car," Gillespie said. "I know there is. I saw it on Eamon Price's face."

Freya stared at him, seeing for the first time how important it was to clear Price's name.

"You really believe him, don't you?"

"He's an innocent man, boss," he replied. "You know when you have a suspect you know is innocent, but you can't prove them innocent, right?"

"Naturally," Freya said.

"Even if they've confessed. You know they're covering for someone, or they're acting out of valour or something," he continued. "Well, take that and then put the investigation into somebody else's hands, on a team who have no part in it. All you can do is sit by and watch as an innocent man's life is about to go down the drain."

"Quite the speech," Freya said. "But I hear you. We can't help them all, you know? We have a tool kit based on procedure, logic, and historical crimes. For the most part, those tools work. But every so often, they fail us, and when that happens, we must be sure to move on. We must believe in what we do, or, as Ben put it before you came in, what's the bloody point?"

He cocked his head to one side, listening intently.

"Why do I get the feeling you're preparing me for something, boss?"

Freya smiled at him. He was the very definition of a loveable rogue. His methods had been questioned on more than one occasion, and his views on specific topics were antiquated, to say the least. But, there was no questioning the man's heart.

"Just..." she began. "Just believe in the process, Jim. That's all I ask."

"Boss?" Nillson called out. She was halfway through the door, leaning back into the corridor.

"What is it, Nillson?"

"Detective Superintendent Granger asked me to send you in," she replied, refusing to look in Gillespie's direction. "He wants a word."

"Very good," Freya said, then found Ben. "Take over for me, will you? Alibi Harris, if you can, and then line up Reilly for a chat." She turned her phone off and slid it onto her desk. "I have a feeling I'll need some fresh air when I get out."

CHAPTER FORTY-THREE

"Ah, Bloom," Granger said, proffering the visitor's seat with a sweep of his hand. "Come in, come in. Sit, please."

She purposefully left the door open and took a few steps toward the spare seat, adopting the expression and body language of somebody surprised to be called in for chat.

Granger rose from his seat, leaned across his desk and shoved the door closed.

"This one's a bit sensitive?" he explained.

"Oh, dear," she replied. "Is it business or something a little more personal?"

He laughed once, then eyed her knowingly.

"I won't beat around the bush, Freya; I've had a rather disturbing discussion with...somebody in your team."

"Oh, don't tell me; Cruz is wondering why he hasn't been made Chief Constable yet," Freya replied. "I keep reminding him of the ladder he has to climb, but he will persist—"

"I won't pretend you're as ignorant as you make out," Granger said, and he watched for Freya to relinquish her naive stance. "The truth is that I've been placed in a rather difficult situation."

He leaned forward and rested his elbows on his desk, interlinking his fingers. "I don't particularly enjoy being in such positions."

Freya crossed her legs and nodded sympathetically.

"I agree," she said. "It is a conundrum, and for what it's worth, I don't envy your position."

"Well, I'm glad we can agree on that at least. The question is, how do we... remove ourselves from this position, without causing an unnecessary scene?"

Freya shook her head.

"I suppose there's always a transfer," she said. "Let's face it, it worked for me."

"That could be difficult. Locally, at least. Reputations are harder to mask than you might think. London might work."

"No," Freya said. "Not the Met. She'd be eaten alive. They won't stand for any of her tactics down there."

"Sorry?"

"The Met, guv," she said. "They won't have her. She wouldn't last a week, and I don't know about you, but I don't want her back on *my* doorstep. No, thank you."

"I was referring to DS Gillespie, as well you know," he said.

"Gillespie? Well, I'm sure he'd be glad to see the back of her as well—"

"Will you stop," he said, raising his voice. His nostrils flared and he stared her down for a moment as his temper abated. "I'm not here to play games. I have heard claims of very serious offences from an officer in your charge. Claims that date back a year or more, and that, according to the claimant—"

"Jewson?"

"Are common knowledge, Freya," he continued. He lowered his voice to a hiss. "Relationships with the mother of a suspect?"

Freya frowned.

"I'm afraid that's news to me, guv. The only relationship I've known him to have is his current one."

It was obvious that Granger didn't believe a word she said but moved on anyway.

"His current relationship? You're referring to the lead CSI, Katy Southwell."

"I am, guv, yes," she said.

"Well, perhaps she'd be interested to hear about his exploits with a particular barmaid who was a key witness in a recent investigation in Horncastle."

"That sounds a little far fetched if you ask me, guv—"

"Or the woman who chased him down her street while he was going door to door?"

"We do meet some characters, guv."

"She was wearing a brassiere and very little else, and made serious claims against him."

"Oh really? What were those claims?" Freya asked.

"Well, I still need to do some background work—"

"Oh, I see," Freya replied. "So, you've been told of these exploits and are yet to evidence them, is that right?"

"I will," he said. "If I have to, I will. If you and your team are reluctant to provide me with the answers I need, then I'll be forced to."

"That's fine," she said. "You should, of course. I mean, until we can actually prove he did anything, Gillespie remains a vital part of my team."

"And then there's the comment he made a couple of days ago."

"Comment, guv?"

"Freya? I'm not playing games, remember?"

She sighed and unfurled her legs as if the whole affair was little more than an unnecessary chore, which, of course, it was.

"I wasn't there," she said, holding her hands up.

"But DI Savage was," he countered. "Come on, Freya. You're about to be married. You can't tell me you haven't discussed this. In fact, I'd go as far as to say that you've preempted every word of this conversation."

"Me, guv? No. I mean, I've thought about it. I had an idea of what you might say, but whatever you may think of me, I'm not a rule breaker, and I do understand the games that people play."

"And what games are they?"

"Games that further the careers of unworthy individuals, guv," she said. "And I'll follow your lead and speak directly. Jewson. She's in for the kill. She's looking for the fast track, and judging by what she told me, her values have no place in the police force."

"What values are those?"

"Values that are based on the theory that fellow officers are guilty until proven innocent and values that toy with the shame and the guilt that a handful of genuinely disgraced officers have caused the force, resulting in every off-hand comment being blown out of proportion, and for officers with exemplary careers to come to a grinding halt and for lives to be ruined." She jabbed an index finger down onto his desk. "She knows damn well that one word to you about some irrelevant comment would result in you shuffling in your seat and panicking about your pension. She doesn't care that Gillespie's career might be over. She doesn't care that the team we've built over these past few years—"

"Freya?"

"No, you listen to me," she told him. "I'm bloody sick of this. She knows that when, not if, when, the media get hold of this, she'll be heralded as some kind of Joan of Lincolnshire figure, fighting for the greater good. Not afraid to speak out or to crush an innocent man to expedite her career. A man, guv. Had I said those words, or Gold, or Nillson, then nothing would have happened. But because it's Gillespie, because he's male, and because in her mind the force is a hive of misogyny, she sees a place for herself in some bizarre reformed version of what we have. She's been planning something like this since the day she came to us."

"During which time you were hospitalised, I might add. And she performed a terrific role, did she not?"

"I doubt it was as terrific as she makes out," she replied. "Knowing her, she wrapped Cruz around her little finger and blackmailed him into putting in a good word for her."

"That's conjecture," he said.

"Yeah, well, when you spend your life dealing with liars and very little in the way of facts, guv, you get pretty good at seeing through it."

He sighed and relaxed a little in his chair.

"So, how do we move forward?"

"Easily," she said. "You do what you have to do, invoke the assistance of the IPOC; they'll carry out an investigation, they'll find him innocent, and we can all get back to doing what we're good at."

"It's not as easy as that," he replied. "he made a comment about..." He checked the door and lowered his voice. "About children, for God's sake."

"And do you know what the comment was?"

"Something about tickling them and gaining some kind of satisfaction about it," he replied.

"Right," Freya said, then held her hands out, hoping he would explain how that could possibly be interpreted as anything but innocent. "So, where's the problem?"

Granger appeared uncomfortable in his seat. He shifted awkwardly. "Well, you see, it wasn't so much as what he said but how he said it."

"How he said it? How he said the words, *tickling children*?"

"There was, so I'm told, at least a certain degree of...pleasure associated with the statement."

"Pleasure? In tickling children?"

"Look, Freya," he said. "You know as well as I do about the safeguarding rules. He said something in a particular way, and now I'm forced to act upon it."

"Yes, you are. You're forced to dismiss the little cow for potentially destroying a man, who, by the way, spent his childhood years going from kids home to kids home, and somehow, not only made it into the force and made sergeant in a major crimes team, but also had such a positive impact on a young boy's life, that that young boy now wants to be a copper."

"I appreciate you feel strongly about this—"

"You're bloody right I feel strongly about it. He's a good copper."

"He has a... questionable history, Freya. One that, when the media get hold of it, will gobble up and cast a shadow over this station so dark that I doubt we'll ever see sunshine again. Do you understand the significance of this?"

"Oh, I understand, alright, guv. I understand that after all this time of doing what you asked, playing by the rules no matter how absurd they might be, that the one time we need you to have our backs, we don't have it."

"You have my full support—"

"We have nothing, sir," she told him. "Nothing. All we've got is a young woman, who by the way, dresses entirely inappropriately for the role, who knows the rules as well as you and I, and has you by the balls." She held up a fist to illustrate her point. "I thought you were made of better stuff," she said. "Or perhaps you have something to hide? Perhaps you're worried about us all being investigated and the IPOC finding something in your past?"

"I'm not worried about my own past in the slightest," he said.

"Well, you should be," she told him. "She needs to be put back in her box. If you give in to her, then who knows what's next? You'll have people making all sorts of claims. We'll all be written off."

"My hands, Freya—"

"Don't say it," she warned, but his expression remained unmoving.

"They're tied," he said, eventually. "If you want to send him in, I'll be the one to—"

"No," she said. "No, if anybody is going to tell him the force he's given his life to for the past decade sees greater value in that little cow than they do him, then that's going to be me." She shoved herself out of the seat and tore the door open, but just had to say one more thing. "God help you when the day comes when you need our help, guv," she said. "This is the beginning of the end."

"It's no such thing—"

"And when the next unsupported claim lands on your desk, and the next one, and the next one, and when the press are camped on your doorstep, and officers are quitting because they've lost faith in their employer," she said. "You'll know exactly who to blame. This isn't a question of right or wrong. This is a question of loyalty." She shook her head sadly as she reached for the door to close it behind her. "And you just got it wrong."

CHAPTER FORTY-FOUR

"No, she said something about the firm," Gold was saying when Freya got to the incident room doors. She stood outside, peering through the little windows in the doors, exactly as she and Ben used to do in the early days. "Something about Reilly Haulage being made of bad blood."

Ben was at the whiteboard, as lost as Freya had been. He turned to Chapman.

"Can we look into the firm? Make the requests for whatever warrants we need, and take a deep dive into the administration. Who's listed as a director? Is it just Robert? Is Albert still listed? In which case, what is the share split? Would Robert have anything to gain from a business perspective if his dad died?"

"He's got an alibi, though," Nillson said.

"He also has money," Ben said. "He's not exactly a powerful figure, but he does own a haulage firm, and I'll bet there are more than a few people out there who owe him favours."

"Aye," Gillespie said, nodding along. "He strikes me as being someone who would take a backhander here and there."

"Exactly," Ben said. "He's given himself a questionable alibi by claiming he was at home with his housekeeper, but that doesn't mean to say he hadn't arranged it. Who has he been speaking to? Do we have his phone records?"

"He's on the phone twenty-four-seven, guv," Gold said. "We were looking through his phone records earlier."

"Have we put names to each of the numbers?"

"Most of them," she replied, slipping a piece of paper from her file. "Most of them are drivers of his or employees of some description, and then there are customers of his, but there are a few numbers we couldn't pin down."

"Unregistered?"

"International," she replied. "Most likely customers. There's an engineering firm in Holland he speaks to frequently, quite a few in France, Spain…" she looked up from the paper. "The list goes on. We have managed to segregate some of the international mobile numbers and pair them with their respective businesses. For example, there's only one customer in Holland, so we've grouped the Dutch mobile numbers together with it. The same for a few others."

"Good idea," he said.

"Well, it's not that good. We've still got two dozen numbers we can't identify."

"Okay," Ben said, pacing back and forth while Freya watched on with pride. "What about frequency? Who does he speak to most?"

"Nadia," Gold said. "At least every hour."

"His housekeeper?"

"Well, she probably does more for him than clean his house," Gold said.

"Aye, ain't that the truth," Gillespie said with a long exhale and a mucky smile. All eyes turned on him, and he held his hands up in defence. "I know, I know. Think before I speak, yada yada—"

"Anyone else?" Ben said. "Who does he speak to regularly? Or, more to the point, is there anyone he's been speaking to recently that he doesn't usually speak to as often?"

"Ah, gotcha," Gold said.

"That's one for you," Ben told her. "Did he speak to anybody around the time of the murder or shortly after?"

"I'm on it," she said.

"Good, Cruz, I need you to go back to Pound Road, please," Ben continued.

"Eh? Not door to door, surely?" he replied. "I thought Jewson was the new door knocker? Where is she, anyway?"

"Who cares?" Gillespie added.

"I need somebody I can trust for this,' Ben explained. "And no, you won't be knocking on doors. I need you to walk the length of the street searching for the murder weapon. I know we've had uniforms go over it, but we weren't necessarily dealing with a murder then, and they don't have your experience."

'Oh, right," Cruz replied, his tone altering into something far more positive. "Just in the gardens, then?"

"The gardens, the gutter, under cars. Somebody hit Albert Reilly with something with a sharp corner. They left the house through the rear door, turned left onto the road, and then, I don't know, either got on their bike or in their car. If it was Harris, he'd have been carrying it on his bike."

"He could have dropped it when the lorry hit him," Nillson said, to which Ben clicked his fingers. "Good, good. Get hold of Souness and see if anything was found at the scene. Don't take his word for it. I want a list, an inventory."

"On it," Nillson replied.

"Cruz, you're on street detail. We're closing in, now."

"All good," he replied. His back straightened, and his chest filled, giving him the look of a randy grouse. "If we need my experience, then, of course."

"Gold, what was in Harris' possessions? Did he have a weapon of any sort? Was he carrying a bag?"

"Want me to call Katy back? She might be reluctant to give us any more information—"

"No, you're right; we'll need to go through the correct channels, which is Souness."

"I can reach out to him," Gillespie said.

"No, not you," Ben said, closing him down. "Nillson. We don't want to put Southwell in a difficult position, so I need you to get to know Souness. Get him on our side."

"Gotcha," she said.

"At the end of today, we should know if Harris was either carrying a weapon, dropped a weapon, or chucked a weapon in a hedge. If all of those are negative, then I say, we focus on Reilly."

"What about the blue car?" Gillespie asked. "If Harris was on a bloody pushbike, then who was driving it?"

Ben stopped, and the whole flow came to an abrupt halt as he stared at his old mate. Even through the window, Freya recognised the pain on his face.

"There *was* no blue car, mate," he said, shaking his head. "Sorry, fella. Eamon Price made a mistake."

"There must have been," Gillespie said.

"Look, maybe he was just in shock. You know how the mind can play tricks on you, mate. Some part of his mind probably recalled the car from earlier in the day and just added it in."

"No, he saw it."

"Jim?" Ben said, bringing his old friend under control. "You can't help him, mate. You can't help them all."

The bags beneath Gillespie's eyes were heavy, dark, and laden with what might be. Any hopes he had of a swan song had finally been quashed.

"So, what do you want me to do?" he asked. "I could go with Cruz. With two of us looking, we'd stand a better chance."

It was then that the responsibility shifted. It was unfair to expect Ben to delay the inevitable. Freya pushed the door, and it opened with a long drawn-out squeak.

Gillespie turned on his seat to see who had entered and read all he needed to read in her expression.

"Ah, come on."

"I'm sorry, Gillespie," she said softly, and the air in the room felt weighted by sorrow and injustice and caught the emotion in her throat just in time. "I'll need your laptop, phone, and anything else."

"This is a joke," he said.

"No," she snapped, and had to swallow once more and blink away a few rogue tears. "No, it's not a joke. It's many things, but a joke, it is not." She gestured back at Granger's office. "He's doing what he has to do. His hand has been forced, and before you say anything, just remember that if this goes any further, each of us will be asked to provide a statement." She looked around the room at each member of the team in turn, then returned her attention to Gillespie. "You will leave and wait to be contacted. Please do not call in, please do not implicate any one of us by calling us on our personal phones. We need to play by the rules."

"I'm on my own, then?"

"No," she said. "But we need to play by the rules. When the time is right, we'll be in touch. All being well, this will be over in a day or so, a week tops."

Slowly, he rose from his chair. His fingers slid over his laptop, as if he was considering shutting it down, but then thought better of it. What was the point?

"So this is it, then, eh? This is how it ends?"

"Just remember what I said," Freya told him. "Believe in the system. We have to believe in the system."

He laughed once, but it was weak and nothing at all like his usual laugh, the memory of which must be embedded in the very fabric of the walls.

"Aye," he said, eventually. "But you know, you're all I've got. I've Katy, and I've you lot. You're like my bloody family."

"Just...just trust in the system," she said again. He cast his gaze at every one of them, offering a silent goodbye in the form of a nod to them all. To Cruz, he reached out and ruffled the young constable's hair. "You'll be alright, Gabby. You'll be alright."

Freya hated to rush him, but now that the order had been given, lingering would only allow for questions to be asked at a later date. She could picture the scene at the inquest, with some judge or other questioning why it took longer than twenty-minutes for Freya to deliver the news and then a further twenty-minutes for Gillespie to leave the building. It was tiny pieces of evidence like that that created doubt and discrepancies.

Slowly, he walked towards the door, pulled it open, and then stepped through with one final look back.

"Jim?" Ben called out, and Freya glared at him, shaking her head.

"Ben, no—" she started, but Ben waved her off, irritated at the interruption.

"Aye?" Gillespie said from the corridor, his voice cracked and dry.

"I can't change what happens in here, but you're a good mate. You should know that. You're a bloody good mate. You're the best mate I have," he said, and Gillespie nodded his gratitude.

"I didn't think you had any mates," he replied, revealing a hint of his former self.

"Well, I don't. Not really. Only you lot. But if somebody deserves the title of most reliable, funny, best company, or whatever, then that's you, mate," Ben said. "In fact, I want you to be my best man."

"Eh?"

"At my wedding. At me and Freya's wedding," Ben said stiffening and filling his chest. "I need you by my side, mate."

CHAPTER FORTY-FIVE

The drive was silent, yet for the first time in as long as Ben could remember, the cause of the silence wasn't their relationship. It was a similar feeling that coursed through Ben's mind, as when his father had called time on their ageing Spaniel. There had been an intangible void in his life, in their house, that was never quite filled, even by subsequent dogs.

The haulage yard was how Ben had imagined it. A pair of fork-lifts were doing the bulk of the work while men in hi-vis vests to-ed and fro-ed. The smell of diesel hung in the chill air as if the low clouds formed an impenetrable barrier. The offices were in a single-storey brick building with a large flat roof and were adjacent to two huge gates. Thankfully, the entrance was a stone's throw from a little greasy spoon cafe, from which far more appealing aromas emanated and were trapped by those heavy clouds: bacon, sausages, even chips. Ben could almost taste the breakfast he would never be allowed to eat.

"Don't even suggest it," Freya muttered.

"What?" he replied innocently and followed her gaze to the cafe. "I wasn't going to—"

"You forget," she said. "I know when you're lying. If I wasn't here, you'd have put an order in already, so it would be cooked by the time you were done with Reilly."

"Oh, leave off—"

"We are getting married in two months," she reminded him. "Do you want to waddle up the aisle, or do you want to look back on the day with fondness?"

"Bloody hell, here's me telling you just to be yourself and that I'd love you no matter what, and the moment a bacon sandwich is on offer, you pull me up on my waistline." He tapped his stomach. "I'm fine. I've got room for a bacon sarnie if I want one."

"So you *were* thinking about it?"

"No, I wasn't," he said, then grinned. "But I am now."

"No," she said. "Aside from the wedding, you would not catch me dead in one of those places."

"Well, we can get a takeaway. Come on, think about that delicious bacon on buttered bread, oozing red sauce when you squeeze down on it."

"If you honestly think that will entice me into stuffing what I can only describe as junk food into my mouth, then you have grossly misjudged me, Ben."

"Have you never had a bacon sandwich? Come on, surely not?"

"Of course, I've had a bacon sandwich," she replied. "The difference is that when I have a bacon sandwich, it is a fine cut of pork with sage in a quality baguette, served with a side of real apple sauce. It is *not* two rashers of cheap bacon, hastily defrosted, stuffed between two slices of Tescos own bread and smothered with tomato ketchup from a bottle that several hundred builders have had near their chops."

"You don't know what you're missing," he told her.

"Oh, I know what I'm missing," she replied. "And you can keep it."

She looked past him, waiting for him to open the door, which he did, and then he held it for her so she could enter. Ben took one last look at the cafe, sighed, and then followed her inside.

"We're here to see Robert Reilly," Freya announced to a young woman who wasn't sitting behind a reception desk but rather occupying the desk nearest the door. She wore boots and an anorak, over a hi-vis vest, which gave Ben the impression her role entailed her popping outside from time to time.

"I'm afraid he's not here. Have you got an appointment?" Slightly bemused, she reached for an A4 diary, flicked it open, then, after tonguing her index finger, whipped through the pages until she found the right day. "He's nobody booked in."

By the time the woman looked up from the diary, Freya was holding her warrant card up for her to see, and the young woman suddenly caught on.

"Ah," she said. "Right. I'll just get him on the phone. He won't be too far away." She reached for the phone but stopped when Freya let the printed search warrant unfurl. "What's that?"

"Do I really need to read it to you?" Freya asked.

"A search warrant?" she replied. "There's nothing here. What do you hope to find?"

"Nothing,' Freya said. "I hope to find absolutely nothing." She peered about the room, her eyes settling on a closed door. "I doubt I will, though."

"You can't go in there," the woman said when both Ben and Freya marched towards the door. "What do you mean, you doubt you will? You doubt you'll what?"

"Find nothing," Freya replied as Ben reached past her to open the office door. She gazed at the woman until she stepped out of Freya's way. "I never have been one to cling to hope."

The office was large enough for the business owner to demonstrate success to prospective customers, yet Ben doubted it had been decorated since the little sign on the desk read *Albert Reilly*. There were framed photos of the fleet over the years; Leyland DAFs parked in formation with a young Albert Reilly standing proudly before them. Other photos showed a young Robert tailing his father as he oversaw the offices being built. Each photo depicted a milestone in the firm's success. Even the evolution of the logo was evident in the timeline, which was little more than a blue arrow but had somehow been modernised to reflect the digital world.

"Right, you start with those filing cabinets, Ben," Freya said. "I'll start over here."

"What is it you're looking for?" the woman asked.

"A cup of tea," Freya said. "I don't suppose you know where he keeps them, do you?"

"Tea?"

"Oh, you are kind," Freya replied with a smile, and Ben had to turn away so as not to spoil the effect. "Neither of us has sugar, thank you."

The woman seemed startled and confused at being tricked until Freya stepped over to the door, coaxed her out, and then closed it.

"Photograph everything," Freya said, her tone sharp and focused. "We haven't got the luxury of half a dozen officers, and we can't take all this away, so photos will have to do. Send them to the team so Chapman can get to work on them."

"I'd love to know what it is you think we're going to find," Ben mused as he tugged open the top drawer of the first of three filing cabinets and found it fit to burst. "Christ."

"I hope to find nothing," Freya said again.

"So what the hell are we doing here?"

Freya took her time to answer. She poked her way through Reilly's desk drawers like a bored teenager on a 'bring your child to work' day.

"Harriet Underwood told Gold that this business was started with bad blood, didn't she?"

Yes, but—"

"Albert Reilly took early retirement, unannounced, and seems to have washed his hands of the place. He wasn't living in splendour as his son is."

"Right, so? My old man is worth a few quid, but he's been wearing the same pants since mum was alive. It's a generation thing. They just manage money better than the younger generations. They've experienced hardship. I don't know why, but they'd rather see it in their bank than spend it."

"Right now, little miss-whatever-her-name is switching on the kettle. While that's boiling, she'll find somewhere discreet to call Robert Reilly, after which two things will happen. Reilly will drop whatever it is he's doing and come storming in here making all kinds of demands and threats, but before that, he'll make a call."

"Who to, his lawyer?"

"No, somebody...involved," she said. "He's up to no good. Do you remember how he watched us from his window on Monday morning?"

"Oh, you mean the man we'd just informed his father had died. Yeah, I remember."

"He's got something to hide, and all credit to him, he's hiding it well so far."

"Freya, you're not making sense—" Ben started, but the door burst open and in walked one of the men they had seen outside.

"What the bloody hell is going on in here?" he said, and Ben waited to see how Freya wanted to play this particular scene she had envisaged.

"Oh, you must be Mr Reilly's colleague," she said, making a show of fishing her warrant card from her pocket to show him. "Detective Chief Inspector Bloom. This is Detective Inspector Savage. We're here to conduct a search of the premises."

"You what? You can't do that—"

"I assure you I can, and I am," she continued. "Why don't you make yourself useful and give Inspector Savage a hand? Now, do you know if the files are arranged by date or by customer?"

"This is an outrage—"

"I'd appreciate it if we could differentiate between customer files and employee files."

"What are you looking for?"

"I don't know," Freya said. "That's why we're searching the place." Her smile left him no room to argue. He just stood there, aghast. "Sorry we didn't catch your name, Mr..."

"Shaw," he said. "Graham Shaw."

He was a burly figure, a man's man, who, despite his fifty-something years, was confident enough to make his presence known.

"Thank you, and what is it you do here, Mr Shaw?"

"Foreman," he said. "I run the place."

"Oh, so you manage the lorries in and out, I suppose?"

"Aye, s'right. I create the routes."

"Is that difficult?" Ben asked.

"Harder than you think. You've got to know the customers, see? We send a lorry to Holland to deliver a load; we don't want it coming back empty, do we?"

"So, you line up other customers who might have an inbound cargo?" Ben said. "To make the trip worthwhile."

"Something like that, yeah."

"And who would you say is your biggest customer?"

"Do you mean which of our customers is the most successful, or which of them uses us most?"

"The latter," Freya said.

"Frenchies," Shaw said. "Harry French and Co.. They make cable up in Yorkshire. Fibre or something, I don't know. Anyways, they do alright. We cover their internationals. They keep the domestic stuff in-house."

"I see," Ben said. "And where would I find Harry French's file?"

Shaw appraised Freya, then studied Ben and smirked.

"Something funny?" Ben asked.

Shaw tore open the second drawer down, flicked through the files, and then heaved a stack of them out before slamming them on the desk in front of Freya.

To Ben's surprise, Freya reached up and scooped her hair into a bunch. With a few deft movements, she tied it in a bun atop her head, revealing the true extent of her scar from the cheek up to her eye. She watched as Shaw stared unabashed, then lowered his gaze.

"No," he said, finally. "There's nowt funny at all."

Freya reached forward, grabbed a file and opened it flat before her. She paused after a second or so and looked up at Shaw. "You might want to give what's her name a shout," she said. "She's just putting the kettle on, and I rather suspect we're in for a long day."

CHAPTER FORTY-SIX

"Oh my!" Chapman said, which wasn't necessarily what surprised Cruz when he heard it. It was more the fact that she had said anything at all. He could go for days without hearing her utter a single word, and even then, it was often just, 'Yes, guv,' or "I'm on it.'

"What is it?" Gold asked, always one to offer help when one of them needed it. She was like the mother of the group. In fact, she was the only one of them who actually had children.

Chapman pushed her seat back from her desk, staring at her screen as if it was on fire.

"Ben's sending me some docs to go through," she said.

"So? Oh, don't tell me they're images of—"

"No, they're just the Reilly Haulage docs," she said, then turned her screen for them to see an endless list of emails feeding into her inbox. Even in the short space of time that Cruz looked, at least a dozen more came in. "I thought he'd just box everything up."

"They didn't have time to get a team together," Cruz told her. "I suppose it beats heaving them into the boss's car."

"Right," Chapman said, resigning herself to the task ahead. "There goes my evening."

The printer suddenly whirred into life like an ageing bear waking from a long winter.

"Speaking of evenings," Gold said to Nillson. "How did yours go?"

"Sorry?"

"I heard you had a date. How was it? Anyone we know?"

Nillson opened her mouth to speak, but no words came out.

"Oh, didn't it go well?" Gold said.

"It..." Nillson started, then, shaking her head, she shoved herself out of her chair and stormed out of the room. The doors slammed closed behind her as if having picked up on her mood.

"Was it something I said?" Gold asked nobody in particular.

Of all of the people in the room, Cruz empathised with her. If there was something to put his foot in, he'd been there, done it, and bought the T-shirt, and having worked with Gillespie for what felt like decades, he guessed the source of the issue.

"I'm not sure the date was common knowledge," he said quietly.

"What? Course it was. I heard Ben talking about it this morning."

"Right, and who do you think told Ben?"

Gold shrugged.

"Freya?"

Cruz shook his head.

"Who was working with Nillson last night?"

Gold looks away as if trying to recall.

"Her and Jim went to the forensics place, didn't they?"

Cruz nodded.

"Yep," he said. "What you have there is the direct result of our old mate, Jim Gillespie and his giant gob, which, by the way, knows no boundaries."

"Ah, Christ," Gold said. "Well, why did she tell him?"

"He has a way of getting things out of you," Cruz said confidently, having fallen foul of Gillespie's mouth on more occasions than he cared to remember. "My guess is that they went to the forensics unit. Gillespie was fart-arsing around looking at all the cars, or maybe he stopped for a burger, and Nillson told him to hurry up because she had a date to get to."

"Eh?"

"It's as easy as that," he said. "That's how he gets you. You let one little secret slip out, and…" he clapped his hands together. "Bang, he's got you in his trap."

"You're a fine one to talk," Chapman said without looking up. The printer was in full flow now, and she was in some kind of trance, printing documents and then scrolling to the next email.

"What's that supposed to mean?"

Chapman tore herself from her screen for a moment.

"Who told that little minx all about Jim's affairs?"

"Eh?"

"It wasn't me," she said. "Was it you, Jackie?"

"No, of course not," Gold said.

"And it certainly wasn't Jim," Chapman continued. "Which leaves…"

She stopped short of saying his name, and despite wanting to, he couldn't bring himself to lie to them.

"Well, I might have mentioned a few things in passing," he said. "You know what it's like. You're sitting in a car with someone, waiting for something to happen, and you know? You just get talking don't you?"

"And I suppose it had nothing to do with the fact that you fancy her?"

"What? No—"

"There goes DC Cruz, offering all his worldly experience to the young, inexperienced lass in his passenger seat."

"It wasn't like that—"

"There she is, listening intently with her blouse ready to burst open," Gold added. "You stuck up for her."

"I did what?"

"You stuck up for her. When she made a thing about what Jim said, you were the only one who stuck up for her."

"Well, yeah, but—"

"You took her under your wing in the hope that she would look up to you, didn't you?"

"No, she was a cow," he said.

"You gave her all the ammunition she needed to make a scene," Chapman said. "If she hadn't known all that stuff about what he got up to before he met Katy, she wouldn't have said anything. All she needed was a way in, and you gave it to her."

"I didn't."

"What's this?" Nillson asked, having reentered the room far more quietly than she had left.

Gold caught her attention as she took her seat.

"Sorry, Anna," she said. "I didn't know it was a secret. I never would have—"

"No, it's fine," Nillson said. "And you're right. It didn't go well."

"Well, I'm sorry," Gold said again. "I hope he paid for the meal."

Nillson smiled back at her, unwilling to reveal any more.

"We were just saying it's all Cruz's fault that Jim's been suspended," Chapman said.

"Oh, really?"

"Yeah, it's quite simple, really. She sat in his passenger seat, undid a few buttons on her blouse, and when he finally stuffed his tongue back into his mouth, he told her everything she needed to know about Jim."

"That sounds about right," Nillson said. "She'd eat you alive, Gabby. I'd steer clear if I were you."

"I do not fancy her," he said. "Besides, she hasn't exactly shown me any decency."

The three women stopped, and he suddenly realised he'd taken the first shovel full of soil from a hole he hoped he would never have to dig.

"What do you mean?" Nillson asked. Had the question come from Gold or Chapman, he might have been able to deflect it or tell a half-truth. But Nillson could floor him with one stare, and the tone of her voice was enough to shake the truth from him. "What did she do to you?"

"Oh, you know," he said.

"No," she replied, short and curt. "No, we don't."

He took a deep breath and closed his eyes, then, like a suspect staring at infallible evidence, he confessed.

"She isn't as good as she makes out," he began. "Remember the quarry job? I told everyone how it was her that found the body and the evidence and the rest of it?"

"Yeah?" Nillson said, her voice probing like a tiger's claw coaxing a mouse from its hole.

"She accused me of being sexist."

"What?"

"She accused me of saying something sexist, but I didn't. I swear I didn't."

Enough time had passed since Chapman had right-clicked on a document and sent it to the printer that the print queue had depleted, and the old machine wound down with a tired sigh.

"She blackmailed you?" Nillson said, to which he nodded.

"I didn't mean for it to go this far, but it just got out of hand," he said. "Next thing you know, she's wormed her way in here, and I couldn't say a thing against her."

"Because you feared she would use it against you?"

"Yeah," he said. "It wasn't my fault she did what she did to Jim, but you're right," he said quietly. "This is all my fault."

CHAPTER FORTY-SEVEN

As with all monotonous tasks, they developed a system. Ben would take a file from the filing cabinet and open it on Reilly's desk before turning every page for Freya to photograph. She would then send the photos to Chapman while the woman, they had subsequently learned was named Lucy Froggart would reassemble the file and return it to the cabinet. Shaw's role was to answer any questions Freya had, which were many. What did this customer want moving? How long have they been customers of Reilly Haulage? Where are they based?

The answers spawned very few noteworthy matters, but the point was that Shaw was with them, and while he was with them, he was unable to contact Reilly.

Two hours had passed when Freya, who was waiting at the desk with Ben's phone ready to take the next batch of images, looked up at Ben, who stood beside the filing cabinet with hands empty.

"That's it," he said. "That's all of it."

"We done then, are we?" Shaw grumbled. "I've work to do, you know?"

"This can't be it," Freya said. "Reilly Haulage has been going since the eighties. You're not trying to tell me that four decades of invoices and employee records are stored in three filing cabinets?"

"No, the rest is archived," Froggart said, which earned her a glare from Shaw. "What?"

He shook his head discreetly, but it was obvious enough for Freya to notice.

"How interesting," Freya said. "And where is this archive?"

Shaw pulled a face to Froggart as if to say, 'Well, go on then, you might as well tell them now'.

"We use an independent firm," she said. "Lindum Records and Digital Archiving."

"Go on," Freya said.

"Well, we're obliged to keep records for ten years," she said. "So, every year, we do a kind of a clear out. They collect the old files, scan them, and then store the originals."

"And what is it that determines an old file?"

"Oh, you know," she replied. "One-off customers, finished contracts, that type of thing. Anything we don't need to access on a day-to day-basis, really."

Ben looked quizzically at Freya, whose mind was interrogating the system for a flaw or a thread to pull on." She reminded Freya of Chapman. Perhaps it was the way she held the collar of her blouse together; it was a defensive posture that might have been the result of working in a male-dominated environment.

"So, therefore, the files we've just photographed are only the most recent customers—"

"Within the last year, yes."

"Or, perhaps the up-to-date contracts with long-standing customers?"

Froggart considered the question, then nodded.

"Sounds about right, yeah."

"There were two files that were significantly larger than the others," Freya started.

"Harry French and Co. and Gdansk Tanks," Froggart said.

"Gdansk Tanks?"

"Oil tanks," Shaw cut in. "They supply most of Europe."

"And they're called Gdansk Tanks, are they?"

"No, they're called Zawsze Zbiornik, but it's a bit of a mouthful, so the old man nicknamed them Gdansk Tanks."

"The old man? Albert Reilly?"

Shaw shrugged. "Course."

"So, they've been customers of yours since Albert Reilly was in charge?"

"As has Harry French, Dolomites, Wonder Weld...do you want me to go on?"

"No," she said. "No, but I'd like a list of customers that Albert Reilly worked with and still have a live contract."

"What? That'd take ages," Shaw said.

"Well, you'd better get started then," Freya said, looking up at Ben. "Shall we take a look outside?"

"I could show you around if you want," Shaw said. "Lucy'll put the list together, and we can't have you wandering around on your own. It's a health and safety thing, forklifts and whatnot."

Freya eyed him, studying his body language. He was doing his best not to seem too keen, but the idea of them walking around the yard had clearly piqued some kind of anxiety.

"Can you manage that, Lucy?" she asked, to which the young girl nodded. "Should be easy enough."

"Very well, Mr Shaw. You shall be our chaperone," Freya said. "Lucy, how long do you need?"

"An hour or so," she replied, and Freya wrote Chapman's email address on the back of one of her contact cards. She handed it to Froggart. "Send it to this email address for my attention, will you?"

Froggart nodded and watched as Freya led them from the office.

Shaw followed up on his health and safety concerns by

retrieving two hi-vis vests from a drawer. The company name was printed on the back, and they were clearly a one-size-fits-all affair.

"Should have hard hats really but I won't tell if you won't," he said.

"Let's just hope nothing lands on my head," Freya joked, to which Shaw said nothing. Instead, he held the door for them. "So, let me get this straight," she continued once they were all outside and the stench from the cafe next door filled the air. "One of your longest-standing customers is this Harry French?"

"Aye, s'right."

"Who are based in the UK but require Reilly's to take their cables to Holland?"

"Aye. They've got a disti near Rotterdam."

"A disti?"

"Distributor," he explained. "From there, the cables go all over Europe."

"But, it would be bad business for one of your lorries to come back empty-handed. So...?"

"So, we line up a collection destined for the UK, Ireland, or wherever really. If we can get some return work from Rotterdam, then great, but sometimes we send the drivers on to make a collection. It's all about striking a balance between fuel, wages, and the value of the load."

"So, for example," Ben said. "You could send a lorry load of cables to Rotterdam, then send the driver on to Albania, France, or something?"

"Potentially, yes. I mean, if we sent them on to Albania, we'd need a full load to make it work. Wouldn't send them on for one box, like. But a lorry load, then, yeah. If it's worth our while."

"You make regular journeys for Harry French. Presumably, you have some regular return trips?"

Freya listened to the two men discussing logistic efficiencies, but busied her mind with the proceedings before her. The forklift trucks were whizzing around, loading two lorries with cargo from an area at the far end of the yard.

"What's happening here?" Freya asked, interrupting their conversation. She gestured at the melee of activity.

"Loading up," Shaw said, pointing to the furthest lorry from them. "Dolomites going down south."

"Dolomites?"

"Bathroom fittings," Shaw said. "He'll be coming back with a load of recycled paper, believe it or not."

"Recycled paper?" Freya said. "You drive recycled paper across the country in a diesel lorry? Doesn't that defeat the purpose?"

"They could always cut down more trees," Shaw replied.

"What about that one?" she said, pointing to the second lorry. "The one with the side thing open."

"That's a curtain sider," Shaw explained.

"And what are those things being loaded on?"

"Tanks," Shaw said. "Oil tanks."

"From Gdansk?"

"Aye," he said. "Those are going down to Grantham. There's another lot going up to Glasgow."

"And you've been doing this for Gdansk Tanks since Albert Reilly was in charge, have you?"

Shaw nodded.

"I tell you what, we must have had thousands or more come through here. They're awkward, though. You know, because of the size and shape of them. Can only get eight on a load. But it makes the return trip worthwhile."

"You must have a good relationship with Harry French and the owners of Gdansk Tanks," Ben said.

"Not me," Shaw said. "No, that's all down to Albert and Robert. Things were easier back then, I s'pose. Fewer firms to compete with. These days, any bloke with a van thinks he's a haulage firm. They don't understand, though, see? Licenses, legislation, tax. Changes all the time, it does. We've got a bloke in there who does nothing but keep us on the right side of the law. S'like a moving bloody goalpost."

"Well," Freya said. "As interesting as all that is, I think we've taken enough of your time."

"Eh? Don't you want to see the maintenance log?" He pointed to what looked like an old shed beside the River Witham, with huge double doors, and from which the local radio station blared.

"We're not really interested in how you maintain the lorries, Mr Shaw."

"What?"

"But you can expect another team to pay you a visit for that. I imagine they'll be keen to see which corners are cut."

"Well, aren't you going to wait for Robert?"

"Why, is he coming?" She grinned at him, knowing full well that the first thing he would have done when he found out who they were would be to have called his boss.

"Well, I mean, you've been through his paperwork. He's going to want to know why, surely?"

"I rather expect that if Mr Reilly was going to show up, he would have done so by now," she said. "Which tells me he has a more pressing engagement." Shaw studied her as if bewildered by the way her mind worked. "And I, for one, would love to know what could be more important than the police searching his premises."

It pleased her to see him squirm. It wasn't a confession as such but it was a clear indication of guilt. Identifying the cause of the guilt was another challenge altogether, but at least she had a strong inclination to delve deeper into the Reilly Haulage business.

"He said he needed to go to Lincoln nick," Shaw said reluctantly as if they had shone lamps in his eyes. "Something to do with the accident. Some copper said it would be in his interest to go in voluntarily; Souness or something."

"Sergeant Souness?" Ben said.

"Yeah, that's him," Shaw replied. "Look, he's a good man, a good employer. He don't deserve none of this."

"None of what, Mr Shaw?" Freya asked.

"Well, this," he said. "The searches and the interviews. He's done nothing wrong."

"Well, perhaps when Sergeant Souness has finished with him, and I've finished with him, and if we find that he, as you say, is not responsible for any shortcomings," Freya said, and she took a step closer to him so that she might look closely into his eyes. "Then perhaps we'll be forced to look further afield."

"I see," he replied, forcing himself to meet her inquiring gaze.

"Thank you for your time, Mr Shaw," she told him as she handed him her hi-vis vest, then turned to walk towards her car. She stopped as if struck by a thought. "Oh, and by the way..." he raised an eyebrow in waiting, and she smiled at the confidence he had found. "Don't go anywhere, will you. I think you and I will be getting to know each other quite well in the not-too-distant future."

CHAPTER FORTY-EIGHT

For as long as Nillson could remember, Cruz had been the butt of all jokes in the team, and even when they had both reported to DI Standing, he had been the gopher, the coffee boy, the door knocker, and the one to type up reports.

He had kept the lowest rung of the ladder warm for far longer than he deserved to. He had earned their respect in more ways than one. There had been numerous times when an investigation had had them all stumped, and he had spurted some random fact he had learned at a quiz night or a game show, which had led them down new avenues. There had been a period when being laughed at or belittled had got to him, and during times of duress, his bladder had been known to let go.

Yet, still, he persisted. Any lesser man would have handed in his warrant card and sought a new career, but not Cruz. There was a strength to the smaller-than-average young man she had come to respect. So, to see him on the verge of tears, genuine tears, was a sight she couldn't bear.

"You can't blame yourself, Gabby," she told him, to which both Gold and Chapman agreed. "She played you, and she's using Jim to further her career. That's all there is to it, and if Jim doubts it, you can be sure we'll put him straight."

"He could lose his job, Anna," he said. "He might be a bloody bully and an idiot sometimes, but he doesn't deserve to lose his job. I should have said something. If I had have, then we wouldn't be in this position, would we?"

"You can't change the past, Gab," Gold said. "Besides, you don't think Freya is going to stand for it, do you?"

"She can't save him."

"Right, but she can stop her from doing any more damage."

He smothered his face with his hands and peered through the gaps between his fingers.

"I sometimes wonder if I'm cut out for this," he said. "We're supposed to be upholding the law. It's hard enough to do that, let alone fight battles on the inside."

"Oh, shut up," Nillson told him.

"Eh?" He dropped his hands and stared at her, aghast.

"I said shut up," she repeated. "Look at you. Look at how far you've come. Most people would have given up by now, but you haven't. No, you've stuck it out. Honestly, I've seen the crap you've had to put up with, and if it had been me, I would be working in an office or joined the RAF or something. Alright? Buck your ideas up, and get on with the job. If we let Jewson get to us all, then she's won. I want her to swan back in here, see us all working, succeeding, and realise her efforts have achieved nothing but lose a good man his job."

"A good man?" Gold said. "I thought you were mad at him?"

"I am," she said. "I'm always mad at Jim, but he doesn't do these things out of malice. He just doesn't think, that's all. He's a brilliant copper, but when it comes to social affairs, the man's a moron. He'd be the first to admit it."

"Sorry to break the party up," Chapman said. "But can I ask for some help here?"

She had printed out every document Ben and Freya had sent and laid them all out in piles across the spare desks.

"What do you need?" Nillson asked.

"Well," she began with a sigh. She pointed to two of the desks. "Those are employment records, management accounts, and regulatory files." She turned to the other five desks she had commandeered. "Those are the customer files."

"Right, so what are we doing?" Gold asked, coming to Nillson's side, ready to help.

"I don't actually know," Chapman replied. "I'll get them on the phone."

Chapman picked up the nearest desk phone, dialled Ben's number, and then routed the call through to loudspeaker.

While the call connected, Nillson took a stack of papers from the first two desks and slapped them down in front of Cruz.

"What's this?"

"They look like bank records to me," she said.

"Right, so...?"

"So, look for something," she said as the call was answered.

"DI Savage," Ben said.

"Ben, it's me. Us," Chapman said. "You're on loudspeaker."

"Ah, and I imagine you're staring at a pile of papers as tall as me?"

"No, I've split them out into what I think is internal admin and customer records," Chapman replied. "I've taken over the incident room, actually."

"And you're wondering what on earth is it you're looking for, I presume?"

"Well, yes, actually."

"Well, the bad news is that we don't know," he said. "But Freya is adamant something is either going on or has been going on, and if we can't find it in there, then there's an archive firm we'd need to look into to get the rest of the files."

"Bloody hell," Gold said aloud.

"Bloody hell indeed," Ben said. "We've spoken to the foreman at the haulage yard, and Freya has somehow managed to convince herself, which means that we need to do the spade work."

"I haven't managed to convince myself," Freya cut in. "I'm just sure that there's something here. Gold, when you spoke to Harriett Underwood, what was it she said?"

"Harriet?" Gold said, recollecting the visit to the old lady's house. "Only that the firm would be the death of Robert. Something along those lines, anyway."

"Right, and when we spoke to Mr Shaw, the foreman, he made it quite clear that the largest of their contracts have been going since Albert Reilly was in charge, and given that Albert quit the business in a hurry, leaving everything to his son to manage, I suspect the answer lies in the historical data of those clients."

"Right..." Chapman said, clearly unsure what this meant.

"Chapman, if you check your emails again, you should find a list of customers dating back to when Albert Reilly was in charge," Freya said, and Chapmen stepped over to her computer.

"Yep, it's an email from Lucy Froggart," she called out.

"Good, those are the customers I want you to focus on," Freya continued. "I imagine you've drafted in the team?"

"I had to, guv," she said. "It's colossal."

"That's okay; we'll be there soon to help, as well. I'm afraid it's going to be all hands on deck," Freya said. "Is Jewson there?"

The room was silent for a moment, and Nillson obliged to respond.

"We haven't seen her since she went to meet Granger, boss," she said.

"Oh, that's a shame."

"I'm sure we'll manage without her, though," Nillson added.

"Oh, I'm sure we will," Freya said. "I just wanted somebody to send to the coffee shop, that's all." At this, Cruz raised his head, and his shoulders sagged at the prospect of falling to the lowest rung yet again. "We'll have to swing by on our way back and pick some up," Freya said, to which Cruz appeared perplexed at first and then smiled to himself. Nillson observed this little rise and fall of hopes and dread in private but hoped he would glean some understanding of how far he had come from it. "In the meantime, let's see what we can find, eh?"

"Actually, I have found something," Cruz said, and the whole team turned to face him. He rose from his seat, carrying a few pieces of paper, and came closer to the phone. "Sorry, boss. It's just there seems to be a few discrepancies."

"Such as?" Freya asked.

"Well, I've been through Reilly's personal accounts," he said. "I did all that yesterday and didn't see anything really suspicious. He receives money in the form of dividends from Reilly Haulage, he then splits that out into his pension, an investment GIA, and puts some into an ISA. But he also takes dividends from another firm; an umbrella firm."

"That's standard practise, isn't it?" Ben said. "Tax efficiencies, and all that."

"The thing is, the umbrella firm is a mechanism to invest the profits from Reilly Haulage. I suppose the return is better than a bank can offer."

"Are you going somewhere with this, Cruz?" Freya asked.

"Well, there are payments going into the umbrella account on the fourth of every month. They're from a foreign bank account," he said. "Reilly Haulage also has a payment on the fourth of every month. Without fail."

"What are you saying?"

"I don't know," he said. "It just strikes me as odd. The payment to Reilly Haulage is from a Polish sort code. The payment into the umbrella firm has the same sort code. Different account number, but the same sort code."

"The same bank?" Ben said.

"Looks like it," Cruz said. "The thing is, everything on Reilly

Haulage's side of things ties up. There are invoices here to support each payment."

"Who's the customer?" Freya asked.

"It's a name I can't actually read," Cruz admitted. "But I looked them up. They manufacture oil tanks and fuel tanks, that type of thing."

He waited for the boss to respond, but all they heard was silence.

"Boss?" Nillson said. "Did you hear all of that?"

"Chapman, send me the relevant files, will you?" Freya said eventually. "Build me a case I can use in an interview."

"Will do," Chapman said, taking the files in question from Cruz.

"There's one more thing," Cruz said. "I've got a bloke named Shaw who owns twenty-five per cent shares of the umbrella firm."

"Shaw?"

"That's right. He's the foreman at Reilly's Haulage," Cruz said. "Might be nothing, but—"

"No ideas are nothing, Cruz," Freya told him. "Good work."

"Cheers, boss."

"Nillson, Reilly is with Sergeant Souness," Freya continued. "Call him, will you? Make sure he doesn't let Reilly go, and ask him if we can use one of his interview rooms. Ben and I are taking a detour. Coffee will have to wait, I'm afraid."

"On it," Nillson said, leaving Cruz and Gold to finish the call.

"Gold, while Reilly is with Souness, can you head over to his house?" Freya asked as Nillson stepped over to her desk and dialled the number she had scribbled on her pad.

"Erm, yes, sure," Gold said.

"Talk to the housekeeper, Nadia," Freya said. "See if you can use some of that feminine charm of yours, or whatever you want to call it, to get through to her. You never know; with Reilly out of the house, she might open up and reveal something. There's a link there."

"Okay," Gold said. "Want me to go now?"

"The sooner, the better," Freya said, and in a heartbeat, Gold had scooped up her bag and coat and was heading towards the door. "Cruz, I want you to go through the Polish account. Marry up invoices with payments, and then line them up beside the mystery payments into the umbrella firm."

"I thought you'd ask that," he replied. "It'll take a while."

It was good to see Cruz so engaged. If his discovery broke new ground in the investigation, it could be the boost he needed.

"Souness," a voice said after a few rings.

"Sergeant Souness, it's Sergeant Nillson. We spoke an hour or so ago."

"Oh yeah. I remember," he said. "You're Jim Gillespie's mate."

She winced at the description but let it slide.

"Listen, I understand you have Robert Reilly in custody. I need you to keep hold of him for a while. DCI Bloom and DI Savage are on their way; they want to conduct an interview there while he's in custody. Are you able to facilitate that, or do I need to arrange transport to bring him here?"

"Reilly?"

"Yes, Robert Reilly. Owns Reilly Haulage?"

"Well, I'd love to help," he replied. "But we've only just got the forensics report back, and from what I've read, I've no reason to bring him in at all."

"Sorry?"

"He's not here, Sergeant Nillson," Souness said. "Whoever told you he is is gravely mistaken."

CHAPTER FORTY-NINE

One of the benefits of having such a large property was the privacy the dozens of trees afforded a man like Reilly. One of the drawbacks, however, was that should the owner of such a property decide to have an impromptu bonfire in the far corner of his garden, the smoke could be seen for miles, and the culprit was immediately obvious.

Freya pulled the Range Rover to a stop beside Reilly's Jaguar. Gave the house a cursory glance, then immediately set out, pulling her coat on as she strode around the side of the house. Ben followed, finishing a call with Cruz, but then called out.

"Hold up," he said, and Freya stopped to see what the hold up was. A little black Toyota pulled into the drive and ambled up to where Freya had parked her car.

"Is that—"

"Gold," he finished as Jackie climbed from her car.

"What are you doing here?" she called.

"Long story," Ben said. "Keep Nadia inside. I don't want them conferring."

"Got it," Gold replied as she hurried towards the front door.

The rear gardens weren't exactly manicured. The shrubs were

clipped, and the leaves had been raked, but Freya supposed it pleased Ben to see the molehills that plagued even Reilly's lawn, knowing how it was a topic his father often brought up when they visited. However loathsome the molehills were, their quarry lay further away, in a conclave of what appeared to be old stables.

"Want me to call it in?" Ben asked.

"It wouldn't hurt to have some support en route," she said as they neared. "How's Cruz getting on?"

"Put it this way," he said. "I sometimes wonder if he wouldn't have been better off working for HMRC." They rounded a large apple tree, as Ben explained. "He has an eye for numbers."

Ahead of them were two rows of stable buildings, and on the concrete hardstanding between them, Robert Reilly was busy feeding an old incinerator. He had his back to them, and between feeds, he rested one foot on an old wheelbarrow and leaned on his knee, resembling a farmer watching over his flock.

"Bit damp for a bonfire," Ben called out, startling Reilly. He turned in surprise and made a show of being taken off-guard, presumably a tactic to buy time while he considered an explanation. "We saw the smoke from the road."

"Just having a bit of a clearout," he said. "I suppose you have a warrant."

"We don't need a warrant, Mr Reilly. We're not here to arrest you," Freya said, and thankfully, Ben had the foresight to take a peek inside the incinerator, saving Freya from having to stare into the flames.

"What are you burning?" he asked.

"Oh, just some old papers," Reilly replied.

Freya took a peek inside the wheelbarrow, where a few bundles of paperwork remained.

"Can I see?"

"Do you have a warrant?" Reilly asked then sighed. "Look, I'm looking at a manslaughter charge. You said it yourself: I'm going to have to step up to save Eamon from going down. He's got a family. I haven't. I'm just having a clearout, that's all. I've got no one left. If I go away, who's going to go through all my stuff? The council? No thanks. I'm burning the lot."

"Well, that's interesting, Mr Reilly," Freya said. "Because we spoke to your foreman today: a Mr Shaw?"

"Right, so?"

"Well, he explained that you're obliged to keep certain records for ten years. Is that right?"

"Aye, it is."

"Well, if that's the case," Freya said, and she peered into the wheelbarrow before he could stop her and withdrew the topmost sheet. "Then why are you burning records that belong to your umbrella company?"

"Well, it was just lying around. It must have got caught up in all my personal stuff—"

"Speaking of Mr Shaw," Ben said. "I spoke to one of *our* colleagues just now. He's quite good at spotting trends and anomalies in numbers. He has one of those brains, you know?"

"Right?"

"He did a little digging, and it seems that your umbrella company has been receiving regular payments from a Polish bank."

"So?"

"Well, we were wondering why somebody might make payments to your umbrella firm and not to Reilly Haulage."

"Sorry?"

"Is it to avoid paying tax, Mr Reilly?"

"Look, if you're going to ask about the business, then I'll need to call my lawyer."

"One more question, Mr Reilly," Ben said. "Why does the foreman of Reilly Haulage own twenty-five per cent of the shares in the umbrella company?"

"What?" he said, buying himself more time.

"Did you pay somebody to murder your own dad, Mr Reilly?" Ben asked.

"What, no!"

"Was it Mr Shaw?" Freya asked. "He seemed like he was on your side. I imagine he's quite capable."

"I did nothing of the sort—"

"Why did your dad suddenly give up the business, Mr Reilly?" Ben asked. "The business he spent his life building up, and even went inside for?"

"I don't know. I've never known why he did it."

"But you were glad he did, weren't you?"

"I don't know what you're talking about."

"What is it, drugs?" Ben asked. "Is that it?"

"Drugs?"

"You send a lorry out to Holland to deliver cable for Harry French; they pick up a legitimate load from Gdansk Tanks and fill them up with drugs. Is that it? Your driver brings it all back to the yard, where the drugs are moved on, and the tanks are sent on to the customers. Is that it?"

"I don't know what you're talking about?"

"Let me guess, Mr Reilly," Freya said. "When your father went inside for manslaughter, you took the reins, didn't you? You found a way of balancing the books that he didn't approve of."

Reilly stiffened. He held his head up straight in defiance, and his nostrils flared.

"There we go," Freya said. "The question is, why wait all this time to kill the old man? Was he planning on shopping you in?"

"No comment," Reilly said, which Freya took to be confirmation of guilt.

"What a racket," she said. "But not something you could do on your own, I suppose. That's where Mr Shaw comes in, isn't it?"

"No comment," he replied.

"You give him twenty-five per cent of the shares in the

umbrella firm, and he helps you bring the drugs in. Not a bad little deal, really."

"You don't know what you're talking about," Reilly spat.

"Call your lawyer, Mr Reilly," Freya said. "Ask him to meet you at the station." She nodded at the incinerator, and with a heave, Ben kicked it over. He grabbed Reilly's shovel and, wincing at the flames, dragged the contents onto the hardstanding, treading on the embers to preserve as much evidence as he could.

"Robert Reilly, I'm arresting you for conspiring to murder your father, Albert Reilly," Freya said. "You do not have to say anything, but it may harm your defence if you do not mention, when questioned, something that you later rely on in court. Anything you do say may be given in evidence. Do you understand?"

"What about Souness?" he said, and Freya followed his gaze to the house, where from a ground-floor window, two faces peered out at them.

"I wouldn't worry about him if I were you," Freya said, as she pulled his arms behind his back, ready to cuff. "A manslaughter charge is the least of your worries right now."

CHAPTER FIFTY

Nadia Bartosz was a petite little thing. She wore smart jeans and a black blouse, and she had pulled her hair back into a half ponytail. To top it off, her perfume was delicate yet alluring, not cheap.

Jackie had looked like her once upon a time, before Charlie was born, when she could fit into a size eight or even a six, although she liked to think she was happier. Nadia stared out of the kitchen window, watching as Ben and Freya led Robert Reilly away.

"He is coming back?" Nadia asked.

"I suppose none of us can know that for sure," Gold replied, and Nadia stared at her as if deciphering her response. "What I mean is, it depends."

"This is for the crash? The dead man?"

"No," Gold replied, and Nadia nodded.

"His father, then?" She stared at the man, who was being handed over to two uniformed officers who had met Freya and Ben on the lawn.

"Nadia, is there something you want to tell me?"

The young woman met Reilly's stare as he was led past the house.

"No," she replied. "There is nothing."

"You know, he told us he was with you when his father died. Is this true?"

"Yes, of course," she said. "We were...together. Mr Reilly and me."

"In a professional sense, or...?"

"I don't understand."

"What I mean to ask is, were you and Mr Reilly in a relationship?"

"Relationship?" She said. "Like lover?"

"Well, yes," Gold said. "Do you have feelings for him?"

"Feelings, yes?" She said, and she turned to face Jackie. "Not all good feelings."

"Oh?" Through the window Jackie watched Ben and Freya returning to the outbuildings at the far end of the property. She wanted to bang on the window and ask them to come and help, but they were deep in discussion.

"Mr Robert is sometimes not nice man. Not all the time. Sometimes. Only sometimes."

"Nadia, there's a chance that Mr Reilly will be facing a lengthy prison sentence. If that's the case, then he won't be back here. You can speak freely. Talk to me. I can help."

"No," she said. "No, you cannot help. What can you do? Mr Robert goes to prison; I have nothing. Mr Robert does not go to prison. Then nothing changes. I am in... trap, yes?"

"There are people who can help you, you know?"

"Nobody can help me," she said.

"Nadia, if Mr Reilly acted inappropriately, then you should tell me. We can prosecute. If anything, it'll go against his character, and he won't be able to... he won't be able to hurt anybody else. Do you feel like you could talk to me about it?"

"About it, about what?" Nadia said, shoving herself from the kitchen sink to pace a few steps. "What I say? I say he did... these things, he say no. He say I tell lies. No dowód."

"Dowód?"

She fumbled for the right word.

"Proof," she said. "I have nothing proof."

"We can help you," Gold said, and she stepped up to Nadia to look her in the eye. "If he's touched you or... hurt you, then we can help. We can make sure he never does this again."

"And me?" She replied. "What I do? I get other job?" She shook her head gravely. "This good job," she said. "Money good, time good, work easy."

"So you would let him get away with what he's done so you can keep your job?" Gold asked. "Nadia, that's crazy—"

"Crazy, no," she said. "In my country, all men want this. It is power. My power. Our power. They have money but want this." She waved a hand over her chest. "I have this but want money. It's nothing."

"Nadia, if he assaulted you—"

"What is this, assault? Mr Robert took only what I let him to have. It is man and woman. Business."

Jackie shook her head at what she was hearing.

"And if he goes to prison?" She asked. "What will you do? You can't stay here."

"Maybe I go home," she said, and she seemed to brighten at the thought. Jackie wondered what that home would look like. She imagined thick jumpers, open fires, and a large family where everyone has to shout to be heard.

"There is an alternative," Gold said softly.

"Alternative?"

"Another option," she explained. "Another outcome."

"He go to prison or he not go to prison. What is this other outcome?"

"You could be charged, Nadia," Gold said, which seemed to alarm her. "You could have to go to court."

"Me? I'm nothing. I'm housekeeper. I cook, I clean, I... I take care Mr Robert."

"You lied to us," Gold said.

"Lie?"

"You told us that Mr Reilly was with you when his father was killed. But he wasn't, was he?"

"Of course," she replied, then busied her hands with her hair. "I was here. He was here. We were upstairs. His room—"

"I think you're lying, Nadia," Gold said as nicely as she could. "I think you're scared."

"Why you think this? You come in here, think you know everything."

"Because I've seen it before."

"Scared? What for scared?" Her expression was one of utter disgust like being scared was beneath her. "I have nothing for to be scared."

"If Mr Reilly goes to prison, Nadia, you lose everything."

"I have nothing," she replied with a shrug. "I cannot lose what I do not have."

"You know, if you help me, then I can help you? There are programs. You'd have a new name, a nice house, a new start, Nadia. Do you have family here?"

Nadia listened, then shook her head.

"No family."

"I can make you safe. You never need to worry about him."

"Who said I am worried?"

"I can see it," Gold said, and she tugged on Nadia's shoulder to look her in the eye. "I can see it in your eyes. You're scared. It's not weak to be scared. It's a good thing. It means you're intelligent." Nadia turned her head away and closed her eyes. "Did he pay you?"

"For sex?" Nadia asked. "Not for sex. I am not prostitute."

"I meant to lie," Gold said. "Did he pay you to lie about Monday morning? Is that it?"

Nadia's gullet rose and fell as she swallowed hard, and finally, her eyes rolled round to meet Jackie's. She took a deep breath and for the first time during their conversation, Jackie saw the little girl inside.

"I don't want new name, new place," she said eventually, and she peered out of the window once more. "I want to go home."

CHAPTER FIFTY-ONE

The very thought of going home to wallow in self-pity seemed absurd to Gillespie. There was a real danger of him ordering a curry and cracking open a tinny or two, which meant that when he didn't show up at Kate's that evening, and when he wasn't answering her calls, she would pay him a visit and find him sprawled on the sofa with his belt undone and a line of dried dribble across his cheek. That was one slippery slope he was keen to avoid. Besides, there was no way he was going to let that little minx destroy his career, and there was no way he was going to let her shocking behaviour send an innocent man down.

It was wrong, what he was doing - completely wrong. In fact, it was the type of thing that would destroy any chances he had of salvaging something of his career should the enquiry fall flat and by pure chance he was reinstated. The alternative was drinking himself into a stupor and letting it happen, and he wasn't quite ready for that.

"Mum?" a young child yelled when he rang the doorbell, and he dreaded the idea of having to navigate unruly kids while asking difficult questions. The problem when questioning parents was that they were never quite engaged. They always had an ear out for their bairns, or an eye on the laundry or dishes. "Mum!"

"Alright, I heard you the first time," the mother yelled back. "There's nothing stopping *you* from answering the bloody door, you know?"

"Can't," the boy replied matter of factly. "I'm in the middle of a game. Besides, it could be a strange man. I'm not allowed to speak to strange men."

The woman was cursing under her breath when she answered the door, flopping a grubby old tea towel over her shoulder. She looked him up and down.

"Yes?"

"Ah, you must be Anita," Gillespie said. "Anita Stone. Is that right?"

"Yes," she said, growing curious.

Gillespie tapped his pockets, making a show of searching for his warrant card.

"Damn it," he said, turning away. "I'm sorry to have wasted your time. I've left my ID somewhere."

"What ID?"

"Oh, sorry, I should have explained," he said, taking a step closer to her. "I'm Detective Sergeant Gillespie; I believe you spoke to my colleague a couple of days ago. A PC Jewson?"

"Jewson?"

"About so high," he said, holding his hand at shoulder height. "Mid-twenties, long hair."

"Ah, how could I forget?" she said.

"Aye, she has that affect," he said, feigning embarrassment.

"To be honest, I was surprised she's allowed to go about like that."

"She's not," Gillespie assured her. "But you know what these youngsters are like. They've no idea about the real world, eh?"

"Hear, hear," she said. She eyed him as if making a judgment call. "What is it you need to speak to me about?"

"Well, first of all, may I just say that I'm so sorry for your loss. It's a terrible thing, and if we can do anything at all, you should know we're here. It was about your wee chat with PC Jewson," he said. "You see, she's young, and well, this is a wee bit embarrassing, but she didn't write anything down."

"I see," Anita said.

"But look, I'm just as bad. I haven't even brought my ID."

"It's fine," Anita said. "Look, I can give you a few minutes."

"Aye? You sure? I mean, it's no bother. I can just nip back to the station. I'll be half hour or so."

"No, no," she said, opening the door for him. "Come on. I'd rather not have this hanging over me."

"Aye," he replied. "Well, that's very kind of you." He stepped past her and took in the decor. It was a nice house, or at least it would have been had the hallway not been filled with black bags and a roll of carpet.

"Not getting rid of a body, are you?" he asked as she closed the door behind him.

"Sorry?"

He pointed down at the carpet.

"There's no body in there, is there?"

"Oh, no. Of course not. It was damaged when the burglar broke in, and to be honest, I don't really want to be reminded of it."

"Ah, that's good. Carpet's no good anyway."

"Sorry?"

"A roll of carpet," he said. "It's a terrible way of getting rid of a body. Plastic sheeting is the best. Stops all the fluids from spilling out, if you know what I mean. Lighter too."

"Right," she said, suddenly seeming unsure of her decision.

"Sorry, I'm just trying to lighten the mood. The fact is that I come cap in hand if you get me. She really ought to have made notes or at least written them up when she got back to her car.

But I suppose we all have to learn, don't we? And what with the government making police work harder, we have to be grateful for what we can get."

"I doubt she'll make the same mistake again," Anita said, then gestured at the kitchen at the end of the hallway. "Please, go on through. Just don't break an ankle. My public liability isn't up to date?"

"You what?"

"That was *me* trying to lighten the mood," she said.

"Ah, right," he said as he clambered over the carpet. "Made a right old mess, didn't he, eh?"

"It's not the mess that's the bother," she said. "It's the fact that he's been in here. You know? He's been through our things."

"Have you heard anything from the team investigating the burglary?"

"Have I hell," she said. "And I don't expect to, neither. He's long gone, isn't he? With all due respect, love, you haven't a hope in hell of catching him. He would have slipped into the crowd by now, Never to be seen again."

"Well, you may be right there," Gillespie told her. "In more ways than one."

"Sorry?" She said, her head cocking to one side. "You know who he is?"

"Well, it's hard to know for sure," he said.

"Have you got him?" Anita said. "Have you got him, yes or no?"

He smiled weakly.

"Off the record? Aye, we think so."

"Jesus, some good news at last. I've been sitting here thinking about him and my dad and wondering what the point of it all is. How did you do it? Did he hit somebody else's house? That's what they do, isn't it? Do a few houses at a time."

"Well, I'm not sure if we can really take the credit for catching him, per se," Gillespie said, and she studied him as if she was reading something in his expression. "If you were to thank somebody, then you should probably start with the man who was driving the lorry that your...well, you know?"

"The lorry that killed my father? Sorry, I don't understand."

Then it hit her, and her expression altered entirely.

"Sorry. Bitter sweet, eh?" he said.

"Are you saying he's dead?" she asked, to which Gillespie nodded.

"He was riding the bike the lorry was overtaking when somebody pulled out on him."

She leaned on the wall and stared into space.

"You alright, love?"

"I'm sorry," she said. "I'm not sure how to process it. I should be pleased, but..."

"Aye, " he said. "Aye, it is. Listen, Anita, I'm sorry to ask, but can you remember what else you told her? PC Jewson, I mean. What else did you discuss?"

"Well, there was a bit of mix-up to start with," she said. "Poor girl. She thought somebody had already told me."

"Told you?"

"About my dad," Anita said. "I thought she was here because of the robbery; she didn't know there'd been a robbery and was talking about the..." she broke off, lost in thought.

"Sorry, are you telling me that you found out about your dad through PC Jewson?"

"Well, yes. But she didn't know. How could she have known?"

"That's beside the point, Mrs Stone," he said. "There are ways to deal with these things. I expect that made things awkward. I mean, I can give you the number of somebody if you want to report it; make a complaint."

"No," she said quietly. "No, she had a way about her. You know, she moved the conversation on."

"She manipulated the conversation, you mean? After she just delivered that awful news?"

"She seemed quite persistent," Anita said. "She wanted to know about my father's relationship with Albert."

"Look, Mrs Stone, I can only apologise for what she put you through—"

"There's no need," she replied. "He's gone. It doesn't matter how I find out. What matters is that he's gone."

The door along the hallway opened, and a young boy stepped out.

"Mum?"

"One minute, love," she said.

"Mrs Stone, I think I've taken enough of your time. It's clear you need time to grieve," Gillespie said.

"Mum?"

"Just a minute," she snapped, then looked up at Gillespie. "Sorry. I've been a bit short recently. Having to deal with all this on my own."

"Ah, sorry. I saw the van and figured you were married."

"Oh, I am," she said. "Sorry, he's just... he works a lot. That's all."

"Ah, good. Well, as long as you're not entirely alone," he said. "What does he do? Your husband? Where does he work?"

"Oh, boring, really. He's in logistics. Travels quite a lot, but he'll be home tomorrow." She stared at the mess in the hallway. "We were supposed to go away, but then all this happened, and well, he got a call, so I ended up with it. Hopefully, we can get all this sorted so we can go away."

"Well, Mrs Stone, thank you for your time, and once again, I'm so sorry about the erm..."

"Misunderstanding?"

"Aye," he said. "The misunderstanding. I'll see to it she doesn't make that same mistake again, eh?"

"Ah, let her be. There're far more important things in life to worry about," she said. "Anyway, was it helpful?"

"Was what helpful? The chat?"

"No, what I told her," she said. "I mean, the way she reacted when I told her, I got the impression I'd just cured cancer or something."

"Sorry, when you told her what, exactly, Mrs Stone?" He said. "What is it you told her?"

CHAPTER FIFTY-TWO

"Look at all this," Ben muttered as he sifted through the ash. It was one of the many reasons Freya admired him. He was never one to shy away from getting his hands dirty; a real boy at heart. "God knows what he's burned here." He pulled a partially burned piece of paper from the embers, blew the ash from it, and then carefully dabbed at the glowing edges to prevent any more evidence from being incinerated. "It's disappearing before our eyes."

"Photograph it," Freya told him. "Photograph every last scrap before it's gone."

At this, she pulled her own phone from her pocket and crouched beside him. Some pieces of paper were barely touched, while only fragments of others remained: corners and indecipherable segments.

Ben grabbed the shovel to scoop a large stack of papers from the ash, then upturned it to spread the documents out on the concrete hardstanding. The naked flames had all but abated, but the gentle breeze that wandered across Reilly's expansive, mole-ridden lawn kept the cinders alight, and slowly, they ate away at the evidence before them.

"Reilly Holdings and Investments," Ben said, waving the corner of a piece of paper at Freya. "His umbrella firm." He set the scrap of paper down, photographed it, and then added it to the pile they were making, which they weighed down with a heavy rock. "Having a clear out, my backside."

"It's my fault," Freya told him, to which Ben stopped and stared at her.

"Sorry, did you just admit to being wrong?"

"I thought that when we turned up at his yard, he would come flying in," she said. "I should have foreseen something like this."

"I'm not sure you can beat yourself up about this," he said. "How were we to know he had all this, whatever it is, at his house?"

She held up a scrap of paper.

"Most of this is in Polish," she said.

"Gdansk Tanks?"

"That would be my guess," Freya replied. "Although, I dare say we'll need to find a translator if we're to make any sense of this at all."

She held a sheet up to the dim sunlight while he studied his phone.

"This one has some payment details on it," she said, then caught the shift in his expression. "What is it?"

He held the phone up for her to see the name of the incoming caller.

"Gillespie?" She said. "Don't answer it."

"Freya, the poor bloke is—"

"We are very likely going to be investigated," she said, tugging the phone from his hand and hitting the red button to reject the call. "Imagine what the IOPC would say if there were records of either you or me or anyone on the team, talking to him on the phone a matter of hours since he was suspended? How would that look?"

She handed him the phone back.

"No contact," she said. "Let's just get through this investigation so I can put time into developing a plan. I can't do both, I'm afraid; not well anyway."

"Ah, you're probably right," he said, staring at the phone. "Maybe some time on his own is what he needs? Better not leave it too long, though. He'll be buried beneath a mountain of empty Stella Artois cans and pizza boxes."

"I doubt Katy will let that happen," Freya said. "I get the impression she enjoys order. The slightest hint of dirt or germs in her kitchen, and she'll be whipping her microscope out. Are they living together?"

"No, he still has his place. I think they stay over more often than not, but they're not quite ready to give up their freedom," Ben replied. "So what's the theory here, then? Albert Reilly established a contract with the long-term customers, and when Robert took over, he exploited those contracts and their...logistical know-how by using the return journeys to bring in drugs?"

"I wouldn't call it a theory," Freya said. "It's an idea. I mean, why else would he be buying all of this? Why else would Shaw have been so confident we wouldn't find anything, despite there clearly being something amiss? Reilly Haulage is as clean as a whistle, Ben," she told him. "The dirt is in...what did you say it was called? Reilly Holdings and Investments? What we need to find is evidence of a crime."

"Alright," Ben said. "Alright, let's say we do find something. Let's say you're right; they are bringing in drugs. How does this link to Albert Reilly? We are, after all, investigating a murder. The last time I looked, we don't represent His Majesty's Customs and Excise."

"That's the tricky part," she replied. "But I'm not giving this lot up." She jabbed an index finger at the mess before them. "The answer is in here, even if we can't bloody well read it." She slapped the papers to the ground. "Something happened," she said. "Albert

Reilly was running a successful business right up to the point he went to prison."

"Hardly a measure of success," Ben said as he set to work with the shovel.

"The accident was unfortunate," Freya said. "But it speaks volumes. Albert Reilly took ownership. He held himself accountable and served the time for it. Don't you see what that means?"

"That he was a naive old man with a guilty conscience?"

"That he was a good man," Freya said. "With a good heart. Who ran the business while he was inside?"

"Well, I suppose Robert stepped up," Ben said, jabbing the shovel into the ashes.

"How long has Shaw worked there?"

"Eh?" He said. "I don't know."

"Get Cruz on the phone, will you?"

Ben leaned the shovel against the incinerator, navigated his phone, and then initiated the call.

"Any particular message?" He asked.

"I want to know when Shaw joined the business," she replied, as Ben dropped to a crouch and then set the call to loudspeaker.

"Ben?" Cruz said when he answered the call.

"I think I've got something."

"Go on," Ben said.

"I've...well, Chapman and me, we've managed to link up every transaction from the Polish bank to a return trip. Every month," he continued. "Every month, Reilly's send a shipment of cable to Holland, then return via Gdansk with a legitimate load of industrial tanks, and every time they do that, which is around the fourth of every month, Reilly Holdings and Investments receives a sum of money from the Polish bank."

"How much are we talking?" Freya asked.

"Fifty-thousand Euros, ninety-thousand Euros, seventy-thousand," Cruz said. "It's big money."

"Cruz, have you got the employee records there?"

"I've got them," Nillson cut in. "I'm just looking for any anomalies."

"You won't find any," Freya said. "Reilly Haulage is watertight. When did Shaw begin there?"

"Shaw?"

"He's the foreman," Ben added, and they waited a few seconds for her to find the right file.

"Graham Shaw," Nillson said. "Jesus. He's been there since nineteen-eighty-four."

"Working as the foreman?" Freya said. "I don't know about you, but if I was in a job for three decades without receiving a promotion, I'd have a few questions."

"What are you saying?"

"I'm saying we need to do some digging on Shaw," Freya replied. "Where does he live?"

"One sec," Nillson replied. "Oh, blimey."

"What?" Freya said. "What is it? What have you found?"

"Well, put it this way, I'd be surprised if the foreman of a haulage firm could afford a postcode like this one."

"Right, let's pull this together," Freya replied. "You can be sure Reilly Haulage is as clean as a whistle. They would have gone to great lengths to see to that. But Reilly Holdings and Investments is where the issues are." Freya stood and paced, gathering the information into some semblance of order. "Nillson, get this onto the whiteboard, will you? I need a timeline."

She heard the young Sergeant move across the room and the faint click of a pen lid.

"Ready when you are," Nillson said.

"Roger Havers works for Albert Reilly," Freya began.

"He started in the early eighties," Nillson added. "I saw his record a while ago."

"Right. Roger Havers has an accident which leads to a death."

"That was mid-eighties," Chapman added.

"Albert Reilly takes responsibility and is handed a

manslaughter sentence. Meanwhile, Robert Reilly takes command," Freya said. "The firm probably received some bad press as a result of the accident, who knows. But what I am certain of is that while his father was serving time, Robert Reilly and Graham Shaw sought other ways to increase the firm's revenue."

"Drugs," Ben added for clarity.

"Right. But all we have is a pile of mostly burnt paperwork to go on, so we'll need a Polish interpreter."

"How does this link to Albert Reilly's murder?" Nillson asked. "Sorry, I just can't make it out."

"Well, what did Albert do as soon as he was out of prison?"

"He retired," Cruz said. "He gave it all up."

"And why did he retire?"

"I suppose he'd just spent the best part of a decade inside, so he was looking to enjoy the rest of his life."

"Yet, he took no assets from the business. He didn't cash in his pension or his shares. He simply handed it all to his son. Why would he do that?"

A moment of silence followed, and to Freya's joy, it was Cruz who made the connection.

"He didn't like what they had been doing while he was inside," he said.

"Bingo," Freya said. "He wanted no part in the new enterprise. He was a good man, so the only motive I can glean from all of this is that he was preparing to spill the beans on his own son or ruin it somehow."

"We've got no evidence of that, Freya," Ben said.

"Well, find it, then," she told him. "Albert knew about whatever it was they were doing. There has to be a reason Robert waited all this time. Maybe he was waiting for the old man to pop his clogs naturally. Maybe Albert threatened to shop them all in. Maybe he was writing his memoirs. I don't know. But the answer is in there, somewhere."

"Freya?" Ben said, but she ignored him; she was on a roll.

"Chapman, pull what you can together on the umbrella firm," she said. "Nillson and Cruz, I want you to deal with Shaw. Grab some uniformed help and get down to the haulage yard. I want to know where he was on Monday morning and if he hasn't got a good enough answer, I want him in a cell."

"Freya?" Ben said with a little more urgency this time.

"What is it?" She said, irritated, and she turned to find him sifting through the very deepest part of the ash pile with his bare hands. Carefully, he picked something up and tossed it onto a pile he had been making.

"What are those?" She asked, eyeing the dark blue pieces of charred card.

"What do they look like?"

"They look like..." she paused, and the gap in her narrative hit her in a moment of hallelujah. "Right," she said, for the benefit of those on the call. "It's not drugs."

"Eh?" Cruz said.

"The umbrella firm. It's not drugs they've been importing, it's bloody people," she said. "Ben's found the remains of some old passports."

"There must be a few hundred here," he said.

"Passports?" Cruz said.

Ben took the phone from Freya's hand.

"Chapman, look something up for me, will you?" he said.

"Go on," she replied, like a reliable hound.

"What's the name of the firm Eamon Price was delivering the tanks to when he had the accident?"

"What's that got to do with anything??" Nillson asked, but Freya had an inclination of where he was leading.

"Just trust me," he said. While they waited for Chapman to search through the invoices, Freya began to study the small pile Ben had been making, comprising the remains of various passports.

"Oh, would you look at that," Chapman said. "Grantham Metals."

Freya felt Ben turn to face her, but she was fascinated by the burnt documents.

"Right, well if that isn't enough to convince the home office, I don't know what is," he said. "They're shipping in industrial fuel tanks for them to be scrapped immediately."

"I don't get it," Cruz said. "How does that help us?"

"They are importing illegal immigrants," Ben explained. "The poor sods climb into the tanks for the journey. The tanks are steel lined so x-ray wouldn't pick them up, and they can be closed from the inside, so the carbon dioxide probes that customs and excise use on the ports wouldn't flag any high levels of CO_2." He took a few steps back and forth. "As soon as the tanks reach the haulage yard, the immigrants are moved out, and the tanks are sent on to Grantham Metals for scrapping. It's a front."

"Ben?" Freya said, finding interest in a fragment of a passport.

Alive with the revelation, he bounced over to her, and she held up one particular page from one specific passport.

"Read that," she said. "Get Gold back to the station. I think I know what's happening here."

CHAPTER FIFTY-THREE

"Ah, for Christ's sake," Gillespie said as he ended the call, which had been directed straight to voicemail. "Somebody pick up the bloody phone, will you?" His growl faded to a disappointed mutter. "Only been gone two bloody hours, and they've forgotten me already."

He tried Nillson's number, and when he heard the ring tone, a glimmer of hope showed itself but then faded on the fourth ring. By the time the polite young lady, whose voice was the very epitome of disappointment, announced that he could leave a voicemail if he wished, that hope had all but dissipated.

"Bastards," he grumbled as he climbed from the car and strode over the gravel car park. He then shoved his way through the door and immediately took in the aroma of what smelled like dead farm animals but was very likely the trays and bags of animal feed.

"Now then," somebody called, and he found an ageing man behind the counter. "Looking for something, are you?"

"Miracles?" Gillespie replied. "Don't suppose you've any on sale, do you?"

The man smiled back at him.

"We're all out of miracles," he replied. "I can offer you a wide selection of animal feeds, Calor gas bottles, or perhaps some candles."

"Candles?" Gillespie said. "Who buys candles these days?"

The man smiled again, although Gillespie was sure it was to hide his truest thoughts.

"It's funny; you're not the first person to say that."

"Truth is pal," Gillespie continued. "I'm Detective Sergeant Gillespie. We're investigating a murder up the road."

"Ah, right," the man replied, looking a little taken aback by the introduction. "Well, it wasn't me, if that's what you want to know."

"Aye, I'm sure it wasn't," Gillespie replied. "The thing is, we have a colleague, a young female officer named Jewson. I'm afraid to say that my boss sent her out to do a few bits and bobs that she wasn't quite ready for. If you know what I mean? Made a few wee mistakes."

"Right?" The man said. "So?"

"I'm sorry, didn't catch your name."

"I didn't give it," he replied, then relented. "It's Rosford. Arthur Rosford."

"And is this your place?" Gillespie asked.

"You're on about the lass, right?" he asked, then held his hand up to shoulder height. "So high?"

"That sounds like her," Gillespie said. "Did you speak to her by any chance? It would have been the other night, around five-ish."

"Course I did," he said. "I was just locking up. Said she needed to see my CCTV."

"And did you let her see it?"

"Course," Rosford replied as if Gillespie was a persistent child.

"And do you think you could perhaps tell me what she found when she saw the footage?"

"No," Rosford replied curtly.

"No, as in she didn't find anything, or no, as in, mind my own business?"

"No, as in, I don't know what she saw. A car. I can't tell you much else."

In an effort to control the multitude of questions that were vying to escape his mouth, Gillespie took a breath and closed the gap between himself and Rosford. He stepped up to the counter and hoped his subdued tone expressed the gravity of the situation.

"Listen, Mr Rosford, this is a matter of some urgency. It's a significant detail in a murder enquiry. Do you understand what that means?"

"I know what a murder enquiry is, yes."

"Right, well then you should understand what it means to hinder said enquiry," Gillespie continued. "It's a criminal offence; not many people realise that."

"I can't tell you what she saw because she deleted the files."

"What?"

"The files," he said. "She deleted them. Took a photo on her phone, then deleted the lot. I couldn't believe it, if I'm honest. I mean, she made out it was a mistake, but—"

"It wasn't a mistake," Gillespie told him. "She's just a bit... bitchy."

"You're telling me," Rosford said. "All I can tell you is that it was a car. A blue one. Hatchback, I think. Yeah, that's right. She made a point of looking for a little blue hatchback."

"But she deleted the files?"

"Like I said—"

"Bitch, right, yeah, I hear you," Gillespie muttered. "Do you have a backup, or something?"

"A what?"

"A backup," he said. "You know, a hard drive or something where the files are backed up to."

"I don't know," Rosford said. "I've got an IT guy who comes in and does it all. Don't bloody understand it. I deal in animal feed, not bloody megabits."

"Can I see?"

"What? No—"

But Gillespie ignored him, telling himself that he was already in this up to his eyeballs, another complaint from a member of the public would hardly be the cherry on top of the cake. He strode into the back office, glanced around and then saw the little desk with the old computer monitor.

"Oy," Rosford called, but by the time he had walked around the counter and into the back room, Gillespie was already in the process of waking the old PC with a few deft shakes of the mouse and a couple of taps on the space bar. "I suppose you've got a warrant?"

"I suppose I can get one," Gillespie replied, checking under the desk and spying a USB hard drive. "And while I'm at it, I can also request an arrest warrant for obstructing police procedure."

"This is a joke," Rosford said, and in response, Gillespie pushed the seat back, inviting the owner to enter his password. "For Christ's sake."

He leaned forward and did his best to shield his fingers, but even Gillespie, who was awful at anagrams, could make out that the letters F, R, M, H, and P, when combined with the numbers 4, 5, and o, made farm shop.

"You may as well drive," Gillespie said, inviting him to open the CCTV software, which Rosford did with obvious reluctance.

"I'll be making a complaint about this," he said as he opened the software.

"Well, then I'll make sure our secretary sends you the thank you hamper before you get a chance," Gillespie replied, then pointed at the screen. "This it, is it?"

"Like I said, she deleted everything."

Few pieces of software came naturally to Gillespie. In fact, computers were not his strongest point. However, after a decade in the force, he had become quite adept at surveillance software. They all worked the same way; they just had different logos on. The layout was nearly always the same, the timeline looked almost identical, and the location of the digital storage device was nearly always under File and then Preferences.

"Can I?" he asked, and Rosford handed him the mouse. It took a few moments, but he found the USB hard drive, and then the files that had been backed up to it, and in under two minutes, had navigated to the early hours of Monday morning.

"There," Rosford said. "That's it."

Gillespie hit the pause button, freezing a light blue hatchback passing the farm shop on the main road.

He considered calling Ben, Nillson or even Cruz, but if they hadn't called him back by now, then no doubt either Granger or somebody higher up had issued the orders not to speak to him. So he called somebody else, somebody who was about to owe him a favour.

"Souness," the voice said when the call was answered.

"Hey, sarge," Gillespie said, hoping his accent was enough of an introduction. "Remember me?"

How could I forget, Sergeant Gillespie?"

"Look, I need a wee favour."

"Another favour?"

"I've got the blue hatchback," he said. "If I'm right, then Eamon Price is telling the truth, and your investigation is about to fall flat on its backside."

There was silence for moment, and Gillespie thought he heard the atmosphere shift as Souness left whatever room he was in.

"What's the favour?"

"A number plate check," Gillespie said.

"A number plate check?" Souness repeated. "Surely you have your own resources to do that sort of thing?"

"Well, aye—"

"Which makes me wonder why an officer from the major

crimes team would be calling little old me to ask for a favour," Souness said. There was no real malice in his tone, only a smugness that Gillespie could handle given the circumstances. "That's against regulations. I would have thought an officer of your experience would know that."

"Aye, well," Gillespie replied. "Let's just say that regulations aren't my strongest point right now."

"How soon do you need it?"

"Immediately," Gillespie replied, to which Souness sucked in an audible breath, making him wait for his prize.

"Read it out," he said. "And Gillespie?"

"Aye?" he replied.

"Don't make me regret this, will you?" Souness said.

"Believe me," Gillespie told him. "The only person regretting anything about today will be me."

CHAPTER FIFTY-FOUR

She could picture the scene when Detective Superintendent Granger rose from his tired desk chair, straightened his tie, and leaned across his standard-issue desk to shake her hand.

'Good work, Jewson," he would say, making a point to maintain eye contact. "Bloody good police work."

And that was as much of the little daydream her imagination would allow for the time being. The moments that followed when she strode into the incident room were a bit of a blur, a fog of ill-feeling, resentment, and helplessness.

She checked the rearview mirror, then reversed the police Astra into a spot, out of sight of the little blue hatchback on the driveway, one hundred and fifty yards away.

The hatchback had been reversed up to the house; the boot lid and the front door to the property were both open, meaning the occupant was either unloading or loading.

Then she saw her heaving a heavy case into the back of the car and slamming the lid with surprising strength, so much so that the car rocked on its suspension.

That was it. That was the car loaded. There were two possible courses of action. Firstly, she could wait for the vehicle to move off, pull into the road, and perform an arrest right there on the street, or secondly, she could enter the house through the open door, no warrant needed, and catch them in the act of hurrying away.

She snatched the handbrake on, checked her side mirror, and then eased herself from the car as inconspicuously as she could, which was fairly difficult given the livery and the blue light on the roof.

The route she took to the house was indirect, keeping out of the eyeline of anybody peering through the front windows, at least until it was too late for them to slam the front door closed. The last resort would be to call in and request a local unit stop by, but somehow, the thought of that diluted the daydream of Granger bestowing his gratitude.

Besides, it was just one woman. How hard could it be?

She stopped at the front door to listen for a moment. Had she been seen passing the windows, she would have heard the sound of a panicked escape, maybe even a rear door slamming. But she heard nothing of the sort, only a few dull thuds from an upstairs room, as the occupant retrieved a few last-minute things, a passport maybe or some cash to make the journey easier.

The house had a smell to it, as they often did in Jewson's experience. Foreign foods with all those weird spices and the God awful meat they buy, which was probably roadkill. She turned her nose up at the stench, and with an eye on the stars, she made her way across the hallway and leaned into the first doorway. There were two sofas, a coffee table, and dust hung in the air as if somebody had shaken an old rug.

She took a single step inside, keeping an eye on the stairs, turned, and then nearly jumped out of her skin. Behind the door an old man sat in an ancient and tatty armchair. His head rested on his right shoulder, and that side of his face had succumbed to gravity, revealing yellow teeth behind those cracked lips.

His dark brown skin was peppered with grey hair and wiry

with age, the very opposite of the bum fluff she had noticed Cruz cultivating.

The only part of him that resembled life were his eyes, and they followed her as she came to stand before him and placed an index finger to her lips.

"Shh," she hissed quietly. They were big and round behind sagging eyelids, and red arteries crisscrossed what she imagined was once bright and white and filled with life and joy. She tugged her ID card from her pocket, and it fell open before him. "Don't say a word."

He blinked once, and some tiny backstreet in her mind tried to recall if a single blink was the standard signal for the affirmative or if one blink was no and two was yes.

"I won't be long, Dad," the voice called from upstairs, deep and heavy with assertion and laden with the delicate fruits of some other language.

Jewson watched him, almost daring him to open his mouth, and although his fist balled on the arm of the chair, his lips were lifeless.

"Good boy," she whispered.

And that was when she saw it. A white paper bag adorned with the Co-op Pharmacy's recognisable branding was on the little side table beside him, along with a plastic beaker and long plastic straw, the type MacDonalds used to give away for free before the annoying European girl guilt-tripped the world into using paper straws that go soggy before you've had a chance to finish the drink.

She fingered the bag's opening and peered inside, aware of his ever-watchful eyes. There was a little box inside, not unlike the Sertraline she had taken, but it wasn't Sertraline; it couldn't have been, could it? Anti-depressants like that would kill the old boy, surely?

She pulled the box from the bag, noting a plastic syringe

beneath it and a pack of disposable needles. The label read Warfarin, which gave her no clue as to its purpose.

That was when she read the little printed label a little closer, and saw something quite amiss; something that made her gasp in shock and caused her eyes to widen as the missing piece of the puzzle became evident, and then her brow furrowed as a shadow passed across the man's face, and something connected with the back of her skull, sending lightning flashes through her eyes, a sine wave through her ears, and the irony taste of blood that pooled at the back of her throat.

CHAPTER FIFTY-FIVE

"You beauty," Gillespie shouted down the phone. "You bloody beauty."

"Like I said," Souness replied when Gillespie had calmed down. "You didn't get that from me."

"Scout's honour," he replied. "Thank you, Sergeant Souness."

"What?" Rosford asked, taking a step back. His face was a picture of panic, as if Gillespie might hug him or wrestle him to the floor.

"You, my friend," Gillespie said, finding Ben's number on his phone and hitting the green button to dial it, "might just have saved a man from going to prison."

"Is that man me?" He asked as Gillespie strode from the back room and made for the door. "Are you done here?"

Gillespie ignored him. A hundred scenarios played out in his mind: what Jewson was doing, what her end game had been, and how her actions could affect the team as well as innocent people like Eamon Price.

The polite young lady returned to inform him that Ben was still unavailable and invited him to leave a message.

By the time he had climbed into his car and started the

engine, another young lady on Nillson's phone had given him a similar message. By the time he had pulled onto the main road towards Billinghay and was working his way through the old Volvo's gears, various similar-sounding women on Gold's phone, Chapman's phone, and even the boss's phone had all, by way of a group effort, informed him that his call was not welcome to anybody on the major crimes team and that he should just give it up.

"Bugger," he spurted in a fit of rage that he tried his best to keep a lid on. But the frustration was all too much. He slapped his hand against the steering wheel in time with his outbursts. "Bugger, bugger, bugger, bugger," he yelled, stretching that final effort out like an eighties rock singer until his eyes watered with the effort.

He was left with one final choice, and he considered it with a heavy heart before giving in.

He dialled the number eased off the accelerator and flashed his lights at the car in front. It was a fifty miles per hour zone, and the daft sod was barely doing forty.

"Come on, you old bastard," he muttered as the tone shifted in the call. He half expected one of the women to greet him like an old friend, but instead, he heard a voice that, right there, right then, he would have paid good money to hear.

"Jim?"

"Cruz?" he said. "Ah, Gabby, Gabby, Gabby. What would I do without you?"

"I'm not supposed to be talking to you—"

"Never mind that," Gillespie said. "This is important. I need you to—"

"I could lose my job," Cruz said.

"Well, I have lost my job," Gillespie snapped at him, then softened. "Well, nearly, anyway."

"Listen, I'd love to talk, mate, but honestly, the boss would hit the roof if she knew I'd spoken—"

"Gabby!" Gillespie yelled. "Don't hang up. Please, just hear me out."

"Granger's on the warpath, as well," Cruz continued. "I'm telling you, this is serious, mate."

"I just need a favour."

"I can't do it, Jim," Cruz said, and there was genuine sorrow in his voice. "I can't do it."

"Not for your old mate, Jim, eh?" Gillespie said, finding his powers of manipulation weakening by the minute.

"There is something I want to say, though."

"Yep, anything," Gillespie said. "But just let me—"

"It's my fault," Cruz said.

"Never mind all that—"

"But I do mind," Cruz said. "I really do. I've got to say it. I can't stop thinking about it. It's all my fault."

"Yeah, yeah, I get it. She let a button or two pop open on her blouse; you wanted to make a good impression and found yourself telling her a wee anecdote about the good old days, eh? I know, and I don't blame you, Gabby. If I was a few years younger and if I weren't with Kate—"

"No, before that," Cruz said. "At the quarry. When the boss was in hospital, Ben said I had to work with her. She accused me of touching her bum."

"She did what?"

"She accused me of touching her, and then she reckoned I'd behaved inappropriately. Made some sexist remarks."

"And did you?"

"No!"

"I mean, you can tell me, eh? Your old mate, Jim."

"I didn't," Cruz said, his voice rising to fever pitch. "But she blackmailed me, and like an idiot, I fell for it. If I'd stood up for myself, she would have gone back to working the beat, and none of this would have happened."

There was an echo to his voice that enabled Gillespie to place

Cruz with sniper-like accuracy. He was standing on the top step of the fire escape, from where he could see down to the ground floor and up to the floor above in case somebody caught him.

"Gabby, listen, she's a piece of work, mate."

"I know, but I just can't help feeling that it's all my fault. She's bloody horrible, Jim. Honestly, once she's done with you, she'll work through the team. The boss reckons she'll stop her, but I don't know. I reckon she's met her match with this one. It's like she's playing a game. All she had to do was report that you had made a comment about children, and she knew Granger would have to follow up on it."

"Aye, that's about the size of it," Gillespie said. "Listen, you know I would never...you know. I'm not like that, right?"

"Yeah, I know," Cruz said before a loud bang echoed through the call. "Gotta go."

"No, wait," Gillespie said, but a few digital notes indicated the call had ended. "Gabby? Gabby, you there, pal?"

There was no answer, and he was approaching the turning.

"Ah..." he hesitated in a whirlwind of frustration searching for the right word, then settled on an old favourite. "Bugger!"

The man in front of him was driving so slowly that there was barely a need for Gillespie to slow down to make the turn. He slewed the car into the turning, feeling the tyres roll beneath the old Volvo, and then gunned the engine. He passed a liveried Astra in a blur of silver and orange, then, using all his weight to turn the wheel, he pulled onto the next street in a chorus of tyre rubber.

Had he actually maintained his car, or better still, invested in a newer model, the handbrake turn he performed before the little blue hatchback might have been effective, impressive even. Instead, when he pulled on the handbrake and dragged the wheel to the left, the old car rolled to one side and came to a leisurely stop like a fairground ride for under fives. A few seconds later, the drink bottles in the rear footwell settled.

The car door creaked open, a Kit Kat wrapper took flight, and

Gillespie approached the house with caution, running his hand across the blue hatchback's bodywork. Gently, he tried the passenger door handle and felt the mechanism click, then slowly and quietly opened the door. It was cleaner than his own car, but not anally clean like Freya's. Some clothes were in the passenger footwell and a scarf. He brushed them to one side and heard the crinkle of a plastic bag buried beneath. Using the scarf as a glove, he tugged the bag open and peered inside.

"Jesus," he whispered to himself, then glanced back at the house before leaving the car and stepping up to the front door.

"Jewson?" He called out. "Jewson, it's Gillespie. You alright, love? Need a wee hand?"

No answer came, and he hesitated. It was one of those protocols that were ingrained into every police officer: never enter a property alone, never risk the life of an officer or a suspect, and bravado never prevails.

It was also one of those protocols that, less than six months after hearing it for the first time, he realised it had been dreamed up by an officer with either very little imagination or experience or had written one too many condolence messages to families of fallen officers.

"I'm coming in," he called and stepped into the house. He inhaled. The smell reminded him of the Sudanese restaurant Katy had taken him to. There was a pungency to the meat like it had been cooking for a week and was as rich in flavour as could be. "Jewson, can you hear me? Call out if you can. Make a noise."

He peered around the first door and realised almost immediately that she wouldn't be calling out.

Her hair was blood-soaked and matted, and she was lifeless on the ground at the feet of an old man, who seemed to stare up at Gillespie with his lip snarled.

"You did this, eh?" Gillespie said, and the old man balled his fists. Gillespie dropped to a crouch, keeping the old man at a distance. He felt for Jewson's pulse and found it steady but weak.

"You daft, wee cow," he muttered at her, and as he shoved himself to his feet, something caught him on the back of the head. He stumbled forward, tripping over Jewson's body with a billion tiny lights dancing before his eyes. He groped for the mantelpiece to keep him upright when another blow hit him, and despite every bone in his body telling him to stay on his feet, there was no way he could. He sank to his knees, turning to see his attacker, when another blow rained down on him.

Warm, sticky blood gushed from the back of his head, and he fell forward, then rolled to stare up at his attacker as she prepared for one final swing.

There were no words exchanged, just grunts from them both and a wheezing from Jewson.

"You hang in there, Jewson, eh?" He grumbled, but so distant was his mind that he didn't even recognise his own voice. It was negligible, like a dying animal.

Through the swirling lights, he studied her. She wasn't a killer. She was like every other person he'd nicked during the past decade: somebody who had made a mistake and let things escalate.

And it was wildly out of control.

"What you going to do, eh?" He asked her as she fought with herself, with some kind of medical appliance held above her head like a yobbo with a brick. "You going to hit me with that, are you? What is that? Is that a CPAP machine? Help me sleep, will it?"

"Don't..." she started, and Jewson woke with a start. She rolled onto her side and then slid across the floor to get away. Immediately, James stepped over him. He saw her raise the machine again, and just as she was about to bring it down, he leaned forward and bit down on the back of her calf.

James yelled and kicked him off, by which time Jewson had crawled further away.

Gillespie was lying at the old man's feet. He wasn't sure why; there was little chance of old Pa James intervening in the ruckus, but he glanced up at him and spat his daughter's blood onto the carpet. Whereas before, the old man had been relatively still, and only his eyes and hands had moved. He now jolted like a current pulse through him. His face was a picture of torment, and saliva as white as fresh snow formed in the corners of his mouth.

"Dad?" James said, and she stepped over Gillespie and instinctively felt for a pulse. "Dad, no. Dad, come on."

"He's gone, love," Gillespie told her. Despite the less-than-favourable situation, there was rarely a time to use such news as a weapon.

"No," she said, panicking now. She loosened his shirt and felt his wrist, checking her wristwatch to time the nonexistent pulse.

"Terri, love," he said. "He's gone."

The energy seemed to dissipate from her like smoke through an open window. Her shoulder sagged, and she buried her face into her father's shoulder, crying out over and over.

"Oh, Dad," she said. "Oh, Dad, no."

Gillespie braved another wave of bright lights and turned his head to see Jewson. She lay at the foot of the sofa, eyes closed, and a fresh wound on her temple.

"You daft wee lass," he whispered and then regretted the effort. "For what it's worth," he said to James, and she turned to him, a grimace of pure hatred across her lips and in her eyes. "You couldn't have cared for him where you're going."

She laughed, but it wasn't a laugh. It was a breath, a fatigued, despondent and arrogant breath.

Slowly, she reached out to the little side table where she set the bloodied CPAP machine down, and she held it in a familiar grip.

"I'm not going anywhere," she told him, then brought it down onto his skull one final time.

CHAPTER FIFTY-SIX

"Jeeyagh," Gillespie yelled the moment he came to, saw Freya's face inches from his own, and he sat bolt upright.

"Easy now," Freya told him, her hand on his shoulder. "You've been hurt, Jim. Take it easy."

"Ah, Jesus Christ," he said, grabbing hold of his head and wincing. "What the hell?"

"Just...take a moment."

"James?" he mumbled. "Where's James?"

"We've got people looking for her," she replied.

"How's the patient?" Ben asked from the doorway with his phone pressed to his ear.

"Ben?" Gillespie said. "How's it going?"

"Never mind me, Jim," he replied, then the call must have been answered. "Hi, I'm Detective Inspector Savage, I need ambulances. One dead, two more with severe head wounds, one of which is unconscious..."

His voice trailed off as he paced the hallway, leaving Freya to contemplate the mess.

Jewson was sprawled on the floor on the far side of the room as if she had been caught crawling to safety.

"I tried to save her, boss," Gillespie said. "Honest. I did what I could."

"I know," she replied, leaving him to help the young woman who had caused them all so much grief. She checked her pulse again. It was weak but steady. The urge to roll her onto her back and slap her face was strong, not necessarily just as a means to wake her up. "What happened here, Gillespie?" Freya asked quietly. "What the bloody hell happened?"

"Ah, where do I start," he groaned. "I couldn't just go home, boss. I couldn't just let her get away with it."

"I told you to trust the process," she said, not sternly, but as a mother might when soothing a child's grazed knee.

"I didn't trust her," he said. "I didn't trust that she'd told us the truth." He closed his eyes and lay back on the carpet, his hand fixed to the side of his head. "I went to see Anita Stone."

"You did what?"

"It was the only thing I could think of. Jewson had been there," he said. "We didn't send her there. I was scratching for... something, anything."

"And what did she say?"

"Well, there were a couple of things our little madam omitted to tell us, eh? First of all, Jewson told Anita Stone that her father was dead."

"She did what?"

"Apparently, it was a misunderstanding and that she thought she already knew."

"Why do I doubt that?"

"Aye, well," he continued. "Then she said about how Havers was worried about his old mate."

"Worried, how?"

"His health," Gillespie said. "Apparently, she invited her old man to go away with them for a few days in their camper van. Anyway, he declined the offer, stating that he needed to keep an eye on Albert. He was worried about him."

"Ambulances are on their way," Ben said as he re-entered the room. "Jim, keep still, mate. You've lost a lot of blood."

"Apparently, Havers was concerned about Reilly's health," Freya told him.

"I hope somebody thinks as much of me when I'm that old," he said. "Who told you that?"

"His daughter," Gillespie said.

"Anita Stone? You went to see Anita Stone?"

"It's okay. We've been over it," Freya said, shaking her head."

"Well, what about Terri James?" Ben said. "How does she fit into all this? We're going to need more than an old burned passport if she's going to hold her hands up."

"We've got every officer in the county looking out for her car, so she won't get far," Freya said.

"Yeah, but then what? The most we can charge her for right now is assaulting a police officer."

"Not necessarily," Gillespie said. "I also went to the farm shop up the road. Turns out that Jewson stopped by there the other day to look at the CCTV."

"That's right. She said there *was* no blue car."

"Ah, well. Not quite. The footage shows James heading towards Martin and then, less than half an hour later, heading back towards Billinghay. It all fits the timeline."

"Jesus," Freya said. She stared down at Jewson, shaking her head, and felt her pulse again. Aside from keeping her stable, there was very little they were equipped to do. "The little cow was planning on taking it all to Granger, wasn't she? There's us lot chasing after a bloody human trafficking ring, and she's here catching the actual killer."

"There's another thing," Gillespie said. "I checked inside the car. Before I came in, I mean. I had a wee look inside."

"And?"

"Bloodstained clothes in the footwell and a plastic shopping bag."

"Containing?"

"Bloodstained latex gloves, an old Nokia phone, and a broken picture frame."

"The phone must be Albert Reilly's," Ben said. "Who was the picture of?"

"It wasn't a photo. It was a letter from the Queen. Sixty years of marriage."

"Amazing," Freya said. "So he was a family man at heart, was he?"

"You think that's what she used, then?" Ben asked.

"I'm pretty sure," Gillespie said. "She's no killer, eh? When she hit me, she picked up the first thing she could grab. A bloody CPAP machine. What gets me is why James would want to kill the old man. I mean, he was her bread and butter. Without him to care for, she's got no income."

Freya studied the old man in the chair, the elephant in the room, as it were.

"What's that?" she said, pointing to the little paper bag on the table.

"Medication," Ben told her at a glance.

Slowly, Freya rose and made her way across the room.

"He's had a stroke," she said. "Look, you can see the side of his face. The entire side of his body is different."

"Aye, he was alive when I came in," Gillespie said. "That happened while his daughter was beating the living hell out of me with his CPAP."

Freya snatched up the bag, tore it open and studied the contents.

"Warfarin," she said.

"Any paracetamol in there?" Gillespie asked. "My head is banging."

"These are blood thinners," Freya said, emptying the bag onto the little side table. A plastic syringe fell out, along with a carton of disposable syringes. She looked up at Ben, who seemed to be following but hadn't quite made the connection.

Then she held the box up to the light so she could see the printed label.

"Albert Reilly," she said.

"Eh?"

"Albert Reilly," she said. "These are Albert's."

"But—"

"No, buts. This medication belongs to Albert Reilly."

"Why is it..." Ben started. "Oh, Jesus. She was nicking the old man's medication. It's got nothing to do with Robert Reilly's sideline."

"She was keeping her dad alive," Freya said, cutting him off.

"Why wouldn't he just get his own meds?" Gillespie asked. "And what's the sideline?"

"Short answer?" Ben began. "Robert Reilly imports industrial fuel tanks from Gdansk through Reilly Haulage. All above board. He then fills those tanks with people—"

"With what?"

"People," he said. "Immigrants. The tanks are then scrapped. The paper trail is neat and tidy. Nothing amiss, except for a payment from a foreign investor into his umbrella firm every month."

"Jesus," Gillespie said.

"We caught Reilly burning the evidence at his house. Documents and passports?"

"Passports?"

"One of which belonged to a man named Joseph James." Ben placed a hand on the old man's shoulder. "My guess is that Terri James came to the UK as a carer and then tried to get her father in, but he was refused a visa, so she sought other means to get him in. This man then endured a God-awful journey inside a fuel tank on the back of a lorry so his daughter could take care of him."

"For Christ's sake," Gillespie said.

"They keep the passports to maintain control," Ben explained. "The victims can't leave without going through them, and they can't prove who they are. The only options available to them are to hand themselves in and claim asylum, risking deportation or staying below the radar. Many of them fall into the world of crime or find cash work. Whatever way you look at it, they have very bleak futures."

"Ben, get Chapman on the phone, will you?" Freya said seeing the conversation was becoming more conjecture than potential theory.

While he did as she asked, Freya returned to Jewson's side and checked her pulse again.

This time, she stirred at Freya's touch. She opened her eyes and tried to clamber away in a panic.

"Easy now," Freya told her.

"What the...?" She started. "How——?"

"Just take it easy," Freya said.

"Freya?" Ben said, putting the call onto loudspeaker.

"Chapman, are you there?" Freya asked once Jewson had settled.

"We're all here, guv," Chapman replied.

"Good, we're looking for Terri James."

"Eh?" Cruz said.

"We've got officers on the lookout for her vehicle."

"I didn't think she drove?" Cruz said. "She said she used public transport."

"And did any of us check with the DVLA?" A silence followed. "Chapman, I'm going to need an ANPR alert set up, and while you're at it, get onto the borders. She is not slipping the net."

"Got it," Chapman replied, the tasks being nothing short of easy for her. "I just need the number plate."

"Gillespie will send it to you now."

"Gillespie?" Cruz said. "I thought——"

"Long story," Freya said, cutting him off. "Before she's caught and brought to the station, I want every aspect of the following theory fact-checked and proven," Freya said. "When I sit down before her in an interview room, I want her to have no room to manoeuvre. Is that clear?"

"We'll do what we can," Nillson called out, which was as good as Freya could hope. "Right, pay attention," Freya began, and she left Jewson to her own devices and closed her eyes to put the events into a comprehensible order. "Terri James was a self-employed carer. Her one and only patient was Albert Reilly. At some point, Robert Reilly helped her get her father into the country."

"Was that before or after she started caring for his dad?" Gold asked.

"Doesn't matter," Freya said, picturing their confused expressions in the incident room. They would all be looking at each other, bemused. "What matters is that she recognised her father's symptoms and, seeing as Joseph James didn't exist, she had no option but to steal medication from Albert Reilly. Sadly, that is not a plan with legs."

"What do you mean?" Cruz called out.

"I mean, Albert Reilly died, Cruz. He had a stroke, didn't he?"

"I thought he was hit over the head."

"He *was* hit over the head, but that was after he died. She went to his house to steal some medication, found him dead on the floor and realised that somebody would work out that he died because he hadn't been taking his medication."

"Because she had been pilfering it off to keep her dad alive?" Gillespie said.

"Exactly," Freya continued. "She stages a break-in that's gone wrong, hits him over the head with the nearest thing to hand, escapes out of the back door, breaks the window, locks the door, and then calls Havers. She knew he lived opposite, and she knew the pair were always arguing. Why not muddy the waters a little?

Havers runs over and finds him. Meanwhile she escapes down the side of the house. What she didn't expect was for him to come running out quite so quickly. Quick enough that he saw her and had presence of mind to jump in his car and go after her."

"Jesus," Gillespie muttered, turning to look at Jewson. "And I suppose you knew all this, did you?"

"I was piecing it together," she replied.

"Well, you won't be piecing much else together for a while, Jewson," Freya said, nodding through the front window at the two ambulances and three police cars that were struggling to get past Gillespie's old Volvo, which looked like it had been abandoned in the middle of the road. "The cavalry has arrived, come on."

"What are we doing with her?" Ben asked.

"Throwing her to the wolves," Freya replied, making no effort to hide her disdain. "Place her under arrest and get one of them lot to take her back to the station."

"You what? You can't arrest me?"

"Oh, I think I can, young lady," Freya said, turning on her heels in an instant. She closed the gap between them, bent until her face was just inches away. "You endangered every one of us today. Sergeant Gillespie could have died, and you withheld vital evidence, perverting the course of justice. Now let me tell you something; that does not look good on a police officer's resume."

Jewson closed her eyes, then winced at the wound on her temple.

"Officer Jewson," Ben began. "I am arresting you on suspicion of perverting the course of justice and conspiracy to endanger the life of a police officer. You do not have to say anything, but—"

"Alright, alright," she said, and Freya smiled inwardly at the tears in her eyes. "I'll talk to Granger. I'll withdraw the complaint. I'll tell him I misunderstood or something."

"Have you finished?" Freya asked.

"Didn't you hear me? I said I'd make it right. I'll request to go back into uniform or transfer somewhere. Come on."

"What do you think, Freya?"

"What do I think?" she said. "I think I'd like to focus on the task at hand, given that we've already lost over a day. Hand her over."

"You heard the guv, Jewson," Ben said. "Come on, on your feet."

"I'm injured," she said, but when Ben reached down to help her stand, she shrugged him off. "Leave it, will you?"

It was a sight to behold, Freya thought, watching him grab her by the elbow and hand her over to the uniformed officers who burst into the room a few moments later.

Amusingly, it was Frobisher, and he took in the sight in utter bewilderment: the dead old man, the injured Gillespie, and Jewson with her hands pulled behind her back.

"Crikey," he said. "What the hell happened here?"

"Funny you should ask," Gillespie replied as he struggled to his feet. "The good news is that you won't have any more burglaries to deal with for a while."

"What?"

"Take her away, will you?" Freya said. "And I want a unit to pay a visit to Reilly Haulage. You're looking for a man named Graham Shaw."

"Graham Shaw," Frobisher said by way of confirmation. "What's the charge?"

Freya gave it some thought.

"You can always recite section two of the human trafficking act; see where that gets you."

"Section two?" he said, and he pulled a face as he recalled, from memory, the crime in question. "Arranging or facilitating the illegal travel of others?"

"Very good," she replied. "Can you handle it?"

"Yes, guv," he said. "Leave it with me."

He gave Jewson a nudge and left the three of them alone with

Joseph James, who stared at the spot on the floor where Gillespie had been lying.

"What about us?" Ben asked.

"Us?" Freya said. "We're going to bring Terri James in, of course."

He stared at her, ran his tongue around his lips, and then nodded.

"You know where she is, don't you?"

"Terri James has just lost her father, and her job, and very soon, she'll lose her liberty," Freya said. "I think I know where she's gone."

"And me, boss?" Gillespie asked. "What do I do?"

"You can go and see one of the paramedics," she told him. "When you're done, I want you in the back of my car." She grinned at him, then cut the moment short by looking at her watch. "You've got three minutes."

CHAPTER FIFTY-SEVEN

Freya drove surprisingly slowly, considering the urgency, and for the entire journey, Gillespie groaned and moaned about his headache, clutching a bunch of blood-soaked wadding to his head.

The sun was sinking in the sky behind them, and still, onwards, she drove through Woodhall Spa and Horncastle, where she cut beneath the lower part of the Wolds to Alford. Still, she didn't stop. She didn't even use the sat nav, which was surprising given that Freya usually had to look at the dashboard screen more often than she did the windscreen.

It was only when they had passed through Alford and were on the little lanes he remembered from his teenage years that Ben understood where they were going.

But he didn't say anything. There was no need. He knew as well as she did that it was a calculated risk.

As it turned out, Freya's intuition was as accurate as ever.

A man-made sand dune ran the length of Huttoft Beach, through which a gap had been dug to provide access to the small car park. During the summer months, the car park would be rammed, but given the drop in temperature and fall in daylight hours, Ben wasn't surprised to see just a handful of cars: a Volkswagen van, a Ford Mondeo, a sleek Jaguar, and of course a light blue hatchback, parked at the far end.

Freya approached slowly and blocked any attempts to escape.

"She's not inside," Ben said.

"Of course, she isn't," she replied. "You don't come to the beach to sit in your car, do you? You come to breathe the fresh air."

"Like him, you mean?" Ben said and nodded at a man three hundred yards away atop the dune, staring out to sea with his coat tails flapping in the breeze.

There was something familiar about the man; perhaps it was the way he stood with his back ramrod straight and his hands buried in his pockets. He looked lost or lonely, or just plain depressed, even from afar.

"Just like him," Freya replied as she climbed from the car.

Considering all he had to work with was a handful of alcohol wipes and a thick bunch of wadding, Gillespie had done a decent job of cleaning himself up. The paramedic had, according to him, advised him to leave the wound open, but Ben wondered if he was just saying that to avoid wearing a bandage on his head.

"There," Freya said, pointing to a lone woman on the distant shoreline. Unlike the man on the dunes, she wore no coat. Her shoes were in a heap in the sand behind her, and despite the icy North Sea, slowly, she walked forward.

"Christ, what's she doing?" Gillespie muttered.

"What would you do?" Freya asked. "You said it yourself: she's not a killer. She didn't plan any of this. She just reacted. She was trying to keep her dad alive."

"She's going in," Ben said, and he took a step forward, readying himself to run, but Freya discreetly caught his arm and held him there.

Gillespie's eyes, however, didn't leave the woman, who was now up to her knees.

"Ah, I can't watch this," he said, pulling off his coat.

"You'll need these," Freya said, stopping him in his tracks. She tossed him a pair of handcuffs from her pocket, then nodded at him reassuringly before he sprinted across the sand.

"Freya?" Ben said, pulling his arm free. "What the hell?"

"Just..." she began. "Let's just watch, shall we?"

"She's going to bloody—"

"No, she's not," Freya told him. "If we'd arrived five minutes later then maybe, but look. Look out there, and tell me what you see."

Ben studied the scene. Gillespie was just twenty metres or so from her, already splashing through the water. Maybe it was her state of mind or the noise of waves, he couldn't tell, but Terri James was oblivious to his approach. The water was above her waist now, and she held her arms up as she waded out slowly, giving Gillespie the perfect purchase when he closed in from behind, stopped and wrapped his arms around her, and, despite her kicking and thrashing, dragged her from the water.

"I see something I should be helping him with," Ben said.

"No, Ben," she replied. "What you see is an officer with an outstanding record, who was recently accused of a God-awful fabrication, and suffered the manipulation of what I can only describe as ineffective policy. You're looking at a man who, unlike the rest of us, believed in Eamon Price. If it wasn't for Gillespie, Ben, I'd have given up on that little blue car a long time ago," she said, beaming at him. "And there he is, saving a woman's life."

He grinned and shook his head.

"Only you could have seen that."

Gillespie had wrestled James to the beach and held her face down in the sand while he handcuffed her.

"You're not telling me you let him do that alone to convince Granger of how good he is, are you?"

"Oh, come on, Ben. Give me some credit," she replied. "Do you honestly think Granger needs convincing of how good Gillespie is? The man might be a spineless old fart, but he does have eyes, and as much as it pains me to say it, he didn't get to where he is without some kind of acumen." He stared at her, waiting for her to finish the explanation. "I let him do it alone, Ben, to convince Gillespie of how good Gillespie is. Nobody else. Everybody else knows it," she said. "He knows, or at least, he knew it. He just needed reminding, that's all." She adjusted her coat against the breeze and raised her collar. "Message Chapman, will you? I don't want her in my car. Have her contact a local unit to pick her up."

"That was a bloody risk. She could have died. He could have had trouble dragging her out."

"In which case, you would have been there in a heartbeat," Freya told him.

Down on the beach, Gillespie had hauled James to her feet and was leading her towards Ben and Freya.

"You realise where we are, don't you?" Ben said.

"I do," she replied, pointing up at the dune where the man was still motionless, lost in thought. "Two years ago, I walked onto that dune, and you were staring down at the body of Jessica Hudson."

"Do you think he realises?" Ben asked, and he nodded at the man, who was in his late fifties or early sixties.

"I think he has other things on his mind," she replied.

"Like what?"

She turned to study the man from afar.

"Well, he hasn't moved an inch since we arrived. He hasn't even glanced this way. He didn't flinch once when James tried to end her life, and I'd be surprised if he even realises there are other people on the beach."

"Very astute," Ben muttered, but then the man did move. He pulled something from his pocket, a pot or a bottle or something. "Oh, good Lord."

Freya didn't even need to look. She lowered her head and, probably out of respect, masked the grin that formed on her face as the strong breeze caught ashes from the urn in the man's hands, and scattered the remains of whoever it was, far and wide.

"You bloody knew, didn't you?" he said, trying not to make a show of wiping his eyes.

"I had an idea," she replied, and she glanced up at the man as he replaced the lid on the urn and tossed it to the ground at his feet. "Poor man."

"It's quite fitting, really, isn't it?" Ben said as Gillespie and James neared. "Us being here, I mean. This is where we met, and in a matter of months, we'll be man and wife."

She ignored him, as she so often did when he spoke of matters of the heart and called out to Gillespie.

"Well done, Sergeant Gillespie," she said. "There are towels and blankets in the back of my car."

He stared at her, shivering and incredulous, as if he expected her to have fetched them for him. Ben gave him a knowing nod, and the big Scotsman strode back towards the car, his feet squelching with every step.

"As for you, Terri," Freya began. "At this point, I would normally provide a summary of the facts to give you a chance of denying them." James was shivering; her loose clothes were taut against her sodden skin, and she was far too shamed to meet Freya's stare. "However, seeing as there's a bag in your car that will prove you murdered Albert Reilly, plus statements of two injured police officers, CCTV footage showing you travelling to and from the scene of the crime, a lorry driver who claimed you caused a fatal accident, and a corpse in the morgue who hasn't seen an ounce of the medication he was supposed to be for God knows how long, I really don't think there's much point is there?"

"Do whatcha got to do, lady," she replied.

"I will say this, though," Freya said as Gillespie returned with a bundle of blankets, one of which Ben took and wrapped around James' shoulders. "As far as motives go, yours was a noble one. It's just a shame that you let the evil inside you rule your heart. You can never run now, Terri. You can never run from who you are, and you have a long time to live with the consequences of your actions." James looked up at her, understanding every single word Freya spoke. "I only hope that when that cell door closes behind you, you spare a thought for the lives you've destroyed." She left the sentiment where it lay in the sand. "Anything to say?"

"He was a good man," James said. "Albert. He was a good man, and I'm sorry. I'm sorry for it all."

Freya gave Gillespie the nod.

"Make her aware of her rights, Sergeant Gillespie," Freya said. "Sit her in my car until the local boys turn up,"

"Aye, boss," he replied.

"And Gillespie, you need to get out of those wet clothes if you're coming back with me," she called out, then muttered under her breath. "I don't want my car smelling like a wet bloody dog."

"Well?" Ben said as they turned their backs on the sea and faced inland.

"Well, what?"

"We'll be married," he said. "In a few months' time, there'll be no escape from me. I hope you know that?"

She laughed, and the breeze blew her hair from her face, but she made no attempt to pull it back into place.

"Oh, Ben," she said, and she closed the gap between them, glancing back at Gillespie to make sure neither he nor James were looking, then reached up and kissed him. "I knew there was no escape from the very first moment I saw you."

The End.

ALSO BY JACK CARTWRIGHT

The Deadly Wolds Murder Mysteries

When The Storm Dies

The Harder They Fall

Until Death Do Us Part

The Devil Inside Her

The Wild Fens Murder Mysteries

Secrets In Blood

One For Sorrow

In Cold Blood

Suffer In Silence

Dying To Tell

Never To Return

Lie Beside Me

Dance With Death

In Dead Water

One Deadly Night

Her Dying Mind

Into Death's Arms

No More Blood

Burden of Truth

Run From Evil

Deadly Little Secret

The DCI Cook Murder Mysteries

A Winter of Blood

A Secret to Die For

VIP READER CLUB

Your FREE ebook is waiting for you now.

Get your FREE copy of the prequel story to the Wild Fens Murder Mystery series, and learn how Freya came to give up everything she had to start a new life in Lincolnshire.

Visit www.jackcartwrightbooks.com to join the VIP Reader Club.

I'll see you there.

Jack Cartwright

A NOTE FROM THE AUTHOR

Locations are as important to the story as the characters are; sometimes even more so.

I have heard it said on many occasions that Lincolnshire is as much of a character in The Wild Fens series, as Freya is, or Ben. That is mainly due to the fact that I visit the places used within my stories to see with my own eyes, breathe in the air, and to listen to the sounds.

However, there are times when I am compelled to create a fictional place within a real environment.

For example, in the story you have just read, the towns and villages mentioned are all real places. However, the houses that are described are entirely fictitious.

The reason I create fictional places is so that I can be sure not to cast any real location, setting, business, street, or feature in a negative light; nobody wants to see their beloved home described as a scene for a murder, or any business portrayed as anything but excellent.

If any names of bonafide locations and businesses appear in my books, I ensure they bask in a positive light, because I truly believe that Lincolnshire has so much to offer and that these locations should be celebrated with vehemence.

I hope you agree.

Jack Cartwright
AUTHOR

AFTERWORD

Because reviews are critical to an author's career, if you have enjoyed this novel, you could do me a huge favour by leaving a review on Amazon.

Reviews allow other readers to find my books. Your help in leaving one would make a big difference to this author.

Thank you for taking the time to read *Run From Evil*.

Best wishes,

Jack
Cartwright
AUTHOR

COPYRIGHT

www.ingramcontent.com/pod-product-compliance
Ingram Content Group UK Ltd.
Pitfield, Milton Keynes, MK11 3LW, UK
UKHW040230070425
457122UK00001B/21